CARTOON CITY

CARTOON CITY

FERDIA MAC ANNA

review

First published in 2000
by REVIEW

An imprint of Headline Book Publishing

10 9 8 7 6 5 4 3 2

ISBN 0 7472 7341 3

Typeset in 12.25 on 14pt Perpetua by
Palimpsest Book Production Limited
Polmont, Stirlingshire

Designed by Peter Ward

Printed and bound in Great Britain by
Clays Ltd, St Ives, plc.

Headline Book Publishing
A division of the Hodder Headline Group
338 Euston Road
London NW1 3BH
www.reviewbooks.co.uk
www.hodderheadline.com

To:

Kate   Kate   Kate
Sienna Sienna Sienna
Bessa   Bessa   Bessa
Finn   Finn   Finn

Somatomegalic Epiphyseal Dysfusion Syndrome:

A rare medical condition whereby an adult suddenly begins to grow again. First described by Vladimir Gobowski in Prague, 1912. Credited in English medical literature to Adiref Anna Cam.

PROLOGUE

Pals

'Hey Goalpost, what's the weather like up there?'

Dez's voice sneered out of the darkness ahead, causing Myles Sheridan to freeze suddenly in the long grass. He had known him just a few hours yet somehow Dez had discovered the nickname that had followed Myles since childhood. A name that resurfaced every couple of years like a curse.

'Same as it is down there,' Myles said, disappointed that he couldn't think of a better reply.

Six foot six inches tall since the age of thirteen, Myles had attracted a lot of nicknames – the Lighthouse, the Crane, the Moving Lamppost, the Eiffel Tower. For some reason, perhaps because he was skinny, Goalpost was the one that had endured, and the one he most hated. It was as though he was branded.

The worst thing was that a couple of weeks ago he had started growing again. And this morning, when he had checked himself with the tape measure, he discovered that he had grown by yet another quarter of an inch. Now, at thirty years of age, he stood six foot six and a half inches tall. There was no telling where this thing was going to stop.

The last thing Myles needed was to be teased about his height by a teenage scumbag. Dez was small, wiry and hyperactive, with lively blue eyes and a face like a demented leprechaun's. Despite his youth, Dez came across as the sort who would relish the chance of a scrap with a tall guy. The first and most important lesson a tall guy learned was to steer clear of fights with guys small enough to loaf you in the balls.

As Dez sniggered from the darkness ahead, Myles felt an urge to turn around and walk back down the hill. After all, if this young scumbag was going to take the piss . . .

Just then he felt a strong hand on his shoulder and Pat's familiar, soft voice said calmly, 'Relax the head. Your man's been eating too much red meat.'

'Did you tell him?'

Pat squeezed Myles's shoulder. 'Not at all man, I would never do a thing like that to a pal.'

Pat was just under six feet tall, big boned and chunky, with hands like shovels. Even in the pale orange light from the street-lights, Myles could see Pat's deep-set gentle brown eyes twinkling at him. After so many years it felt oddly normal and uplifting to be on a dark hill at night with Pat. Like boys out for mischief.

'Sticks and stones man. Rise above it, you know what I mean?' Pat swished past, leaving behind a pungent blast of aftershave.

Myles's shoulder felt as though it had been clamped briefly and then freed. He heard frantic whispering from up ahead.

'I know he's a guest,' Dez hissed. 'What I'm saying is who in their right mind takes a bleeding "guest" along on a gig?'

'Let it go,' Pat said firmly. 'He's a mate and he's here because I want him here. Right?'

'I've spoke my bit. Now I'm saying nothing. See this mouth, it's bleeding zipped tight.'

'Good.'

'You won't hear one single solitary bleeding word out of this mouth for the rest of the night, right?' Dez continued.

'Proper order.'

'I'm a professional, that's why.'

'Fair enough.'

'This mouth is bleeding professional too, in fact it's—'

'Then shut your professional mouth and come on,' Pat said.

Ahead, Myles heard feet swishing through wet grass. He walked on, treading carefully lest he skidded.

Once, when he was thirteen, Myles had been cornered in the school toilets by a bunch of sixth years who were angry at him for being taller than them. They had told Myles that his growth hormones were out of control. Then they had turned him upside down, inserted his head in the toilet bowl and flushed the handle repeatedly to shrink Myles back to normal size. 'It's for your own good,' their leader had explained.

Upside down and dripping, Myles had observed Pat stroll in and lean casually against the wall. 'What's the story, lads?' Pat had inquired in a soft voice, as though breaking the noses of a bunch of sixth years would be a pleasant break from classroom routine. After a few face-saving smart comments, Myles had been placed right way up again and the older guys had drifted away like smoke. When Myles had thanked Pat for saving him, Pat had just shrugged. 'I was kind of wondering,' he had said, 'if maybe you could give me a bit of a hand with the algebra.'

From then on Pat had dubbed Myles 'Big M'. Pat became 'Big P'. 'Big P' protected 'Big M' from assholes while 'Big M' helped 'Big P' with homework. They had stayed best friends throughout school. The only rupture between them occurred when Big P got off with Big M's first girlfriend behind the bicycle shed at a school ceilidh. The rupture lasted a week, until Pat apologised to Myles and broke it off with the girl as a renewal of friendship. After that, the bond between the tough guy and the tall guy had grown stronger in a way that neither could explain.

Upon graduation, Pat had gone to England to work on sites, earn money and 'sleep with tons of women'. Myles had stayed home, tried college and ended up a sub-editor on the *Evening News*. They kept in touch sporadically. A few years ago, contact ceased altogether.

Until last Friday, when the phone rang on Myles's desk as he was subbing a bought-in article about how to put the 'zest' back into lovemaking. The receptionist informed him that a Mr 'Big P' was downstairs to see him. After nearly ten years, Pat had grown broader and tougher and now sported a beard that made him look like a mature Kris Kristofferson. 'Are you bored, man?' Pat had inquired. 'Want to come on a gig next week?'

Now the Tough Guy was back protecting the Tall Guy again. Only this time from Dez, a seventeen-year-old leprechaun. Myles moved forward, taking precise steps, careful not to rest his entire weight on either foot lest he go tumbling into wet blackness. A cool breeze washed over his face and gently flapped his jacket collar. The initial rush of annoyance at Dez was giving way to a feeling of relief. In truth, he was glad of the diversion. Before this he had been feeling panicky, wondering if he was out of his mind to be tramping through long grass on a hill on the north-side. He recalled Dez's elfin face, bright with jealousy in the pub earlier after Pat had informed him that Myles would be accompanying them. 'Might as well bring women and six-packs and throw a party,' he had snorted.

Be positive, Myles told himself. This story will make your career. No more being a 'scullery-maid' of journalism. No more subbing pieces, laying out pages and correcting copy written by people who hadn't the literary skills of a badger. Think about the three hundred quid plus expenses that Migraine McGann, the features editor at the *Daily News*, had promised him if the story made an entertaining colour piece. 'Crime is big stuff,' Migraine had drawled when Myles had run the idea past him. 'This is your big chance to become a features ace. Gimme a thousand words first thing Friday morning.'

Myles followed Pat and Dez up to the top of the hill, where the glow of streetlights sat like an orange fringe. Below, a long, sleek container truck gleamed under the lights like a shiny new dinky toy waiting to be played with. In a few moments Pat and Dez would walk down the hill to 'liberate' the truck and drive it to a location somewhere in the inner city. Once there, the cargo of smuggled cigarettes would be unloaded and transferred to other vehicles to be distributed and sold on the streets later. The cigarettes were 'dirty' anyway, Pat had explained. It wasn't as though they were really stealing. Instead, they were simply 'redistributing' someone's illegal profits. 'It's dead simple. Officially the cigarettes don't exist; therefore the crime doesn't exist either.'

Now Myles eased forward to stand alongside Pat on a narrow, slippery ridge overlooking the street. Pat turned to him, smiled, and removed a small pair of binoculars from his pocket. He scanned the area for a few moments. Satisfied, he handed the binoculars to Myles. Myles experienced a pang of delight, as though he had just been made a member of an outlaw gang. Being here with Pat was more exciting than squatting on a barstool in his mother's pub, larruping pints and whiskeys and staring at the soccer on TV until his eyes boiled. More stimulating than getting out of his cranium in The Nerve nightclub and shifting some wagon who had a face like a roadmap. Better than being at home.

Looking through Pat's binoculars at the street below, Myles became exhilarated; it was just like the moment at a rock concert when the lights come up on your favourite band and the guitarist strikes a power-chord. He checked out rows of identikit houses with their eyelids shut, then panned along lines of gleaming cars. Finally, he focused on the truck, which glowed like a beacon. Not even a cat stirred. He handed the glasses back to Pat.

'Well, what do you think?' Pat asked him quietly.

Myles blinked giddily for a moment, surprised to be put on the spot.

'A bit like robbing an orchard,' Myles replied. 'Except the apples are already packed,' he added, and immediately felt foolish.

Pat looked at him blankly for a moment, then gave a quiet snort.

'What did I tell you?' Dez said. 'Goalpost thinks we're doing an orchard.'

'That's enough,' Pat said sharply. 'No talking while we're working. Keep it clean till we're off the scene, right?'

They moved forward quietly. Dez led the way down the hill, followed by Pat and then Myles.

Myles considered leaving Dez out of the article altogether. Perhaps he'd refer to him throughout as 'The Leprechaun'. He decided to call Pat 'Black Pat'. It sounded mysterious and romantic, like a storybook pirate or a wild west outlaw. Definitely more intriguing than 'Big P'.

Halfway down the hill Myles's foot hit something soft and he wobbled forward slowly like a reluctant ice-skater. He slid past Pat and Dez so gradually and lugubriously that he would have had time to shake both their hands and exchange tearful goodbyes.

Pat reached for him but missed. Dez glared at him as though this type of stupid behaviour was exactly what he had expected of Myles all along. Myles himself hit a bump and soared into space with the effortless grace of a champion ski-jumper in a slow-motion replay. For an instant he hung in the yellow beams of the streetlights, before plunging, ears ringing and arms flapping like a shirt inside a tumble dryer. He closed his eyes momentarily and when he opened them it seemed to him as though he was falling upwards. He had already died, he thought. This was how it felt to be hurtling towards the hereafter. How serene it was. How at peace he suddenly felt.

Then he smacked into wet grass, the impact knocking the breath out of him. Lying on his back panting up at the dark, he felt a sensation of wetness flooding his body, as though a water hose had doused him. He wiggled his fingers and toes. Moved an arm. Raised a leg. Nothing felt broken. He saw a sneering headline in the *Evening News* : 'Goalpost Falls Off A Hill'.

Immediately a curious sense of disappointment flowed through him, as though his body secretly yearned to keep on plunging through space.

'Hey man, you OK?' Pat said.

'I'm grand,' Myles croaked. 'No sweat.'

There was a shuffling sound and then Pat and Dez towered over him. Pat looked concerned. Dez's tiny face sneered at him.

'Hey Goalpost, enjoy your trip?' he said.

ONE

Outlaws

Dingo's Auto-Parts looked like a car graveyard. Fenders, radiators, windscreen frames and rear axles, as well as other bits of cars, lay about the yard as though tossed there by an explosion.

As Pat turned the truck into the yard, the beams from the headlights played across a rusted, wheel-less Mercedes that was propped on breezeblocks alongside a funeral mound of old tyres. The khaki-coloured turret of a light tank sat by the far wall like a mute overseer of destruction.

'One great thing about this place,' Pat said, 'Never any problem with parking.'

He negotiated a way through the debris and drove around to the back, where he pulled up alongside a pair of large doors covered in graffiti. Then he cut the engine. Silence poured in on them. There were no stars in the sky. It was as if a vast black curtain had been pulled over the place.

After Myles's fall down the hillside, being driven away in the cab of a stolen truck had seemed an anti-climax. They had passed no other cars on the road, seen no sign of police, pedestrians or motorcyclists, and noted scarcely a light on in any of the houses. Instead, rows of streetlights stood stiffly to attention like an honour guard. The city's population had gone away for the night.

The only glitch in Myles's relaxed state was the sensation of spreading dampness on the seat beneath him. He felt like a child who had wet himself and was afraid to say anything. Pat was still being friendly to him, but perhaps only out of sympathy. Dez ignored him. The trick now was to act as though nothing untoward had occurred. 'If you put your mind to it you can do anything,' his father, Big Paddy, had drummed into him. Myles recalled his father's favourite motto: 'Never let the bastards see you cry. Too many of them would only enjoy it.' Big Paddy had loved to strut around the pub in his captain's uniform spouting these and various other insights. He had been large, loud and brimful of his own wisdom up until the moment he died. 'He saw everything coming,' Myles's mother, Stella, said after the funeral. 'Except the grenade that blew him to bits.'

For a moment Myles saw his father's shagged-out face in the rear-view mirror. Big Paddy curled his lip at his son, 'Don't be a long, lean, lanky layabout all your life.' Myles turned away and looked out of the window at the rusted hulks.

Dez scratched his nose. 'How long do you want to give it?'

Pat squinted at his watch. 'If nobody shows in five minutes, we vamoose.'

It had been ridiculously easy. They had simply walked across the road and taken the truck. Just like that. The ease with which the crime had been accomplished gave Myles an angle for his article: 'Crime Pays – and that's why people do it'. He wondered if the Thought Police at the *Evening News* would let that one through.

Migraine would publish any article that would sell newspapers. Myles wondered what was in it for Pat. Pat must have a plan. Even in school, Pat had liked being notorious. Maybe he just wanted to be a superstar gangster.

'What are you smiling about?' Pat's face was amused as well as intrigued.

'This is cool,' Myles said. 'It'll make a great piece.'

'It's not over yet,' Dez said, indicating the far side of the yard where a dirty white transit van was nosing around the corner with its lights off. They watched the van glide over to where they were parked and pull in alongside. Following it was Pat's Volvo estate, also with its lights off.

A long-haired hippy in his thirties with a straggly beard and a hook-nose got out. The hippy nodded in the direction of the truck's cab.

'The skull on that,' Dez said. 'If he'd a nose like that on the other side of his head, he'd make a great pickaxe.'

Pat opened the door and got out, followed by Dez and Myles.

'How's it going Alvin?'

'Depends what you've got for me.'

'Only the very best, as usual,' Pat said.

Myles looked around. No sign of an ambush. But then it wouldn't be much of an ambush if you could spot it. He tried to blank his mind of all thoughts, which he hoped would give him a cool, inscrutable expression. He followed the others to the back door of the truck. Two other men had appeared. They stood alongside Alvin, shining flashlights. The one who had driven Pat's Volvo, a surly looking weasel, glared at Myles as though he couldn't believe anyone could be that tall. As Pat and Dez opened the back doors, Alvin's men illuminated piles of neatly stacked boxes.

Pat climbed up and lifted down a large cardboard box. Alvin placed it on the ground, ripped off the top and began examining a carton of cigarettes. Pat handed another large box to Myles. Myles took the box from Pat and held it, unsure what to do.

Now he was an accessory, Myles thought. His fingerprints were on the box.

Pat was about to jump down when a sudden rustling came from inside the truck. An overhead light buzzed into brightness and there was movement behind the stacks of boxes. The weasel quickly reached into his inside pocket. Everybody froze as a wild-haired man with a bare chest and black underpants emerged blinking into the light. The man shielded his eyes to squint at them. A young blonde woman appeared alongside him, clutching a sleeping bag to her bare shoulders.

Myles let go of the cardboard box. It hit the ground with a

thud, spilling cigarette cartons. Everyone turned to stare at him.

'Sorry,' he said.

Everyone dismissed him and turned back to the occupants of the truck.

'Howaryis,' the man said politely. 'Do you mind if I ask yis what yis think yis are doing with my truck?'

After that, things became heated.

Alvin adjusted his collar and picked a bit of fluff off his shoulder. 'This has nothing to do with me,' he said, before walking away, taking his men with him.

'I know where you live,' the truck driver shouted after him.

'I'll move,' Alvin shouted back.

'Yeah, well you won't be able to move far enough. I've got pals.'

The truck driver turned to Pat, Dez and Myles. 'My pals will take a dim view of this hijacking,' he said.

'He's right,' the blonde woman assured everyone. 'He has absolutely stacks of pals.'

Pat spread his hands, like a pastor giving absolution.

'I'd hate you to think of it as a hijacking. Think of it as a misunderstanding,' he said.

The driver looked hard at him. 'I can find out where you live,' he said. He swept his hands out to include the other two. 'I can find out where all of yis live.'

'Youse better listen to him,' the blonde nodded. 'He has done a lot of work on himself.'

'Shut your jaws, you silly wagon,' Dez said.

Pat stepped closer as the truck driver braced as though about to launch himself at Dez.

'I'm sure we can work this out between ourselves,' he said.

'Are you starting with me?' the man yelled. 'Come on then, I'll take the lot of ye.'

'Excuse me,' Dez's weedy voice interrupted the driver's rant. 'Does your missus know that you're doing the horizontal mambo with a young one in the back of your truck?'

'Huh?' the driver said.

The blonde burst into tears and the man immediately sent her to the back of the truck. Then he sat down on the tailboard. He weighed things in his head for a moment, and then he smiled. The smile made him appear like a very nice man. 'I'm sure we can work this out between us,' he said.

Following an intense discussion, the driver agreed to forget about tonight if everyone else would forget about the blonde.

'Agreed,' Pat said.

They shook on it.

Negotiations over, Pat, Dez and Myles got into Pat's Volvo and the truck driver and the blonde climbed into the cab of the truck. Pat waited until the truck had driven off before starting the Volvo's engine and turning the car in the opposite direction.

Dez hunched in the passenger seat like a disappointed child. Myles sprawled along the back seat so that he wouldn't bang his head on the underside of the car roof. They sat in silence until suddenly Pat snorted.

'The face on your man,' he said.

Pat and Dez looked at each other then erupted. They laughed like helpless children until their faces turned red and puffy. Eventually it became so intense that Pat pulled into the kerb so that the waves of hysteria could wash over them.

At first Myles was surprised that they could be so blasé about having wasted a night's work, and at considerable risk to themselves. The hilarity was infectious, however. Gradually he was sucked into the mood, and without really knowing why, he laughed too.

'I bet your man has a colour telly back there,' Pat said.

'And a fridge,' Dez spluttered.

'Wouldn't surprise me if he has a Jacuzzi too.'

'Not bad going for a wrinkled old prune.'

'He must be fifty.'

'Easily sixty.'

'You could hang your washing from his beer belly.'

'What age is the little honey – seventeen?'

'Sixteen.'

Dez smiled. 'You notice the way she had eyes for me?'

'No,' Pat said.

Dez puffed himself up. 'You're just jealous cos I have that special something that ladies want from a bloke.'

'What's that – bad breath?'

'I have what they call "The Touch".'

'The touch?' Pat winked at Myles in the mirror.

'A woman only has to look in my eyes when I'm doing her hair and they're gone. The secret is you go slowly. Caress and tease. Treat each hair like it's a person. I don't "do hair". I make love to a woman's follicles.'

There was silence for a moment as Dez let this sink in.

'Follicles?' Pat said.

'Follicles,' Dez nodded. 'Come round to the salon someday and see how it's done.'

Pat thought for a moment. 'Thanks, I might. Follicles, that is interesting.'

'Afterwards,' Dez continued, 'the towels come off, the curlers come out, and the women look me in the eye and say, "Dezmondo, you're an artist."'

'What about that woman last week whose "follicles" accidentally got dyed blue?'

'She wanted blue.' Dez looked at Pat. 'Hey, can I help it if she changes her mind?'

As Pat restarted the car and they drove away from the kerb, Myles concluded that tonight's cock-up would make a good gang-who-couldn't-shoot-straight type of colour piece. He would have to take care not to paint Pat as a ludicrous figure. It didn't matter about Dez, but Pat had done Myles a great favour by bringing him along. The gig had gone smoothly, except for the last bit. How could Pat or anyone have been expected to know that the truck driver had built himself a love nest in the back of his own wagon?

Pat reached into the glove compartment and rummaged about. He took out a cassette and inserted it into the tape deck. The sound of REM singing 'Driver 8' filled the car.

'I hate these bleeding wankbags,' Dez said.

'You had your Puff Daddy earlier. Now it's my turn.'

'At least that was real, this is just whingeing.'

'What's wrong with REM?'

'They're fuckheads. I have proof.'

'What are you on about?'

'Listen. I'm at the Shelbourne bar minding my own business one night and who do I see? Michael Stripe, that's who.'

'It's Michael Stipe,' Pat said.

'Stipe, Stripe, who cares? Anyway, he is all on his owneo. That man is such a complete poser that even the people of Ireland won't drink with him.'

'He's a good songwriter.'

'Hey, I could write a better song than REM anyday. I have a good friend in the music biz. Know what he tells me?'

'No,' Pat said. 'But I've a feeling you're going to tell me.'

'It's a well-known fact that Michael Stripe—'

'It's Stipe.'

'OK, OK. Michael "Stipe" writes lyrics by cutting words out of magazines and mixing them all together. Boom, boom – instant songs. I could do that.'

'You could write better songs than REM?'

Pat caught Myles's eye in the rear-view mirror and winked to show that he was winding Dez up.

'Of course. Listen, there are hundreds of better songwriters than Michael Stipe. I just happen to be one of them.'

'How are we gonna break the news to all the millions of REM fans?' Pat said.

Dez snorted. 'They're only fans cos they've been brainwashed. That Michael Stripe is a waste of space.'

'Michael *Stipe*.'

'Him too.'

'You've a lot in common then,' Pat said. 'What do you think Myles?'

'REM are OK,' Myles said diplomatically. 'But I like Van Morrison.'

'He the bloke that sings the song about "The Brown-Eyed Girl"?' Dez asked.

'Yep,' Pat said. 'Van the Man is a genius, isn't he Myles?'

'Absolutely.'

'He's another massive poxbottle. What's so genius about writing a song about a brown-eyed girl? Now, if he wrote a song about a red-eyed girl, I'd be impressed. Even a song about a pink-eyed girl might make him a genius.'

Pat laughed and turned the music up. Dez turned it down. They kept this going for a while until boredom set in. Myles got the impression that they went through this type of routine many times. It probably kept them sane on gigs.

When they were finished messing, Pat caught Myles's gaze again. 'Pity about tonight.'

'Well,' Myles said. 'It was different.'

'Hey listen, I don't want my real name used,' Dez said. 'In fact, I don't want to be in this article at all, OK?'

'Fair enough,' Myles said.

'Keep quiet, Dez,' Pat said. 'Listen Myles, tell you what. Forget tonight and I promise you a really sweet story by the end of the week.'

'I don't know,' Myles said. 'My deadline is Friday morning.'

'What's the use of a deadline when you don't have a story?' Pat handed Myles a small silver hip flask. Myles took a sip. Brandy scorched his lips and throat but it made him feel alert and glowing inside. He handed it back.

Pat's eyes glinted in the murk. 'Put it off a while. I've got a really sweet piece of action for you. Worth waiting for, I guarantee. Trust me.'

Myles didn't want to tell Pat that this was a make-or-break story. If he didn't have the piece ready for Migraine on the agreed deadline then he might lose his chance of being a features ace, not to mention three hundred smackers. Migraine believed in deadlines, but he seemed to believe in Myles too.

'I'll see what I can do. Maybe I'll say I need more time.'

'Now you're talking.'

'Take a right-hand hammer,' Dez said. 'Short cut.'

Pat turned off the main road onto a side street. Halfway up, a red-haired girl on a bicycle suddenly appeared in their headlights. Myles saw the girl's shocked expression just before Pat hit the brakes and she disappeared. The car jerked violently. There was a clump followed by a loud clattering. A bunch of flowers hit the windscreen then scattered.

Pat cut the engine. After a moment, he reached over to the tape deck and turned down Michael Stipe singing 'This one goes out to the one I love'.

'Jesus.'

'You hit her or what?'

'What do you mean "I hit her?" She came out of nowhere.'

'Get out and look.'

'No, you go.'

Nobody moved.

Then the red-haired girl popped up from directly under the front windscreen. A pale face framed a long nose and full lips over a delicate chin. Vivid green eyes glared accusingly at them. Unusual looking yet attractive in a sultry sort of way. Early twenties, dressed in a red duffel coat. Middle-class rich kid living on Daddy's money, Myles guessed.

The girl approached the driver's window. Myles noticed that Pat was smiling now, as though he no longer saw this incident as an accident, more as a chance for a pick-up.

Typical.

During the Leaving Cert, Pat had skipped the geography paper in order to chat up a pretty shop assistant. It had been worth it, he had said afterwards. He had brought the girl down to Stephen's Green during her lunch break and they had made love in the bushes with a bunch of ducks looking on. He had learned all the geography he would ever need, he told Myles afterwards.

Pat rolled down the window. 'You alright?'

'You could have killed me,' the red-head said, fighting to keep her voice steady. 'This is a one-way street.'

'We are only going one way,' Pat twinkled at her. She ignored his attempt at wit.

'You need your eyes tested,' she said.

She turned away from them and walked over to where her bicycle lay. She picked it up, knelt down to check for damage, then wheeled it over to the footpath where she stood, bewildered. She looked at all the flowers lying around. A striking, medium-sized girl with unusual features, yet who was far more attractive and interesting than most pretty girls Myles had seen. He noticed that she was wearing flowery Doc Martens.

On impulse he opened the door and got out of the car to help.

'Where are you going?' Pat asked.

'Back in a moment.'

Myles picked up some flowers and handed them to the girl, who took them without looking at him.

'Are you OK?'

'Go back to your friends.' She walked past him.

'I was just—'

'I can handle this by myself.'

'It's no trouble.' Myles watched as she gathered the remaining stems.

The Volvo's door opened and Pat got out. 'Since when is this a one-way street?'

The red-head calmly arranged the flowers into a bundle and tied them with an elastic band. 'Since ages ago. Reverse and take a look if you don't believe me.'

Dez leaned out of the passenger window. 'Hey, she's alive, so what are we waiting around for?'

Pat ignored him. He studied the girl with new interest.

'Maybe you are the one who needs their eyes tested,' he said softly. 'I know this area all my life and never once do I see a sign that says—'

'Yeah well, they changed it,' she said abruptly.

'When?'

'Ages ago. To stop guys like you speeding around like they're at the Monte Carlo rally.'

The girl and Pat looked at each other for a moment. A challenge passed between them.

She shrugged. 'Go and see for yourself.'

'OK, I will,' Pat said, and got back into the car. In a moment he had started the engine, shifted gears, and began to reverse back up the street. Alongside him, Dez's livid face spat out curses.

The red-head finished tying her flowers, picked up her bike and carefully remounted. She gave Myles a quick look that hardly seemed to register him at all. He may as well have been a bus stop for all the notice she took of him. He felt a sudden urge to do or say something that would force her to engage with him or at least acknowledge his presence. He wanted to ask her where she was going with a bouquet of flowers at four in the morning. He wanted to protect her in case she got knocked down again.

A small envelope lay on the ground. She had her back to him and was about to cycle off after the car. Quickly, Myles bent down and picked up the envelope. It was addressed to 'Barry'. Lifting the flap, he noticed a card inside. He put the envelope into his pocket, and ran after the red-head.

'Hang on,' he yelled. 'What's your name?'

'You don't need to know that,' she said, speeding away without looking around. 'Thanks for the help anyway.'

She pedalled until she reached the end of the street where the Volvo had pulled up. Pat climbed out of the car with a triumphant smile on his face.

'See. There's no sign,' he shouted. 'I come all the way back here for nothing.'

The girl sped past, legs pedalling furiously. 'Yeah well, you're a right eejit for believing me then aren't you?' she shouted back, just before she shot around the corner and disappeared.

The smile dropped off Pat's face as though he had been slapped. It was replaced by a sudden dark look of rage. Dez shouted something from inside the car. Pat jumped back in and smacked his fist into the horn. A long loud blast ripped through the night. For a moment, Myles thought that Pat and Dez had decided to go after her. Then Pat saw Myles arriving and immediately his expression softened. He leaned back and opened the back door. When Myles climbed in Pat was all smiles again.

'Nice to have a bit of diversion now and again,' he said.

'Well, nobody got hurt,' Myles said weakly. 'That's the main thing.'

'Little Miss fucking One-Way Street,' Dez hissed.

They drove in silence for a moment. REM gargled quietly amid the engine noise. Nobody bothered to turn them up.

'Listen,' Pat said softly. 'If you like you can come back to my place for a few jars and a bit of blow. Finish the night on a high.'

'Oh,' Myles began. 'Maybe next time. It's a bit late.'

'Suit yourself. But the offer stays open.'

Dez turned around and looked at both of them. 'Wanna know what I think?'

Pat sighed. 'What do you think?'

'I think we should have run the bitch over.'

T W O

Black Pat

Myles woke up in the bath with a rolled up towel for a pillow and a tap dripping cold water onto his forehead. He saw his own legs extending halfway up the far wall as though he had been capsized.

Slowly, he untangled himself and climbed out, feeling shivery. There was a distant high-pitched whining in his ears, which sounded like a small animal being sawn in half. In the mirror, he loomed pale and stubble-jawed. His light blue eyes were clear but the skin beneath was flaky and angry-looking. Shafts of his fair hair stood at odd angles as though he had been electrocuted.

He looked almost normal.

Last night he had only meant to take a short nap. He hadn't felt like tiptoeing down the corridor to his bedroom. But the large swigs of brandy he'd gulped from Pat's hip flask, along with several tokes from a joint, had ensured that he passed out the instant his head hit the towel. He checked his watch. Almost eight. He didn't feel too bad considering he had only had around four hour's sleep. A delicious buzz ran through him as he recalled the events of the previous night. There he had been, strolling like a desperado across the wet-nosed tarmac to the glistening truck. He remembered the mixture of fear and excitement that had gripped his insides as they sped along sleeping city streets. It was like rewinding highlights from the hit movie of his life.

Pat had promised to call later this afternoon with details of a 'really sweet story'. He had a good feeling about where all of this was going to lead him. Pat had returned and had helped to pull him out of a rut. Life had come into focus again. Now there would be possibilities.

After combing his hair, he straightened his shirt and picked bits of fluff from his jacket and jeans. Then, cupping his hand over his mouth and nose, he blew into his palm to find that his breath stank. He drank cold water from the tap. Next he brushed his teeth. He took his shaving kit out of his kit bag, lathered his face, then shaved himself slowly and carefully. Didn't gouge his skin once, which proved he was in good mental shape. He checked his clothes in the mirror and decided against trudging down the corridor to change. What he had on may look a bit crumpled but it would do for another day. He found a tube of Lifeguard deodorant, opened a button on his shirt and sprayed under his arms, across his chest and finally around his groin. He gave the latter another shot to be sure.

One last thing. He got out his tape measure, kicked off his shoes and measured himself. Six feet six and a half inches. No change. Perhaps he had stopped growing. He certainly felt less anxious now. Then he had a chilling thought. What if the weird growing process suddenly began reversing itself? What if he started shrinking?

He put the notion out of his mind, tidied up his shaving things and went downstairs.

As he descended, the distant whining noise grew increasingly shrill and urgent. At the kitchen door, he hesitated. The whining came from inside. He paused and listened. From within a woman's voice coaxed, 'Go easier on the bow, darling, it's not a toy.'

Resisting the urge to sneak down the hall and out the front door and away, he entered the kitchen. Inside, the familiar, large, gloomy room of his childhood greeted him. The doorknob came away in his hand.

His mother stood by the cooker with her back to him, smoke

rising over her head, radio softly babbling beside her. Lucy sat at the table keeping an eye on five-year-old Justine who had set up her violin stand in the middle of the room and was sawing away with grim concentration. No sign of Myles's sleepy-eyed elder brother Philip who was probably in his room on the top floor messing with his model trains until it was time to open the family pub. Big Paddy, wearing his starched green captain's uniform, looked down from his portrait above the cooker, keeping an eye on everything from the next world. A similar portrait hung over the bar of the pub next door. Others were distributed throughout most of the rooms in the house, except the bathroom. Nobody wanted Big Paddy looking at them in the bathroom.

'Morning everyone,' Myles said, attempting to force the handle back on the door.

'Daddy,' Justine said. 'I'm practising.'

'It sounds great darling.'

'Good morning,' Lucy said.

He was relieved that she didn't appear too depressed this morning. At least she had said 'hi'. His mother turned around and studied him with one watery pale blue eye through thick-rimmed glasses. Her other eye was hidden by a large black patch. Her good eye glanced at the doorknob in his hand.

'I only super-glued that yoke back on yesterday.'

'Sorry about that,' Myles said, pushing the knob back into its hole in the door and giving it a final twist. 'Look, it's grand now. How's the eye?'

His mother turned back to her cooking.

'Oh it's alright. As good as you can expect at this stage. Those doctors don't know anything about a woman's eyes.'

A year ago, she had accidentally poked herself in the eye with a teaspoon during a big drinking and singing session with her traditional musician friends. Next morning, she told everyone that she had contracted a rare ailment of the iris that might lead to her losing her sight. Even those who were present at the teaspoon incident had gone along with her. In case anybody should fail to notice her misfortune, Stella had bought the largest and most dramatic eye-patch she could find to cover her wound. Now she was considering having a gem sewn into the centre of the patch to make it more impressive. Some eejit in the pub had told her that opals were great for healing eye wounds.

'OK Justine, that's plenty,' Lucy said. 'We'll do more practice tonight.'

Myles walked briskly across to the table, ducking to avoid the bare lightbulb, and bent to kiss Lucy on the cheek. She received his peck icily and watched Myles with curiosity as he sat down at the table. 'Sleep comfortably last night, did we?'

'It was OK,' he said, and reached for the teapot.

'You must have had a very tiring evening.'

'Very.'

Lucy gave him a smile that started as a smirk and turned into a grimace.

'Dad.' Justine laid her violin and bow down on the table and started on her breakfast. 'We're having sausages. Want to share one?' She held up a ketchup-smeared banger that looked like a newly severed finger.

'No thanks honey, you go ahead.'

Justine popped the severed finger into her mouth. 'Why did you sleep in the bath, Daddy?' she asked with her mouth full.

'Because I was very tired, honey.'

'Did you fill it with hot water or cold water?'

'There was no water, love. That would be dangerous.'

'Mammy, can I sleep in the bath tonight?'

Lucy grimaced. 'No you can't.'

'Why not?'

'Because you're too young,' Lucy said, throwing Myles a murderous look. 'See what you've started.'

A plate of bacon, eggs and sausages appeared in front of him. His mother stood alongside, her head indistinct in a mist of cigarette smoke. She seemed to be mulling over something she wanted to say.

'Thanks very much,' he said.

Stella took a drag on her cigarette. 'God, I opened the bathroom door this morning and I swear I thought you were a corpse lying there.'

'I didn't want to wake anyone,' Myles said.

'No movement, not so much as an eyelid stirred. Dead he was, just like his father.'

'I was just taking a nap.'

'Don't interrupt, darling. There was me thinking to myself, "Here we go again with the agony. How can one woman stand so much heartbreak?" It's not fair.' She took a pull on her cigarette. 'Aw well, I suppose it saves the walk from the bedroom in the morning.'

She sighed, cigarette dangling on her lower lip. 'I had your coffin picked out. I was going to line it with blue velvet to match your eyes,' she said.

Myles said nothing as his mother walked back to the cooker. He watched her lift a small white cup from the counter and drink from it. Then she let out another sigh. In a short while she would go to the pub and welcome the first customers of the day. At lunchtime she would start drinking seriously. By teatime the traditional musicians and poets and people who had fought in the GPO in 1916 and other freeloaders would have occupied the pub like an invading army. At first, Mother would resist all urgings to sing, but after an appropriate interval she would give in. She'd perform rousing versions of 'The Long Black Veil', 'As I Roved Out', 'Do You Love an Apple', and her favourite, 'The Night They Drove Old Dixie Down'. Everyone would tell her that she was the best singer in Ireland and she would instruct Philip to pull free pints.

It had been Lucy's idea to move in with his mother while their new house was being built. 'Think of all the money we'll save,' she had argued. For some reason, he had allowed himself to go along with the plan. 'It'll only be for a couple of months,' Lucy had promised. 'The time will fly.' That had been four months ago, and there was still no sign of Maguire the builder finishing the job, and Myles was running out of money. The other thing he hadn't counted on was that Lucy would get on so well with Stella. It was like having two mothers.

He hated having to live in his old room again. In amongst his old toys and posters and even his thirty-year-old teddy bear that his mother had saved. Only now with Lucy and Justine for roommates. It seemed as though Myles was stuck in his mother's house forever.

He glanced up at the portrait of Big Paddy. His father winked at him. 'Never get off one horse till you've another one waiting.' Myles bit off a piece of a rasher. Then he chewed a piece of toast. The food warmed him but it tasted of stale brandy.

'You haven't forgotten our appointment later on this afternoon, have you?' Lucy asked.

'No,' Myles lied. 'Of course I haven't.'

What was she on about? It wasn't the anniversary of their moving in together, though he usually forgot that. And it wasn't like her to remind him anyway. She preferred to let him forget under his own steam, then twist his guts about it afterwards. Perhaps it was her birthday.

'You have forgotten,' she announced. 'I recognise that vacant expression.'

'Ah, the vacant expression.' Stella blew smoke. 'Sure, he got it from his father. Paddy was a virtuoso of the vacant expression.'

'I haven't forgotten anything,' Myles said.

Lucy smiled as she handed him a piece of paper. 'Fitzwilliam Square, number 40a, eleven-thirty a.m. Here, I've written it down just in case. The counsellor's name is Frank Forage.'

'Thanks,' Myles said.

Another session to assist with Lucy's battle against depression. Another useless diversion that he would have to fork out for. Only this time she wanted him to come along to lend support. That was OK. He could sit around and act glum for a while; fifty quid a session was enough to depress anyone. He had already missed two. He couldn't let Lucy down again. Unless he forgot. He could feel himself beginning to forget already.

'By the way, these came when you were in the bathroom.' Lucy passed him a sheaf of ESB bills, Visa demands, phone and gas bills, and some other letters.

'Thanks.'

As he placed the counsellor's address and the bills into his pocket, his fingers made contact with an unfamiliar object. He pulled out the envelope from last night, addressed to 'Barry'.

Opening the flap, he lifted out the small card and glanced at it: 'Molly's Flower Shop, flowers for all occasions', it read. Underneath was a squiggly hand-written inscription that he couldn't make out. The signature was illegible. It began with an 'M'. Mary? Maria? Maeve? Impossible to tell.

'Fan-mail?' Lucy asked.

'It's nothing,' Myles said, quickly thrusting the card and the envelope back into his pocket. 'Just the usual rubbish. Listen, I've got to run.'

He stood up from the table, went over to Justine and kissed her on the forehead before heading for the door.

'Good luck everyone,' he said cheerfully. 'I'll see you later.'

'Myles,' Lucy said sharply. 'You can't leave now.'

He stopped. 'Why not?'

Lucy smiled, as if she were addressing a child. 'You've got muddy marks all down the back of your trousers.'

Myles contorted in the doorway, examining his trousers. From behind, it looked like he was wearing a field. The evidence of last night's fall down the hillside.

'It must have been a *very* tiring night,' his mother said.

The newsroom seemed uncharacteristically calm. People stared into their computer screens, as though meditating. There was no sign of the editor or his staff, just subs and reporters. Some people noticed Myles passing through but few acknowledged him. Myles worked in features, an inferior area as far as news people were concerned. To news people, features people were the wimps of the industry.

At the entrance to the features department he ran into Bob Casper, a skeletal man with a hook nose on a thin, bird-like face, who always displayed a childish delight in the misfortune of others. For some reason Myles was still trying to work out, Bob Casper had become his best friend at work.

'Heard the news boyo?'

'No,' Myles said.

Bob Casper's face lit up. 'Migraine's dead.'

'What?'

'Deceased. Passed on. Shuffled off this mortal coil. Isn't that fucking brilliant news?' Bob made a grand gesture with his hands. 'Migraine is no more.'

'I get the picture. When did this happen?'

'This morning boyo, at around six. Massive heart attack. Who says there's no God, eh?'

Myles didn't know what to say. 'I was wondering why things were so quiet.'

'They're all delighted. They just don't want to show it in case someone gives them something to do, like write a news story.'

Myles didn't share Bob's delight. Migraine McGann had been a gruff, overbearing bully, but he had had a soft spot for Myles. Four years ago, Migraine had been instrumental in promoting him from copyboy to sub-editor. He had commissioned him to write a rock column, encouraged him to express himself through occasional four-hundred-word features. Migraine had believed in Myles. The fact that he and Myles's late father had been best friends in the army was entirely incidental.

Bob Casper chattered amiably about the various contenders for the job of features editor. The smart money was on Gargan, a blustering red-faced news hound with big blond hair who was known as 'The Sperm with the Perm'.

'Tell you boyo, if Fowler gives the gig to The Sperm, I'm joining the *Catholic Standard*.'

'You wouldn't go for the job yourself?'

Bob waved away the thought. 'Not at all. Sure, I wouldn't want to peak too early. Anyway, that's all the good news. The bad news is that Brazil are going to stuff Holland tonight.'

He had forgotten about the Subbuteo table soccer championship. Every year a dozen features hacks hunched together excitedly over a green baize tablecloth to flick miniature footballers on stands at a tiny plastic ball. The prize was an inch-high, made in Taiwan replica of the World Cup. In reality the whole shebang was an excuse to get trashed. Even so, they took their table soccer very seriously. Last year there had been arguments and several walkouts. During the semi-finals, Lola Wall, the tragic-faced assistant features editor who wouldn't swot a fly, had attempted to strangle ace crime writer, Jarlath Boon.

'Oh God, is that tonight?'

'Don't tell me you're chickening out on us. Five o'clock, the back room of the Nerve, right?'

'Right,' Myles said.

Bob walked off, looking happier than Myles could ever remember seeing him. Nothing like the sudden death of an editor to cheer up a colleague.

Features was a long, musty smelling room with grey walls. Cream-coloured computer terminals rested on brown wooden tables. There were no posters on the walls; no decorations at all. It might have been a waiting room in limbo.

Myles said hello to Dogbrain, a flabby white-haired ancient sub-editor who had been sitting at the same desk since the Civil War and who had been unable and unwilling to master new technology. Everyone else used computer terminals except Dogbrain, who still tapped away with two fingers on an old portable Remington.

'Everyone was looking for you,' Dogbrain said cheerfully.

Dozens of messages lay piled on Myles's desk. At least half seemed to come from Jarlath Boon, ace feature writer and grade A pain in the arse. There was also a message from Pat with a phone number to ring.

'See Migraine's dead,' Myles said.

Dogbrain stopped typing. His wrinkled face turned youthful in shock. 'Get away. You're codding me right?'

Myles explained what he knew and Dogbrain listened attentively, then shook his head.

'Couldn't have happened to a nicer fellow,' he said.

Just then Dogbrain's phone rang and he answered.

'Call for you,' he said, holding up his phone. 'It's Jarlath Boon.'

'Tell him I'm not in.'

'He says to tell you that he saw you come in.'

'Then tell him he was mistaken.'

Dogbrain spoke quietly into the phone. 'Jarlath, Myles says that you were mistaken.'

Myles groaned, then sat down at his desk by the window and phoned the number left by Pat. Dez's voice answered. 'How's it goin' Goalpost?'

'Alright till I spoke to you.'

'Pat wants you to meet him Friday lunchtime. Says to tell you it'll make up for last night. Got a pen?'

'Fire away.'

Dez gave Myles the address of The Crazy Horse, a pub on the docks famous for its pints of Guinness and its ballad sessions.

'Try not to fall off any hills,' Dez said, then the line went dead.

On a whim, Myles removed the card from his pocket and examined it. He lifted down the Yellow Pages from atop the cabinet and looked up florists. He found a number for Molly's Flower Shop, and dialled. A woman's voice answered. Myles launched into a big story. He said he had found a card belonging to a girl he had met and whose name he couldn't decipher, and that he was very keen to return the card to the girl personally. The woman replied that it was against the policy of the shop to give out the name or the address of any of their customers. Anyway, the woman said, the owner wasn't there at the moment so there was nothing she could do. Myles thanked the woman and hung up.

As he placed the receiver back in its cradle, he became aware of a figure standing by his desk. He looked up to find Jarlath Boon glaring down at him.

'Crime is my area,' Jarlath said. 'You're double-jobbing.'

'It was Migraine's idea,' Myles lied.

Jarlath gave him a sarcastic smile. 'That's odd. He said it was your idea. Pity the poor man's dead now so we can't prove it.'

'Yes it is. He was a good man.'

'You'll never publish that article in this newspaper. I'll go to Fowler if necessary.'

Myles stood up, towering over Jarlath Boon to make him feel insecure. 'Well, I'm sorry you feel that way. I have to go now. I'm late for an appointment.'

'You knew it was my area. Why didn't you clear it with me?'

'You mean you didn't get my message?'

'No,' Jarlath said, momentarily thrown by Myles's lie. 'You could have phoned me at home.'

'I tried, you were constantly engaged.'

He took advantage of Boon's confusion to break away and head for the door.

Outside in the corridor Jarlath caught up with him.

'You're being bloody immature.'

'Sorry Jarlath, I'm in a fierce hurry.'

'You just got here.'

'We'll talk when I get back, I promise,' Myles said, and skipped down the stairs as fast as he could. Jarlath caught up with him again and continued to harangue him without looking where he was going. Jarlath had worked in the building for over thirty years, he said. He was not going to take this kind of interference from a 'lanky poxbottle' like Myles.

'It's no good running away from me. I deal with hard chaws every day. A lad like you is no bother. Doesn't matter to me how bloody tall you are.'

Downstairs, Myles pressed the buzzer that released the lock on the doors to the newspaper lobby and went through, followed by Jarlath.

'I never liked you from the moment you joined. You only got in here because of your father. You'd never have made it on your own merits.'

'I'm sorry, I really have to run.' Myles rushed out the main door and down the steps.

Once in the street, he broke into a run. After a few moments Jarlath appeared at his elbow, also running.

'I was a champion distance runner in college,' Jarlath said breathlessly. 'You can run, but you can't get away.'

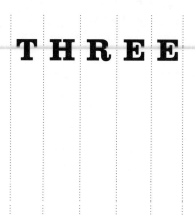

T H R E E

Lucy

At the first knock the imposing Georgian door swung open, revealing a large bearded man with ginger hair and glasses. The man wore a billowing Hawaiian shirt with palm trees on it. He beamed hugely at Myles.

'Hello, I'm Myles Sheridan—' he began.

The ginger man cut him off. 'Of course you are. I've known all about you for so long, I feel as though I'm married to you myself.' He had a melodic English accent that would have sounded cheerful announcing an earthquake. 'Frank Forage.' He extended his hand. 'Pleased to meet you.'

Frank Forage had an extremely powerful grip and long curling fingernails. It was as though Myles had put his hand into a Venus flytrap.

'I'm afraid I haven't got long, I've got to be back at work in—' Myles began.

Frank stopped him. 'Now this will take only about half an hour and it'll be quite painless really. There's a bundle of us but don't worry, we won't eat you.'

'Oh.' Myles hesitated. 'I thought it was just Lucy and myself, em, with you.'

'Heavens no, dear heart, that would be no use to anyone.' He glanced up at Myles. 'Gosh, you're a tremendous height really, aren't you?' Myles knew what was coming. 'What's the weather like up there?'

'Same as it is down there,' he said.

'Ha ha ha, very good,' Frank Forage said.

He led Myles down a bright hallway and through an open doorway into a large room. Inside, Lucy and a group of other women sat in a semi-circle of hard-backed chairs, drawn up like covered wagons against an Indian attack. Lucy gave him a radiant smile, all the proof he needed that he had walked into an ambush.

'Here we are. Everyone, this is the famous Myles.'

'Hello,' Myles said. The women gave him guarded smiles, as though he was a guest on Rikki Lake who had been dragged on to be ripped apart by his loved ones. Lucy's best pal, Annette, sat there with her arms folded like a boxer waiting for the bell. That was a bad sign. Annette, a small frumpy thing, had always hated him. She figured that he was morally inert, whatever that meant.

The thing was to stay cool. If he let women in therapy see that he felt rattled, they would fall upon him like wolves. So he put on a big, false car salesman's grin.

'Hi,' he said jokingly to Lucy. 'Haven't we met somewhere before?'

She gave him a big smile. 'I'm glad you're here.'

He took a chair next to Lucy and listened as Frank Forage gave a run-down on what the sessions were all about. Myles lost interest after Frank started going on about 'personal affirmation'.

Sitting with her trim ankles crossed and wearing a loose green dress, Lucy looked as fresh-faced and attractive as when Myles had first met her at a gig in the Baggot Inn seven years ago. Back then, she had been sitting at the next table with friends, and because he was a bit drunk he had immediately started flirting with her, which she hadn't seemed to mind. Lucy's pout and her giggle had delighted him. After the gig, he had been captivated by the nonchalant way she rode her Honda 50 without a helmet, long blonde hair streaming like an actress in a French movie. At a party afterwards, he had followed her around, pouring her glasses of Valpolicella out of a two-litre bottle, cracking corny jokes to get her to giggle some more. She was five foot four and he had had to bend down to be heard over the party din. Eventually they had ended up sitting together on a window-ledge. Emboldened by wine and mindful that she appeared shy, he had wrapped the curtains around them. They had kissed while Dexy's Midnight Runners sang, 'Come On Eileen'.

'I suppose a ride is out of the question?' he had asked her. He thought he had blown it until she started giggling again. Later, she had given him a lift home on her Honda. He had stuck out behind her petite frame on the tiny bike like a totem pole. Before parting, he had persuaded her to scrawl her phone number in biro on the leg of his blue jeans. The next morning he had decided that he was in love with her and phoned her to tell her so.

That night, at a party in someone's flat, they had made awkward, gasping, elbows-at-all-angles love inside a spare sleeping bag behind a sofa. A week later she had told him that she was in love with him. His friends had told him that it was a 'phase he was going through'. Her friends had warned her about falling for a tall guy. 'The height difference is too great,' her best friend Annette had protested. Height didn't matter to Lucy; she thought that Myles was sweet and funny and a bit different. Somehow they had scraped together enough money to place a deposit on a semi-detached two-storey in Lucan. Almost three months to the day after they had first met, they had moved into their new home. March twenty-first.

After that the trouble had started.

First Lucy cut her hair. Then she had expected him to mow the lawn every day. She had also insisted on teaching him how to cook. Now her giggle wasn't so appealing or sexy, and her pout seemed more like sulking. Every weekend they broke up. By the Monday evening they were usually back together again. Lucy insisted on celebrating the twenty-first of every month as though it was their wedding anniversary. Or rather, she celebrated it while he always forgot and had to be reminded, which caused them to break up again. He told her that she had become a very different person to the woman he had fallen in love with. She told him that he was dreamy and vague and self-centred and as a lazy as a lump of coal and not half as useful. After a year of incessant strife and walkouts, they had finally agreed to separate for good. That night, to celebrate their amicable parting, they had shared a bottle of wine and retired to the sofa to watch *Friends*. Nine months later, Justine was born. To prove that he cared and took his responsibilities as a father seriously, Myles had moved back in.

For the next four years they had existed in a strange limbo world, where both of them tried hard to put on a nice, politely loving and respectful front for the sake of their child. In reality, neither had much to say to the other. She felt neglected. He felt trapped. Both had quickly got used to it. Neither, though, could find the courage or the willpower to separate again. They never rowed in front of Justine. They always waited until the child was asleep before getting stuck in to each other. Occasionally, they shared a bottle of wine, forgot about their differences and went to bed. Always aware of the permanent after-effects of a good night on the sofa, Myles always used a condom. Once every six months, there would be vague talk about getting married.

Over the past year he had started to stay late at work. At weekends he usually went drinking with his friends. Sometimes, when he was drunk, he had messed around with other women, but had never got into anything too serious. He figured that he would wait until Justine was at least ten before moving out. He didn't want to traumatise the child unnecessarily. Also a year ago Lucy had announced that she was depressed and started going to therapy. The rows had stopped. Instead, they settled for long silences. After he had agreed to pay for the therapy, the silences also stopped and life in limbo was resumed.

Despite everything, Justine had grown into a bright, lively and mischievous five-year-old.

Now here he was, sitting at Lucy's therapy session waiting to be dissected by a gaggle of strangers. Afterwards, Lucy would hand him the bill. He would pay it and everything would be back to normal until the next session.

'This is such a big day, I can't tell you, wait till you meet the gang.'

As Frank Forage introduced the 'gang', Myles noticed that the therapist's accent had taken on an American twang. Frank introduced Harriet, elderly and prim, followed by Jesse, small, young and tidy, and then Claire, a pretty but anorexic twenty-something who looked familiar.

'And, of course, Annette and Myles know each other well,' he said.

'Yes,' Annette said. 'We certainly do.'

'Hello Annette,' Myles said.

'Whatever.'

Frank Forage held his hands in the air. 'OK everyone, I'd like us all to officially welcome Myles to the group. Go on, make him feel at home.'

The women broke into a round of applause that echoed off the walls. Lucy gave him another radiant smile.

Perhaps this wouldn't be so bad. He was being overanxious because it was a new experience. There was nothing wrong with new experiences. He caught Annette giving him a leering grin. Then again, they could be lulling him into a false sense of security. Frank brought the applause to an abrupt close by drawing his finger sharply across his throat.

'Now, this morning we're talking about Unblocking.' He turned to Myles. 'Unblocking is a way of releasing frozen energy. We've unblocked quite a lot of frozen energy in the past few weeks. So Lucy, why don't you talk us through your situation.'

Lucy composed herself, then began, 'Well, I've been thinking about what we were discussing the last day. How each person can play an active role in sorting out their own problems.'

'That's correct,' Frank Forage said. 'What we like to say is that "Every Problem is Simply a Task Designed by Our Inner Selves". That little sentence gets me through many dark days in my own on-going battle with alcoholism.' He paused for a moment to reflect on his struggle. Then he sighed, 'Hey, that's enough about me. Please go on.'

Lucy continued, 'I used to dismiss my own anxieties by helping others. I realise that I blocked up all my energies by focusing every-thing on my family.'

She glanced up quickly at Myles, then back to Frank Forage. 'I would help anyone as long as it wasn't myself.'

'Yes, that's the pattern,' Frank said. 'Absolutely classic. Did the same thing myself.'

Myles sat like a garden gnome as Lucy talked about how she had recently begun to 'explore her inner self' and 'release bottled up aggression and other energies'.

Discreetly, he looked around the room. No posters on the walls. Not even a No Smoking sign. Nothing to distract or daydream upon. He noticed that Claire was peeling some loose skin from the back of her wrist.

Lucy began an indictment of him: Myles responds to this, Myles does not respond to that. She was talking about him as though he hadn't been properly housetrained. Then came the list of war crimes.

Rarely helps with the housework.

Always working late.

~~Blames every row they have on her PMT.~~

Messes around with young women.

Says he wants to marry her but refuses to set a date.

Shows no interest in getting the new house ready.

Never cleans the toilet.

She had been tricked into pregnancy and trapped into a sham common-law marriage.

Throughout the litany, he noticed that she wouldn't meet his eye. None of the others were looking at him either. They all appeared spellbound by Lucy's bid to turn herself into a martyr. If this were a whingeing session, nobody would take any notice. Call it 'group therapy' and a bunch of sad women will gladly fork out fifty quid a week for a good moan that was just as easy to do down the pub. Anyone could see that Frank Forage was a conman. People can be such morons.

He concentrated on blanking his mind, staring ahead of him at the white wall. After a while it became a swirling fog. He allowed his consciousness to drift, a technique he had perfected in school to avoid maths and other boring stuff. Lucy's voice became a far away whirr that he found peculiarly comforting. A feeling of peace overtook him. Moments later, he felt his inner self separate from his body. He floated slowly towards the ceiling. Looking down upon his body seated on the edge of the group, he noticed that he had a bald patch on his head, just off-centre. It was the sort of thing you would never catch in a mirror. Nothing much he could do about it. No point trying to hide it either. He would tell people that it wasn't a bald patch at all; it was simply evidence of his head expanding. He wondered why the body he had left behind didn't just topple onto the floor. After all, he couldn't be in two places at once. How would the group react if his body fell over? Frank Forage would probably try to 'unblock' him. Just then Frank held up a hand and Lucy's voice was cut off. Instantly he was yanked back to earth.

'Is your partner, Myles – is he consistent in his attitude to you?'

'How do you mean?'

'Does he always treat you the same?'

'Well, he forgets our anniversary every year.'

Myles froze. The gravest war crime of all. He had come here in a spirit of goodwill and ended up at the Nuremberg trials. You would think they were married or something. He decided to leave Lucy the moment Justine turned eight.

'So how do you cope?'

She shrugged. 'I used to get angry. Then I got depressed and now I just mope around.'

'Classic,' Frank Forage wagged a long fingernail. 'You see how not coping can devitalise us. Self-pity is another name for self-indulgence. That was the way I was before I found the courage to admit to myself that I was and am now and always be will an addict. Be it alcohol, drugs, gambling or sex. It never fails to amaze me how much life has to teach us and how much we all have to learn. But hey, this isn't about me, this is about you.' He turned to Myles. 'Myles, perhaps you'd like to join in here?'

Sensing a trap, Myles coughed. 'Oh, well, I wouldn't wish to interrupt.'

'There are no interruptions here, Myles, just healing.'

'Right,' he said. 'Well, the first thing I'd like to say is that I don't forget every year.'

They all looked at him.

'Just most years,' he said with a weak grin, hoping to raise a laugh or at least a smile or two.

Nobody laughed, nobody smiled.

'I know I may not the best, em, man in the world, but I hope I'm not the worst either.'

Stony looks.

He continued. 'The other point I wanted to make is that, em, Lucy and myself are not actually married.'

'You're the father of her child,' Annette said crisply, then raised her eyebrows. 'Amazingly.'

'Please,' Frank Forage said. 'Allow Myles the space to unblock.'

'Sorry,' Annette said.

'Myles, please carry on,' Frank urged.

This lot were not going to let him away with anything. He got the impression that they had already made up their minds about his qualities. He would have to take a different approach.

'I admit that it's all my fault,' he said. 'But I do put out the bins and I always put the dirty dishes in the dishwasher.'

'Huh,' Annette said.

Frank Forage leaned across and touched his arm. 'Remember, this isn't about blame. This is about coping and healing.'

Myles pointed at Annette. 'Well someone should tell her.'

Frank Forage shrugged. 'Annette will be unblocking next week. Until then we'll just have to be patient. Remember, coping and healing.'

'Right, coping and healing,' Myles said, softening his voice and adopting a contrite tone. 'I'm beginning to understand that. This has been a real eye-opener for me. I realise that I've been living for over seven years with someone I scarcely know.'

He turned to Lucy. She was eyeing him suspiciously, trying to figure out what he was up to. He tried to think of a sad moment so that he could summon a tear. He settled on the bit where Spock died of radiation poisoning in the second *Star Trek* movie and got shot out into space.

'Lucy has done brilliantly with Justine. She's the creative as well as the driving force in our household. Everything good that happens is as a result of her goodwill and common sense. All I can say is that I realise now that I am going to have to do a lot more if I want this relationship to work.' He saw the faces of Captain Kirk and the crew as Spock was buried at space. He felt a tear begin to roll slowly down his cheek. His voice cracked. 'And I do want this relationship to work. Very much.'

There was silence.

The women looked at him with stunned faces. Even Annette was wide-eyed. Some of them looked at Frank Forage to see what he thought, while others glanced at Lucy.

'Thank you Myles,' Frank Forage said. 'I'm sure we all applaud your candour and those moving sentiments. What do you say, Lucy?'

'I don't know,' she said. 'He's said stuff like this before.' She looked at him. 'But crying, that's new.'

Myles wiped his tear away and gave a small embarrassed laugh. 'I don't blame you for being suspicious. All I can say is that I hope you won't write me off completely. I'm just asking for a chance.'

A compassionate, sincere smile appeared on the therapist's face. Myles decided that he despised Frank Forage.

'Well, I sincerely hope that this session marks a breakthrough. That would be great because you're the first of the partners to come along and participate.'

Myles caught Annette and Jesse exchanging smiles. This was working. He was turning it around. Show a bit of emotion to women and they immediately appoint you an honorary girlie. Even Lucy's expression had softened. Everyone appeared impressed, except for the pretty anorexic, Claire, who sat rigidly with a small hand raised. Frank nodded to her.

'Oh yes, Claire, I hadn't forgotten about you. Lucy, are you comfortable with Claire unblocking with us?'

'I suppose so,' Lucy pouted.

'Good.' Frank Forage turned to Myles. 'Claire unblocked last Tuesday,' he explained. 'Go ahead Claire.'

'Thanks,' Claire said quietly. 'I had a long talk with Lucy about what happened and she has forgiven me. Now I'm working on forgiving myself.'

Myles sensed a sudden tension in the room. Everyone was looking at their feet again. Expecting something dramatic. There was something familiar about the way Claire was looking at him.

'It's just such a coincidence that we should end up in the same group. I wonder if Myles remembers me?'

'I don't think so. Do I know you?'

Claire smiled. 'I worked in the Nerve a few years ago. You used to come in a lot.'

Even though he felt his memory stir, Myles shook his head. 'Sorry.'

'Once you gave me a lift home.'

'I don't remember.'

'You should do. I gave you a blowjob in the back seat.'

After the therapy session had finished, they all went out into the hall where they milled about awkwardly. He expected Lucy to tear into him. Instead he was pleasantly surprised when she came up and kissed him on the cheek. 'Thanks for coming. It meant a lot to me,' she said.

'You're welcome,' he said. 'Thanks for still speaking to me.'

'Of course I'm still speaking to you. We could grab a table at the Elephant tonight,' she said. 'Then maybe a movie with tons of popcorn, the way we used to before Justine was born.'

'Gosh I'd love to,' he said. 'It's just that I'm already committed to playing Subbuteo with the lads from work.'

Lucy's face shrivelled. 'Table soccer?' she said in disbelief, as though she had just been told that she had a month to live.

'It's the finals of the World Cup,' he explained. 'I can't get out of it. How about tomorrow night?'

Lucy smiled and shook her head. 'Myles Sheridan, you're incredible.' She gave him another kiss and went off to talk to Frank Forage.

Myles said goodbye to everyone and walked briskly from Fitzwilliam Square to St Stephen's Green. Walking around the city was a good way to clear the mind, particularly after a stressful experience. It was lunchtime and the streets buzzed with harassed shoppers and stylish young people, as well as packs of office workers on their break. He was due back at work by three so he had a couple of hours to just ramble. The only problem was that the socks he had worn since last night had turned rancid. It felt as though the fabric had burrowed into his flesh. By the time he reached Stephen's Green, his feet itched so badly that he yearned to tear off his shoes and socks, plunk down on the footpath and give the soles of his feet a vigorous scratching.

Apart from the tricky business with Claire of the Blowjobs, he thought the session had gone remarkably well. He remembered Claire as a frisky waitress who worked nights at the Nerve Nightclub a few years ago. She had been so well endowed that Bob Casper had joked that she must be carrying her groceries down the front of her shirt. After one very drunken night in the Nerve, he, Bob, Claire and another young one had driven to Dollymount Strand in Bob's Mazda. He had grappled with Claire in the back seat while Bob had fun with his girl in the front. Just kissing and a spot of groping, followed by some yanking and a bit of caressing. No riding and definitely no blowjobs. A blowjob was not something you'd forget, no matter how drunk you were.

At the top of Grafton Street he came upon a Sock Shop. He went inside and rummaged among the racks until he found a black pair his size. Outside, he walked across to the Green and found an empty park bench by the duck pond. He removed his shoes and quickly changed out of his old socks into the new pair. Instantly his feet felt tranquil. He tossed the old socks in the bin and strode out of the Green, across the pedestrian crossing and over the traffic island past a line of jarveys seated on horse-drawn carriages.

Before turning into Grafton Street, he waved to ancient crumple-faced Johnny Bones, his mother's brother. Johnny tipped his black bowler hat in reply. When Myles was a boy, Johnny had given him summer work driving the tourists around the Green for ten pounds a spin. He looked upon Myles as one of his own boys.

Long before his fingers began toying with the card in his pocket, Myles knew where he was headed. Within minutes he found himself standing outside Molly's Flower Shop. He stopped at the window display, momentarily paralysed by the colours and aromas. Suddenly he wasn't sure if he wanted to go ahead with this. Perhaps he should just throw the card away and forget it. It might look as though he was a stalker. Then again, it would be interesting to see if he could discover the girl's identity. It might turn out to be a useful exercise. Another thought struck him. He would send flowers to Lucy. It would be the last thing she'd expect, and it would make up for not going out with her tonight.

Inside, a small round lady with a pleasant face greeted him. He ordered a bunch of flowers. When the lady asked which flowers he wanted, he paused. He looked around at the various displays astonished by his own ignorance. He recognised roses and possibly marigolds, and the long droopy yokes with helmets in the corner which he suspected were lilies.

'Maybe you'd like me to make up a bouquet?' the lady suggested.

'That would be brilliant,' he said, relieved.

She asked him how much he'd like to spend and he told her around twenty-five quid. She said that he would get a fine bunch for that. He gave her Lucy's name, the address of his mother's pub in Dorset Street, and then he signed a small card: 'To Lucy, x Myles'.

When that was done, he removed the girl's card from his pocket and handed it to the woman, saying that he was keen to track down the girl who was the owner of the signature on the card. He needed to return it to her in person, he said.

The woman studied the card for a moment, and then she smiled at him.

'Gosh, you've just missed her, she was standing right where you are now only ten minutes ago.'

Myles took a step backwards as though he had been pushed.

'She was?'

'Oh yes, sure, she's been expecting you for ages.'

FOUR

Players

Brazil and Holland were level at one goal each in the World Cup Final. With seconds left, the ball landed at the feet of Ronaldo who had only the Dutch goalkeeper to beat. Before he could shoot, Jaap Stam kicked him off the table. Ronaldo hit the floor and his legs broke off.

'Foul,' Bob Casper roared.

'He dived,' Myles said.

In the back room of the Nerve, Dogbrain put his hand in the air, calling for hush.

'Penalty to Brazil,' he announced.

A dozen hacks from the *Daily News*' features department shouted and stamped their feet.

'Ah referee,' Myles protested.

But Bob Casper was already placing the tiny black and white ball on the penalty spot.

Myles had been unbeaten for two years. Fifty-six victories and eleven draws. Last year he had beaten Bob four-nil in the final. The current situation was completely unfair. Myles illegally tilted his goalkeeper to one side to cover as much of the goal as possible.

A shadow loomed over him. 'Goalpost, you're only a lanky poxbottle,' Jarlath Boon's voice slurred.

Earlier, Myles had beaten Jarlath's South Korean team by two goals to nil, despite Jarlath's incessant under-the-breath taunts of 'scab' and 'double-jobber'.

He was about to tell Jarlath to fuck off when Brazil's captain, Rivaldo, flicked the penalty past the Dutch keeper.

'Yesssss,' Bob jumped in the air while Myles picked the tiny ball out of the back of the net.

Within seconds of the restart, Dogbrain blew the whistle for full-time. Brazil had won the World Cup.

Jarlath Boon leered at Myles. 'Told you.'

As the other hacks swarmed around Bob offering congratulations, Myles decided to be gracious in defeat. He gave Bob a forced smile and raised his pint in salute. Then he withdrew to a table at the far end of the room as a photographer snapped Bob attempting to slurp champagne from the mouth of the miniature World Cup.

OK, he thought, let's keep things in perspective here. Bob had won tonight, but that didn't make him a winner and Myles a loser. Guys like Bob got lucky for a while, then one day, for reasons nobody can explain, their run of luck ended. Even the greatest winner has to lose sometime. 'It's never for ever,' Big Paddy used to say. Myles reasoned that all of this was happening for a purpose. Perhaps to indicate that he had lost his passion for the game and that it was now time to retire. Dogbrain handed Myles a fizzing glass.

'It was a good game. Shame there had to be a loser.'

'Yeah,' Myles said. 'Shame you had to award a penalty in the last minute.'

'Yes,' Dogbrain said. 'That was a pity, wasn't it?'

Bob came over, beaming. 'No hard feelings, boyo?'

'Congratulations,' Myles said.

'How long was that unbeaten record of yours?'

'Two years,' he said.

'Had to happen sometime though, didn't it?'

'I suppose so.'

'Ah well, there's always next year.'

'Maybe.'

Bob looked at him, 'Sure it's only a game. But it was a definite penalty.'

'It was only a nudge.'

'You clattered my player.'

'He took a dive.'

'Sure look at him.' Bob opened his palm to reveal Ronaldo broken into tiny pieces. 'Mind you, I think the referee might have stepped on him as well.'

Myles shrugged. 'I'll buy you a new one.'

Bob grinned as he dumped Ronaldo's remains into the ashtray. 'Ah sure, plenty more where he came from. These things happen in football. Cheers.'

Bob raised his glass in a toast to the beautiful game and Myles joined him. They watched as two of the copyboys tidied away the soccer equipment. Last year, after Myles had beaten Bob in the final, Bob had refused to talk to anyone for an hour. Only a game, yeah right. Depends who's winning at the time. Myles decided to change the subject. 'Do you remember a waitress called Claire who used to work in the Nerve?'

Bob considered, 'You mean the one with the big bust who gave you a blowjob on Dollymount Strand?'

'Thanks. That answers my next question too.'

'Any time boyo. Glad to be of service.' Bob paused meaningfully. 'Just like she was. Are you seeing her again?'

'No, not really. I met her today, socially.'

Bob gave him a playful punch on the shoulder. 'You lad you,' he smirked.

Myles decided against telling Bob anything about the therapy session. He regretted mentioning Claire at all in fact, and he was deeply embarrassed that Bob had such a good memory. Dogbrain came over to sit with them. Then two of the other subs, short tragic-faced Lola Wall and baby-faced Cliff Mangan, joined them. Bob ordered more champagne. Myles noticed Jarlath Boon skulking in the far corner with a face on him like a boiled squirrel.

Today had not been great. First there had been the wake-up in the bath, next the hassle at work with Jarlath, followed by Lucy's humiliating therapy session. Migraine, his mentor, was dead and now he had lost his status as table soccer champion. The only interesting aspect of his day had been the visit to Molly's Flower Shop, but even that had been accompanied by the disturbing news that the red-head had been 'expecting him'. What did that mean? The small, round flower shop lady had reminded him of the type of easy-going primary schoolteacher who could never control her class. She had had to search around for ages for the message the girl had left for him.

Eventually, she had discovered a piece of paper sticking out from under a plant. 'Yes, here we are. I knew I wrote it down. She says she'll be working in Roolaboola's all this week if you want to call in.' She hadn't been able to tell him why the girl had been expecting him. 'You'll have to ask her that yourself,' she'd replied in her soft northern burr. All she would tell him was that the girl was an excellent customer, purchasing expensive flowers at least once a week. 'Now, I've probably said too much.' Myles had thanked her and left the shop. Outside, he had immediately swung on his heel and re-entered to ask if the lady could tell him the girl's name. She had smiled softly; sorry, she couldn't tell him that either.

Roolaboola's was a new nightclub on George's Street. Reputedly the coolest nightspot in the city, it catered mainly for students and clubbers. He could walk there in less than five minutes. It might save tonight from being just a bad memory. Bob leaned over to him. 'I'm in the mood to get rat-arsed tonight. What do you say?'

'Game on,' Myles said.

The queue snaked along the street and around the corner from Roolaboola's. Clubber girls posed in skimpy tops and luminous pants, retro hippychicks wore flowery pants and dresses. The boys played it cool in lumberjack shirts, combats and trainers. It was cold but everyone looked youthful, perfect and cool, with shiver-proof skin. By the time they had walked to the end of the queue, the combined array of style, bare flesh and surface poise made Myles, Bob and Cliff feel like has-beens.

'We'll never get in,' Cliff Mangan said.

'Look at all the hippy crap,' Bob said. 'Sure, none of these fucking teenyboppers was even born in the 70s. We're too mature for this.'

'Speak for yourself,' Cliff said. 'I was born in seventy-five.'

'Don't worry, follow me,' Myles said, determined that the evening was not going to be a dead loss.

He led them past the waiting punters to the entrance and showed his press card to the bouncers, telling them he wanted to review the night for the *Evening News*.

'You'll have to ask Garvin,' a bouncer said, beckoning to someone inside.

Garvin was a young, good-looking, black man with a crew-cut, purple lipstick and a bright purple sequinned dress.

'OK,' Garvin said in a whiney voice. 'But you'll have to promise me that you'll write nothing unpleasant about the club. I'm not letting you in if you say nasty things about us.'

'Cross my heart' Myles said, and Garvin waved them past.

Bob walked slowly with a superior smirk as though he were doing people a favour by being there. Myles kept an eye out for the red-head as he and Cliff guided their colleague through the throngs clogging the passageway into the main dance area. Streams of cheery, sweating young people passed them, dancing their way towards the cloakrooms or the toilets. Some just seemed to be bopping about aimlessly.

Inside, the place heaved to harsh beats that sounded like speeded up jackhammers. Strobe lights pulsated across a hive of spinning bodies. Pale shrouds dangled from the rafters like hanged monks. They made their way across the sheeny metal floor as youngsters undulated in an ocean of pink and green with occasional detonations of dazzling orange. From a metal cage in the centre of the room a pair of dreadlocked fire-eaters in black leather took it in turns to spew crimson flames at the ceiling. A control box high on the far wall displayed a ghostly pink-tinged figure that was hunched over a set of turntables like a supernatural priest.

Cliff Mangan pointed to the ghostly figure in the control box and shouted, 'That's Boy George.'

'Get away,' Myles said.

'It's true, he's an international club DJ now.'

'My granny's bollocks.' Bob's face registered disbelief. 'What would Boy George be doing in a kip like this?'

They hit a sudden bad smell as they moved through the middle of a clump of E-heads who danced with their chins out as though pleading to be punched. E-heads break wind like donkeys because the drug relaxes muscles in their lower bodies. Myles had never been very impressed by the drug. What was the point of taking something that turned you into a fart machine? They went upstairs to a small bar that overlooked the dance area. Half a dozen over-30s sat at small tables, trying to look cool but seeming desperate and a bit sad. They chose a window table that overlooked the throbbing dancefloor. Thick walls reduced the music to a dull pounding. A heavy-set waitress with a beehive hairdo arrived to take their order.

'Are you on the menu?' Bob leered.

'You couldn't afford me, pal,' the beehive drawled.

After a few moments of banter which failed to impress the waitress, Bob ordered champagne and she went away.

'Champers lads?' Bob slapped his hands together. 'Might as well rip it up tonight, what do you say.'

'Grand,' Cliff Mangan said. 'Long as you old-timers are paying.'

Myles scanned the downstairs area. He watched as a dozen E-heads gently ran their hands over the body and face of a young man who stood with his eyes closed as if in a trance. He looked for the red-head but saw nobody he knew. Everyone was dressed glam casual. People danced or moved all the time, even those who were standing talking constantly made little movements. Immediately beneath Myles's window, a nerdy photographer snapped pictures of two attractive blonde girls. Good-looking girls who didn't appear to sweat were ideal for the weekend papers. Can't have young ones with dripping armpits and stains on their dresses. Nobody seemed to be getting off with anyone or even to be hitting on one another. This club was strictly about dancing, not sex. The girls were Teasers and Leavers, into posing and dancing only.

'I preferred him as a singer,' Bob said.

'Who?'

'Boy fucking George. What's he doing playing this diarrhoea?'

'Some of it's alright,' Cliff Mangan said. 'You have to be into it, you know?'

'It's not music. These kids wouldn't know music if it bit them in the goolies.'

'Young people today,' Myles said sarcastically.

Bob pointed a finger at him. 'Do you know what this sounds like? It sounds like someone recorded a power drill up close then mixed in the noise of a jumbo jet going through a hangar. Where's the melody? Where are the songs? I'd even prefer Hawkwind to this, and they're crap.'

'That's a bit harsh,' Myles said.

'Oh yeah, well you're the fucking rock critic so you'd know all about it wouldn't you? Go on then, Mr Critic, name the band playing now?'

Myles listened. A swamp of thumps and glooping noises and a beat over which a distant disembodied voice wailed repeatedly something that sounded like 'Lick me all over'.

'See? I knew it. You don't know.'

'Yes I do. It's System X,' Myles lied. He wasn't going to let Bob have everything his own way. Cliff threw him a meaningful look but Myles ignored it.

'Very fucking impressive. Now what do you want – a medal? This stuff is complete cack. How come nobody plays Bob Marley anymore? That was real dance music.' Bob glanced around him. 'I betcha it's not Boy fucking George at all. They've got some looka-like in from one of those agencies.'

Myles glanced through the window just as the red-head emerged from a group of dancers below. As he watched, she made her way through the dancefloor towards the main entrance. Only Little Miss One-Way Street had such vivid red hair. If he wanted to intercept her, he would have to move now. He stood up, his rapid movement taking the others by surprise.

Bob's face suddenly became concerned. 'You still mad at me for winning the World Cup?'

'Not at all,' Myles said. 'I've just seen someone I know.'

Bob spread his hands like a preacher. 'It's no good being angry. You have to learn to accept these things. Losing is part of life. Just like winning.'

'I'm not angry,' Myles said, beginning to get annoyed with Bob for delaying him. 'Listen, I'll be back in a while.'

'There's no need to get so uppity. You've been acting the grump all night. It was only a game.'

'Well done. The best team won. What else do you want me to say?'

Bob turned to Cliff. 'See what I'm up against?'

Myles hesitated as Bob turned back to him with the face of a jilted lover. 'You've always been a bit too good for the likes of us, haven't you?'

'What are you talking about?' Myles demanded.

'C'mon boyo. The son of the army hero mixing with the plebs out of the goodness of his heart. You can't fool us, can he Cliff?'

Cliff cleared his throat. 'Well, maybe if we could all sit back down and have a talk.'

Just then the beehive arrived with the champagne and Bob switched his attention to her.

'Ah, the return of the beautiful woman with the big hair. C'mere, we know that's not Boy George, we've sussed out that much, haven't we boys?'

The beehive pointed to a poster on the far wall that read: 'DJ Tonite, Boy George.'

'That clear enough for you?' She put the bottle and glasses on the table and accepted two twenties from Cliff, who fetched his wallet out when it became clear that Bob had lost interest in paying.

'I don't believe it,' Bob addressed her. 'I think you're conning us. It's a scam isn't it? The DJ's a lookalike isn't he?'

'Whatever you're having yourself.' The beehive shrugged and walked away.

Bob beamed triumphantly. 'See? What did I tell you?'

'No, it's definitely him,' Cliff Mangan said. 'I can tell by his nose. Look at it.'

As Bob and Cliff began to argue about the size of Boy George's nose, Myles seized his opportunity to leave. 'See you in a few minutes,' he said.

He walked away quickly, ignoring Bob's shout of, 'Hey, don't be a sore loser.'

He ran down the stairs three at a time, descending into an inferno where beats and dancing and the pungent pong of sweaty bodies had coalesced into a ferocious assault on his senses. In the short while that he had been upstairs with the others the dance-floor had become even more crammed. He spotted the red-head about twenty yards away. He moved through the gyrating bodies, striving to keep an eye on her.

Just when he thought he'd lost her he spotted her at a table in an area by the main entrance arguing with a fair-haired man. As Myles moved a few steps closer, a weed in a lumberjack shirt wearing glasses blocked his way, indicating that he wanted a word. Myles bent down as the weed shouted, 'Would you know anything about any Es for sale?'

Impatient that this four-eyed E-head was delaying him, Myles shook his head and attempted to pass by. The weed wouldn't budge.

'Why not?' he shouted. 'I just want six.' He held up six fingers. 'See? Six,' the weed explained.

Myles beckoned to him. 'I'm a cop,' he shouted into the weed's ear.

The E-head looked startled. 'Oh, that's unfortunate,' he said, and melted away into the sea of bodies.

The red-head was still toe-to-toe with the man. Myles stood a few yards away and watched as they yelled at each other. He noticed her strong face and her long bump of a nose and the way her mouth curled to one side when she was angry. She made to walk off but the fair-haired man grabbed her arm. She tried to pull away but he jerked her sharply and she spun into his arms. She pulled free and slapped him hard on the face. Stung, the fair-haired man released her, holding up his hands as though her motives were beyond him. The red-head moved past him towards the exit. As Myles started to push his way through the crowd, something made him look back over his shoulder. From the window of the bar above, he saw Bob and Cliff looking down on him, solemnly. Bob waved the tiny World Cup at him. 'Nana-na-nana,' Bob mouthed.

He caught up with her in the narrow passageway.

'Excuse me,' he said loudly, then, when she didn't react, he shouted louder. 'Excuse me, Miss.'

The red-head pulled up and turned. Her fists were clenched at her sides, her face firm, indicating that she had been anticipating another round with the fair-haired man. It took her a few seconds to focus on Myles.

He smiled to put her at ease. 'Hi, do you remember me?'

'No.'

Her answer shook him. Hadn't she been expecting him? Hadn't she invited him herself? Or had the flower shop lady got it arseways? He tried to appear cool and debonair, but that was difficult because he was still a little breathless from chasing after her.

'I was in the car that nearly ran you down last night.'

She softened. 'Oh yes. The one who got out to help me. That was good of you. Now I suppose you expect a reward.'

'No, I don't.'

'Good,' she said and turned around. 'See you.'

'Hang on,' Myles said, and caught her up again. 'Wait. I have something of yours.'

She turned around and he took the card from his pocket and presented it to her. She looked at it and her expression changed.

'Thanks,' she said. Her brilliant green eyes looked up at him as though she were searching for a switch on a tall lampshade.

'I, em, found it on the ground last night. I thought I should give it back. It looked private so I didn't read it. Em, except for the name of the shop,' he said, inwardly wincing as he realised he sounded like an eejit.

'Thanks,' she said again, softly. 'Are you trying to hit on me?'

Myles found that he couldn't speak for a moment. 'Em, well, I wasn't trying to – em, I just wanted to—'

She smiled, revealing perfect tiny teeth. 'It's OK. Listen, don't mind me, I've had a rough night. It really was good of you to keep the card for me.'

She glanced off to Myles's right side and her face suddenly turned hard. The fair-haired man appeared at Myles's shoulder.

'What do you want?' she said.

'Here,' the fair-haired man said, and tossed her a long black coat. 'A witch needs her cloak.'

The red-head nodded to Myles, indicating the fair-haired guy.

'Hit him,' she said.

Myles blinked. 'Ah, well, I—' he began.

'It's OK, I'm going.' The man gave Myles a sympathetic look before disappearing back into the throng of clubbers. Myles noticed that he had a red mark on his cheek where the red-head had struck him.

She seemed suddenly cheerful. 'OK, Mr Tall. You can walk me to the door.'

'That's no use. How about walking you to a taxi?'

'I'm up for that.'

At the door they passed Garvin, who stood alongside the bouncers, shivering as the night air cut into him. They said 'Goodnight' and he wobbled his head at them.

Outside, the cold bit into Myles's face but he didn't notice. He was excited just being with this girl. He felt like Sherlock Holmes after cracking a difficult case. He forgot about Bob and Cliff in the upstairs bar. He forgot about his World Cup defeat. She put on the long, black velvet coat. It came down to her ankles and made her look much taller and aristocratic. He guessed that the coat was from the 50s, or earlier. A coat peculiar to a disappointed life, he thought to himself, for no good reason.

'Where do you live?'

'Stop fussing, I'm fine.'

'Just trying to help.'

'You make quite a habit of that don't you?'

'I've got lots of bad habits. Some I really enjoy.'

'Where's your Volvo and all your rally driver friends tonight?'

'It wasn't my car and I wasn't driving.'

'They all say that.'

Myles shrugged. 'In that case I'm sorry we missed.'

The red-head giggled through her teeth. It was the first time

Myles had seen the girl smile or heard her laugh. He found it very attractive. Like everything else about her.

They walked up George's Street, then turned down Exchequer Street on their way to the top of Grafton Street to hunt for taxis. There were few people about. Just rows of parked cars and silent shops. He wondered what age she was. Twenty-two? Twenty-three? Born in the 70s, no doubt. What kind of music did she like? Perhaps she'd have some of his favourite bands in her CD collection. Please God she wasn't into Hip-Hop or rap. He could never be with anyone who liked rap. He wanted to make her giggle again. After a while, he noticed that she had begun to limp.

'Are you alright?'

'I can take care of myself.'

'Yes, I saw that. I meant, can you walk?'

'I was dancing earlier. I think someone reefed a lump out of my hoof.'

They stopped by traffic bollards at the junction of Nassau Street and Grafton Street. She hobbled across to a low shop window-ledge where she sat down. She took off her flowery Doc Marten boot and examined her foot. He sat alongside her. After a few moments, she placed her foot across his knees, the sudden familiarity sending a thrill up his backbone.

'Does that look like a bruise to you?'

He touched her slim ankle, then briefly scrutinised her pallid flesh, careful not to hurt her. He saw no marks. He felt an urge to fondle her cute pudgy toes.

'You'll live,' he said. 'It's just a bruise.'

She pulled her foot away and put her sock back on. He felt a pang of regret as her petite foot vanished back inside her flowery boot.

'You haven't told me your name,' he said, as he laced it up.

'You're right, I haven't.'

She looked at him.

'I'm Myles Sheridan.'

He offered her his hand and she shook it. Her small hand in his. She had sharp fingernails. 'I'm six foot six and a half and I specialise in offering a personalised chauffeur service to young ladies in distress.'

'That's nice. But I'm not sleeping with you.'

'Who said anything about sleeping with you?'

'Good, that's settled then.'

'I only asked what your name was.'

'Maybe I'll tell you my name when you get me home,' she said, then added, 'If you can get me home.'

'I can give you a piggy-back, if you like.'

'What if I live miles away?'

'Then I'll give you a piggy-back to the taxi rank.'

She blew air through her teeth. 'Can't you think of something more original than a taxi? I'm sick of taxis. You can never get one and when you do you have to fork out all this money.'

'Where do you live?'

'Mountjoy Square.'

'Leave it to me.'

A mad thought struck him. He was on a roll. This was turning into an interesting night; he didn't want to quit now. 'Wait here for a few minutes, will you?'

'How many minutes?'

'A few.'

'How many's a few?'

'Ten, maybe fifteen at the max.'

'OK, Mr Tall,' she smiled. 'You've got ten minutes.'

'What will you do if I'm not back before then?'

She sighed. 'I'll have to make alternative arrangements.'

'Right, don't budge.'

He ran up Grafton Street, past the darkened windows, the discarded burger boxes and stray cans, dodging a lurching couple and several noisy late-night revellers. This was a risk, he knew. But if it worked, he would be away.

On the corner of Stephen's Green, he found ancient stooped Johnny Bones amongst a group of other jarveys and their wagons. Johnny was about to take his horse and carriage home for the night.

Johnny wasn't surprised to see him, but then, having been a jarvey on Stephen's Green for twenty years, Johnny wasn't surprised by anything anymore.

'Lookit, if it isn't the long fellow,' he said.

'Uncle Johnny, I need a huge favour.'

Clopping down Grafton Street atop the big black and white speckled horse, Myles rode high above the drunks and the garbage and the couples who called out to him.

'It's Clint Eastwood.'

'What's the weather like up there?'

'That's the only ride you'll get tonight.'

Myles saw the red-head seated on a traffic bollard at the bottom of the street with her back to him. He didn't want to call out to her because that would be extremely uncool. Surely she must be able to hear the hoofbeats by now? They were ringing off the buildings around him like gunshots. He was twenty feet from her when she eventually turned around. He saw no hint of surprise on her face. She watched him with a curious, detached expression. She could have been watching a screen far away. Perhaps it was no big thing for her to see a man riding a black and white speckled horse down Grafton Street to give her a lift home. He experienced a twinge of disappointment. He had been expecting to make a bigger impression. He had been expecting to be made for the night.

He reined in the horse in front of her. Instantly her fog cleared. She gave him a big smile and giggled through her teeth. He felt rewarded and even vindicated.

'Not bad,' she said. 'Actually, I'm impressed.'

'Room for one more on top,' Myles said, leaning over and stretching out his hand.

She took it and he pulled her up behind him. She was as light as a child. She made herself comfortable on the saddle then put her arms around his waist and instantly he felt like a hero.

The horse clopped down Suffolk Street and out onto Dame Street. They rode past Trinity College which was lit up and glowing brightly like a church. People called out to them. Cars beeped as they passed. A bunch of scumbags in baseball caps ran alongside. 'Hey mister, giz a go,' a scrawny blond scumbag shouted. 'Sorry lads, full up,' Myles said.

The blond scumbag gave him the finger.

'Ye lanky fuckhead,' the scumbag shouted as he was left behind.

Somehow it felt natural to be riding down O'Connell Street seated atop a sunken-backed nag with an attractive red-head whose name he still didn't know and with all the lights of O'Connell Street shining down on them like it was St Patrick's Day.

It had taken some hard pleading and eventually thirty pounds of Myles's cash before Johnny agreed to part with the horse. 'Tie her to the railings outside your mam's pub and I'll collect her at six a.m.,' Johnny had said gruffly. Myles had even promised to give him a write-up in the *Evening News*. 'About time,' Johnny had grumbled.

As they trotted into the blank-eyed gaze of the Anna Livia statue residing long-legged in its splashing fountain, Myles felt euphoric. Even the empty crisp bags and the burger cases floating among the other rubbish in the glistening yellow water failed to deflate him.

He saw his father seated on the wall of the fountain in his captain's fatigues, chewing a burger.

'Can't that thing go any faster?' his father said as they passed.

When they arrived at Mountjoy Square, the red-head directed him to a large Georgian house on the corner. Myles reined the horse to a standstill outside. The girl climbed down and stood stiffly for a few moments, rubbing her legs. Myles bowed and removed an invisible Stetson.

'Will there be anything else, Ma'am?'

She looked up at him. 'I suppose you expect to come in for ritual sexual intercourse now, do you?'

Myles shrugged. 'What makes you think I want to come in?'

They looked at each other for a moment. The horse neighed and shook its head. Myles stroked its neck. A car beeped at them as it drove past.

She opened the door and turned to him. 'You can come in for a cup of peppermint tea, but that's all, Mr Tall.'

'Best offer I've had all night,' he said.

He climbed down and tied the horse to the railings. Then he followed the girl inside.

FIVE

Red-head

'Come on Mr Tall.'

She led him up the wooden stairs. Her straight-backed posture made her appear noble and self-possessed, and he was excited at the way her black jeans highlighted a strong behind and firm legs. She wasn't skinny; instead she had an attractive, firm roundness about her that made her appear mature and confident. She was a sensational invitation to make babies. He must be away now. He made a list of reasons:

She had accepted a lift home on the back of his horse.

She had brought him home to her apartment after midnight.

She had laughed at his jokes.

The trick now was to show restraint, appear casual, almost uninterested. Women didn't like it when a guy was too keen or made the big move too soon. They enjoyed a build up. Soft talk, cup of tea, bit of banter. Once a woman felt relaxed, then she would get down to it. It was all a matter of keeping his cool.

He was glad that he wasn't drunk, though he regretted not changing his clothes that morning. His underpants felt as though they were welded to him. If he was lucky, she might think that he was sweaty from the nightclub earlier.

The third floor light was on a timer that clicked off as they reached the apartment door. He heard her fumbling with her keys in the darkness.

'Shit balls fuck,' she said. 'This always happens.'

Eventually, after a lot of messing, she opened the door and went inside.

'Wait here,' she said, and disappeared.

He stood by the door, trying to make out his surroundings in the murk. He heard cars swish by outside, and what sounded like an alarm going off somewhere down the street. Far off, Johnny Bones' horse neighed.

Inside the apartment, a match flared, illuminating the red-head hunched over a table fiddling with some type of small oil lamp. The soft light spread, making everything look spooky. She gave him a lopsided grin as she blew out the match, indicating that she enjoyed the effect. She beckoned him inside. He stepped in and closed the door quietly.

They sat on creaky skinny-backed chairs at a round table by large windows that were hung with heavy drapes that blocked out light from the street. The lamplight lent her hair an auburn tint, emphasising her large nose and full lips, her vivid green oval eyes under slender arched eyebrows. She smiled at him as though this were all a game, shook her hair and blew a strand out of her eyes. She seemed sparkling and mysterious and fun. He liked the cute way she chewed her bottom lip as she concentrated on adjusting the wick.

'I don't want to open the curtains,' she whispered as the lamplight grew brighter. 'I can't abide the glow of streetlights. They're so smarmy, don't you think?'

'Oh yes.'

'Streetlights mess up the nighttime and I love nighttime,' she whispered.

'Me too,' he said quickly. 'It's much better than, em, daytime.'

The apartment was a modern open-plan job with almost everything contained in one room. A flight of wooden steps by the doorway led to a bedroom area that was directly over the compact wooden kitchen. He noticed a sliding door at the far end of the room that he presumed led to a bathroom.

'How's your foot?' he whispered, enjoying the feeling that what they were doing was secret and fun.

'It'll do,' she whispered, looking him in the eye. 'Nothing like a good ride late at night to sort out a personal injury.'

He wasn't sure what to say to that. Women liked a man to show subtlety and restraint, even when they themselves were being a bit forward. At least, he presumed that they did. It was difficult to tell exactly what the red-head might look for in a man. She wasn't like any other girl he had ever been with. She seemed more self-assured, less worried about what others thought. For instance, she hadn't asked him what he thought of her apartment. Strange then that he felt a powerful urge to protect her. He could still see her bewildered expression the night that Pat had nearly run her down.

'Listen,' she stood up. 'If you're thinking of making a move on me, just hold off for a while, will you?'

'What makes you think that I—' he began.

'I need a cup of peppermint tea first,' she said.

'Oh, right,' he said, confused. 'Why are we whispering?'

She pointed to the bedroom area. 'Because I don't want to wake Lorcan. Listen, you can hear him.'

Lorcan? It had never occurred to Myles that she could have a male flatmate. He made out the rise and flutter of gentle breathing from the area above the kitchen, a sound that had utterly escaped his attention until now. That explained why she was so relaxed. His conviction that he was going to get laid evaporated.

'We can do anything we want as long as we're quiet,' she said, which did little to restore his optimism.

How could you shag someone when at any second this bloke Lorcan was liable to pop up over the wooden balustrade above?

'Do you have any chocolate on you?' she asked suddenly. 'I'd murder a Crunchie.'

'You must think I'm Father Christmas.'

'You know what they say? The first disappointment of growing up is when you find out that there is no Father Christmas; the second is when you find out that there are no adults.'

'Anything else you don't believe in?'

'Lots of things. Marriage, the church, men who always carry their own condoms.'

'Horse rides home from Grafton Street?'

'I'm still trying to decide about that one.'

'Well, I'm sorry that I don't carry any Crunchies.'

'You're forgiven,' she said. 'How about a cup of peppermint tea?'

'What makes you think I like peppermint tea?'

'You'll like *my* peppermint tea.'

She walked over to the kitchen and flicked a switch on the wall. A small light buzzed on above the cooker. He heard her fiddling about with jars and cups, then the soft, hollow rush of water filling a kettle. As his eyes adjusted to the light he noticed that different sizes of paintings hung on every available space. The walls looked like a mad gallery with exhibits stuck up without concession to method or appearance. In the murk, he could make out paintings of various flowers, while a large canvas over the fireplace appeared to represent a huge medieval stone tower.

'It's Mia,' she said.

'What is?'

'My name, silly,' she said.

'Mia,' he repeated.

The name suited her. Mia, it was gentle, yet it implied resilience and mystery.

'I was beginning to think that names were something else you didn't believe in.'

'Oh, I have no problem with names. It's the people they're attached to that I sometimes object to.'

'How do you feel about the person attached to Myles?'

'The person attached to Myles is doing fine,' she said, before adding, 'So far.'

When the kettle boiled she made two cups of peppermint tea and brought them over to the table. He noticed that her limp had gone. A strong aroma of mint wafted over him, reminding him of the cinema when he was young. His father had often taken him to the Savoy and left him with one of the ushers, a former army buddy. The usher had always plonked Myles in the centre of the front row, and for some reason had always handed him a bag of Fox's mints with a conspiratorial gleam in his eye. Perhaps the usher believed that a bag of Fox's mints was the ultimate treat for a ten-year-old boy. The experience had left Myles with an obsession for sitting in the front row at the movies, but it had put him off mints for life. Now, as he sipped a rancid brew that tasted like warmed-up liquid toothpaste and contemplated the obstacle of Mia's sleeping flatmate upstairs, he began to concede that the evening was turning against him.

'Don't you like it,' she said, watching him intently.

'Oh, it's grand,' he lied. 'Just a bit hot.'

She watched him with concern until he took another sip. To distract her, he indicated the makeshift gallery.

'Are you a painter?'

She eyed him warily. 'No. I don't consider myself a painter. I'm an artist.'

'Well excuse me,' he smiled, but she didn't smile back and that threw him. 'What do you paint. I mean, what art do you practise?' Now he couldn't think straight. He gathered his words. 'What subject matter inspires your work?'

That wonderful sexy giggle again.

'If you're good, I'll give you a tour later.' She paused. 'That is, if you're still here.'

She smiled to show that she wasn't about to throw him out that minute. 'I've been a painter for three years, ever since the College of Art.'

'You mean an artist,' he said.

This time she gave him a look that was a cross between wariness and appreciation. 'That's what I meant,' she said. 'Mr Tall Smartypants.'

She told him that she had nearly had an exhibition last year but the cow that was organising it had wanted sixty per cent of all sales. He expressed surprise at the high percentage, but Mia told him that splitting sales fees fifty-fifty with a gallery was quite commonplace; it was just that she hadn't cared for the way the woman had proposed to market her work, as though she was some boring landscape hack. She had decided to hold off on an exhibition of her work until the time was right. One of her best friends, Aisling, had just opened a gallery on St Stephen's Green and there was a strong possibility that she would exhibit there before next April. In the meantime she made a living handing out events leaflets in pubs and nightclubs with her friend Stick at weekends, while most weekdays she worked as a waitress in the Elephant.

'So what do you do?' she asked him.

'The best I can,' he smiled.

'Sounds illegal,' she said.

'Only sometimes,' he said.

'Is that why you hang round with the shady types who nearly ran me over?'

'Yes, well.' Myles gave a mock yawn. 'It's hard to get good help nowadays.'

'So is Mr Tall a gangster or what?'

'Would that make a difference?'

'Depends what sort of a gangster you are?'

'How about the kind who can conjure up a horse on Grafton Street after midnight?'

He had expected her to giggle at that but she just sat there considering him for a moment, with her cup of peppermint tea steaming in front of her face. He figured that he might have gone too far with the gangster spoof. She seemed to be taking him terribly seriously all of a sudden. He didn't want to tell her that he was just a journalist. That would only make him look bad because nobody was very impressed by journalists. Especially if the journalist turned out to be a sub-editor on a tabloid.

'All right then Mr Tall,' she smiled. 'Maybe I know a girl who'll hire you to do a job for her. Would you be up for that?'

He was relieved that he had gotten away with it.

'That depends.'

'On what?'

'Well,' he was beginning to enjoy playing this role, 'What's she like – this girl?'

'She's cool.'

'Can she afford me?'

'What's your fee?'

'Depends on the job.'

'She's very resourceful. I'm sure she'll find a way.'

Myles leaned forward. 'First I would have to find out what the job involved. Then, of course, I'd have to agree a fee with the girl. Talking about fees, we still haven't discussed my fee for tonight.'

'You're drinking it,' she said.

She stared calmly and cheekily at him, a flop of red hair dangling over her left eye.

Sensing that the mood was now in his favour, he leaned forward. 'You know what I think?' he said.

'What?' she brushed away the hair.

'You're sitting too far away.'

'Am I now?'

'Yes. I think that I should move closer. For ease of communication.'

'Do you?'

'I mean,' he whispered, 'if you know a girl who's going to hire me to do an important job for her, then we can't afford any misunderstandings.'

'I don't believe in misunderstandings.'

'Neither do I.'

She shrugged to indicate that it was his choice where he sat, and if he decided to sit closer it wouldn't bother her.

He creaked his chair a foot closer.

'Are you hitting on me?' she asked for the second time that evening.

'Would you believe me if I said no?' he asked.

'No.'

'Then, I am, yes.'

Figuring that he had nothing to lose, he got down off the chair and crawled over to where she was on all fours. That made her smile.

'Why are you crawling?'

'So that we can be the same height,' he said.

She threw back her head and giggled, and when she had finished she let him put his arms around her and she responded when he pressed his lips to hers. A long slow kiss. She tasted of mint, but this time the taste didn't bother him. She chewed his top lip and he sucked on her slim juicy tongue. They were really getting into it and beginning to speed up when she suddenly broke off. When he tried to kiss her again she put her palm up to his mouth and gently held him away.

'Down boy,' she said. 'Let's not go mental.'

He stayed where he was for a moment until it became clear that she wasn't going to resume kissing him. Courage flagging, he crawled back to his own chair. It wasn't a total rejection. At least he had got a kiss, and a long slow exciting kiss too.

She said, 'That's plenty for a first date.'

'Second date,' he protested. 'What about last night?'

She shook her curls. 'Trying to run someone over doesn't count. I never change my rules. Anyway, I have my period. Unless you feel like turning into Dracula.'

Quickly, perhaps too quickly, he gave her a big smile to show that turning into Dracula wasn't really such a big problem to a man like him.

'Well, do I at least get your phone number?'

'If you behave and drink up your peppermint tea.'

Now that amorous activity had ceased, both appeared relieved, as if an invisible wall of pressure had been dissolved. They talked about nothing much for a short while. Anything so that he wouldn't have to drink any more liquid toothpaste. She asked if his parents were still living. He told her that his father had passed away a few years back but that his mother was hale and hearty. He decided not to tell her that his mother ran a pub. Some people could never get their heads around the fact that his mother was a publican.

'What did your father do?'

'He was a captain in the army.'

He thought for a moment, then decided to continue along a course he had traversed in the past with some success.

'He got killed in the Lebanon a few years ago.'

'Oh, I'm sorry to hear that. Were you very close?'

'Yes,' he said. 'Like father and son.'

She gave a small smile at that.

He continued, 'Dad wanted me to follow in his footsteps and join the army but they wouldn't take me. I was too tall. Easy target. Wouldn't last ten minutes in a firefight, they said.'

'Was he——?' she began.

'He was killed in a dispute with a local militia. He had sort of blown up one of their tanks and had kind of carried a couple of his wounded men to safety. He was going back for a third man when they got him with a rocket launcher.'

Noticing that he now had her undivided attention and reluctant to let go, he plunged in all the way.

'They couldn't find enough of him to send his body home so we never had a proper funeral. Just a presentation ceremony at the barracks where they gave my mother a medal that he'd won for valour. She keeps it on the mantelpiece at home in a glass case. It's all we have of him now, apart from his captain's cap.'

He saw that she was deep in thought and he felt a glow of satisfaction. People rarely asked questions after he told them a tragic story about his father's violent demise. His mother always said that his father had died in the Lebanon, which was true, strictly speaking. Big Paddy had been blown to bits in a Portaloo by one of his own grenades after a night's drinking. 'A tragic latrine accident,' the army had called it.

That made three crucial things he couldn't tell her about: subediting, publicans and latrine accidents.

They sat quietly for a moment, just looking into each other's eyes. Nothing else was going to happen. He figured that he had better be off.

He stood up. 'Time to take my horse and ride into the sunset.'

'What about your tour?' she said.

'Tour?'

'Of course. You can't leave without your tour.'

She picked up the oil lamp and escorted him along the rows of paintings. He looked at the first few out of polite curiosity, scarcely hearing her whispered commentary. 'This is the stuff I'm working on for my first exhibition. I'm going to call it "Origins". I'm tracing my own origins and the origins of every woman.'

He suddenly felt exhausted, like a child who had been wandering around lost in a shopping centre for hours and now wanted someone to come and take him home. He had viewed over a dozen works by the light of the lamp before it dawned on him that he was looking at paintings of male genitalia. Some penises were represented as flowers, others as pillars or plants, and a few as microphones on stands. The medieval tower turned out to be a giant stone phallus rising from between two soft mounds of earth. There was a complete wall of erect penises, including a few at half-mast and one that skewed alarmingly off to one side. Skinny ones nestled alongside fat ones. Some penises rested on testes that were bigger than the penises. A few had no balls at all. Each penis was a different size, shape and colour. The most disturbing was a big blue volcano with throbbing veins and an ugly red helmet that seemed about to erupt in their faces.

The wall opposite was devoted to limp penises. He began to feel slightly disturbed and disorientated at the mass of phallic imagery. Perhaps women felt this way when they looked at paintings of other naked women or at the nude spreads in *Playboy*. He wondered how she came by her subject matter. Did she employ real models or did she simply use her imagination? He was afraid to ask. He imagined a line of half-naked guys shuffling about outside Mia's apartment, comparing their erections in readiness for her penis auditions.

'What do you think?' she asked quietly.

'Extraordinary,' he said. 'I've never seen anything like them.'

'Thanks,' she smiled. 'I have high hopes.'

After looking at a few more paintings, he told her that he really should go. She led him to the door and they kissed briefly. She wrote down her number for him and he promised to ring.

'Yeah, sure, they all say that,' she said.

'So what's this job you want to hire me for?' he asked, thinking that it might somehow involve her gaining some form of retribution on the fair-haired geek who had pissed her off in Roolaboola's earlier.

'I don't want to totally wreck your head,' she said.

'Try me.'

'OK. How much would you charge to kill my father?'

'Em,' he said.

'It's alright. You can think about it,' she said matter-of-factly. 'Give me a ring when you come up with a price.'

Then she smiled warmly at him, waved goodbye and closed the door.

He went downstairs, feeling as though he had just woken from a trance. Had she put something in the peppermint tea? Maybe he was having a weird dream.

The light clicked off halfway and he descended the rest of the stairs in darkness. In the hall he clanged his head off the chandelier. It took him ages to locate the front door handle. Emerging into the orange glow of streetlights, he felt refreshed and free. He also experienced a curious lightweight sensation between his legs, as though he had left something behind. Like his genitalia. Feeling foolish, he put his hand down the front of his jeans to check himself.

It was only after he was satisfied that everything was present and intact that he noticed that the horse was gone. The only trace was a pile of smouldering dung on the steps outside the house.

SIX

Dogs

In the back room of The Crazy Horse, the crowd roared when the Rottweiler suddenly straddled the Airedale, biting into the other dog's neck. Three bare bulbs hung from the rafters, illuminating a makeshift ring of pale tarpaulin raised on breezeblocks and covered with sawdust upon which the dogs fought. Shadows reeled like drunken sailors across the walls as 400 dogfight lovers at twenty pounds a head suddenly surged forward.

Carried by the crowd's momentum, Myles feared that he would end up in the ring with the dogs. He'd make the late edition of the *Evening News*: 'Dogs Bite Goalpost'.

To his relief, the movement subsided at the tarpaulin's edge. The faces of the spectators were grimly focused on the dogs. Some men anticipated moves, replayed each snap and lunge. Alongside Myles, Pat lifted his small son onto his shoulders for a better view.

'Darren, where are we this minute?' Pat said.

'At the movies, Da,' Darren said.

'What are we seeing?'

'*A Bug's Life.*'

'Very good. Be sure you remember that.' Pat winked at Myles. 'His Mam would go spare if she found out.'

An illegal lunchtime dogfight was 'the sweet story' that Pat had promised him. Top of the bill later this afternoon was Buster from Liverpool, unbeaten in twenty-six fights. 'Buster is something special,' Pat had promised. 'Once seen, never forgotten.'

As soon as Myles had arrived, Pat had arranged interviews with the dog-owners and promoters, and he had also lined up several of the more enthusiastic punters. Nobody wanted him to use their real names, though they all begged to be quoted. Myles also agreed to keep the location a secret. They all told him that dogfights weren't about money or cruelty; they were about sport. Pat had even supplied photographs, glossy black and whites of some of the dogs in today's contest, including a couple of action shots of a previous fight. 'Ma took them,' he explained. 'She likes to keep mementoes.'

As Myles watched the fight, he jotted down his observations along with overheard snippets of punters' conversations. Two previous bouts of snarling and gnashing and yelping had given him some good material, but he yearned for something more. This feature had to be really hot; it should be an exposé of an illegal racket, but it could also give an insight into ordinary life on the streets. This piece had front-page potential. It was the sort of thing that could win a Pulitzer.

Pat tapped him on the shoulder. 'Do not worry, man, we will find that horse.'

'Cheers,' Myles said.

It was two days now since Sheba had disappeared. At first, Johnny Bones had been very understanding. 'Ah well, these things happen. As long as I have her home be teatime.' When the horse still hadn't shown at teatime Johnny had become less agreeable. 'Tomorrow morning without fail or things will get heavy,' he had warned, but Myles's efforts to track down the nag had come to nothing. When there was still no sign of her this morning, Johnny had phoned Myles at work.

'Where's me Sheba? What have you done with me bleedin' horse?' Myles had until six that evening to return her. Otherwise

Johnny had threatened to go straight to Myles's mother for satisfaction. 'I trusted you,' he had whined. 'That horse was like a sister to me.'

Myles could picture himself at the next therapy session, attempting to explain to Lucy's group why he had felt compelled to give a good-looking young woman a lift home late at night on a borrowed horse. They would want to know what exactly he had been doing in the young woman's apartment until three in the morning. Well, first she made peppermint tea. Then she showed me her penis paintings. After that she asked me to kill her father. He could see that it would be difficult to clarify the situation without a risk of serious misinterpretation. This morning, in desperation, he had asked Pat for help to find the horse. 'No problem,' Pat had said. 'I know just the man for the gig.'

He had put Dez on the case. 'If the nag hasn't been turned into horsemeat, I'll find it,' Dez had reassured him. 'Just get one thing straight. I'm not doing this for you,' Dez had explained to Myles. 'I'm doing it because I love animals, right?'

'Right,' Myles had agreed. Declaring that he had a hunch, Dez had disappeared just as the fights began.

Now the dogs had ceased struggling. They remained locked together as if awaiting instructions. Pat's ma stepped onto the parapet; a big white-haired woman in a blue cowboy shirt, embroidered waistcoat and long leather skirt with boots. She looked just as Myles remembered her from schooldays. Pat's ma fingered a whistle that she used to signal the beginning as well as the finish of fights. At the opposite side of the ring, the dog-owners stood looking fretful. Before the fight started, they had fussed over their pooches like Hollywood agents. The prize money was three hundred for a win. Second prize was a bin-liner to haul away the loser. Now the Airedale's owner, a slight balding man with a big nose and small thick glasses, shouted at his dog.

'Get up and fight will ye?'

At the sound of his owner's voice, the Airedale attempted to break free. The dogs rolled around for a moment before the Rottweiler reasserted its grip. Roars from the crowd drowned out the Airedale's stricken yelp. Flecks of blood speckled the sawdust underneath the animals. The baying of the crowd subsided to a murmur. The dogs suddenly froze again, as though by mutual agreement. After a few moments of inactivity, the crowd grew restless.

'Throw in a cat,' someone yelled.

A wave of shouts and boos and shut ups ran through the crowd. The dogs remained oblivious to the commotion.

'Why aren't they scrapping, Da?' Darren asked.

Pat winked at Myles. 'See the one on the bottom?'

'Yeah.'

'Well, he's just offered the one on top six bones to let him go.'

'Quit it, Da.'

'It's true. The one on top is still thinking about it.'

'Can I have a fighting dog?'

'Who's gonna feed it? Who's gonna scoop out its shit?'

'I will.'

'Maybe when you're nine, and then only if you're good.'

Pat's ma nodded at the two dog-owners, each of whom held a long wooden pole with a hook on the end. The owners prodded their dogs with the poles but the dogs wouldn't budge.

'Money back,' someone shouted.

Just then the dogs broke into a sudden violent flurry of movement that culminated in the Rottweiler ripping the Airedale's throat out. Blood splattered the sawdust once again as the victor shook its adversary's body. The dog-owners leapt into the ring to separate them. The ringmistress blew her whistle to officially end the fight.

'Well that's that,' Pat said. 'Short and sweet.'

'Get your bets down for the next contest,' his ma called out. 'Buster the Undefeated versus The Terrorisor.'

'He can't take the excitement. Back in a minute,' Pat said, as he carried Darren off towards the toilets.

Myles watched as the ring was cleared and the remains of the Airedale stuffed into a bin-liner. All around people were laying bets with Pat's ma as well as with each other. A buzz of expectation and excitement rippled through the crowd. A pitbull on a leash appeared at the edge of the ring, followed by a squat red-faced man in a 'Terrorisor' T-shirt.

Myles decided that he was obviously in the grip of some kind of destiny. He had landed here today because of his ambition to become an ace journalist. The assignment with Pat and Dez had led him to the accidental meeting with Mia. He was certain that he had found and pocketed the card for a reason, because the card had led him back to her. After that came the horse. Now this dogfight. It was all linked and he was positive that it was leading him somewhere good; it was just that he couldn't make sense of it yet. He had decided against phoning Mia. It would be uncool for him to appear too anxious to start something. Far better to just bump into her in Roolaboola's some night. Make it look like a coincidence. See what happened then. He had met her twice, kissed her just once for less than a minute and already she was leaping with complications. The stuff about killing her father must be a joke, though her face had stayed deadpan throughout. Perhaps she was testing him. Or maybe she was an even bigger liar than he was.

What was obvious, though, was that she fancied him. He liked the way she looked – those green eyes, that strangely appealing large nose, the odd way her unusual features combined to make her attractive and different. He found her fascinating, but no way did he want to get in too deep. He did not want another Lucy. In the beginning Lucy too had appeared sexy and fascinating. The really smart thing to do was to keep things light between them, enjoy a little innocent fling, then forget about her and get on with his life. She couldn't have been serious about wanting her father bumped off. And who was the fair-haired geek? Why did she buy expensive flowers once a week? Who was Barry? What sort of woman would want to mount an exhibition of penis paintings? He was reluctant to discover the answers because he didn't want to shatter his perception of her as mysterious and elusive. It would be tragic if she was suddenly to become ordinary or predictable or even, God forbid, a Nice Girl. Everyone knows that Nice Girls are lousy shags.

Behind Myles, a door opened. A hush fell as a strong light blazed into the room and three figures appeared in the doorway. Shielding his eyes, Myles made out a man in a cape alongside two burly minders.

As the entourage approached, the minders walked either side of the figure, shining flashlights. The crowd parted to let them pass. The man in the cape was a small, brawny black man with a pockmarked face wearing a leopard-skin headband. He stopped at the edge of the ring.

Pat reappeared beside Myles, Darren still high on his shoulder. 'See. Didn't I tell you Buster was something special?'

Buster allowed the cape to swish from his shoulders, revealing a muscled body tramlined with scars.

The pitbull stared across the ring at Buster. Everyone in the back room stared at Buster. Buster stared ahead of him grimly, seemingly at nothing in particular.

The pitbull climbed into the ring and pulled up, held back on its leash. Buster stepped onto the parapet, stood for a moment, then silently dropped into the sawdust.

Dez appeared between Myles and Pat, craning for a look.

'Listen,' he said. 'I brought some mates who know about the horse.'

'Where are they?' Pat said without taking his eyes from the ring. Myles also could not shift his gaze.

'In the lounge,' Dez said. 'They said they'd talk to you.'

'Let them wait,' Pat said, giving Darren a playful joggle on his shoulders. 'We wouldn't want to interrupt the lad's education, would we?'

It took Buster five minutes to strangle The Terrorisor and toss its lifeless body into the corner, whereupon its owner fainted. Immediately afterwards, Buster's minders draped his cape around him and escorted him from the room. The crowd gave him a standing ovation. Buster neither acknowledged the applause nor celebrated the victory, remaining expressionless throughout. People waited until he and his minders had gone before collecting their winnings or lamenting their losses. Pat walked up to his ma and handed over the boy. 'Take Darren for a few minutes, will you Ma? I've got a bit of business. You remember Myles, don't you?'

'Aw Jaysus, Myles how are ye?' she said.

'I'm grand,' Myles said.

'Enjoying the afternoon I hope?'

'Yes, very much,' he said.

Pat's ma gestured around her at the ring and its surroundings. 'We've come up in the world since you were last over.'

'So I see.'

'Well, don't be a stranger. Drop in to see us anytime.'

'Thanks, I will.'

Putting his notebook and biro into his pocket, Myles followed Pat and Dez to the front lounge.

'Leave this to me,' Pat said. 'It's only a couple of scumbags. It shouldn't take long. Might even be a bit of craic.'

Two scrawny young lads in Manchester United tracksuits sat at a table by the door with orange drinks in front of them. They looked about sixteen or younger. Myles recognised the cheeky blond scumbag with the baseball cap who had asked for a ride on the horse on O'Connell Street.

'Ah, if it isn't the rustlers.' Pat sat down across from the scumbags. 'How's it going, Mixer?'

'OK,' the blond crew-cut nodded.

'How's Earl?'

'Earl's grand,' Earl said.

'Right boys, what's the story with the horse?'

Mixer and Earl looked at each other. They didn't say anything. Mixer looked embarrassed.

'Listen lads,' Pat said. 'The longer we have to wait the more pissed off we get.' He smiled reasonably. 'You do not want to piss us off, do you?'

Mixer shrugged. 'We find a horse tied to a railing. How do we know it belonged to you?'

'I don't care about that. I want to know what you did with it.'

Mixer thought for a moment. 'It's like this. A pal from Finglas offers us thirty sheets so we think to ourselves, "thirty's good business". Every day on my patch we buy stacks of stuff and sell loads of other stuff. All we ever look for is a fair deal. We never let our mates down.'

Pat pulled out his wallet. He removed some bills, folded them and handed them to Mixer.

'OK, let's do business. Here's a ton. Have the horse back tonight, right?'

Mixer looked surprised, then he beamed. 'There is just one thing.'

'What's that?'

'We already sell the horse to our pal from Finglas.'

Pat smiled at them. 'That is your problem, lads.'

Pat rose to leave but Mixer stopped him. 'I've got a question.'

'Fire away.'

Pat waited to see what Mixer had to say.

Mixer smiled. 'Say we bring the horse back tonight and it's game ball and all that?'

'I'm listening.'

'Well, any chance of a gig for me and Earl?'

Pat snorted. 'You mean with my crew?'

Mixer nodded. 'We do fine with our own thing, but we think that it's time we move up.'

'What makes you think I need you.'

'Dez says you're understaffed.' Mixer pointed at Myles. 'He says your mate Goalpost is a disaster.'

Dez looked embarrassed. Jesus, Myles thought, now even the scumbags knew his nickname.

'Dez says that, does he? What's Dez to you then?'

Mixer looked sulky. 'He's me cousin.'

Pat slapped Mixer on the shoulder. 'First the horse, then we talk, right?'

'Right,' Mixer said, and he and Earl got up and headed for the door, beaming as though today was both their birthdays.

Pat turned to Dez. His face was dark, his fists clenched. Dez backed away.

'I swear to God I——' Dez began.

'Don't ever go against the family again, right?'

Dez looked at Pat. 'Right.'

'If you do you're a dead man, do I make myself clear?'

'I hear ye,' Dez said, and walked off.

He reached the door where Mixer and Earl waited for him with stunned faces, having overheard the exchange between him and

Pat. Silently they went out. Delighted, Pat turned to Myles and slapped him on the shoulder.

'Every once in a while you have to let everyone know who is boss.'

Next morning, Myles wrote the dogfight feature in two hours. He had been up most of the night making notes, so when he finally came to write he felt possessed. He was amazed at the ease with which full sentences seemed to pour out of his fingers and through the keyboard to appear on the screen in front of him. For the purposes of the story, he called Pat 'Black Pat' and Dez 'The Leprechaun'. Myles portrayed the pair as the modern equivalent of Butch Cassidy and the Sundance Kid, whose lawless acts were assertions of individuality against a bland, conformist and unfair society. He concentrated on making it entertaining as well as funny, including snippets of punters' dialogue along with witty observations. He made great play of the episode when the pair stole the truck, only to discover the driver inside with a teenage blonde.

The final section was almost entirely devoted to the dogfight. Here, he dropped the light touch in favour of the chilling and bizarre to give the feature a punch. Buster was portrayed as a cross between 'The James Brown of Dogfighting' and a zonked-out zombie. As an epilogue he tacked on a short made-up section in which 'Black Pat' advises his son against a life of crime.

He ended up with over nine hundred and fifty words, a lengthy essay for a tabloid. A page and a half spread unless they decided to cut it. He would have finished sooner, except the phone kept interrupting him. First it was Johnny Bones to say thanks for getting Sheba back, and by the way Myles now owed him three hundred quid in lost earnings. Then Lucy rang to ask him which restaurant he wanted to take her to tonight. Finally, he got a call from Jarlath Boon to say that he was going to make a formal complaint to the NUJ about, as he put it, Myles's 'blackleg double-jobbing yellow-pack scabbing'.

Myles proofed the piece over and over, making minor changes. Then he reread it several times. When he was sure that it was ready, he pressed the Send button on his keypad to dispatch the piece to Lola Wall, acting features editor. Next he sent Lola an e-mail to tell her that his feature was in her 'in-basket', awaiting her attention. Then he sat back in his chair as his nerves began to eat at him. After ten minutes a message appeared on his screen from Lola Wall, saying that she had sent on Myles's piece for the immediate attention of the editor, Fowler. She gave no indication whether or not she liked it. That made him even more nervous.

Ten minutes passed, then thirty. Finally an hour. Myles attempted to lay out a health features page for Saturday's edition but found that he could not concentrate. Maybe he would phone Lola. No, better to let this matter take its own course. No point aggravating things. It would only make him look like an amateur. 'Never let the bastards see you crawl,' Big Paddy always said. 'Too many of them would enjoy it.' He had just lifted the phone to call Lola when Bob Casper appeared at his desk.

'Well boyo, how does it feel to be the manager of the world's second best team.'

'Hey Bob, the very man. Listen, sit down, I want you to read something for me.'

'Of course, boyo. Delighted.'

He pulled up a chair and sat down beside Myles while Myles pressed a key that called up the feature onto his computer screen.

'Be honest,' he said, and paced around while Bob read. He walked over to where Dogbrain sat picking out a story on his Remington.

'Some girl was looking for you,' Dogbrain said cheerfully.

'Who was she?' Myles asked.

'Dunno. She didn't leave a name.'

'Thanks,' Myles said.

He was sure that he heard Bob snort, then he thought he heard tut-tutting. After a few minutes he couldn't stand it anymore and he went back to his own desk. He stood and waited for Bob to finish reading. Then he sat down beside him.

'Well?'

Bob nodded his head sagely. 'Interesting.'

'Is that all? Just interesting?'

'Well, let me ask you this. Is this the first major colour feature that you've ever written?'

'Sort of. Well. In a way. Alright, yes,' Myles said.

'Hmm,' Bob said.

'What does that Hmmm mean?'

'Do you have pics?'

'Yes.'

'That'll help.'

'Did you like it or didn't you?'

Bob shook his head. 'I only wish it was that straightforward. I'm just thinking of your career.'

'So am I,' Myles said.

At that moment a chiming sound on Myles's terminal indicated that he had just received an urgent Internal e-mail. He hit a key and the message flashed up on screen. It read: 'Well done. Best colour piece this paper has had for years. Am pulling tomorrow's feature and running yours instead. Talk to me later. Congrats. Fowler.'

Myles read the message twice, then he looked at Bob who gave him a weak smile.

'Well there we are now,' Bob said after a moment's hesitation. 'That's taken the words right out of my mouth.'

SEVEN

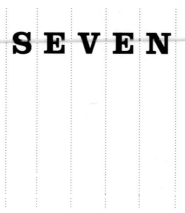

Mia

He stood next to a litterbin across the cobbled street from the
Elephant. Through the large windows he watched as black-clad
waiters and waitresses served lunchtime customers with orders of
burgers and fries or tall dessert glasses of Death by Chocolate.
There wasn't a single red hair between the lot of them.

Perhaps she was on a day off. Maybe she had been lying to him.
At this moment, she could be meeting Lorcan the invisible flatmate
or Barry of the bouquets or the fair-haired geek from Roolaboola's.

It had been four days and nights since the horse ride. He hadn't
phoned her even though he had promised that he would, and she
had made no effort to contact him. Today, he had kidded himself
that he was taking a lunchtime ramble around the streets when all
along he had known exactly where he was going. He just felt like
catching a glimpse of her. No big thing.

He was about to give up and walk away when he saw her
emerge from the kitchen carrying a tray of chicken wings. His guts
burned. She chewed gum and looked cool and invulnerable. He
knew that she was wearing the flowery Docs. His reflection in the

restaurant window grinned back at him like an escaped mental patient. If she were to glance out now and see him staring at her she would definitely think that he was a stalker. He should go in and order lunch. 'Hi, happened to be passing and suddenly got a craving for Death by Chocolate.'

She would never fall for that. Once a woman even suspected that a guy might be seriously into her, she would rather swallow live worms than go out with him.

Anyway, he wasn't hooked, just intrigued. He had caught a glimpse of her, and that was all he had wanted. Hands in overcoat pockets, he walked away briskly until he was out of sight of the restaurant. He felt disappointment mixed with relief. But life had been going well for him of late and he did not need any sudden complications. Yesterday, even the copyboys in the paper had read his dogfight article. Another sure sign of success was that Jarlath Boon had immediately taken a week's leave. Marian Finucane had mentioned his article on RTE radio. The word was that the whole question of illegal dogfights was now going to be raised in the Dail. The Gardai had apparently been in contact with Fowler about the identity of Buster, and there had been irate faxes from the animal rights crowd. Pat had phoned to say that he loved being Dublin's answer to Butch Cassidy and arranged to hook up in the Banshee tonight for 'a few scoops'. Best of all, Fowler had e-mailed him, commissioning further articles. 'The paper needs more of this kind of funny stuff,' he had written, leaving Myles feeling uncertain whether or not he was being paid a compliment.

Lucy had read the article and told him that she was proud of him. She seemed to have forgiven him for the Claire business. Going out to dinner last night, for a moment he had even considered taking her to the Elephant. That would have been a sure way to piss off two women at once. In the end they had gone to Café Caruso, a glitzy place in Dawson Street, with waiters who sported colourful paintings on the backs of their waistcoats and where he had joyously blown most of the three hundred he had received for the feature.

Later, in his mother's house, they had made love for the first time in months. Downstairs in the front room on the rickety old sofa, he had experienced the same delicious guilty feeling that he remembered from sneaking girls into the house as a teenager. One way of keeping a relationship alive was to have sex on the sofa while your mother was asleep upstairs. He had used a condom. At least, he thought that he had. Suddenly he couldn't remember.

This morning he had finally managed to convince Justine that it was not a good idea to sleep in the bath. Daddy had only done it once, he had explained, and only because he had been very tired. Justine had finally agreed to move back to her own bedroom. She was getting creaks in her neck anyway, she had admitted.

From now on Lucy had decided to personally supervise the work on the house in Wicklow. Maguire the builder had told her that the house could be ready at the end of next month. He had also told her that they needed to come up with extra money – over fifty grand extra. Funny how Lucy had waited until after he had paid the bill at the Café Caruso before telling him about the money problems.

Myles saw an ancient white-haired figure approaching. Dogbrain carried a large holdall and appeared to be in his customary muddled condition. He passed Myles without seeing him, whereupon Myles had a lightbulb moment. He caught up with Dogbrain and greeted him warmly.

Dogbrain adjusted his spectacles. 'Ah, the man himself.'

Myles smiled. 'Listen, have you ever experienced Death By Chocolate?' he asked.

'I don't think so.' Dogbrain looked puzzled. 'Nobody's ever asked me that before.'

Taking him by the arm, Myles gently steered him towards the Elephant. A man had not lived, Myles explained, until he had experienced the most excellent lunch that the city could provide. Dogbrain grinned, revealing four and a half teeth distributed along banks of glistening pink gums. 'I'm doing nothing,' he said. 'I don't mind.'

Myles congratulated himself. Dogbrain would unwittingly act as cover, enabling Myles to see Mia without feeling that he was chasing her, which of course he was.

They entered the restaurant and waited to be seated. It was dark inside and cool, with a large fan ticking sluggishly overhead. Business suits huddled together blathering about cars, while stylish, good-looking women stabbed at salads. Here and there a few arty types sulked. An harassed-looking couple sat in the far corner, struggling to prevent their toddlers swallowing the salt. Not a glimmer of Mia.

A tall waiter with a goatee seated them at a No Smoking table. Myles sat with his back to the wall so that he could have a clear view of the restaurant.

'This is a nice place,' Dogbrain said. 'It's a wonder I never noticed it before.'

'You never notice anything,' Myles said.

'That's a bit harsh.' Dogbrain adjusted his glasses. 'True, but a bit harsh.'

After a few moments, Mia came out of the kitchen and began clearing a table at the opposite side of the room. She stopped when she saw him. 'Hi,' she mouthed, giving him a little wave. He waved back. Using signs, she indicated that she was busy now but would come over later. Myles affected a hurt expression, slowly dabbing at his eye. She raised the back of her hand to her brow in mock-exasperation and flounced dramatically through the kitchen doors.

Dogbrain hadn't noticed Myles's face pulling. He studied the black and white photographs of Hollywood legends that adorned the walls, his hands clutching the hold-all to his lap as though it contained precious gems.

'Look, there's a picture of Clark Gable,' Dogbrain said.

When the goatee reappeared, Myles ordered a crispy chicken salad while Dogbrain opted for a chilli burger and fries. Dogbrain declined Myles's invitation to put the hold-all under the table.

'It's got me sister's private things in it,' Dogbrain explained. 'I'm minding it for her while she's having her toes done.'

Myles realised that this was the first occasion on which he had actually had lunch with Dogbrain. With horror he also realised that he didn't know Dogbrain's real name. What if he had to introduce him to Mia? Perhaps using him as cover had not been such a brilliant idea.

Dogbrain leaned over. 'Clark Gable was a great actor all the same, wasn't he?'

'He was OK,' Myles agreed.

'Why do you think they never gave him the Oscar for *Gone with the Wind*?'

'Not a notion,' Myles said.

Dogbrain took Myles's ignorance as a cue to launch into the Clark Gable story. He spoke rapidly, as though he felt compelled to cram in as much as possible before the arrival of the food spoiled his flow.

'Gable didn't get on with Marilyn Monroe, would you credit that? You'd think they would have clicked together, wouldn't you? When they did *The Misfits* she drove him mental with her tantrums and her lateness and because she wouldn't learn her lines.' Dogbrain lowered his voice conspiratorially. 'Some people blamed her for giving him that final heart attack.'

To Myles's relief, the goatee finally arrived with the meals. Myles toyed with his crispy chicken salad. The image of Dogbrain's sister having her toes 'done' had somehow put him off eating anything crisp. Dogbrain lifted his knife and sliced his burger in half. He placed one half on a side plate, then carefully unzipped the hold-all and dropped in the other half. From inside the bag came a series of chomping and slurping noises.

Dogbrain turned to Myles, beaming. 'Did you know that Clark Gable's ears were so big that people said he looked like a taxicab with both doors open?'

'No, I didn't know that,' Myles said, staring at the hold-all which had suddenly become animated.

As Dogbrain began his own half of the burger, Myles noticed that their table had suddenly become the focus of attention for the people at the next table. After a few moments, the slurping noises changed to coughing, followed a few seconds later by a piercing yelp that froze everyone at the nearby tables.

'Ssssh,' Dogbrain said into the bag. 'Hush now or you won't get any dessert.'

There was another shrill yelp.

'What's going on?' Myles asked.

As Dogbrain bent down and buried his head inside the hold-all, Myles caught a brief glimpse of a tiny canine face with big scared eyes peeping out. Dogbrain pulled his head back out. 'It'll be grand now,' he winked at Myles. 'Bit too much chilli on the burger.'

That was when Mia arrived.

'Hello you,' she said, smiling at Myles before glancing at the hold-all which was moving about on Dogbrain's knees.

'Hi,' Myles said.

Mia asked if they were enjoying their meals and they both replied that the food was fine.

'You didn't ring. I hope that means that you were out of the country.' Mia looked pleased to see him. Myles knew that he had been right to let things lie for a few days.

'Things got a bit on top of me.'

'Did they now?' Mia said.

Myles decided to be brave. 'Listen, what are you up to tonight?'

She shrugged. 'You know where to find me.'

'That an invitation?'

'You decide.'

'OK. See you tonight then.'

'You hope.' She smiled.

'I'd just like to say one thing,' Dogbrain said. 'These chips are truly exceptional.'

'Mia,' Myles said, 'I'd like you to meet a colleague of mine. Em . . .' He stopped there as Dogbrain gave a gap-toothed grin.

'Sylvester Dolan,' Dogbrain said after a pause.

'How do you do, Sylvester?' Mia chirped. 'Are you a gangster too?'

Dogbrain looked perplexed. 'No, I'm a sub-editor. Same as—'

He was about to indicate Myles when Myles kicked him under the table, but missed, hitting the hold-all instead. A series of fierce yelps erupted.

'Sssssh now,' Dogbrain said to the hold-all. 'Or no ice-cream.' The yelping ceased. The restaurant was silent except for the ticking of the overhead fan.

'The ice-cream is a powerful force all the same,' Dogbrain said. Myles felt activity beside him. The toddlers from the harassed couple in the far corner stood by his elbow with bright smiles on their tiny faces.

'Can we see the doggie?' the little girl asked.

'I'm afraid that we don't allow dogs in the restaurant,' Mia said diplomatically.

'Sorry about this,' Myles said.

'No problem,' she said. 'I'll be happy to wrap your food for you to take away.'

'He loved the chips.' Dogbrain looked stricken. 'But there was too much chilli sauce on the burger.'

He arrived at the Banshee after nine. The pub was on six levels, each with its own bar and piped music, except for the top floor where an electric blues band played on a small stage. He found Pat and Dez watching the band. Pat immediately bought him a pint of Bud. Dez said 'Hello Myles' instead of 'Hello Goalpost'. That was a good sign. They brought their drinks to a table at the back where they could talk without having to shout.

Pat slapped his shoulder. 'Best bleeding write-up I ever see in me life,' Pat said. 'Good as the essays you did in school. Remember that one about the spaceship? You should have sent it to Spielberg.'

'Thanks,' Myles said.

Dez nodded. 'Me new girlfriend calls me Sundance now.'

Pat said that now he knew what it felt like to be a pop star. 'Every place I go people give me high fives. This morning, there I am strolling out of me local Spar when what do you think? A piece of paper containing a scribbled phone number is pressed into my paw. I look up and there's this good-looking babe of my acquaintance who happens to be a mother of four.'

Dez smirked. 'Nine months after today she'll be a mother of five.'

'What would you know about it?' Pat dipped his fingers in Guinness froth and pretended to slick back his hair. 'A gentleman should always honour a lady's request or he is no gentleman.'

'A request?' Dez said. 'Is that what they call it now?'

When Myles finished his pint, Pat immediately bought him another. 'Tonight, you do not put your hand in your pocket at all,' he said.

'Unless you need to scratch your balls,' Dez added. Dez looked at Pat. 'Is it OK to tell your mate he can scratch his balls? I wouldn't like to offend him.'

Pat made as though to punch Dez, but Dez dodged out of range.

In an hour, Myles drank three pints of Bud while Pat and Dez matched him with pints of Guinness. The drink had little effect except for a slight giddiness.

Pat took him aside. 'Listen, I loved those words you wrote. The way you put things together, man, I could see everything – the truck glistening like a Dinky, the dogs going at each other, even Buster's black skin train-tracked by scars. Just brilliant. Now I've got a bit of a plan. I need to ask you about it.'

Myles smiled. It was like hanging around the yard in school again. He and Pat had always had some kind of scheme going. They drove their schoolmates crazy with envy.

'Man, I've done so many interesting and mad things since I left the city. I've been meaning to write it all down, my own story. After your article I jotted a few things down. Very rough. I need a bit of a leg up, you know. Would you fancy having a look at this stuff for me?'

'No problem,' Myles said. 'I'll even ghost-write your auto-biography with you if you like.'

'I appreciate that, I truly do,' Pat's eyes twinkled. 'People like to read about outlaws. It brings a bit of colour into the lives of ordinary folk, because deep down we are all of us ordinary folk. Isn't that right, Dez?'

'No,' Dez grinned. 'Deep down we are all outlaws.'

Pat reflected. 'I suppose I would have to go along with that,' Pat said.

Pat and Dez gave the impression that they had been drinking for hours before he arrived. Yet neither slurred or behaved boister-ously, nor did they appear to be out of it. However, they shared a knowing air, as though they had taken coke or a similar substance that mellowed out the effects of alcohol.

At the next round Myles ordered a glass. He wanted to be more or less sober when meeting Mia later in Roolaboola's. The good thing about Bud was that you needed to drink a couple of barrels of the stuff before you got langered. He decided against inviting Pat and Dez to accompany him to Roolaboola's. He wanted to keep Mia to himself for the time being. He would have a few drinks and a few laughs with the lads, then slip away afterwards.

At closing time, they moved outside to the street where they hung around talking until Pat produced a joint and lit up in a doorway. They passed the joint around as they walked through Temple Bar. The combination of fresh cold air and strong dope elated Myles. It now seemed obvious to him that he was an ace journalist on his way to the bigtime. He had blown Jarlath Boon out of it. The dogfight feature had opened the door for him. He owed a lot to Pat. Even Dez didn't seem so much of a prick now.

Myles went into a spiel on life and journalism and girls and dope smoking and several other issues that he suddenly felt strongly about. He realised that he was babbling but he didn't care. The city buzzed, the lights inspired him, and the excitement of the night sang from every corner.

Not even the sight of his father glaring at him from the traffic island in the middle of Dame Street could puncture his mood.

He decided that they should all go to Roolaboola's. He would spring the big surprise on them after they got inside. His new friends would be gobsmacked when they saw that he had clicked with the red-head.

At Roolaboola's, they skipped the queue and proceeded directly to the entrance. The bouncers remembered Myles from the last time. Garvin appeared in a yellow mini skirt and matching headband and said hi to Myles before giving Pat a high five then kissing him on each cheek. After that he waved them past.

'You know Garvin?' Myles asked. 'I'm impressed.'

'Man, I know everyone,' Pat said. 'But not everyone knows me.'

Inside the walls throbbed and the floor vibrated like the wobbly room at a funfair. Tonight, everyone was dressed as characters from James Bond films. They brushed through monkey-suited Sean Connerys, Roger Moores and Pierce Brosnans, who danced with various Pussy Galores and Octopussies. They passed assorted Rosa Klebs, Oddjobs and several undersized Jaws, as well as a Blofeld who stroked a fluffy toy cat – at least Myles assumed it was a toy.

They made their way to the bar where they ordered lagers. Myles tried a sip but the loud bass and drums pounded his insides to mush. The beer had no place to go.

He looked for Mia but saw only Bond characters as well as an Indiana Jones who appeared oblivious that he had got the night wrong.

When the noise got too much, they went upstairs to the over-30s bar. Myles steered them to a table overlooking the dancefloor. Pat produced another joint and they lit up. A waitress with gold-painted skin materialised, wearing a gold dress, gold fingernails and a gold wig.

'You'll have to cut out the blow lads or I'll ask you to leave,' she said.

'Don't worry, we're friends of Garvin's,' Pat said. 'We'll put it out in a minute.'

'Yeah,' Dez said. 'When we finish smoking it.'

'Well, if you're friends of Garvin's . . .' The golden waitress shrugged.

Pat ordered champagne and the waitress left. After his next drag on the joint, Myles's head began to flutter, and he began to tap his feet.

'This must be strong stuff,' he said. 'I'm starting to enjoy this music.'

'Nothing's that strong,' Pat said.

'This music is cool,' Dez said. 'You guys are just ancient.'

When the bottle arrived, Pat popped the cork off the ceiling and spilled most of the froth on the table, which Dez thought was really funny.

'Back soon with a big surprise,' Myles said. 'Keep my place.'

He went downstairs in search of Mia. He eventually found her sitting at a table under the DJ box. She was dressed as Pussy Galore in a shiny purple jumpsuit. She was talking with a couple of Bond girls, but was glad to see him.

'You came,' she said and kissed him on the lips, a brief full contact that sent a tingle through him.

'Of course I came. You should have told me it was Bond night.'

'I didn't want to spoil the surprise,' she said.

She introduced him to the Bond girls. Stick was a tall, skinny blonde wearing a 60s-style mini skirt, who gave him a firm handshake. Aisling was an attractive Asian girl, medium height, slightly plump with dark hair. She had a sour expression on her pretty face.

'So you're the gangster?' she said cheekily.

'Em,' Myles said.

'You don't look like a gangster.'

'Why? What do gangsters look like?' Myles said, trying to appear blasé and urbane.

'Hard.' Aisling studied him. 'They look hard. You just look soft.'

Stick punched Aisling on the shoulder. 'Myles you look top. Don't mind your woman here. She is savagely fucking pissed on Slippery Nipples.'

'Like arse,' Aisling said.

'Fuck off you bitch,' Stick said lovingly, and they blew kisses at each other.

Myles looked quizzically at Mia. 'Slippery Nipples?'

'Sambuca mixed with Baileys,' she explained. She studied him with a mixture of concern and amusement. 'C'mere, Mr Tall, look at the big drinking head on you. Are you feeling OK?'

'Just a bit frisky.'

'That's completely allowed,' she said. 'Everyone should feel frisky when they want to.'

'Come on,' he said. 'I want you to come upstairs to meet some friends of mine.'

'The shady gangsters?' Mia asked.

'Yes, em, kind of,' Myles said.

'Cool,' she said. 'Is the one who nearly killed me up there?'

'He is.'

'Upstairs?' Aisling said. 'Don't be soft.'

Stick leaned over. 'We never go upstairs.' She shook her head. 'Way uncool.'

'We've got champagne,' Myles said.

'That's different,' Stick said, taking his arm. 'Why didn't you say you were minted? Come on girls.'

'OK,' Aisling shrugged. 'Seeing as there's champers going, I'll give it a wallop.'

They all went upstairs, Myles with Mia on one arm and Stick on the other, Aisling trailing behind complaining about how much effort it was to move, and the chronic distance they had to cover to get upstairs.

Pat and Dez were surprised to see Mia and intrigued by the Bond girls. Mia said hello and sat down while Aisling and Stick chose chairs either side of her. Mia showed no sign that she recognised either Pat or Dez.

'Fair play,' Pat nodded at Myles. 'You're a fast mover.'

Pleased with Pat's reaction, Myles ordered more champagne. This time, the cork rebounded off a metal light shade to zing past Myles's ear. Dez thought this was hilarious. Pat poured them all foaming glasses.

Myles talked with Stick for a while, but none of the conversation made any sense to him, though she giggled a lot so he figured that he must not have been doing too badly. When he looked around he noticed Mia and Pat deep in conversation. An arrow of jealousy zipped through his stomach.

He was about to interrupt them when Dez leaned over to Myles and snorted, 'So Little Miss One-Way Street is now Goalpost's current squeeze.'

Myles glared at him. 'Her name is Mia, and you can call me Myles.'

Dez gave him a look. 'Relax the head, Goalpost.'

Myles kept glancing over at Pat and Mia. He was relieved when Mia appeared to snub Pat and move away. Myles sat silently for a while, sipping champagne, not looking at anyone. Mia came over to sit beside him, which was exactly what he wanted. She looked different somehow, but then he remembered that she was Pussy Galore and that made him laugh.

'What's funny?' she said, but he wasn't able to reply for laughing. 'Mr Tall's turned into Mr Giggles,' she said.

Stick and Aisling leaned over to ruffle Myles's hair and tickle under his arms. After a while Mia got tired of Myles laughing all the time and talked with Aisling instead.

Myles felt his stomach rushing to his mouth. He got up quickly and rushed downstairs. In the toilets, he dashed into an empty cubicle where he threw up.

Ten minutes after the last heave, he felt sober again.

By the time he got back, Pat had moved across to chat up Aisling and Dez was trying without success to put the bite on Stick.

'I've got a Porsche,' he said to her. 'I could give you a lift home.'

'Porsches are cool,' Stick said, trying to be polite. 'Maybe I'll take you up on that.'

'Course,' Dez leaned over, bleary-eyed. 'If I give you a lift home, I'll expect something for it.'

'What do you mean?'

'I want at least a blowjob,' he said.

Stick looked at him. 'Well you can give it to yourself,' she said, and got to her feet.

'See you later,' she said to everyone as she headed downstairs.

'Thanks,' Dez shouted after her. 'It's been crap.'

Aisling rose and went after her.

'Hang on,' Pat shouted. 'You haven't heard all my chat-up lines.'

'I have now,' Aisling replied.

Dez slumped back, his chin buried in his chest. Pat left to look for the two Bond girls and Myles, tired of trying to keep up with all the activity, closed his eyes.

When he opened them a few seconds later Mia was standing over him asking him something about a party. He said yes even though he couldn't understand what she was saying. Then she was leading him by the hand through the club, with tidal waves of music gushing over them. Goodnight to Garvin at the door, a peck from him on Mia's cheek, and then freezing air on Myles's skin. He galloped into a speech about why dogs should be allowed to wear mini skirts in restaurants, especially when drinking peppermint tea. Mia thought he was amusing, but Aisling, who had popped out of nowhere, told him to keep his voice down, he was frightening the pigeons.

Suddenly they were in a car with Stick driving and he was in the back seat with Mia on his knees, kissing her. They bumped along as

Maria McKee sang, 'My Girlhood among the Outlaws'. 'Play that one again,' Myles shouted, and Stick had to slow down to wind the tape back. They seemed to be driving for ages. He nodded off on Mia's shoulder. She smelled of peppermint.

Next thing, he was inside a warm room with soft music playing and little hippy people springing up from the floorboards to dance in slow rhythmic waves. He smoked another joint with a curly-haired fellow who introduced himself as Lorcan. 'That's a good one,' Myles said. 'Lorcan always sleeps upstairs.'

The curly haired fellow who thought he was Lorcan smiled then got up and disappeared. Later, Myles danced with Mia and they kissed and he was proud of himself for being able to hold it together.

'Play Maria McKee again,' he shouted.

Sometime later Mia led him by the hand out of the warm party and into a dark garden, with lights twinkling at them from across the bay and a wind slicing the ears off him. We're going to the chalet, she might have said, or she could have said that they were looking for a Chevrolet. There was a fumbling of keys and he bumped his head on a doorframe going into a darkened room.

'You OK?' Mia said.

'Story of my life,' he said, rubbing his forehead. Mia lit a candle.

'Poor Mr Tall,' she said, and kissed him.

They flopped on top of a large bed. In a little while he was naked except for his socks. He saw by candlelight that she was naked too.

'Hey, this is finally getting serious,' he said.

'Well, it is our official second date,' she said.

They got inside the sheets, and when their cuddling bodies had warmed them sufficiently she climbed on top of him and they began fucking. She sat on him, pumping up and down, her head back, and he put his hands on her small breasts and tried to get a late night radio station on her cute button nipples.

'Play Maria McKee,' he whispered.

He managed to stay hard most of the time and that surprised him because he felt completely out of it. Mia helped a lot. Whenever he flagged she closed her eyes, hissing, 'Come on come on.'

That got him excited again.

For some reason he felt removed from the action, as though he was just an observer inside someone else's body. Next time he wouldn't smoke any joints. Next time he would bring her to a fancy hotel room. Next time he would really blow her away. They finished and she rolled off him. They lay together watching the tiny reflections of the lights from the bay flickering off the ceiling.

'Play Maria McKee,' he said.

'Go to sleep,' she told him.

He dreamed that he was on top of his father's shoulders going down a busy street. He was so high up he could see over the roofs of all the buildings and reach up to run his hands through the clouds. He wanted to get down so that he could walk alongside his father but when he shouted his father ignored him. He passed a tall building where people opened the windows to look out at him. Dez leaned out of one of the windows. 'What's the weather like up there?' Dez shouted. 'Cloudy,' Myles shouted back and Dez laughed. 'Ha, Goalpost says it's cloudy.' Then all the people in the windows laughed too, and he reached out for Dez to give him a box in the gob for himself but instead he overbalanced, and tumbled from his father's shoulders headfirst towards the street.

Then he woke up. Dazzling sunlight filled the room, turning it white and pristine as a hospital ward. He was alone in the bed.

After a while, he raised himself up on his elbows and looked around. A middle-aged man with a boyish flop of black hair sat on the end of the bed looking at Myles. The man held a gun pointed at Myles's chest.

'Good morning,' the man said. 'We need to have a little talk.'

EIGHT

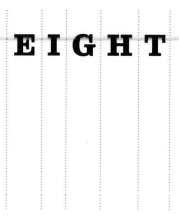

Mr Tall

The man was built like a barrel, with small slitty eyes in a round, genial face. He seemed relaxed, as though it was perfectly routine to hold a gun pointed at a naked man's heart. The flop of unnaturally black hair that lay across the man's forehead, made him look boyish. He dyes his hair, Myles thought. As though this observation somehow gave Myles an edge.

He became acutely conscious of his inappropriate morning erection that bulged the bed sheets. He was too scared to cross his legs, however, in case that drew attention to it. Instead, he prayed that the man with the gun wouldn't notice. Myles yearned to put on a shirt. As though denim might somehow deflect a bullet.

This situation was his own doing. Just when things had been going so well. Nobody had forced him to go out drinking and smoking dope, or get trashed in a club for people who were born in the 70s. It was his fault that he had ended up at a party God knows where and slept with Little Miss One-Way Street, who was even more of a mystery to him now than she was when he first met her. She wasn't even a great shag, just an energetic one.

Now here was a stranger with dyed hair holding a gun on him. 'Think carefully before you answer this question.' The man's voice was clear and pleasant with a pronounced American twang. 'Don't try to bullshit, OK?'

It took Myles a few seconds to summon his voice.

'OK,' he croaked.

'Alright,' the man said. 'Did you ride my daughter last night?' Myles watched the man's face for clues as to how he should answer. The man's affable expression remained unchanged. OK. The man wants to know if I rode his daughter. Whose father is he? Mia's? Aisling's? Stick's? Myles didn't even know whose party he had been attending. He concluded that there was no right way to answer the question. If he said 'No', the man wouldn't believe him. If he said 'Yes,' the man might shoot his prick off.

'I wasn't with anyone last night,' he lied.

The man didn't blink. He seemed to be waiting for a further explanation. Myles watched as the gun's ugly snout shifted to point at his bulge.

'Talk to me,' the man said. 'Make it good.'

Myles blabbed, 'I was a bit out of it. There was this party in someone's house and I sort of woke up in this bed.'

'Where are your clothes?' the man said.

Myles looked about him. The room was bare except for a chair in the corner and a bedside table upon which a candle had melted into a saucer. Perhaps his clothes were under the bed. He didn't feel that it would be wise to attempt to look. Not while a guy held a gun on him. Not while he had this massive hard-on.

'I don't remember much about last night. Someone must have put me to bed. I don't even know where I am,' Myles said, then tried a smile. 'If it's not too much trouble, could I *ask* where I am?'

The man did not give any indication that he had heard the question. Keep talking, Myles thought. He won't shoot you if you're gabbing.

'We were at a club in town and we ended up in someone's car and Mia said—'

'Mia?' the man spat it out and the affable expression abruptly changed to one of contempt. 'Is that what she's calling herself now?'

Myles was so confused that he couldn't continue. If Mia wasn't Mia who was she?

When the man rose suddenly, Myles stopped breathing. Any second he's going to squeeze the trigger. Myles wondered if it was true that you never heard the shot that got you. Instead, the man threw him a bath towel. 'Get up and come with me.'

He climbed out of bed, feeling exposed and stupid and conscious of the lance sticking out between his legs that had grown bigger. He draped the towel around his middle. Now he towered over the man who was around five foot five and suddenly seemed less menacing.

The man walked over to the chalet door, opened it and held it for Myles to walk through. Myles scraped his head off the doorframe again. Outside, the light hurt his eyes. It was a clear, bright day. Small puffy white clouds sailed across a blue sky. Myles could see fields of gorse winding down to a shimmering sapphire sea. So calm, so exquisite. Refreshingly unimpeded by city bustle and worry.

Apart from your man with the gun.

Where was this place? Malahide? Howth? Skerries?

'Keep walking.'

Myles's bare feet trod on soft grass mixed with hard pebbly grains of earth. He walked slowly, trying to pick his way along. Daylight gave him the illusion of safety. Nothing could happen to you in daylight, could it? He saw a gate at the bottom of the hill and beyond that what looked like a cliff path. Jesus, a cliff. What was this man going to do with him? His legs felt hollow. Chilly fingers played along the back of his neck.

'Open the gate,' the voice behind him said.

He lifted the latch on the wooden gate and went through onto a narrow pathway. Beyond was an abrupt drop to jagged rocks and swirling water. A body could be tossed into the waves to be pounded to bits against the rocks. His remains would be washed out to sea, never to resurface. His father had never given Myles advice on what to do when you were naked and scared on top of a cliff with a psycho holding a gun on you. He looked around but there was no sign of his father either.

As the man closed the gate, the latch made a sudden clacking noise like a rifle being cocked and Myles jerked involuntarily.

The man leaned over the gate and held out his free hand. Assuming that for some inexplicable reason he wanted to shake hands, Myles extended his own hand.

The man slapped away Myles's hand.

'My towel,' the man said gruffly.

Myles unravelled the towel and handed it back over the gate. He felt mortified and isolated, with a sore hand, but at least his erection had gone.

'Don't ever let me see your mug again,' the man said. 'Go on, scat.'

'What about my clothes?' Myles said.

The man pointed the gun at Myles's feet and fired a sharp crack. A shower of earth stung his legs.

He took off down the cliff path. He was too terrified to look behind until he had turned several corners and put a lot of distance between himself and the man with the gun.

The gunshot had sounded flat and unreal, like someone snapping a stick. Only a distant cousin of the gunshots in the movies or on television. Maybe it wasn't a real gun. It could have been a starting pistol. But the guy had seemed like he meant business. That American twang. Mixed uneasily with a Dublin accent. Like someone who had been unable to shake off an old identity to properly absorb the new. Myles guessed the man had been Irish to begin with. The way he had said 'ride' instead of sleep with or fuck or seduce. Perhaps he was a drugs baron. There were a lot of shady rich people around these days.

He stopped to rest on a corner. The ocean stretched out before him, vast and blue, unimpaired except for a small island on the horizon as well as a few sailboats. Below, a huge outcrop of jagged rock reared up from the swell like a great sculpted dinosaur. The sweat felt cool on his skin. He was surprised how natural it felt to be running around naked on a cliff path.

Far off he heard voices and splashing. He leaned over to scrutinise the line of the coast until he made out a beach in the distance with tiny figures on it. Swimmers. Where there were swimmers there would be swimmers' clothes. He could lift someone's gear and get onto a roadway. Somehow get back into the city. Out of this mess.

He began to walk in the direction of the beach. Above him, on the hill, he could make out the tops of houses over the gorse and trees. Sometimes he caught a glimpse of a large mansion far above. All the houses he passed seemed to have extensive areas of land around them. All owned by drugs barons, probably.

Rounding a corner, he saw two people on the path ahead. An elderly couple out for a stroll. There was no point turning around, so he broke into a run. The couple might not notice that he was naked. They might mistake him for a jogger on a morning run. Or they might start screaming. As he drew closer he saw that the man had a long stick and the woman wore a scarf around her head. They looked at him with friendly smiles.

'Good morning,' the man said cheerfully.

'Morning,' Myles said as he passed.

No fuss. No screaming. The man hadn't even taken a swipe at him. Perhaps the old couple were half-blind, or they could have been well disposed towards naked joggers. Maybe he was in a nudist area.

He continued running. Further along the path, he came upon a scatter of skateboards. They were parked together like a row of shrunken motorbikes on a small clearing above a cliff path. The path obviously led down to the beach he had seen earlier. Kids. Perhaps teenagers. If he wanted to grab someone's clothes, he would have to follow the path. If they were all youngsters none of their clothes would fit him. Unless he chanced upon the clothing of a teenager who happened to be six foot six and a half. What if he was seen? He would risk being labelled a flasher, or worse, some kind of child molester. He was trying to decide what to do when a small boy and a woman appeared below on their way up the path. They were accompanied by two scrambling dogs – massive ravenous-looking black brutes with bright pink lolling tongues.

The boy looked up just as Myles took off.

'Mum, that man's starkers,' he shouted.

'Ignore him, Austin, he's sick,' the woman replied.

He heard barking behind him, followed by what sounded like hundreds of paws scrabbling up a dirt track. The woman's voice yelled instructions to the dogs, something that sounded like 'Eat him, lads.'

He came upon a small gate and jumped over. Anything was better than letting the dogs catch up. He ran along a small path that led through thick gorse, brambles whipping at his legs. A few seconds later, he heard the dogs skid to a confused halt at the gate, then bark like maniacs. Far above, he spotted the roof and high chimneys of a mansion. He ran up the path until gradually the sound of the barking faded. He slowed, then pulled up to lean against a tree stump, exhausted, and panting. After he got his breath back, he noticed a silver of blood between his toes. He'd been shot, he thought. He'd lost a toe. Examining a gash along the side of his little toe, he couldn't tell if the wound had come from the bullet or something that had grazed him on his run. It didn't hurt so it must not be serious. Keep going, he decided. Get out of here first, worry about gangrene afterwards.

He walked forward purposefully. He would try to make it to a main road. If he met anyone who looked reasonable he would explain that he had been for a swim and that someone had stolen his clothes. That sort of thing must happen a lot in seaside places. The people who owned the mansion would surely lend him a coat or a pair of trousers. Even a drugs baron might give him enough for a taxi home.

The mansion looked drab and desolate; tall dusty windows that hadn't been cleaned or had their frames painted in years were set among dismal grey concrete walls. He walked through an overgrown back garden to the pockmarked back door where he gave three loud knocks.

The knocks echoed gloomily. No hint of activity. Looking around, he tried the side door that presumably led to the front of the house but it was locked. The surrounding vine-covered garden walls were too high even for him, and he could find nothing to use as a ladder.

He was about to give up and head back down to the cliff path when he noticed that a second-floor window was half-open. The window looked relatively easy to reach. He could climb onto the ground-floor ledge then scale a series of protruding blocks up to the second floor. He jumped onto the ledge and began to climb. Even with bare feet, it was easier than he had anticipated. Soon he was standing on the second-floor window ledge. Cautiously, he pushed the window further open then climbed inside.

He stood inside an empty dusty room, then made his way to the door, opened it and went out into a long corridor that smelled vaguely of cabbage and dead flowers. He padded past many large wooden doors until he reached a long spiralling staircase with ornate curved banisters. He descended slowly, his soft footfalls sounding unnaturally loud in the reverential hush. The place seemed deserted. Growing in confidence, he made his way through the hall to what he presumed to be the front of the house. At the front door he tried the handle but the door would not budge. It was locked in three places and bolted in at least a couple more. He guessed that the house probably belonged to elderly and extremely paranoid people who had not bought anything new since the 40s – except maybe door locks. Either that or it had been lying empty for many years. The thing now was to find what he needed.

He walked back along the corridor, opening doors and looking into rooms to see if he could find either a key or some clothing or both. All the rooms were empty and devoid of objects except basic chairs and tables, and occasionally a picture on the wall. Not so much as a wardrobe.

A kitchen was the soul of a house. He would definitely find something useful there. If this place had a kitchen. He walked to the back of the house and opened a large door that looked like it might lead to one. The door opened into absolute blackness. Inching forward cautiously, his fingers discovered material that felt like velvet; a heavy curtain that blocked off the rest of the room. At the top of the curtain he spotted a pinprick of light. He moved along until he found a gap, then he pushed through to the other side into faint light.

It took a few moments for his eyes to grow accustomed to the murk. He had arrived in a sort of chapel. Glancing about him, he saw that he was standing beside an altar. A giant crucifix stood in front of him, lit by a small nightlight. As he moved forward, he saw that the crucifix contained a figure of Jesus, naked except for a loincloth. High above, he made out gloomy stained glass windows, while in front of him were arranged row upon row of pews. The pews were inhabited by dozens of nuns holding beads who sat as still as statues, looking at him as though he were an apparition. The whole scene reminded Myles of an antiquated black and white image in an old photo album.

There was no sound except for a seagull cawing far away, followed by a feeble rustle of breeze from the high windows. Then a small nun in the front row coughed gently, breaking the spell. Myles covered his crotch with his hands and tried not to be so tall.

'Hello,' he began as cheerfully as he could. 'I've been swimming.'

Once Myles had explained his predicament, the nuns were very understanding. They nodded their heads but they wouldn't utter a word or answer his questions. At first he thought that he had stumbled into an order of deaf and dumb nuns. Then the small sister appeared beside him holding a pen and notepad.

She wrote, 'We are a silent order and we are glad to help you.' They gave him a diminutive bathrobe to put on until they could find something more substantial for him to wear. He sat on a pew in the small chapel and admired the stained glass windows and basked in the peaceful atmosphere until a group of nuns returned with a monk's habit and sandals.

'Sorry,' the small nun wrote. 'This is all we have in the way of male clothing. Unless you would prefer a blanket?'

Myles thought that he detected a trace of a smile on her face. He resisted the urge to inquire how it was that an order of silent nuns happened to have a monk's habit in their possession. It might be prudent to let that one pass, he decided.

After he had donned the robe and cowl, a group of the nuns led him to the front of the house. The order had no phone but they offered to send a note to fetch the police if he so wished. Myles declined, explaining that he would much prefer to make his own way home without involving the police. Besides, there was little that the police could do at this stage. A bunch of mischievous kids had obviously stolen his clothing and vanished. No point complicating the situation for everyone. It might turn out to be embarrassing for the sisters if word somehow slipped out that they had been entertaining a naked man.

'We are most grateful for your understanding and tact,' the small nun wrote.

Next he humbly requested money for a taxi home, promising to repay it by money order within twenty-four hours. The nun shuffled away, returning within minutes with an envelope containing six crisp five pound notes.

At the front gate, she gave him a card with an address and phone number of a local taxi that the order occasionally used. The driver's address was in Main Street, Howth. Then she pointed Myles in the direction of the town. He said thanks and started walking. The sandals flapped awkwardly along the ground. Like walking with dead fish strapped to his feet. When Myles glanced back at the front gate, a dozen nuns waved him goodbye.

He made it down the hill to the town without drawing any attention. He found the address on the card the nun had handed him. The taxi driver, a burly red-faced man, agreed to take him home for thirty quid. To the taxi man, Myles was just a monk with hard cash. No big thing.

On the drive into town, he did some serious thinking. The events of this morning had been a warning, he reasoned. Meant to show him that it was time for him to change his life. Otherwise he would end up in real trouble. Perhaps dead. He decided to give up drinking and smoking dope. For a while anyway. He would quit nightclubs and pubs, especially Roolaboola's. He also decided to stay away from Mia, or whatever her name was this week. She had brought upon him this morning's humiliating and petrifying experiences and almost got him killed. Just because of a drunken ride. She was not worth dying for.

Philip did not appear surprised to see Myles enter the pub wearing a monk's habit and sandals. He was used to Myles's ways and rarely paid him much attention. He continued to pull a pint for a customer as Myles the monk lifted the counter flap and came in behind the bar.

'Where's Mother?' Myles asked.

'Out,' Philip said.

'Lucy and Justine?'

'Out.'

Myles went through to the back room and up the flight of stairs that led to the second floor of his mother's house. Once there he made his way to the bedroom and threw off the monk's habit. He showered quickly then dried himself and put a band-aid on his cut foot. He put on a fresh T-shirt and briefs followed by his best Hugo Boss shirt and jeans as well as his leather Armani jacket. He wanted to feel good about himself. He needed to feel that nothing like this morning would ever happen to him again.

Now that he felt refreshed, the experiences on the cliff walk seemed like something from a film. It must have been a starting pistol, he thought. He lay down on the bed in his best clothes and thought over the resolutions he had made in the taxi. Seeing no reason to change any of them, he closed his eyes and went to sleep.

He had no dreams and woke up in the evening, starving but restored. He heard Lucy and Justine clattering about in the kitchen below and hurried downstairs to greet them. He was in great humour now. He had got his life back and he intended to make the most of it from this moment on.

He wanted to take Lucy and Justine out to a restaurant, but Lucy said that Justine was tired and besides they had already eaten McDonalds'. Myles suggested that just the two of them should go out, but again Lucy turned him down saying that she too was pretty flaked out from a hard day. As Myles deflated, she kissed him on the cheek.

'It's really sweet that you want to take us out but we can't drop everything and just go. Maybe tomorrow night,' she said. Myles agreed and sat in the kitchen while Justine regaled him with a big story about getting lost in the supermarket. From the pub next door, he heard music and communal singing. His mother's voice soared above everything: 'The night they drove Old Dixie down, And all the bells were ringing.'

Later, when Lucy was in bed reading stories to Justine, Myles
trudged up the back stairs to Philip's room for the first time in
years. Philip had been shocked when Myles had moved back in. The
brothers had never had much to say to each other. Philip had always
been a mother's boy while Myles had been more attached to his
father. Then again, Philip had never had much to say to anyone,
unless the talk was about hurling or model trains or involved
instructions on the best way to rig up a tap onto a Guinness barrel.
Philip seemed to resent Myles's presence in the house. The other
night at dinner, he had even mumbled something about Myles and
Lucy being better off if they had stayed in a hotel while they were
waiting for their house to be ready.

Outside Philip's door Myles paused. He heard the rattle of
model wheels riding a metal track, the steady drone of small
engines. He tapped on the door. After a while Philip answered. He
looked at Myles like a bouncer waiting to see an invitation.

'OK if I come in for a while?' Myles asked.

Philip shrugged. 'If you like.'

The room had been turned into a gigantic model railway. There
were tunnels and tiny villages and towns and stations and miniature
buses and tiny figures waving and trees and little streetlights that
worked, along with signals that flicked off and on, boulders and
dams and bridges and what must have been at least a dozen trains
pulling various coloured and shaped carriages running on different
tracks and at different levels.

Philip ducked underneath a long bridge and disappeared. After
a few moments he popped up in the centre of the set next to his
bed where he had set up a vast bank of control panels. Philip sat
down, made a few adjustments and pressed some buttons. Then he
beckoned to Myles to join him. Myles ducked under the long
bridge and crawled to where Philip sat, careful not to bump or
dislodge anything. Philip pulled over an extra stool for Myles, then
handed him a control panel. He indicated a goods train that was
just leaving a snow-capped tunnel. Myles nodded and took over. As
boys the only times that they had played together quietly for hours
were those occasions when they were messing about with Philip's

train sets. Something about the mechanical, physical nature of the activity meant they rarely had to bother speaking to each other, so they had got on fine. Now they co-ordinated timetables and sent trains into and out of tunnels, through sleeping villages as well as up and down and around hills and mountains. Time passed quickly and enjoyably.

When Myles eventually looked at his watch it was after midnight. Gradually, they brought all the trains to a halt. Some went into sidings, others to special shelters. Philip turned off most of the lights but left a set of tiny red emergency lights strung through the hills. They gave the model set a fairyland aspect.

Philip crawled out and went over to a small table by the window and put on a kettle.

'Cup of tea?'

'Grand,' Myles said.

He followed Philip out of the set and stood by the door, stretching.

'Thanks,' he said. 'That was great.'

'That's OK,' Philip said. 'It's got a lot bigger.'

'So I see. How many trains do you have now?'

Philip smiled. 'Forty-two.' Then he thought for a moment. 'But six are off the rails right now. It's hard to get parts for the older models.'

Myles walked over to the window and Philip handed him a cup of steaming tea. The brothers looked out at the showers of rain descending through the glow of the streetlights.

Down below, a green Volvo slowed as it approached the pub, as if about to drop a passenger. The window rolled down and a man stuck his head out. From the high angle it was difficult for Myles to see with absolute clarity, but it looked like Dez. The Volvo slowed to a crawl, made as if to turn onto the kerb outside the pub, but then abruptly pulled back onto the road and zoomed away. It screeched around the corner at the end of the street. Myles noticed Philip studying him.

'Someone you know?' he asked.

'No,' Myles said. 'Just another bad driver. Town's full of them.'

NINE

The Sperm

The assembled features staff watched as the Sperm with the Perm punched the air, his pompadour swaying ominously. He looked like a middle-aged singer in an unconvincing glam rock revival band, trying desperately to get the crowd going.

'There are going to be big changes around here. Starting right now,' he barked, pointing a stubby finger around the room. 'There'll be no more sunbathing under the lightbulbs in this department.'

There was something not quite right about the Sperm, Myles reckoned. Probably the weight of all that hair on his brain. He finished his inaugural rant as features editor by announcing that he wanted to see each of them individually in his office beginning right away. He stuck a list of names and times onto the notice board. Then he pelted headlong from the room like a man gripped in a sudden spasm of diarrhoea.

Everyone gathered to examine the list. Bob Casper was first, followed at five minute intervals by Lola Wall, Cliff Mangan, Dog-brain, Jarlath Boon, then the others. Myles was last. Bob Casper sidled up to him.

'If I don't make it back here, do me a favour will you, boyo?'

'Sure, what?'

'Kill his perm!'

'Delighted.'

'Cheers.'

As Bob went off to meet with the Sperm in the features editor's office down the corridor, Myles and the others stood around talking things over. Lola Wall looked even more tragic than usual. She was positive she was about to be shafted. 'The Sperm hates women,' she said. 'I know he's going to yell at me.'

Dogbrain tried to cheer her up. 'Ah, but sure he mightn't mean it,' he said.

Myles caught Jarlath Boon eyeing him. Since Jarlath had returned from his week's leave he had been going round with a smug face as though he had secretly won the Lotto. Myles decided that Jarlath had completely lost the plot and ignored him.

The day after Myles's encounter with the man with the gun, the *Evening News* had run a brief report on page two headed, 'Nude Jogger Horrifies Howth'. The two-paragraph account had reported that Gardai were seeking to interview a mysterious naked man who had jogged past a swimming party of schoolboys and their mothers on a private beach in broad daylight. The man was described as 'of medium height, with a dark complexion and bald'.

In the past week, Myles had steered clear of pubs and night-clubs. He was getting on better with Lucy. Building work had restarted on the new house and the bank had promised to consider favourably their application for a bigger loan. He had written 'Daredevils in Traction', an amusing feature on a group of demented accident prone city centre skateboarders that had been well received by everyone except Jarlath Boon.

Ducking phone calls from Mia had been the only difficult part, along with putting off an invitation from Pat to go for 'another few scoops' to plan his autobiography. Myles had also suffered one nightmare in which his erection had been shot off by the flop-haired man.

Bob was back within five minutes, a long face on him. 'I'm transferred to news,' he said. 'I don't give a flying sideways shite.

At least I'll be out of the Sperm's Perm.'

Lola Wall returned glowing with a two and a half per cent payrise. Jarlath Boon glided back into the room as newly appointed assistant features editor. Cliff Mangan came back as newly appointed deputy assistant features editor. Dogbrain didn't come back at all.

Then it was Myles's turn.

'Sure, you've nothing to worry about,' Bob said. 'You're the new golden boy.'

The Sperm didn't glance up when Myles entered. He was yelling into a mobile phone at a disgruntled photographer. He seemed to be in perpetual motion. He jotted down notes, fiddled with items in a briefcase that lay open on the desk in front of him and occasionally excavated the contents of a gaping nostril. 'Do you know what I'm going to do to your photos? I'm going to dance on them. That's right, dance. You don't believe me? Listen to this then.'

The Sperm stood up and emptied the contents of a brown paper envelope onto the floor. Then he danced on the scattered photographs, holding the mobile out so that the guy on the other end could hear the snaps being trampled. The Sperm winked gleefully at Myles. 'Are you listening? That's what I think of your shagging photographs. You'll get the same treatment if you ever give me rubbish like this again.'

He switched off the phone and dropped it into his open brief-case with a flourish for Myles's benefit. Then he sat down and gave Myles a wall to wall grin. This was unusual because the Sperm was not known for his grins. Apart from his hairstyle, he was renowned for yelling at people and generally being so objectionable that he could give people panic attacks just by entering a room. A grin from the Sperm was either a positive sign or else Myles was about to be fired.

'I'd say that you're the tallest journalist in Ireland,' the Sperm said, scratching under the arms of his white and blue striped shirt. 'You're definitely the highest man who's ever been in this office. How high up are you?'

Myles told him and the Sperm registered surprise. 'Well I

never. God, you could have been a basketball player, couldn't you? Make more money than in this old game I'd bet.'

He offered Myles a pinch of snuff from a small tin box. Myles declined. 'Wise man. Taking this stuff is like having a horse fart in your face, but it's the only thing that can clear the spiders out of me head.' The Sperm snorted a pinch of into each nostril.

He snapped shut the box, put it in the briefcase and closed the lid. All traces of good humour fell away.

'Right. Down to business. You've come a long way in a short time, haven't you? I've been hearing all about your progress. You're definitely the fellow everyone is talking about at the moment.'

'As long as it's all good talk,' Myles said.

The Sperm winked at him. 'Yep, you're the fellow they're all talking about.'

Myles felt a pang of foreboding as the Sperm continued.

'Here's the way it's going to be. I want nice light features. Funny stuff about people and places. None of this robbing trucks shite. And stay away from dogfights. I don't care if you've got a singing St Bernard versus a rabid dinosaur. You got away with it once but it's illegal and I don't want the Guards on my back. Now, I'm not the type to interfere. I just want to know what features you're planning, who you're going to talk to and what you're going to say about them. Apart from that, you're your own boss, OK?'

The Sperm stood up and extended a hand to indicate that the meeting was over. 'Thanks for coming down.' He guided Myles to the door and opened it for him. 'Any problems just talk to the brother-in-law.'

'Your brother-in-law?' Myles said.

'Jarlath Boon, the new assistant editor.' The Sperm slapped Myles on the back. 'He's promised me faithfully that he'll look after you.'

Myles walked down the corridor feeling crushed, as though the Sperm had danced on his career. There had been no attempt to discuss his work or take on board Myles's own ideas. This morning Myles had been an ace journalist. Now he was a scullery-maid again. No more 'Outlaw' stories. Jarlath Boon would look after him all right. He'd send the ace features writer to review dog shows. Myles considered approaching Fowler. But the prospect of Fowler overturning the Sperm's orders was about as likely as Dogbrain swimming the Atlantic with a typewriter balanced on his head. After all, the Sperm was now officially Fowler's right hand. And the Sperm's new right hand was Jarlath Boon. He entered the features room, kept his head down and walked directly to his desk, skirting all eye contact. In particular, he wanted to avoid Jarlath Boon's triumphant leer. He sat at his desk and brooded on the injustice of his life.

He was so distracted that it took him a while to realise that his nostrils were being assailed by aromas – pungent, ticklish, buoyant scents that grew stronger the longer he sat there. His desk was awash with flowers. An impressive bouquet sat cheerfully in front of his computer terminal. A small envelope addressed to him was taped to the stem of a prickly rose. He removed the envelope, opened it and tiny armies started brawling in his stomach as he read the card's familiar scrawl: 'Hello you. How would you like to meet me for a cup of peppermint tea? This offer will not come every day, you know. X. Mia.'

The restaurant on the top floor of the Stephen's Green Centre rang with the brightly deranged chattering of flocks of gaily dressed foreign students. A party of the loudest and most deranged invaded a table beside Myles.

She was late. He would give her another five minutes.

From his window table, he observed the busy streets below. The city looked like a painting by an artist who was big into light grey and dark-grey. Even the colourful horse-drawn carriages on the green appeared drab. He searched for Johnny Bones' carriage but couldn't spot it. The grumpy old fossil still hadn't forgiven him for 'hijacking' Sheba. Johnny was demanding at least three hundred pounds in lost earnings before he would talk to Myles again.

On the phone earlier, Mia had sounded sleepy but delighted to hear from him. 'Oh, it's you. I was just curled up inside a delicious snuggle of sleep,' she had said, giving him one of her giggles.

She had suggested meeting for lunch, and he had agreed. She had a lot to tell him, she had chirped.

It couldn't hurt to meet her one last time. They had shared some intimate moments and he didn't want her thinking back on him as a user. He would keep the conversation light. No mention of fathers with guns or any of the other puzzling stuff, like Barry of the Bouquets or the penis paintings or her invisible flatmate. He wouldn't even ask her if Mia was her real name. He took a sip of his cappuccino, and then poked his spoon into the froth to gather some of the chocolate-flecked cream. What was wrong with buying her lunch, chatting for a while, then at the end wishing her luck with her father and whatever else she had going on in her life. Then that would be that. He didn't care anymore whether or not the man with the gun was her real father.

As he put the spoon in his mouth and sucked, his father's round face frowned from the swirling coffee.

'It's far from cappuccino that you were reared,' he said. Myles put the spoon back in the coffee and stirred until his father's face disappeared.

'Hello you.'

She stood by his table in her long, black velvet coat. She wore a pair of green-tinted rave sunglasses even though the day was dismal. He stood and they gave each other a reserved hug.

'I thought I was going to be stood up,' he said.

'Fat chance,' she said. 'Not when you're paying for lunch.'

He pulled up a chair for her and signalled to a waitress. Mia sat down and gave him a playful look over the top of her rave shades, as though they had resumed a delightful game. He was glad that she seemed relaxed and cheerful. He didn't like to admit that he was pleased to see her. Nevertheless, a feeling of joy surged through him.

She kept her shades on. Perhaps she was keeping them on for protection in case he broke it off and she started blubbing. She must suspect that it was over. Mia didn't seem like the blubbing type, but you could never tell with young ones.

'I phoned you a couple of times,' she said.

'Did you? I didn't get the messages,' Myles lied.

'I thought maybe you were avoiding me after Lorcan's party.'

'No way,' he smiled to show that he was amazed that the

thought should ever have crossed her mind. 'So it was Lorcan's party?'

'You can't have forgotten him? You smoked a joint together.'

'Oh yeah.' Myles recalled the curly-haired fellow who had vanished suddenly. 'Are you having a scene with Lorcan?' Myles heard himself asking and inwardly cringed. What did he care who she was seeing? It was none of his business anymore. It had never been any of his business.

Mia giggled, 'I know I'm bad, but I'm not that bad.'

'Tell me more.'

'Well, for one thing, his hair's too curly.'

'That's a reason?'

'For another, he's my little brother.'

'Lorcan's your brother?'

'Too right. You don't think I'd be sharing my apartment with just any geek. Anyway, I thought I was having a scene with you.'

Myles was saved from having to answer by the arrival of a waitress to take their order. Mia asked for a salad and mineral water. Myles ordered a chicken sandwich. Myles couldn't think of a way to respond without having to break off the relationship and he didn't want to do that just yet. He wouldn't do that to her because he didn't want her to feel rejected. Well, not before she had eaten her lunch anyway. He decided it might be best to change the subject.

'I met your father.'

'So I heard.'

'Has he shot anyone lately?'

'It wasn't a real gun.'

'You could have fooled me. He almost blew my toe off.'

'Yeah, well, sorry about that. I am not my father's keeper.' Mia picked a package of sugar from a bowl on the table and fiddled with it. Her fingernails were painted green, like the shirt she wore, and the rave sunglasses. She was having a green day. 'He was supposed to be in The Isle of Man. He came back a day early. Poor Lorcan had to hide in the coal cellar with dozens of people for like, hours.'

She paused, letting it sink in that Lorcan's experience in the coal cellar was at least as distressing as having a gun pointed at you, if not more. Before he could reply, she put back the sugar package, peeking at him over the top of her shades like a flirtatious schoolmarm. 'You must think that I'm a total looper.'

'No,' Myles said.

'I believe in living in the present. That's why I don't ask you questions about your situation. I don't care about it. As far as I am concerned, when you're with me, then we're together. When you're not, we're not. Know what I mean?'

Myles pretended that he knew. He wondered if Mia had ever been to a therapy session with Frank Forage. What did she mean that she didn't care about 'his situation'? Was she letting him know that she had found out about Lucy?

'I suppose I might owe you an explanation.'

'You might,' Myles said. 'Depends.'

'On what?'

'Is it all going to be angst and misery?'

'Nah,' she said. 'It's got feuding, sex, alcoholism, anorexia, cruelty and death – the usual family stuff.'

Myles was torn between a genuine curiosity to hear Mia's explanation and a desire to avoid any more involvement in her life. What was the point if he was going to break it off? Hearing her story wouldn't change anything, he reckoned. After today, she could hook up with one of her other guys. The fair-haired geek from the nightclub. The mysterious Barry of the Bouquets. Perhaps he and Mia could stay friends, as long as she adopted a mature attitude. Maybe they could be FWBs – Friends Who Bonk. He had heard that that was the latest and best way of having fun without getting into a messy situation.

'I'm listening,' he said.

'Fasten your seat belt,' Mia said.

She spoke clearly, with a slight tone of wonder as though she couldn't quite believe that this stuff had really happened. As a child, she hadn't seen much of her father, she explained; he had always been off somewhere on business. Either her mother had married him in a fog or else it had been after a very long drinking session. Her father had started as a dealer in World War Two memorabilia, which he collected along with landscape paintings and mistresses. Once her father had started bringing women home, and parading them around dressed as Nazi stormtroopers, the magic had gone out of the marriage. Her mother had taken to the whiskey. One Christmas Eve, when Mia was twelve, her mother had fallen asleep in the coal shed after a three-day binge and frozen to death. They had found her on Christmas Day sitting on top of a hill of coal like a mannequin. The only one in the family who got any presents that Christmas was mother, who got a brass and oak coffin. After that Mia and Lorcan had come to regard the coal shed as a kind of mausoleum to their mother. When their father had tried to convert it into a storehouse, they had fought him and won. It was the only victory they had ever achieved over their father, and by God he had made them pay for it.

After her mother died, her father had taken a direct involvement in his children's upbringing. He had been obsessed with her mother, whom he always claimed to have loved deeply.

'Like arse,' Mia said. 'He was just a control freak. Money, people, cars – he just wanted to control everything in his world. He even had a stable of women that he ran. I think he's got brothels and massage parlours all over the country.'

She told him that her father had transferred his obsession to his children, especially Mia. He took an unhealthy interest in everything that she did and he made it a priority to alienate any boy who became interested in her. Once he had even dressed as an SS officer to frighten off her date for the Debs ball. He seemed to be trying to mould Mia into a perfect replica of her dead mother. He swore that he intended to marry her off to a rich oil sheikh, and she had believed him. Which mightn't have been as bad as living at home with him and his dim-witted jack-booted peroxide mistresses, Mia reflected. He only liked blondes, she said. Which was the reason she had dyed her hair red. When she was sixteen, she had changed her name to Mia.

'What was it before?' Myles asked.

'I'll tell you someday,' she said. 'If you're good.'

The waitress arrived with their order. Mia said thanks and ignored her plate. Because she wasn't eating, Myles politely left his

119

sandwich on his plate and decided to go hungry until the story was finished. Mia's family sounded like a complete mess. Then he thought about Lucy's therapy sessions and his mother's bejewelled eye-patch and his brother Philip's chronic infatuation with model trains. He conceded that their families might have more in common than he had imagined previously. As a teenager, Mia had run away a lot. Every time, her father would send someone to find her and bring her back. When she was seventeen, she had made it as far as Venice with a boy she was seeing and they had enjoyed a wonderful month in a magical place before her father had flown over to personally haul her home and scare off the boy. In the end she had given up running away because of Lorcan, a sensitive lad who had ended up anorexic and hospitalised before he was sixteen. Lorcan still needed minding. For a while more anyway. When she was certain that he could look after himself, she would get out of the country and never see her father again. In the meantime, someone had to be there for Lorcan or else her father would just destroy him for kicks. She owed it to her mother.

At this point, Myles debated whether or not it would be insensitive to bite into his sandwich. He didn't want a mouth full of chicken if Mia suddenly launched into a story about her father bayoneting the family cat or ironing Lorcan's pet kitten or biting the head off a budgie.

He decided that his hunger could wait.

When she was eighteen, Mia's father's work suddenly seemed to involve mysterious cheques or bags of money or suitcases that could not be opened. Even his well-groomed associates had shifty eyes. Men came up from the country, bringing bags and suitcases of untraceable money for her father to 'invest' for them. Often, there was four or five hundred thousand lying around the house. Her father had never been in trouble with the police. He was a friend to many politicians. At one stage he had had seven Jaguar cars parked along the driveway. Jaguars were something else that he collected, like women and money. After many battles Mia had finally moved into her own apartment. She always refused to take money from her father. She had put herself through the art college, taking whatever jobs she could, mostly working as a waitress. Her mother had always dreamed that her daughter would become an artist and Mia was determined to fulfil that dream. Painting, she had discovered, helped her to make sense of things. It was also a way of getting back at her father, who had the artistic sensibilities of a piranha.

After college, Lorcan had moved in with her to escape their father's wild stormtrooper parties. Mia kept wishing for a way to separate from her father for good. Like a divorce, only more permanent. A few years ago, her father had again done something horrible to wreck things between Mia and the boy she had run off to Venice with, and whom she had started dating again. The next morning, she had woken up knowing that she was going to kill her father. It hadn't been a shock, more like an acceptance of destiny. It was the only way that she could be truly free of him. Except that she hadn't the courage to do it herself.

'I don't want to spend the rest of my days in jail for that bastard.'

So she had worked out a plan. She would hire someone to bump off her father in the house in Howth on one of the dirty money nights. Payment would be whatever money was in the house at the time, never less than a couple of hundred thousand, often a lot more. The dirty money came from illegal activities including betting, building scams and sometimes drugs deals. Officially it didn't exist. So, with the father dead, all the killer had to do was keep quiet, not flaunt the money for a while and he'd be clean away. She didn't want a penny. She just wanted her father out of her life forever.

'When I met you I foolishly imagined that you were the answer to my prayers. I fantasised that you would do the job on my Psychodad and afterwards we would fly to Venice. Have a magical time together. Maybe make a life there. I realise now that it was a stupid, totally unrealisable daydream. It's amazing all the same what your mind comes up with to keep you going, isn't it?' she said.

Sighing softly, as though she'd just awakened, Mia picked up a fork and tore into her salad. After a couple of mouthfuls, she glanced at Myles to see how he was reacting.

'That's my story so far. Hope you're not too traumatised,' she smiled.

'Not at all. Thanks for telling me,' he said.

Now that Mia had started her lunch, Myles picked up his chicken sandwich. He was intrigued to see that she ate lustily, without much concern for etiquette. She stuffed forkfuls of food into her mouth and gave squeals of pleasure. Talking about her family had obviously honed her appetite.

Finally, she pushed her empty plate away. 'I don't usually smoke,' she said. 'But I could savage a cigarette now.'

Myles rose. 'Consider it done.'

He went over to a table in a nearby smoking area and asked a lady for a cigarette. She handed him one, he put it in his mouth and she lit it for him. He went back to the window table and handed it to Mia.

'Thanks, you're a pet.'

'At your service.'

She took a drag on the cigarette and blew out smoke in an amateurish way, as though she'd only ever done it once or twice before and never in the daytime.

'I was really mad at you for not returning my phone calls,' she said softly.

Myles was about to protest once again that he hadn't received the messages but Mia held up a hand.

'It's OK, I'm not mad at you anymore. I got off with someone and that made me feel a bit better. Only for a little while though. Next morning I rang you twice.'

Despite himself, Myles was stung by Mia's confession that she had shifted another man. However he was impressed by her honesty. At least, he thought he was impressed by it. Why had she bothered telling him? Was she saying that if he wasn't interested in her, she could get someone else without a problem? He wondered who the 'someone' was.

He made a gesture as if doffing his hand to a lady. 'A gentleman should always keep his promises. I apologise for not phoning you.'

'I should think so too.' Mia relaxed. 'Apology accepted.'

Wait a second, he thought. She had just informed him that she had been unfaithful to him, yet somehow he was the one who was apologising to her. Spot the deliberate mistake.

Let her down easy, Myles reasoned. Her confession had given him an opening. He should say what he had to say to her straight and get it over with. It was important to break off the relationship delicately, with due consideration for her feelings. He would emphasise the bit about staying friends.

He cleared his throat. 'Listen, I've been thinking.'

'Let me guess.' Mia expelled a stream of smoke. 'It might be for the best if we took a break from each other.'

He was relieved that she had said it first. He almost asked her to go out with him that night to celebrate.

'It'll just be for a while. OK?'

'Fine,' she said.

'It's not good to rush things.'

'I agree.'

She took a drag on her cigarette and looked at him as though he had just told her something that she had known all along. 'No problem.' Another drag on the cigarette. 'No problem at all.'

Smoke got into her eyes. She took off her shades to dab at them with her table napkin, revealing an angry purple swelling under her left eye. The swelling was shaped like a lopsided half moon. As though someone had struck her there. Or whacked her with the butt of a gun.

Myles's resolve fell away like leaves from a tree. Suddenly he felt like scum. He wanted to reach over to stroke her bruised face. He imagined taking her hand, whisking her out of this place to the airport, and then catching a flight to Venice. He would give her an even more magical time than the one she'd had years ago with the young eejit, whoever he was. She saw him looking at her bruise. She grinned cheekily. 'I got bopped by a champagne cork.'

'Oh,' he said.

She stood up, brusquely arranging herself. 'Look, c'mere, I have to split now. Thanks for lunch.'

Now he didn't want her to go. He thought that he might have made a terrible mistake but he didn't know how to rectify it. 'Next time, you're paying,' he smiled weakly.

'You wish.' She pecked him on the cheek. 'If there is a next time.'

She lurched clumsily into a nearby table, regained her balance then apologised to the table's occupants. He watched as she walked swiftly to the doorway and disappeared into an uproar of giddy students.

TEN

Barry

The second that the basket was opened, Puma attempted to scratch Tinkerbell's fur off. Then Scruffy went for Reginald; Felicia took a swipe at I, Claudius and Mr Bumps chased Picasso into the personal space of Aristotle who attacked with exceptional venom for an elderly animal.

Myles stood at the back of the room and watched as the table convulsed into hissing, meowing, yowling, spitting, fur puffing, back-arching, leaping, slashing, biting and tearing pedigree cats. The exception was Slinker, a streetwise black and white long-hair who wisely leapt to the top of a bookcase to observe the mayhem.

Every time the cat-owners managed to separate their charges, the animals somehow tore free to resume combat. Lennon, the hippy photographer for the *Daily News* snapped away enthusiastically. Eventually, a cat-owner asked Lennon to stop taking pictures because the flashes were exciting the cats.

He came over to Myles to protest. 'I thought that was what you wanted.'

'It is,' Myles whispered, indicating the cat-owners. 'We just can't tell them.'

Myles had been assigned to write a feature about the dedication involved in owning and breeding pedigree cats. Dorothy, the eager-to-please, hyperactive chairperson of the society of pedigree cats and the owner of the prize-winning Puma, had kindly consented to organise an informal get-together; a gathering of twenty pedigree cats and their owners in the drawing room of her house in Terenure. An attempt to line up all the cats on a narrow table for a photo opportunity had proved a miscalculation. The informal get-together now resembled the cat version of the fall of Saigon.

'I'm dreadfully sorry,' she said to Myles. 'This has never happened before. Well, almost never.'

'It's the travelling baskets does it,' a large woman said as she held a wriggling cat. 'They hate being cooped up and joggled about.'

Jeremy, Dorothy's husband, approached Myles. 'I can't understand it,' he said, before casting an accusing glance at Myles. 'They were perfect little angels until you arrived.' Earlier, when Dorothy was preoccupied, Myles had observed Dorothy and Jeremy's ten-year-old son, Francois, slamming Puma's basket repeatedly against the legs of the table. Only when Puma was in a state bordering on madness had Francois opened the basket to let it out.

Lennon took Myles's arm. 'I've got killer pics. I don't need anymore so I'll split now while I'm ahead.'

'You mean in case they ask for the film,' Myles said.

'That too,' Lennon said.

Gradually, the owners managed to entice the cats back into their baskets. Except for Slinker, who elected to stay on top of the bookcase and couldn't be coaxed down, not even with a tin of salmon chunks.

When things were calm, Myles and the cat-owners sat down to tea and biscuits over a sustained low mewling from the cats. Myles interviewed Dorothy and Jeremy and some of the other cat-owners. When he was satisfied that he had enough, he thanked them and made for the hall. Dorothy escorted him to the door.

'You won't say anything about the little misunderstanding will you? It would just ruin the mood at the annual dinner dance.'

'Of course not,' he lied. 'It'll be between us and the cats.'

He drove back to town in a philosophical mood. If the paper wanted him to write about cat shows, then that's what he would do. For the time being anyway. 'It's never for ever,' as Big Paddy used to say. When the opportunity arose, Myles would outflank Jarlath and the Sperm. To do that, he needed a good story, and he needed it soon.

Back at the office, Myles half-expected to find a message from Mia but there was none. He felt guilty about the way things had ended between them a week ago. It was up to him to contact her if he wanted to see her again, which of course he didn't. Well, not right away. He had his own life to lead. He couldn't afford to carry passengers or sort out someone else's problems. By now, Myles supposed Mia's bruise would have healed.

He overheard Jarlath Boon commissioning Cliff Mangan to write a colour feature on a gambling school in the city. A feature that had been Myles's idea. He restrained his anger. Neither Cliff nor Jarlath looked at him for the rest of the morning. Even Lola Wall had begun to avoid him. Myles felt as though he was invisible, except perhaps to his family or the owners of pedigree cats. At least he was still around. Nobody had laid eyes on Dogbrain since the individual meetings with the Sperm. Bob Casper was convinced that he had been 'retired'.

Myles skipped lunch to work on the cat feature. In two hours the piece was finished. He proofed it, made some changes, then pressed buttons on his keyboard to dispatch two copies: the first to the Sperm's in-tray; the second to Jarlath Boon. Then he went out to grab a sandwich.

On his return, there was a message on his screen from Jarlath Boon querying Myles's use of the word 'humungous'. To the best of Jarlath's knowledge and the knowledge of all the subs on the desk there was no such word in the English language. Could Myles come up with a substitute by three o'clock if it wasn't too much trouble? The message added that regretfully, due to pressure on space, Myles's article would now be reduced from five hundred words to three hundred.

That night, after Lucy had left for her therapy session, Myles sat in the front room and watched television. Mother and Philip were working in the pub. They would be there until after midnight, longer if Mother began singing with her cronies. In the meantime, Myles had the house to himself, apart from Justine asleep upstairs.

He watched a programme about lions until a marauding male lion took over the pride and began killing cubs and things got too vicious. He switched to a soap, but after ten minutes of angst he got bored with that. He spent an hour watching MTV, only losing interest once they began showing rap videos. Finally he settled upon a fast-moving US cop show.

He realised that Mia had dumped all her personal shit on him, as though she had been expecting him to turn into the cool, clean hero who would save her from her Psychodad. He knew that he had been right to finish it with her. He couldn't understand why he kept feeling that he had let her down. The truth was that she had let herself down. She should have cleared off to Venice years ago. Lorcan was old enough to look after himself.

He concentrated on the cop show while he picked at his fingernails. On the screen, a psychoanalyst, an attractive blonde, was interviewing a handsome cop who looked like Don Johnson. The analyst kept attempting to get at the root cause of why Don kept blowing away bad guys instead of arresting them. It turned out that Don had suffered a miserable childhood. His father had been a violent dictator. His mother had been a drunk. Nobody had really loved him. 'You're overcompensating,' the beautiful analyst announced.

Myles figured that the cop's problem was a lot simpler: either the cop was worried because he looked like Don Johnson or else he actually *was* Don Johnson.

In US television cop shows things were always predictable. The bad guys had a wonderfully nasty time for most of the show but got shot in the end, while the good guys had a dreadful time until the last five minutes when they shot the bad guy and got off with the babe. The trick in US cop shows, as in life, was to keep going until the last five minutes. Myles took up the remote and flicked channels again.

A psycho in a Ronald Reagan mask menaced a beautiful teenage girl in a big dark house.

He flicked again.

A black woman in leopardskin who looked like Oprah slapped a Harvey Keitel type in a white vest and shorts. Harvey immediately slapped her back.

Flick. A lioness got stuck into a baby warthog. Blood everywhere.

Flick. A Julia Roberts clone wailed her head off as she stumbled into a flower garden in the rain.

The flowers reminded him of Mia's bouquet. He had presented the flowers to Lucy for being so understanding lately. He had been grateful that she hadn't pressed him for details of the night he had stayed over in Howth. She had simply accepted his explanation that he had got drunk after the table football and crashed out on someone's couch. The therapy seemed to have mellowed her completely, or else she was on sedatives. Either way, Myles wasn't complaining.

He flicked back to the cop show. Don Johnson was overcompensating for his miserable childhood by tossing a bad guy off the roof of a skyscraper. Myles turned off the sound before the bad guy hit the ground.

He could drive to Mia's place in less than five minutes. Check to see if her eye had healed. Give her a bit of support in case things were getting her down. After all, they were friends, weren't they? What if she was with one of her guys, though? What if she didn't want to see him? What if he had really hurt her? Destroyed her hopes? Dumped her back on the mercy of her psycho father?

Brooding like this wasn't like him at all. He blamed the uncertainty of not living in his own home. He longed for the old place in Lucan, a place he had hated at the time and couldn't wait to get away from. At least there he had been able to listen to music. Now that his life was in limbo, along with his CDs, he missed being able to anaesthetise himself with *Astral Weeks* or *Dark Side of the Moon* or *Peter Gabriel Live*. It seemed to him that the new place in Wicklow would be ready when he was sixty.

What was that cute thing Mia had said on the phone last week; something about being 'curled up inside a snuggle of sleep'? Myles wondered if Psychodad had really used the butt of his gun on her.

Flicking channels again, he still found nothing that he wanted to see. He returned to the cop show just as the front door slammed.

In a moment Lucy came in, looking windswept but happy.

'How was it?'

'Fine,' she said. 'We met in Frank's house. He says that I'm really making progress.'

'That's nice of him.'

'How's Justine?'

'Upstairs. Conked out.'

Myles got up to let her sit down.

'What's this?'

'Just rubbish.'

'What happened to the sound?'

'It makes better sense without sound.'

He went to the kitchen, made a pot of tea and poured each of them a cup. He sat beside her on the sofa and they watched television for a while. He was glad that she was home. It was important to sit around and watch television with people who knew you and accepted you for what you were. With people who didn't expect you to kill their fathers. Myles let his tea go cold.

'Are you OK?' Lucy said.

'I'm grand,' Myles said.

Lucy studied him for a moment. 'Myles, Frank was wondering if we could have a session here some week instead of in the cold place in Fitzwilliam Square. It would be cosier. Everyone's taking a turn to host a session at home. Would you mind?'

'No problem,' he said quickly. Anything to keep the peace. 'No problem at all.'

'Thanks,' she said.

On television, Don Johnson had been replaced by a Brad Pitt lookalike, who steered a fancy red Porsche along a sunny highway. A beautiful red-head, hair billowing, gazed adoringly at him from the passenger seat.

Suddenly, Myles felt itchy and restless. He had to get away and do something before his brains fried. Handing Lucy the remote, he stood up and stretched, trying to appear casual.

Lucy smiled. 'You only ever hand me the remote when there's

nothing on that you want to see.'

'Listen, something has come up. I have to go out for a little while. Do you mind?'

She didn't look at him. Didn't even ask what had come up.

'I don't mind,' she said.

'Sure?'

'Go out if you have to and do whatever it is you need to do. I'll still be here when you get back.'

'Thanks,' he said, and kissed her cheek.

Then he left the front room, got his coat and paused. What was that supposed to mean, 'I'll still be here when you get back'? He dismissed the thought and went out. He hadn't time to worry about it now. He just knew that he had to hurry, but he wasn't sure exactly why.

Outside, the night was cool and still. Dorset Street was quiet except for the sound of traditional music coming from the family pub. No hint of his mother's voice. She must be saving it for later. He climbed into the Nissan and drove off.

Two minutes later, he turned the corner into Mountjoy Square and found a parking spot that gave him an unimpeded view of Mia's apartment. He saw that there was a light on. Too bright for a candle. Shadows crossed the window. She wasn't alone. He struggled with the idea of calling upon her. A thought struck him. What if she was painting a portrait of some eejit's willy? He didn't want to walk into that. He was wasting his time, he decided. Mia had been an interesting, sexy diversion. A fling, and that's all. It had been fun until Psychodad and the gun. Time to move on. He was about to start the engine to drive back to Dorset Street when the front door opened and Mia came out. She wheeled her bicycle with one hand; in the other hand she carried a bouquet of flowers.

Her third hand gripped Myles's insides.

The flowers were for Barry, Myles knew. Barry must be the guy she had 'got off with' when she had been mad at Myles for not returning her phone calls. 'Got off with' being a polite term for 'slept with', or as Mia would say, 'shagged'.

When she mounted her bicycle and pedalled off, Myles started the engine and followed. He stayed a couple of hundred yards behind. He felt anger boiling inside him but couldn't locate a clear reason for it. Something to do with not knowing exactly why he was following her. Perhaps he just wanted to see where this Barry lived. After that he would head home, secure in the knowledge that he had been right to break it off. In a few minutes they passed the spot where Pat's Volvo had almost run Mia down. Where Myles and Mia had first met. She had not smiled once that night, nor had she given one of her giggles. She had seemed so lively, independent, and confident as well as cheeky. She had worn those flowery Docs.

She went through a red light and turned into a side road and he had to make a sharp turn to stay on her trail. He followed her onto the coast road. He rolled down the window to feel fresh chilly air on his face. The feeling of anger evaporated. Now he felt stimulated, apprehensive and vital. He felt that he was getting closer to the truth about her.

In Ringsend, she stopped at a traffic island across from a pub called The Fountain. Myles pulled into the kerb a hundred yards down the road and turned his lights off. She didn't look round. He sat and watched as she propped her bike against a plastic bollard then carried the bouquet to a lamppost that was garlanded with withered and broken flowers. Slowly and tenderly Mia removed the spent flowers from the pole, carefully replacing them from the bouquet. When she was finished, she hugged the pole.

After a few minutes, she got back on her bicycle and pedalled back the way she had come.

Hunching down in the driver's seat, Myles watched in the rearview mirror until Mia was out of sight.

Then he got out of the car and walked across to the traffic island. He examined the pole.

Aside from the flowers, there was a tattered Manchester United scarf tied to the top. Under the scarf, wrapped in cellophane, was taped a worn colour snap of a darkly handsome boy. Alongside the snap, a card from Molly's Flower Shop.

Myles bent down to read it. 'To Barry, Live Forever, M.'

He stood on the doorstep of the house in Mountjoy Square.

Glancing around, he was disappointed not to find any trace of horse droppings from the night he had given Mia a lift home on Sheba.

He found her apartment on the wall intercom. Mia and Lorcan, apartment five. He raised his finger to the buzzer then hesitated. He looked at his watch. It was now midnight. He had been driving around the city for the last two hours thinking things over until his head felt like the inside of a beehive. Then he had parked outside her apartment. He had been about to drive off when Lorcan had come through the front door and walked down the street in a big hurry. Myles decided it was a sign.

Now here he stood on the doorstep of Mia's place, trying to pluck up the courage to press her buzzer. What was the worst that could happen? She could tell him to get lost. If she didn't wish to see him, then at least he would be able to leave with a clear conscience. He pressed the buzzer.

After a long while, he heard a click followed by a crackle and what sounded like soft jazz piano.

Mia's voice, 'Hello, who is it?'

'It's me,' Myles said. 'I was wondering if it's too late for you to be receiving visitors?'

Her giggle crackled like static over the intercom.

'Of course not, come up.'

Immediately, the buzzer sounded. He pushed the door and went inside. The hall light clicked on and he walked down the hall, and began climbing the dusty stairs. Above he heard a door creak open. The sound of the music spilled down the stairs like a welcome. He recognised the tune: 'Cantaloupe Island' by Herbie Hancock, the only jazz instrumental he liked. If she's waiting for me outside the door of her apartment then it's game on again, he thought.

She stood on the third floor landing, a glass of white wine cradled in her arms. She grinned at him. Her bruise was gone. She looked relaxed and confident and very glad to see him.

'Where's the horse?' she asked.

'Had to let it go,' Myles said. 'It kept asking for peppermint tea.'

As soon as he heard her giggle he knew that everything was going to be alright between them. Now he knew that he had made the right decision in coming here. He got to the top of the stairs then walked over to her.

'I was wondering how long it would be before I heard—' she began.

He leaned forward suddenly, taking her by the shoulders as he kissed her on the lips. It was a delightful feeling as her words flailed against his mouth then fluttered away altogether as she recovered from the surprise and responded to him. Her lips, cold and sweet from the wine, yet soft. He put his arms around her. She untangled her arms from the pressure of his chest pressing against them and circled his neck. A drop of wine splashed on his skin. They locked in a passionate embrace as the hall light clicked off.

She moved away for a second. 'So you have missed me,' she said. 'Listen, I knew you'd be a—' she managed before he kissed her again. 'Mmmmmmm,' she said, and seemed to go weak in his embrace.

He picked her up and carried her towards the light from her apartment's open door. She clung to him. Somehow they continued to kiss passionately without tripping or banging into anything or spilling any more wine.

Inside, he stopped long enough to kick the door shut, before carrying her into cool jazz and soft light and warmth. He laid her down under him on the sofa and climbed on top of her. She managed to prise her lips from his to draw breath.

'Hang on a sec,' she gasped.

'Think of all the time we've wasted when we could have been doing this.' He rose above her, slipping off his jacket and pulling his sweater over his head as he shouted to be heard over the music. 'You know what? First thing tomorrow I'm going to get a big fucking bazooka and blow your father's balls off.'

'Myles—' Mia said.

'Then I'm going to personally roll them down the hill of Howth and kick them into the sea.' Now he was bare-chested. He threw his arms wide. 'Splash. Splash. Bye bye Psychodad.' He was glad to see that she was staring at him wide-eyed, obviously overcome that her cry for help had finally been answered.

He began to open the buttons on her blouse. 'But first I'm going to tickle your belly-button from the inside.' He thought that she'd laugh, but instead she looked confused. Behind him, someone cleared their throat.

When he turned around, Aisling and Stick and at least a dozen others were standing by the fireplace, holding glasses of wine, surrounded by Mia's paintings. The area was lit by small candles, specially for intimate viewing purposes. Mia struggled out from under him. 'We were just celebrating the announcement of my first exhibition,' she gave him a smile. 'You're welcome to join us.'

Myles couldn't speak. He just looked at them.

Aisling raised her glass of wine to him. 'That was excellent,' she said. 'What do you do for an encore?'

ELEVEN

Dez

As soon as the last guest had gone, Mia put on the kettle to make peppermint tea. He sat on the sofa watching her as she moved about the kitchen area. She was the most beautiful and tantalising woman he had ever seen in his life. Her slightly bandy legs only made her more appealing. Her imperfection made him feel more protective towards her.

Earlier, Mia's guests had been very gracious. Everyone had made a point of treating him as though he had just dropped by to view the exhibition. Stick had come over to him at the end to swear drunkenly that the music had been so loud when he had carried Mia to the sofa that nobody could possibly have heard a word he'd said, especially not the bit about blowing Mia's father's balls off with a bazooka.

Mia handed him a steaming cup. 'You don't have to drink it if you don't want to,' she said.

'Are you mad? I love this stuff,' he lied.

For a while, neither said anything. He hoped that he hadn't blown it with his bazooka speech.

'So what happens now?' he asked.

She gave him a dazzling smile, as though she had been waiting for the question. 'Whatever is meant to happen, will happen. Only a complete spanner fights against the unwritten law of the universe.'

'That's deep. I like that, where's it from?'

'Me,' she chirped. 'I made it up.'

He looked at her sitting there, so cheeky and fresh as she blew a hanging strand of red curls out of her eyeline, and he wanted her badly.

'Come here,' he said.

'No,' she said.

'OK, I'll come to you.'

'Suit yourself.'

He moved over to where she sat and they kissed. After a while the peppermint tea went cold.

'Now you expect me to sleep with you, do you?'

'No.'

'What do you mean, no?'

'Who said anything about sleep?'

She giggled, then took his hand and led him upstairs.

'What about Lorcan?' he asked.

'Don't fret. He's gone to stay with his boyfriend.'

'Oh right,' Myles said. 'His boyfriend.'

Mia rummaged in her bedside drawer then handed him a condom. She pulled her dress over her head and dropped it on the floor, then took off her panties. She wasn't wearing a bra. At the sight of her naked body he felt as jittery as a virgin. As he undressed, he glanced about him, half-expecting Mia's party guests to materialise holding little cards awarding him marks out of ten for performance.

'You're so long,' Mia ran her hands across his naked back and thighs. 'I think you're getting taller.'

Then she pulled him into the bed on top of her.

The sex was energetic, awkward and pleasant, but it didn't set either of them alight. It was like a friendly warm-up before the real event. Afterwards he felt deflated and vulnerable. Even though they had just made love and she was lying naked beside him, he felt as though they were in separate beds. For some reason that he couldn't explain, he sensed she had been thinking about someone else throughout.

She rolled over and rested the back of her head on his chest. They watched the headlights from passing cars playing across the ceiling like spooky fairground lights. After a while he began to feel more secure. After all, here he was lying beside her. Both naked. In her bed. What more could he want?

'So how much did you miss me?'

She held her hands a few inches apart. 'This much.'

'That all?'

She spread her hands wider. 'How about this much?'

He shook his head. She spread her hands as far apart as possible.

'That's better,' he said.

'Did you miss me?' she asked.

'You never crossed my mind.'

'How often did I never cross your mind?'

'All the time,' he said, and she giggled.

'Tell me about Venice,' he said.

'No.'

Gently rolling him over, she traced the line of his backbone with her fingernails, sending tingles through him. 'You're so long,' she said again. 'So incredibly long.' She rubbed at a spot halfway down his back. 'How did such a long man get a big whopper blackhead in the middle of his backbone? Hold still.' She squeezed the spot with her nails, making him cry out.

'That hurt.'

She turned him to face her. In the half-light he saw her smiling, dimpled, ecstatic face. She looked as though she was about to tell him that she loved him.

'Are you really going to use a bazooka on my dad?' she asked excitedly.

The question caught him off guard. 'What difference does it make what I use?'

'I want you to use something that makes a nice mess, so you can get his purple Jag as well. I hate that colour on a car.'

'You really don't like your father much, do you?' he said.

She shrugged. 'I'll like him better when he's six feet under.'

'Why can't we just take the money and run?'

'Because he'd come after us. We would never be able to relax with him alive.' She looked at him with big eyes. 'You pulling out on me, Mr Tall?'

'Of course not,' he said. 'Just exploring a few possibilities.'

She sat up in the bed, pulled her legs up and rested her chin on her knees. 'I don't care if you pull out. I can handle it myself.'

'I never said anything about pulling out.'

'You didn't have to.'

She wouldn't look at him. He touched her face and gently turned her towards him. Her expression was fierce, spoiling for a fight. How would Pat handle this? He would coax the girl out of her anger. Promise her anything to avoid a big emotional scene. If Pat figured that there was something in it for him, then he would do what the girl wanted. The point was that he would do it his way, and not allow himself to be emotionally bullied into a rush job.

'Why do you hate him so much?'

She tensed beside him. 'He's scum.'

'Apart from that.'

She shrugged. 'He drove my mother to an early grave.'

'What else?'

'He took away someone I loved.'

'He killed someone?'

She nodded.

'Tell me about it,' he said.

She turned away from him. 'Why should I?'

Roughly he turned her back to face him. She pushed away his hands.

'OK, have it your way,' he said.

She paused. 'You remember I told you about running off to Venice that time?'

'I remember.'

She spoke in a flat voice. 'I went with a boy called Barry. When my father brought me back he threatened to kill Barry if he ever contacted me again. After a while we started meeting again. We thought we could keep it secret. But my father found out. One night he drove after Barry and forced his car off the road into a telephone pole. Barry died instantly. My father might as well have held a gun to his head and pulled the trigger. Barry was the only boy I ever cared for.' Mia thought about it for a while. A faraway look came into her eyes. 'Until recently.'

A surge of power mingled with delight ran through him. Now that she had taken him into her confidence and told him the story of Barry, he felt closer to her. He was relieved that Barry was dead. In a way, Psychodad had done him a big favour by removing the competition.

'Just promise me you'll be patient,' he said, as softly as he could. He smiled.

'OK,' she said.

'I just need some time.'

'Fine,' she said.

He noticed that her eyes were filled with tears. She looked more bewildered and lost than she had that night on the road. 'You don't know how much this means to me.' She threw herself at him and he caught her, but his surprise and her momentum pushed them back onto the bed. 'You're a wonderful man.' She kissed him on the lips, the eyes, the nose. 'I know everything is going to work out.'

They made love again. This time it was passionate and frantic and when they finished they were both panting and exhausted.

'Did you come?' she asked.

'Bigtime. Did you?'

'Absa-fucking-lutely,' she gasped. 'It's never been so good.'

They lay there until they had recovered their breath.

'Where's your favourite place?' she asked suddenly.

'Right here isn't bad,' he said. 'Except for all the pictures of willies on the walls.'

She thumped his arm.

'St Mark's Square in Venice is my idea of paradise,' she said. 'I could live there for ever.'

Resting her chin on his chest hair, she told him that she loved to sit outside Florian's, a gloriously ornate old-style café and drink incredibly expensive coffee. Feel the warm sea breeze on her cheeks. Watch the people in the centre of the square throwing crumbs to the pigeons, disappearing under thousands of flapping, swarming and diving birds. It was like a fantasy place.

'I've always wanted to go on a gondola,' he said.

'No way. Always avoid gondolas,' she cautioned. 'The gondoliers are too expensive and unpredictable.'

She told him that the best and most breathtaking trips were on the Vaporetto – the public water transport buses. Once a person had experienced the sensation of standing on the deck of a Vaporetto as it travelled from the airport onto the main Venetian waterway, they were hooked for life. In Harry's Bar they made this fabulous drink called a Bellini – cold sharp vodka straight from the fridge in an elegant shot glass with a drop of peach. A few of those and you won't be able to leave even if you wanted to, she said.

'Sounds like my kind of town,' he said. 'Except for the gondolas.'

They lay on their backs and watched the headlights flicker across the ceiling some more.

After a while he fell asleep.

He came to with a fierce pain in his lip. In the darkness he thought that some animal had attacked him. Then the animal broke away and he heard it giggle. He attempted to restrain her but she dug her nails into his back like a feral cat.

'Come on, come on, come on,' she sang, savaging his earlobe. He gripped her hands tightly, climbed on top of her. He tried to hold her but she broke free and jumped on his back. Her behaviour irritated him yet it also got him excited. He tumbled her over his head and held her down long enough to enter her. They half-wrestled then half-fucked as they made their way out of the bed onto the floor and down the stairs.

'Go harder,' she yelled.

'Take it easy,' he said.

'Harder. Faster. Harder. Faster,' she chanted. 'Pretend the world is going to end tomorrow.'

They sixty-nined on the downstairs table, a position as exciting as it was unsustainable, particularly after the table toppled them onto the floor. They knocked over a plant as he fucked her from behind. Their knees got mucky in the spilled dirt. She wouldn't let him stop for a breather. When he went soft she clawed at him with her nails.

'Stop that,' he said, but she just giggled.

'Stop what?'

She turned him onto his back on the floor and sat on top with a hand in the air and eyes closed, riding him as though he were a rodeo horse.

'Yee-haw,' she shouted.

'Jesus Christ,' he gasped.

They locked into a deep, satisfying rhythm. She tore at his chest, stomach and hands, moaning as the rhythm increased until suddenly she gave a long series of yelps like she was being knifed. Afterwards, she dropped off him onto the floor, and pulled the cover from the sofa over herself before curling up alongside him.

'That's grand,' she murmured sleepily. 'You can go back to sleep now.'

'Thanks,' he said.

As she snored softly beside him, he ran his fingers along the teeth marks on his arms and neck. He discovered a large bite mark around his belly-button. It felt as though there was a simmering volcano on his bottom lip. Exhausted, he blacked out.

He dreamt that he was flying above the waterways of Venice, scouring the large boats and gondolas and small craft on the glistening water beneath for a sign of Mia. He wasn't worried. He knew that it was all a big game. She would show up eventually. He landed at a small port by a large garish hotel where passengers were lined up waiting for a boat to take them across to the other side. He showed the people a photograph of Mia but everyone shook their heads. Lucy and Justine joined the queue but they hadn't seen Mia either. 'Has that girl not come yet?' Lucy said pointedly before steering Justine onto the boat. Bob Casper arrived dressed as a waiter carrying a tray of gigantic vodka bottles with straws in them. 'Here you go boyo,' he said, presenting him with one. 'Can't let you have all the fun.' He took a drink from the bottle and instead of cold liquid he was delighted to find that the vodka was warm and tasty. A glow spread throughout his body down to his groin where it became particularly pleasurable.

He woke up to find her kneeling over him, giving him a blowjob. She giggled at his surprise but did not look up, nor did she lose concentration. She pushed his head back and held him away from her while she carried on with what she was doing. When he was fully excited and almost on the point of coming, she suddenly pulled away. She placed his hands on his penis. 'Now don't move.'

She grabbed a large drawing pad and felt pen, sat cross-legged on the floor and began to sketch. 'OK, hold it up straight. That's it. Keep it like that.'

As she sketched frantically, he held his penis, afraid to budge in case he put her off her stroke.

'Keep still for a few minutes. I'm going to make you immortal,' she said.

He arrived at work exhausted and hung over, with a swollen lip as well as a line of love bites stitched across his neck like bullet holes. Ignoring the looks from the others, he went straight to his desk and sat down. Carefully, he wrote Mia's words on a piece of card in two separate lines like a poem. He taped the card above the computer screen at his desk.

'Whatever is meant to happen, will happen.
Only a spanner fights against the law of the universe.'

Last night he had agreed to kill a man and now this morning he felt fine about it. Later he needed to sit down somewhere and work out exactly how to get out of it. Nevertheless, he found the prospect of becoming a hired gun exciting. As though he was inside his own movie with himself as star, screenwriter and director. All he needed now was the happy ending.

Jarlath Boon came over. He gave Myles a big mocking grin.

'Sorry Myles. I've no features for you to write again this week.'

'That's OK,' Myles said. 'I've plenty to be doing.'

Jarlath stared at him. At first Myles thought that Jarlath was staring at the love bites on his neck, but then he realised that Jarlath's gaze was focused on the card above the computer screen.

'Is that from *Star Wars*?' he asked.

'No,' Myles said. 'It's from a poem by Yeats.'

'Oh yes, of course,' Jarlath said. 'God, it's amazing how quickly you forget these things, isn't it?'

He phoned Mia on his mobile. The phone rang for a long time. Then her sleepy voice answered. 'I knew it was you,' she said.

'Then why didn't you answer?'

She whispered, 'Because after last night I can barely walk.'

He laughed.

'Will I see you tonight?' she asked.

'Absa-fucking-lute-ly,' he said.

At lunchtime, he went out to the chemists across the street and bought a packet of plasters. He covered the bites on his neck with the longest plaster in the packet. He decided that there was nothing he could do about the volcano on his lip. He would tell Lucy that he had walked into a door. Outside he found Bob waiting for him.

'That's no disguise boyo.' Bob slapped him on the back. 'She must have been a right little vampire. Come on and I'll let you buy me lunch.'

They went to The Surgery, a small coffee shop around the corner where the décor was operating theatre chic and the waitresses wore surgical masks and gowns. At the chrome-plated counter, they bought cappuccinos and Danish pastries and took a metal table at the back. Bob cut his pastry in half with a scalpel.

'You've been leading the wild life,' he said. 'It's a wonder she doesn't throw you out.'

'Lucy and I have an open relationship,' Myles said. 'We don't need to tie each other down.'

'Very civilised.' Bob bit off a chunk of Danish. 'And I'm the Pope.'

They ate in silence for a while. Bob eyed one of the waitresses and even made an attempt to chat her up but was ignored. Myles felt that Bob was jealous of his love bites. The thought that Bob might be trying to compete with him made Myles feel superior.

'I'm thinking of getting out,' Bob said abruptly.

'Getting out where?'

'Out of the job. Out of newspapers. Maybe I'll head for

London. Or I've a cousin in San Francisco. Maybe I'll barrel over there.'

'I thought you liked the news desk.'

'It's alright.' Bob reflected for a moment. 'My talents are unappreciated. Basically they don't deserve me.'

'What will you do?' Myles asked.

'I've a few things planned,' Bob said. 'There's more to my game than newspapers you know. One day soon I'll be on a plane for San Francisco. You wait and see.'

Myles felt sorry for him. He doubted that he would ever find the courage to really leave his secure pensionable job or his wife and kids or his nice two-storey semi-detached house in Cabinteely. If Bob knew the big score that Myles was contemplating he'd probably die of shock.

'Let me ask you a question,' Myles said.

'Shoot,' Bob said.

'Say you had a chance to go for something big. An opportunity that would set you up for life financially as well as emotionally. Only it was a bit risky.'

'How can you be set up for life emotionally? That's a daft idea.'

'OK, financially then. How far would you be prepared to go to get it?'

Bob thought for a moment. 'You mean would I rob a bank if I thought I could get away with it?'

'Something like that.'

'No boyo, I would not.' Bob smiled. 'But I might hire some mug to do it for me. That way I'd be in the clear if anything went wrong.'

'Oh,' Myles said, no longer feeling so confident.

'Why? Are you planning another on-the-spot article with your gangster pals?'

'No.' Myles stirred his coffee. 'There's nothing wrong with just speculating. You know. Like thinking about winning the Lotto.'

Bob looked at him searchingly. Myles looked away, concentrating on his Danish. He had given away too much.

'Well, whatever it is, I wish you luck,' Bob said. 'And afterwards I'll visit you in Mountjoy.'

* * *

'What happened to your lip?' Lucy asked.

'I stayed over at Bob's,' Myles lied. 'I think I picked up a bit of a rash from using his soap.'

'You'd want to watch out for other people's soap,' Lucy said dryly. 'It can turn into a real problem.'

'I have to go back out later,' he said. 'I've a feature to write.'

'I have faith in you,' Lucy said. 'You'll work this thing through, whatever it is.'

'It's just a feature,' he said, irritated.

Lucy must be on medication, he decided. He would have preferred a good row. That way, at least a guy would know where things stood.

'OK,' Lucy said. 'Maybe you'll read Justine a story before you go. She's been asking for you.'

'No problem.'

He went upstairs to change his clothes. Lucy went back to the front room where he could hear her talking to Maguire the builder on the phone. She seemed to have resigned herself to having Myles as a part-time partner who was always working extra shifts or reviewing dance gigs and coming home with plasters on his neck or swollen lips or peculiar scratches on his back. She rarely asked for help with Justine and she never talked to him about the new house anymore. She seemed to have become a Stepford Wife. He shut it out of his mind. He didn't want to think too deeply about the situation because then he would have to work out how he would finish the relationship with Lucy. He would also have to consider his feelings about Justine and he wasn't ready for that yet.

Nor did he want to think about the new house in Wicklow or any of the other stuff about money and possessions. He would face those issues when it became absolutely unavoidable. For the present, things could stay as they were. He changed his clothes, put some cream on his burst lip and went downstairs to read a story for Justine.

Mia sat at a table drinking white wine with Aisling and Stick. She had a sour face on her. For over an hour nothing Myles said drew much reaction from her. Stick tried to liven things up but after a while she too fell silent. They sat around drinking wine and tapping their feet to the music until Stick got up suddenly.

'Hey this is a good beat,' Stick said. 'Come on Ash, let's go bop.'

'Nah,' Aisling smiled knowingly. 'I'll sit this one out.'

'Fuck off ye bitch, we're dancing,' Stick said firmly, and pulled Aisling with her to the dancefloor.

Mia made no effort to get closer to him. He moved next to her. 'Hi, remember me?'

'How could I forget?' she said.

'Has your father been—?'

'What do you care?' she said sharply. 'Maybe it's none of your business anymore.'

She looked at him. Her face had closed down to him, the first time that he had ever seen her so remote and unobtainable.

'What is it? Tell me,' he spread his arms wide. 'I can take it.'

She looked straight ahead at two fire-eaters who were blowing out flames inside a large revolving cage.

'I need to know if you're serious about us. Or are you going to go on playing me along like this until we fizzle out?'

He was surprised at the harshness in her voice. He reckoned that he should try to keep things light. He thought that they had worked it through last night. Now that seemed like an age ago.

'Do I have to make a decision right this moment?' he joked. Her stony expression confirmed that he had hit the wrong note.

'No,' she got to her feet. 'We've got all the time in the world.'

She left the table and moved through the dancing bodies. He got up and went after her. He caught up with her in the corridor to the main entrance, just as he had on the night he had given her a lift home on Johnny Bones' horse.

'Hey, I'm really sorry,' he said. 'Forgive me and come on back and we'll talk this out.'

She allowed him to steer her back through the dancefloor to the table they had vacated. He noticed that Stick and Aisling were dancing close by, keeping an eye on them.

He tried to look into her green eyes, but she avoided him. 'If you care for me then you'll stop using me like this.'

'You think I'm just using you?' he was shocked.

'What else can I think? I don't hear from you for ages. Then you're all over me. You'll make the usual load of empty promises then you'll fuck off when you're bored. I thought we had a deal.'

'You think that this is all about a deal?'

She looked at him. 'Everything is a deal when you get down to it, isn't it? That's the way it works.'

'Well I don't believe that,' he said. 'I'm serious about us.'

'You are?'

'Yes.'

They locked eyes. She was also deadly serious. No more games, no more jokes.

'Come with me,' she said.

'Where to?'

'You'll see.'

He followed her to the upstairs bar. She led him through rows of empty tables to where two figures sat in the far corner. One was Garvin. The other looked like Lorcan with his back turned. Garvin saw Mia coming and alerted Lorcan. He turned, revealing a black eye and a bandage across his nose.

'Hey sis,' he said.

Mia stopped and put a hand on his head. She turned to Myles.

'Just thought you might like to see the latest from the Front,' she said.

'Man, this is a pretty heavy vibe,' Pat said.

They stood on the sideline watching Dez's team of beer-bellies being hammered four–nil by eleven fit, sharp guys who looked as though they didn't have a hangover between them.

'You wouldn't think this was a semi-final would you?' Pat said softly. 'I told Dez that going out to celebrate last night was a bit premature.'

A bitter wind cut through them, made them huddle deeper into their overcoats.

'I don't know why I bother,' Pat said. 'I am not cut out to be a manager. I'm only doing this because the last bloke had a triple by-pass.'

Dez tried a shot on goal from forty yards out and the ball

skewed sideways in the direction of the corner flag. Dez yelled at Mixer for putting him off. Pat held up his hands in despair.

'Look at him. The eejit is living in a flat in Finglas with a sixteen-year-old hairdresser.' Pat shrugged his shoulders. 'He says he's never been happier.'

Pat pondered Dez's happiness for a moment then turned to Myles. 'So, what's this brilliant idea you have?'

'It's the one we've been waiting for?'

'I'm all ears. What's it worth?'

'We walk away with half a million in untraceable bills.'

Pat looked at Myles, concern brimming in his dark eyes. Like an elder brother always looking out for his charge. Or like a guardian angel that was wondering where he had gone wrong. 'So what's the catch?'

'The catch is we have to waste a guy. Otherwise it's no deal.' Myles thought that 'waste' would be a far better word than 'kill'. It made the deed seem more remote, less intimidating. He thought that Pat would be impressed, take him more seriously as a partner.

Pat digested this information for a moment. He didn't appear surprised. Just thoughtful.

'I like the bit about the half million,' he said. 'I would not be so gone on the other thing.'

'It's sort of a double bill. Can't have one without the other,' Myles said.

'You sure about this?' Pat asked.

'I'm sure,' Myles said. 'I'm in one hundred and ten per cent.'

'Do you really want to get into this kind of life? Wouldn't you rather write your book or something?'

'I know what I'm doing,' Myles said. 'It's about time I got off my arse and did something real.'

Pat seemed to accept the explanation. 'Tell me more about the gig,' he said.

They watched the soccer as Myles told him about the house in Howth and the suitcases full of money and the lack of security. He told him that after the gig they would have to keep quiet for a few weeks and not flash money about. Then they would be away clean. He didn't mention Mia or Lorcan. That could come later.

'Do the laundry and get away clean,' Pat smiled. 'I like that bit.'

Pat found the lack of security intriguing. 'It's interesting that such a bloke can get away with his kind of caper without some heavy hitters alongside as a guarantee.'

'He's a smug man,' Myles said. 'He figures that he has already bought everyone.'

'Why can't we just take the moolah?'

'He would come after us. He has powerful friends.'

'Powerful friends are useless if they don't know who pulls the gig. If we lift dirty money then nobody cares except the people who own the dirty money. If we leave a body behind, then the Plods are in as well. It's no good pulling off a good gig if you have to spend the rest of your life ducking and diving.'

Myles considered this. He didn't wish to appear like a flaky amateur who would crumble at the first sign of pressure. The important thing was to get Pat on board, they could work out the incidentals later. The solution would come to him. Pat was right. It was too much to hope that Psychodad would have a heart attack when he saw Pat and the crew coming at him with guns and masks.

'How do you come by this gig?'

'I have a friend on the inside.'

Pat regarded Myles with sudden approval.

'Well, what you are proposing is a sure way for you to become an outlaw,' Pat said. 'I am expressing interest, but I will have to take a look first. It's about time we did a real gig together. Only thing is, you need to be sure that your motivation is clear before you get into something this heavy. You follow?'

Myles nodded. 'I'm just depressed where I am. I'd rather be depressed with a load of money than with nothing.'

'That is definitely something to reflect on,' Pat said. 'I have a pain in my arse sitting around this dump taking minor scores. A big score sets a person up. Who knows, maybe afterwards I can even write *my* book.'

'So is that a yes?'

'Let's put it this way, it's not a no.'

They looked at each other. Then Pat leaned forward and fixed

Myles in a stare. 'Tell me this. Are you doing this for yourself or are you doing this because of a babe?'

'Bit of both,' Myles smiled.

'Little Miss One-Way Street?'

Myles nodded. 'How did you know?'

'An educated guess.'

Pat looked at his feet for a long time. Myles could hear Dez shouting at his team to get their act together. Then Pat folded his arms.

A shout went up from the pitch: 'Goalpost, watch out.'

Before Myles could turn, the ball hit him in the groin, doubling him up and knocking the breath out of him. Myles heard laughter from the pitch. Pat was laughing as well.

'My friend, you are well and truly fucked.'

TWELVE

Jarlath

'Why do we have to go with him?' Mia said, when he told her that Pat would be driving them. 'He's a sleazeball.'

'Because he's the best in the business. He will make it work.'

'I thought that you were going to make it work,' she said, and sat down on the sofa. 'Why do you need someone to hold your hand?'

This morning she had criticised him for leaving the cap off the toothpaste and getting paste all over the glass counter. What was the big problem? She must have PMT.

Earlier, she had picked on him for breaking the handle off one of her mugs. That made four in three weeks. She had called him a klutz.

'That was my favourite mug and now look at it,' she had said, before throwing the bits back into the bin where he had dumped them. 'Nothing tastes as good out of the other ones.' Perhaps he shouldn't have tried to hide the evidence. But it was only a mug. He had accepted the fact that God had made him six foot six and a half and still growing in order to have him walk into doorframes and shatter lightbulbs on his forehead, as well as destroy mugs, plates, doorknobs, television remotes, stereo controls and household ornaments. Mia would have to learn to accept it too. He wondered when she would notice that he had cracked her chandelier.

Mia's antagonism towards Pat was understandable. After all, he had nearly run her down. Myles listened to her rant. Why do we have to have anything to do with a creep like that? Who did Myles think he was going around hiring sleazeballs without first discussing it with her? She didn't want a guy like that knowing her business. Guys like that, you couldn't trust their moral values, she said.

'What moral values do you require to rob and murder someone?' Myles said.

'It is not murder,' she said. 'Don't use that word.'

'What word would you like?'

'It is not murder.' When he said nothing she yelled, 'Not murder!'

'OK,' he said. 'It's pest control.'

Curiously, her anxiety calmed him and made him feel as though he was in control. You couldn't expect to pull off an ambitious score without some strains on their relationship. Now he felt sorry for her. So young and fragile, skin reddening around the eyes as though she wanted to cry but was too proud to give in. He sat beside her on the sofa.

'I'm doing this the best way I can,' he said quietly. 'After today I promise you'll never have to see the guy again.' She was silent for a moment, staring ahead of her. He adored the way her pout grew more prominent when she got mad. It was very sexy.

'You could have warned me,' she said.

'Sorry about that.'

She said nothing. He took this as a good sign. He put his arm around her and held her to him. She relaxed into him, leaning against his shoulder. He gave her a cuddle, stroked her red hair, then let his fingers play on her neck.

With his free hand, Myles encircled her breast. The second his finger touched the outline of her nipple through her top, she exploded off the sofa. Immediately she barged into him.

'That's all you think about, isn't it? Shag, shag, shag. Fuck, cock into cunt, cock into cunt, cock into cunt, isn't that right? You must have been listening to me with your dick. You can't just hold me for a moment without trying it on, can you? You're like a randy dog.'

She stormed off and ran upstairs, leaving him shocked and frozen on the sofa, paralysed fingers enveloping an invisible breast.

Pat's Volvo pulled into the kerb beside them.

Mia climbed in the back carrying a mysterious knapsack that she had secretly packed. She insisted that Myles get into the passenger seat.

'How's it going?' Pat said. 'Hope you weren't waiting too long.'

Mia looked around the interior of his Volvo. 'Where's the furry dice?'

Pat didn't miss a beat. 'I keep them in my other car, the Rolls.' As they drove off, Pat asked Myles to choose a tape to play.

He picked out *Van Morrison live in San Francisco*. They travelled through the city as Van sang 'Dweller on the Threshold'.

'The man's an artist. Every time I hear this I always notice something different, even though it all sounds the same. Know what I mean?' Pat said.

Myles said that he did. Mia looked out of the window. Pat checked her in the rear-view mirror.

'You alright back there, grumpy?' he said.

'I'm grand,' she said without turning around.

'Sorry we don't have an upstairs lounge for you to sit in,' Pat said. 'Maybe after this gig I'll get one put in.'

Mia ignored him.

Myles put his hand behind the seat to give her leg a squeeze, but she just moved it away. Myles asked how Dez was doing and Pat gave an exasperated moan.

'Don't talk to me. He's only got the young one pregnant. He's going to be a father for the third time. If he keeps on like this his kids will end up older than his girlfriends.' Pat shook his head. 'He says he's ecstatic.'

At Sutton Cross, Mia told Pat to turn right onto the scenic route to the hill of Howth. 'This is a good fast road,' she said.

'Going through the town you have to slow down then go up a steep hill.'

'I love it when you give me directions,' Pat said.

'I love it when you just shut up and drive,' she said.

Again, Myles put his hand behind to make contact but she sat back suddenly. She seemed reluctant to show affection in front of Pat.

'You probably don't see the point in a recce, do you?' Pat said.

'If it has to be done then so be it,' she said.

'Are you sitting comfortably?'

'In this heap, you must be joking.'

'Good, then I'll tell you a story,' Pat said.

'Do you have to?' she said.

He continued as though she had told him to go ahead. 'A while back these dudes decide to pull a big gig on a post office in Malahide. They borrow a cool flash car, get masks and shooters, and even remember to bring big bags to stuff the money into. They only bother to do the one recce, and at night too so as nobody will clock their ugly mushes and remember them to the Plods.'

'Fascinating,' Mia said sarcastically. 'Can't wait to hear the rest.'

'Anyway, day of the gig, they pull up outside the post office with their masks on and their shooters and bags in their hands, and what do you know, the post office is next door to a cop shop.'

Myles looked at Pat. 'So did they abandon the gig?'

'These guys? They stroll right on in. Go about their business robbing the post office.'

'What happened?'

'Twenty minutes later they are all flat on their noses wearing cute little iron bracelets. Except for the leader who breaks his leg in three places trying to jump over a Plod car. What do you think of that?'

'I'm gobsmacked,' Mia said dryly.

'Just shows you that it's important to do your homework,' Myles said.

They passed the convent where the nuns had clothed Myles. He remembered that he had forgotten to return the monk's robe. Neither had he bothered to send on the thirty pounds to the small nun as he had promised. He vowed to make amends after the gig. Otherwise his oversight might bring bad luck.

'OK, slow down,' Mia said. 'Pull in here.'

Pat pulled the car in a few yards from the gate of Mia's father's house. They saw a long driveway leading to a garage. Over the garage doors was a square piece of flat, white painted wood that held a rusty basketball hoop. At the side of the garage was a purple Jaguar. Beyond the garage they caught a glimmer of high windows and part of the red slate roof of the house. Mia's father was away. Not due back until the next morning. Lorcan had phoned this morning with the news. He had been keeping an eye on the place but he wasn't there now. Mia described the front area of the house while Pat asked questions about security and alarms. He wanted to know about the neighbours. Were any of them retired policemen or army? Did they have dogs? Swimming pools filled with alligators? Helipads? Anything unusual that he should know about? Mia answered all his questions.

When Pat was satisfied, they drove off. They checked exit routes, side roads and secluded car parks all the way to the summit. From time to time Pat stopped the car and drew little maps in a small sketchbook.

Then Mia directed him to the back road that took them up to the small grassy entrance to the cliff walk. The walk led behind her father's house and wound across the summit down the other side of the hill to Howth town and harbour.

Myles looked at Mia but she was still pissed off. He had never seen her so angry for so long. Perhaps there was something else on her mind as well. The late Barry of the Bouquets, probably.

They got out and walked along the cliff walk. Mia wore her mysterious knapsack on her back. It seemed heavy.

'What's in the knapsack?' Myles asked.

'Personal stuff,' she said.

She led the way, with Myles behind followed by Pat. They did very little talking. The day was overcast and the sky was grey. The dark sea splashed and gushed beneath them as they walked. Flecks of seawater carried in the breeze pitter-pattered off their faces, tingling their skin and refreshing them. In a while they reached the gate to the big house. Myles scoured the ground for signs of Psychodad's gun shot. He spotted a deep gouge near a rock that could have been a bullet hole. Before he could bend down to investigate, Mia was through the gate. They followed her up the long winding slippery path past the chalet to the back of the house. At the back door Mia pointed out the key's hiding place under a rock. She unlocked the door and led them to a back staircase up to her old room. They kept their voices low and conversed only when absolutely necessary. Mia opened the door to her room, but declined to come inside. Myles and Pat walked into a mausoleum to stuffed animals. Shelves of carefully arranged teddies, lambs, puppies and dolphins. Even a shelf devoted to cuddly crocodiles. In the half-light through the open curtains, the animals looked spookily alive. Myles noticed that the room contained no Barbies or Disney characters or creatures from famous storybooks. Mia had only been into anonymous stuffed animals. When they came out she took them through the rest of the house. She showed them the front room where Psychodad did all his business. She pointed out the chest in the corner where he kept the money. Then she led them out to the back garden again and locked the back door.

Pat asked several questions that Mia answered. When he was satisfied, Mia took off the knapsack.

'OK,' she said. 'I just need a couple of minutes.'

From the knapsack she removed a crackly polythene jumpsuit, plastic gloves and galoshes as well as a large tin of green paint. They watched as she put the jumpsuit on over her clothes. Without a word, she put on the gloves and galoshes. Finally, she handed the knapsack to Myles and squeaked off to disappear around the side of the house. Pat raised an eyebrow at Myles. Myles shrugged to show that he didn't know what was going on either.

'Hang on for a bit,' he told Pat.

'Take your time,' Pat said. 'I'm in no hurry.'

Myles followed Mia around to the front of the house. He heard squeaking from the garage area. He walked towards the sound until he came upon Mia alongside the purple Jaguar. She held the open can of paint over the car's roof. When she saw Myles she gave him a dazzling smile.

'You're just in time,' she said.

'For what?'

'Performance art,' she chirped.

She slowly tilted the can so that the paint poured over the roof, streaming onto the windscreen and down the sides. Walking slowly around the car, she poured all the while to cover as much it as possible. The green liquid flowed over the car, trickled off the wipers and formed green pools on the ground. The Jaguar looked as though it was melting. Myles watched the car changing colour and shape as it was enveloped in paint. The effect was quite soothing, almost spiritual. In a few minutes the car was completely green. A work of art. Mia placed the empty can on the roof like an offering to the Gods. Quickly, she ripped off the gloves and galoshes then tore off the jumpsuit. She rolled the items into a tight ball and put them inside a small plastic bag. She tied the bag to her belt.

Then she took an Instamatic camera out of her jacket and snapped a photo of her work. Myles was aware of Pat standing alongside.

Pat whispered, 'Jaysus, this one's really mad.'

Beaming, Mia came over to them, flapping the drying photo in the air as though fanning herself. Behind her, green paint spread out like lava around the gleaming car.

'That was so cool,' she said, as she stretched. 'OK lads, you can take me home.'

It took an hour of rummaging through old stuff in the attic before he found the box. He pulled it from between two large bags and opened the lid. He took out his father's bulky Smith and Wesson pistol. The gun felt heavy in his hand, the heft and scale and cold metal somehow reassuring. Myles could understand why guns were called 'Equalisers'. He found a box of bullets and a small case of cleaning equipment, also a manual. Elated, he put them all back in the box then carried it out of the attic and down the stairs to the top floor. He sneaked downstairs, passing the kitchen where he heard the squawking of Justine's violin practice blending tunelessly with the babble from his mother's radio.

He padded down the hall, carefully opened the front door and went outside. Pulling the door gently shut behind him, he ran down the steps, got into the Nissan and drove off.

His father had had no patience with him. 'Come on out of that,' he had said when Myles missed a large tree from six feet. 'Aim and squeeze, aim and squeeze.' His father had eventually placed his large paw over the boy's small hand and carried out all the actions – loading, flicking the safety catch, taking aim, squeezing the trigger and dealing with the recoil. Even then, Myles had kept missing the tree. After two dozen lessons from his father, Myles had yet to fire a gun alone. The last lesson had been seven years ago. Three years before his father had been blown to bits in the army latrine. At work, he strolled through the corridor to the features department. He felt the reassuring weight of his father's gun in his inside pocket. He said hello to the Sperm, who passed by too preoccupied to return the greeting. He imagined himself spinning around, dropping to a half crouch with the gun in his hand pointed directly at the Sperm's perm. 'Excuse me, I said hello.' As the Sperm dropped to his knees begging for forgiveness Myles would put a bullet into his hair then stroll away with a smirk on his face like Bruce Willis in *Die Hard*.

Inside the office he found the usual suspects. Except for Dogbrain who was apparently now 'on annual leave'. Myles made a point of deliberately saying hello to Lola, then to Cliff. He ignored Jarlath. In a fantasy, he pulled the gun from his inside pocket in one fluid movement, took careful aim then popped Jarlath's nose off, before returning the gun to his inside pocket. He went to his desk, sat down and ignored all the messages on his screen.

Later, Myles intended to take the gun up to Phoenix Park, find the quiet place where his father had taken him and practise blowing away a few cans. As he thought about it, he suddenly realised that shooting at cans was not going to be of much use if Psychodad pulled a Luger on him. Myles would need to practise shooting at something that moved. A target at a rifle range would be ideal, but he could not go to a rifle range without a licence. As the Psychodad gig could happen any time in the next few weeks, he needed to prepare quickly. Another thought struck him. How would he know if he had what it took to shoot a man? He should shoot an animal first. If he couldn't kill an animal then he wouldn't be able to pull the trigger on a man. Going to the zoo and taking a pop at a monkey was out of the question. It would have to be an animal that wouldn't provoke an outcry. That ruled out most of the neighbourhood cats and dogs.

He also wanted to be able to impress Pat by pulling out the Smith and Wesson. That would prove to Pat that Myles was no amateur. Then, if for some reason Pat chickened out or got hurt, Myles would be able to complete the job. As Big Paddy always said: 'If you want something done right, then do it yourself.'

On the drive back to the city three days ago, Mia had been relaxed and playful. This time Pat had been slightly removed, as though her display of performance art had prompted him to re-evaluate the gig. Myles was glad that Pat had never seen the penis paintings. By the time they arrived in Mountjoy Square, however, everyone had loosened up. Mia and Pat were even joking, something that had given Myles a buzz of satisfaction. He liked to see the people he cared about getting on with each other.

Just then a flutter of wings at the window disturbed Myles's reverie. He looked out to see pigeons flapping at each other on the window ledge. Big, ugly, dirty-looking city pigeons with cruel beaks and dark pronged feet. The pigeons were running rampant in the city. Crapping on cars, dive bombing people having lunch in the parks, squawking and fighting outside people's windows. Someone ought to do something about it. At lunchtime, he took the back stairs and made his way to the roof of the newspaper building. Looking about him, he saw that he was alone. Across the rooftops, nothing stirred. He saw a piled up bunch of boxes on the roof of the building directly across. Traffic noise from below. A cloudy sky. The only living things were Myles and hundreds of big, fat, ugly pigeons.

'Here pidgie pidgie, pidgie,' he cooed.

He walked to the centre of the roof and chose a position. He pulled the gun from his inside pocket. He didn't like the way he'd done it so he put it back and pulled it out again, this time turning in exaggerated slow motion to point the muzzle at a waddling pigeon four feet away. He flicked the safety catch, took careful aim at the pigeon's puffed out chest. He pressed the trigger; the gun bucked in his hand and the pigeon disappeared. A riot of wings flapped the air as feathers floated down to land at his feet. A red lump of something plopped down at the edge of the roof. Above him hundreds of confused birds flew around squawking.

Drunk with excitement and achievement, Myles took aim at the circling pigeons and fired again. He missed. Again he fired and again he missed. He wondered what happened to bullets when they were shot up in the air. He had just picked out a tough-looking pigeon that had landed a few yards away and was staring at him menacingly when he heard shouting. He hunched down and looked around him. At first he saw nobody. As the shouting continued he saw two fat men on the roof of the building directly opposite. They stood beside the piled up boxes that Myles could now see were cages. Cages with homing pigeons in them. The men were yelling at him to stop shooting their fucking pigeons.

Keeping low so they couldn't get a good gawk at him, he made it to the door, opened it and crawled inside. Barrelling down the back staircase, he realised that he still held the gun in his hand. Quickly he stuffed it inside his jacket. The barrel felt warm. Reaching the corridor, he walked swiftly to the features department. To his relief, everyone was at lunch. He pulled out the gun and wiped it clean with his handkerchief. Then he walked across to Jarlath Boon's desk, opened the bottom drawer and dropped in the gun. He placed a sheaf of copy paper on top to hide it then shut the drawer.

He left the features room and took the stairs down to the lobby, going out the back way through printing. Once he hit the street he kept his head down and walked.

He was halfway up O'Connell Street when his mobile beeped. He pulled it out of his pocket, pressed the button and put the phone to his ear.

'Hey man,' Pat said. 'How are you?'

'Grand,' Myles said. 'I'm grand.'

'That's good,' Pat said. 'Because the gig is tomorrow.'

THIRTEEN

Howth

It was a wonderful sight, one of the most gleefully enjoyable of Myles's life.

After lunch, he arrived just as Jarlath Boon was being hauled down the front steps of News House handcuffed to a burly policeman. Another policeman carried Myles's father's Smith and Wesson in a clear plastic bag.

Jarlath Boon's square face was purple. 'I swear I have never seen that weapon before in my life,' he roared. 'This is an outrage.'

Myles joined the large crowd who had gathered on the steps. They watched as Jarlath was bundled into a police car and driven away.

'I always suspected that there was something depraved about that fellow,' Bob Casper said knowingly. 'He was forever awarding himself invisible stripes.'

Lola Wall was shocked. 'An animal abuser. Who'd have thought it?' she said. 'And him with three beautiful Dalmatians at home.'

Bob Casper nodded, 'Some people get their kicks in weird ways. I hope he gets life.'

'That's a bit strong,' Cliff Mangan said. 'All he did was blow away a pigeon.'

Bob Casper turned on him. 'It was a racing pigeon you prick. If he tried that in Cork he'd be a dead man.'

Myles and his colleagues went back to work and spent most of the afternoon badmouthing Jarlath Boon.

By the time Myles arrived, The Crazy Horse was packed with men together in drink. He found Pat and Dez in the back room shooting pool. Still buzzing from Jarlath's misfortune, Myles went up to Dez and shook his hand.

'I'd like to offer my warmest congratulations on the pregnancy of your girlfriend.'

Immediately, Dez pointed the pool cue at Myles's nose. 'Are you trying to exacerbate me, Goalpost?' Dez said.

Dez came up to Myles's chest. The tip of the pool cue wavered an inch from his nose.

'Just trying to be friendly,' Myles said.

'Well how would you like this friendly pool cue shoved up your hole?'

Pat stepped between them. 'Now lads, relax the heads. No need for the bitter word.'

Reluctantly, and after a long meaningful glare, Dez broke off to resume his pool game. 'Get him away from me. He's intruding on me personal space.'

After Pat had won the game and Myles had apologised for intruding on Dez's personal space, prompting a mumbled grunt of acceptance, they sat down at a table in a quiet corner and ordered pints.

'OK, time to do a bit of business,' Pat said, spreading a small hand-drawn map of the area around Psychodad's house on the table between the pints.

They went over the plan thoroughly, paying particular attention to arrival and getaway. Myles felt as though he had become a member of an outlaw gang. He was the Tall Texan while Pat was Butch Cassidy and Dez was the Sundance Kid. On reflection, he decided that the Sundance Kid was too grand a title for Dez. The Sundance Leprechaun was more appropriate.

Pat folded the map and put it back in his pocket. 'For the purpose of this operation, I'm Captain, Dez is Sergeant and Myles is a Corporal.'

Dez looked stricken. 'Why do I have to be a sergeant? Why can't I be a loo-tenant?'

'Because Sergeant is easier to remember, OK?'

Dez mumbled something.

Myles thought that he should speak up too. After all, the whole thing had been his idea.

'I've a problem with being a corporal,' Myles protested. 'Why can't I be a sergeant too?'

'Because this is your first gig,' Dez said. 'And you can't have two sergeants.'

Myles pointed out that he had been on gigs before, admittedly as an observer. That experience should be taken into consideration, he argued. After a discussion, Myles was promoted to Sergeant while Dez was made Sergeant-Major.

'Warmest congratulations,' Dez said curtly.

Dez left to procure cars for the job. Pat shrugged to indicate that Dez's grumpiness was beyond even his control.

'He's just pissed off because he is the driver and has to wait outside while you get to come in to do the gig with me. He wanted to bring Mixer and Earl in but I wouldn't wear it. One scumbag on a gig is enough. Don't worry about him. He'll be grand by tomorrow.'

Pat lowered his voice and fixed Myles with a serious stare.

'I have been giving the Psychodad vibe a great deal of serious thought,' he said. 'If bumping off the geezer is the only way that we can guarantee the success of the gig, then so be it. Therefore I have decided to personally handle blowing the head off the bolix, if that's OK with you.'

'Fine by me,' Myles said.

'I always say that if something is worth doing, then it's worth doing right,' Pat said. 'I just want you to know that I do not take this decision lightly. All life is sacred, even that belonging to a real bucket of shite.' Pat paused for a moment to reflect on the gravity of the undertaking. Then he slapped Myles on the back. 'Now here's the business part. Because I am doing the whacking we now split the money seventy per cent for us, thirty for you, agreed?'

'Agreed,' Myles said.

He felt that a huge pressure had been lifted. Psychodad would not vanish in a flurry of feathers like the pigeon, but now at least it was Pat's problem not Myles's. He wondered what had caused Pat to change his mind. Maybe it was the lure of extra money. He knew that Pat could never have killed anyone in cold blood before. The thought put a chill in him so he quickly dismissed it. He didn't like to think of his friend as a murderer. No more than he liked to think of Jesse James as a murderer or Billy the Kid or Michael Collins or Finn McCool or any of the great heroic figures from history. Psychodad was the real villain here. Getting rid of him would rescue Mia and her brother from a nightmare. As well as give Pat and Dez and himself new starts in life. Exchange one life for five. That was a pretty fair deal, he decided.

'Now, let's get some drinks in,' Pat said. 'We've a big day ahead of us tomorrow.'

In the morning Myles phoned in sick. He was put through to features where Dogbrain's slow, suspicious voice answered the phone.

'Hey, you're back,' Myles said.

'No,' Dogbrain said. 'I'm not really.'

Myles told Dogbrain that he was sick and Dogbrain said that he was sorry to hear that and he hoped that Myles would get better soon.

'How are you doing, are you OK?' Myles asked.

'Yes,' Dogbrain said and put down the phone.

He walked to The Crazy Horse where Pat and Dez waited for him in borrowed cars. He climbed into Pat's Fiat. Dez followed in a Volkswagen van.

Myles pulled out his mobile and dialled Mia's number. The phone rang for a while before her husky voice answered.

'Hello you,' she said.

She told him that Lorcan had phoned earlier to say that the gig was still on. Psychodad had blamed local gurriers for the incident with the Jaguar. An hour ago he had left for the airport to pick up the moneymen. He was driving the spare gold-coloured Jag – he always kept a spare in the garage. Lorcan had been about to clear off, leaving the house empty until Psychodad returned. There was a brief pause.

'Sorry for being so irrational yesterday,' she said. 'I think the idea of returning to my old house got me quite emotional.'

'Forget it,' Myles said.

'I'll think of a way to make it up to you tonight,' she purred. 'You just come back safely, you hear?'

'See you later,' Myles said and rang off.

Myles told Pat Mia's news and then they went over the plan until they could recite it by heart. Pat made Myles repeat three crucial instructions.

One: get the money first before whacking Psychodad.

Two: whack Psychodad.

Three: get the fuck out of there.

The plan was that as soon as the guests had driven away, Dez would bleep the all clear and Pat and Myles would put on the masks and sneak downstairs to do the gig. The masks were just in case Pyschodad was not alone. After they had done the business, they would walk up to the front road and Dez would pick them up. That was plan A.

Plan B was to leg it down the cliff walk to the parked Fiat.

'Plan C is every man for himself,' Pat joked.

Pat stuck the new Van Morrison tape into the Fiat's cassette player. Van sang 'Days Like This'.

'This is one of the best ever rock songs,' Pat said. 'It's almost as good as "Alright Now" or "Smoke on the Water".'

At Sutton Cross they turned right and cruised up the hill. They turned off onto the back road while Dez kept going. Pat parked the Fiat at the entrance to the cliff walk. They got out and he locked the car.

'Better safe than sorry,' he said.

They took the cliff walk to Mia's father's house. Pat carried a black hold-all while Myles lugged a large travel bag, empty except for the pair of black and white theatrical masks that Mia had made especially for them. A smiley face for Pat, and a sad face for Myles.

It began to rain, making the ground wet and treacherous.

Soaked and itchy, they reached the back of the house. Myles removed the key from its hiding place and opened the door. They went up the back stairs to Mia's room, where they sat down soggily on her bed. Pat removed a bleeper from the hold-all then stretched out on the bed and closed his eyes, placing the bleeper on his chest.

'If anything exciting happens, wake me,' Pat said.

Dez had the other bleeper. By now, he should have been parked on the main road, pretending to be an ESB meter man with a stack of official-looking charts in case anyone got nosy. As Pat began to snore softly, Myles wished that he could lie down on the bed too but there wasn't room. Instead, he sat in a chair by the window and watched the rain. It was better than looking at all the stuffed animals along the shelves. Keep staring at those things long enough Myles reckoned, and they would begin to talk. Why had she only been interested in stuffed animals? What did that tell him about her? He thought about it for a while, got nowhere and gave up.

He could feel himself growing. He reckoned that he would probably be seven foot tall after this gig. His trousers looked short on him. Today, there was an extra expanse of pathetic looking sock on show whenever he stood up. When this was over, he was going to have to get his trousers specially made for him.

After an hour the bleeper bleeped and the message window lit up. Pat raised himself to his elbows to check the message. Psychodad had arrived with guests. They heard two cars pull up in the driveway. The front door opened and closed. Footsteps and voices sounded in the hallway followed by a door slamming.

Then silence.

Without a word, Pat lay back on the bed. Myles sat and waited. He felt his stomach draining away into his legs and seeping out through the tips of his toes. Occasionally a gust of disembodied laughter floated up to Mia's room. Along with the aroma of coffee.

Right now, Myles didn't feel like a member of an elite army squad. Nor did he feel like the Tall Texan. Instead he was a voyeur in a girl's room. He wondered if Mia had ever sneaked Barry into this room. Had she and Barry ever made love on her bed with Mia singing 'come on, come on, come on'?

Thinking about her and Barry made Myles feel very tired. Giggling gleefully at Jarlath Boon's glorious misfortune had kept him awake most of the night, which was possibly not the best preparation for a gig. Now that this morning's initial excitement and apprehension had faded, he felt that he could use a rest. Even now, the memory of Jarlath's purple face prompted a smile.

Closing his eyes, he allowed his mind to drift. He slowed his breathing until he felt without concern or persona. In a while, he became weightless, liberated and serene. Gently, he floated out of the window and drifted over the roof of the house. Looking back, he saw himself sitting at the window of Mia's room, chin in hand with his eyes closed. The rain lashed down but he didn't feel it, though he was aware of a chill in the air. He floated over the roof to the front of the house where he saw below him the gold Jaguar, parked alongside a battered ancient Mercedes that obviously belonged to the moneymen. Next to the Jaguar was a large, ugly green discharge that looked like someone had tipped a vat of crème de menthe onto the gravel. Myles observed the Volkswagen van parked along the main road. Inside, Dez lay slumped against the door, as though asleep. The road was deserted and gloomy in the rain. As Myles touched down on the roof of the house, his foot made a soft buzzing noise. He immediately pulled away and sought a better landing place. But the next spot his foot touched also emitted a buzzing noise. He was about to drift away when the entire roof started buzzing. Terrified, he shot up into the air like a rapidly deflating balloon.

He snapped awake suddenly to find Pat's massive hand on his shoulder. Pat held the beeper in his hand.

'Come on sleepyhead, we're on,' he whispered.

The sense of terror fell away, and was immediately replaced by relief that something was happening, as well as a craving to move fast and get the thing over and done with. They got up and crept out of Mia's room, leaving the door open. They went downstairs cautiously. From outside came the sound of a car driving off. Pat held a gun in his hand. Myles carried the two bags. He was amazed that he felt so calm and alert. He seemed to be moving on automatic. He kept expecting to hear bells tolling in the distance, twangy guitars, the full Clint Eastwood.

Outside the door to the living room, they paused. Myles handed Pat a mask. They put them on, then immediately took them off again when they realised that they couldn't see anything. Mia had carved tiny slits for the eyes. Pat poked his finger through the holes, making them bigger. Myles did the same. Then they readied themselves to go in. Pat held his gun at the side of his mask, his free hand on the door handle.

Myles could hear his heart booming. Louder than the grand-father clock in the hall.

The happy face opposite him counted softly.

One: Pat's hand tightened on the doorknob.

Two: Myles suddenly wanted to pee.

Three: Pat opened the door.

They charged in. 'OK, get your fuckin—' Pat began.

There was nobody in the room.

They spun around frantically, but the room was empty except for their reflections in the large mirror over the fireplace. Two men in black and white masks, one very tall, the other holding a gun in mid-air.

Happy face looked at sad face. 'Where is he?'

Sad face shrugged. Had Psychodad left with the moneymen? Had he heard them outside? Was he now hiding somewhere in the room? Behind the sofa?

Just then a toilet flushed close by. They froze. Myles was afraid to breathe. A long wall panel that was actually a door to a small bathroom opened and Psychodad walked in. The hidden bathroom was something that Mia had neglected to mention in the recce. Psychodad saw them and stopped buckling his belt, a look of bemusement on his face.

'Hello lads,' he said. 'What can I do for you?'

Pat swung around and levelled the gun.

'Hands in the air,' he shouted.

'Oh I get it, it's a robbery,' Pyschodad said. 'Put the gun down and let's discuss this.'

'Put your hands in the air,' Pat shouted and then Psychodad was gone.

Moving with remarkable agility and grace for a middle-aged man, he ducked and rolled headfirst across the carpet. Pat's view was obscured by his mask. As he stepped back to get a clear view, Psychodad rolled smoothly off the floor and karate kicked him in the stomach. Pat slammed against the wall. The gun flew into the air and plopped onto the sofa next to Myles.

'OK,' Pat croaked. 'Let's discuss this.'

Psychodad rose and landed a rapid series of kicks onto Pat's mask. Pat toppled like a pole to disappear behind the sofa. Myles picked up the gun and straightened up to find Pyschodad in front of him standing in a half-crouch.

'Don't move,' Myles croaked.

'OK son. Let me through and I'll forget you were here.'

Myles had a clear view. One squeeze and Psychodad was dead. 'Stay where you are,' he said.

Pyschodad stared at him contemptuously for a moment, as if trying to decide whether Myles was worth bothering with. Myles was positive that he caught a flicker of recognition on Psychodad's face. A sad-faced mask is no disguise against being six foot six and a half and still growing.

'Think about what you're doing son. Here's the deal. Are you listening?'

Myles nodded.

'Let me go and I'll let you live.'

Myles was paralysed. He couldn't blink. He was the one with the gun yet Psychodad was promising to let him off the hook. After a few seconds, Psychodad abruptly dropped his karate stance. He seemed disappointed.

'OK son, time's up. Either use that thing or get out of my way.'

Psychodad walked towards the open door towards the hall. Instinctively, Myles stepped out of the way.

Pat appeared from behind the sofa. 'Do him for Jaysus' sake,' he gasped.

Pat's voice snapped Myles out of his paralysis. He swung around in time to see a figure disappearing through the door of the front room to the hallway. He pulled the trigger. Instantaneously, the chandelier in the hallway exploded, showering glass everywhere.

Myles heard a curse. Then a rush of footsteps trying for the back door. Myles ran into the hall and followed. In the kitchen he caught a glimpse of movement and fired again. The kitchen window disintegrated. His mask slipped and he smacked into the kitchen wall. Picking himself up quickly, he tore off the mask and threw it from him, then he ran for the open back door. Outside, he saw a small trim figure slipping and bumping down the wet path to the cliff walk, desperately attempting to keep his feet.

Myles took off after the figure. He ran down the path, trying to keep his balance in the rain. Ahead, Psychodad's legs suddenly slipped from under him. He began sliding downhill on his rear end at great speed. Myles tripped and righted himself by grabbing onto a bush. He straightened up in time to see Psychodad crashing like a rocket through the wooden gate, below which the ground seemed to have been turned to play dough by the rain. As bits of gate fell to earth, Psychodad skidded across the cliff path and hurtled over the edge.

Myles heard a long, plunging, oddly feminine-sounding scream. 'Eeeeeeeeee.'

The scream hung in the air for a few seconds, then became lost in the clatter of rainfall mingling with the faraway rush of the sea.

Carefully, Myles slowed down and picked his way to the bottom, steering clear of the long muddy slide that illustrated the path of Psychodad's reluctant descent.

At the bottom, he stepped over the shattered remains of the gate onto the cliff path and cautiously made his way to the edge of the cliff. He looked over. In the rain it was hard to see clearly. Beneath, he could make out waves crashing into jagged rocks. He glimpsed a dark ragged shape being tossed high into the air by a wave. As he watched, the dark shape plummeted into the roiling waters and vanished.

Myles heard movement behind him. He turned as Pat made his way across the cliff walk to join him. They stood together looking over the cliff at the fiercely clashing waves. Myles handed Pat his gun back. They looked at each other and Pat snorted.

'Did you see that?' Myles said breathlessly.

'Absolutely. The eejit jumped,' Pat said. 'A clear case of suicide if ever I saw one.'

* * *

They couldn't find the money. There were no suitcases, bags or hold-alls in the front room and none in the secret bathroom. Pat began to throw accusatory glances at Myles, as if the whole thing was his fault, which, in truth, it was. Myles began to panic. What if there was no money? What if Pat lost his cool and turned the gun on him?

After ten minutes of tossing things about, Myles discovered three suitcases in the hallway, covered in bits of chandelier. A quick check revealed that each suitcase was crammed with wads of notes. Myles touched neatly tied piles of hundreds, fifties, twenties and tens.

It had been worth it. The whole business. The waiting, the fear, the panic, the chase. Here was his new life staring back at him from a cheap suitcase. He stayed looking and touching long enough to savour the sensation of subdued rapture that was spreading through him. Then he called Pat who came skidding.

'Goalpost, you are a genius,' Pat said, and kissed Myles on the forehead.

Myles could take a kiss on the head, but Pat calling him Goalpost was going a bit too far. It showed a lack of respect, not to mention almost ruining a big moment. He knew now that Pat had told Dez about his nickname. Somehow the disappointment of that small betrayal undermined the joy he felt at finding the bags of money.

Pat bleeped Dez to say that they were on their way. Then they grabbed the suitcases and left through the front door. As they passed the gold Jaguar, Pat turned to Myles. 'Listen, do not say anything to Dez about me getting a kicking, OK?'

'Don't know what you're talking about,' Myles said. 'All I saw was an eejit jumping off a cliff.'

'Sound man,' Pat said. 'I greatly appreciate it.'

Myles decided to forgive Pat for his Goalpost slip. What did it matter anyway? Pat could call him anything he wanted once they had split the money.

Dez picked them up at the gate. They climbed in and he drove away. 'Took your time,' he said.

He looked at the suitcases on their knees, observed the look of satisfaction on Pat's face and he nodded.

Pat made the victory sign. 'A perfect vibe.'

Pat opened his hip flask and took a swig. Then he passed the flask to Dez. He cocked a thumb at Myles in the back. 'Your man here is a natural. He chased the bad guy over a cliff, and he found our money.'

'Over a cliff? I'm impressed,' Dez said. 'We'll have to promote you again,' he said, and they all laughed.

'As long as I get a pension,' Myles said, and they cracked up.

'You're holding it,' Pat said, and they nearly crashed.

Dez passed the hip flask back to Pat and he took a drink.

'Did you see the body?' Dez asked casually.

Myles looked at Pat. He shrugged. There was a moment's hesitation. A spasm of doubt gripped Myles's stomach. He had watched Psychodad sail over the cliff, but he had not seen him fall, and he had not seen a body in the surf, only a dark shape that could have been a shadow.

'Did you see a body?' Dez repeated, anxiety in his voice.

Pat took another swig of the hip flask.

'Yes Sergeant-Major,' Pat said. 'We saw a body.'

He handed Myles the flask and Myles took a big gulp.

After dark, Myles arrived at Mountjoy Square full of whiskey but too exhilarated to feel drunk. He was entitled to feel happy. He had pulled off the gravest, most dangerous act of his life and made a big score. In the private back room of The Crazy Horse, they had locked the door and sat down by the pool table to count out over eight hundred thousand quid until the green baize was covered in neatly arranged bundles. After splitting the take, Myles now carried a suitcase containing nearly two hundred grand. Nearly eighty grand was in the hold-all under the back seat of the Nissan, parked in the all-night car park around the corner.

Mia would be proud of him. He was proud of himself, and he wanted to boast about what he had done. Bob Casper would be gobsmacked if he ever found out that a lowly sub-editor had carried out the perfect score. They would all be chewing their penises in jealousy.

His father's face appeared on the door in front of him. Myles had been expecting him to turn up sooner or later. 'You never did anything like this, did you?' Myles said. 'You never held a bag with two hundred grand in it did you?'

Ashamed, his father averted his gaze to Myles's shoes.

'No more long, lanky layabout crap. No more Goalpost. What do you think of that?' Myles said.

'Not much,' his father's unhappy face said as it began to fade.

'Why don't you say congratulations to your son?' Myles said. 'Is that too much to ask?'

'Yes,' his father said mournfully, and disappeared.

Myles pressed the buzzer for Mia's apartment. A man's voice answered. A sharp pain shot through him. As soon as Myles realised that he was talking to Lorcan, the pain went away.

'Let me in, it's Mr Tall,' Myles said. 'I mean, it's Myles.'

'Just a sec,' Lorcan said. The buzzer went and he pushed the door open and went in.

This time no Herbie Hancock music floated down the stairs, and nobody waited to greet him on the third-floor landing. He had to go to the door of the apartment and knock before Mia answered.

'Oh hi,' she said, as though he was an acquaintance from work. She whispered. 'Can't talk, it's my poker night, I forgot all about it. How did it go?'

How did it go? Was that the best she could say to him? He was a fucking hero. Mr Tall had banished Psychodad for ever.

'Perfect,' he said. 'He's gone.'

'Yessss,' she hissed softly, punching the air in slow-motion. He was disappointed that Mia's reaction was so muted. Like she was hearing old news that she had celebrated ages ago. She took him by the hand and led him inside. She didn't even ask what was in the suitcase.

'I broke your chandelier,' Myles whispered. 'Sorry.'

'Don't worry about it,' Mia said. 'I'll buy another.'

Lorcan, Stick and Aisling sat at the table with cards in their hands. On the table stood half-empty bowls of Pringles and nuts as well as messy piles of coins. They nodded to Myles then went back to their cards. Lorcan still had a bandage on his nose.

'Sit down anywhere, we're just in the middle of a hand,' Mia said. She went back to the table and picked up her cards.

Puzzled and disappointed, Myles lounged by the window. Nobody paid any attention to him. He had been expecting to be kissed and hugged and made a fuss off. He noticed that there was a bottle of white wine on the table and four glasses. Mia hadn't asked him if he wanted a drink. Now she wasn't even making eye contact. Perhaps she couldn't in front of Lorcan and her friends. Or did she know something that he didn't? It was almost as though she hadn't been expecting him. Had she already found out all she needed to know about today's events? Confused, he sat on the sofa to watch the poker game, suitcase at his feet.

After the initial nod, Lorcan ignored Myles. Instead, he seemed more interested in behaving as though he was one of the girls.

'Stick is minting it again,' he said to Mia.

'Too right sweetie,' Stick said.

'Jesus,' Aisling said, examining her cards through big round glasses. 'I've a hand like a foot.'

Stick played three kings and two jacks and they all groaned. She gathered in the coins. 'I'm concentrating on what I'm doing instead of moshing about. That's why I'm minting it.'

'You haven't been the same since you gave your bloke the flick,' Mia said.

'You said it girl,' Aisling agreed. 'Bankrupting her friends is Stick's way of taking her mind off sex.'

'You wish,' Stick said.

Aisling leaned over. 'Anyway, I hear you have a new bloke.'

Mia looked at her. 'You mean the dizzy looking barman from The Chocolate Bar?'

'He's not a barman,' Stick said defensively. 'He's a maitre d' and we were just talking.'

'Yes,' Aisling said. 'Astonishing the conversations some people can have when they've got their tongues stuck down each other's throats. What was he looking for anyway — a fishbone?'

Mia and Aisling laughed and Lorcan tittered politely. Myles wondered if he should chip in with a few remarks. They appeared to be ignoring him. He decided to wait a while. He wanted a drink badly though.

Stick waited until the giggling had finished. 'You're right about the dizzy bit.'

'Were you bold?' Aisling asked.

'Might have been, but he passed out.'

'God that happened to me last Saturday. I was gutted,' Aisling said. 'These young blokes with the big drinking heads on them. There should be a rule. If a man goes out with you, he should only be allowed one pint or one glass of wine. That way, if you decide to take him home, he might be able to get it together.'

'Like arse, you'll never make that work,' Mia looked at Myles.

'Myles, you're a man, what do you think?'

'Well,' he was surprised to be suddenly included. Mia gave him a dazzling smile. Everything seemed fine again. How could he ever have suspected that there was something amiss between them? He said, 'It depends on the man doesn't it?'

'Proper order sweetie,' Stick said. 'Anyway, I might give the dizzy barman a second chance.'

'Like arse,' Aisling gasped. 'Are you cracked, girl?'

Stick shrugged. 'I said might.'

This time Stick won with two pairs, aces and twos.

'Any chance of a drink?' Myles said as Lorcan dealt another hand.

'Help yourself,' Mia said, indicating the bottle. 'You know where the glasses are. Oh, and don't break any.'

He went across to the counter and fetched a wine glass. He stood behind Mia while he poured himself a glass. He got no reaction from her or the others, except for a quick smile from Stick who seemed to like him. He got the impression that everyone was gathered, not to play poker but to protect Mia. From what? From him? He noticed Aisling's beautiful handpainted silk dress. Like a kimono only ritzier, with light blues and yellows and soft red colours intertwined like exquisite snakes on a buttermilk background. It looked Oriental so he presumed that it must be Vietnamese. He was sure Mia had told him that Aisling was Vietnamese. Anyway, she looked stunning. Or maybe he was just drunk.

'Getting in touch with your roots?' he said when he caught Aisling's attention.

'Pardon?' she said.

Myles indicated the dress. 'That's a wonderful dress.'

'Thanks,' she said, regarding him with cautious approval.

Myles searched for something classy to say to get Aisling on side. 'It makes you look like a Vietnamese princess.'

She averted her gaze quickly. It seemed to Myles that her eyes were welling up.

'What?' he said. 'Did I say something wrong?'

Stick shook her head. 'It's alright. She's just in denial.'

'I'm not denying anything,' Aisling said quietly. 'It's just that if you want to call me a princess I'd like it if you called me an Irish princess. I grew up here. I live and work here and as far as I am concerned Irish is what I am.'

There was silence for a moment. Everyone looked at Mia. 'He didn't mean anything by it, did you Myles?'

'No,' Myles said.

'That's OK, forget it,' Aisling said coldly, not looking at him. 'My deal, I think.'

Myles lost patience. 'Jaysus, all I said was it's a wonderful dress.'

He went back to the sofa and sat down again. The wine tasted sickly sweet and cold. He wanted a beer or perhaps more whiskey but he didn't like to ask. He didn't want to risk an inappropriate comment. The others played another hand of poker. Stick won again. Mia and Lorcan groaned.

Myles finished his wine. 'Is there anything I can do?' he said, thinking that he might be invited into the game. He fantasised about throwing open the suitcase and depositing the money onto the table. Blow them all away.

Mia and Stick looked at their cards. Lorcan pretended he hadn't heard.

'Well, now that you ask,' Aisling straightened her glasses on her nose and looked at him coolly. 'You could fuck off back home to Lucy and your kid.'

FOURTEEN

Venetians

He stood at the water's edge.

Above him the cliffs leaned out as though they were about to topple. All around him on the slippery promontory lay scattered bits of seaweed, driftwood and other stuff the tide had washed up. The wind had softened so it was possible to get close to the edge to look for signs.

It had taken him an hour to climb down, and while he knew that it was unwise to return to the scene of a crime, he also realised that he had to come back for the sake of his own peace of mind or he would never be able to sleep.

Anyway, there had been no crime. The eejit had jumped. Myles craned over to scour the waves and the surrounding rocks for pieces of clothing or hair or any indication that a man had plunged to his death in this place. He saw only lapping waters and the occasional dull grey shape of a fish passing underneath the surface.

A soft breeze played on his face. Something flapped on a jutting rock just yards from where he stood. It looked like a frayed piece of material, perhaps from a shirt. He could reach it if he lay across a long slab of rock nearby.

He knelt down and arranged himself. He was inches short. Leaning out further, he almost got there. This time he made a huge effort, almost overbalancing, just managing to touch the edge of the stuff.

One more try and he would have it. He leaned out again. With a massive effort, his fingers closed on the loose fold of cloth. Suddenly, a withered bony hand erupted from the water and seized his wrist. The hand began pulling him into the waves. Terrified, he gulped for air as he lost his grip on the rocks. He scrabbled to find something solid to hold onto but the surface was too slippery and he began to slide inexorably into the waves. Beneath the water, a dark shape loomed. As he watched it became a leering eyeless face under a boyish flop of inky black hair.

He yelled as he hit the surface. Immediately, freezing salty water filled his open mouth, choking him.

He sat up in bed, coughing and flailing his arms about, his own scream reverberating in his ears.

As he sat there panting, he heard footsteps pounding up the stairs. The door opened and Lucy appeared in the doorway.

'What is it? Are you alright?'

'Yes,' he said annoyed that he had let himself down. 'I caught myself on something,' he added unconvincingly, casting about for something that he could claim had hurt him. He saw nothing except bed sheets. He felt wet, clammy and embarrassed. He could still feel the grip of bony fingers on his wrist.

'God, I thought someone was being murdered,' Lucy chortled. 'You scared me to bits.'

Trust her to make a big deal out of nothing. He wished that she would go away and leave him alone. He threw off the bedclothes and the air dried the wetness on his skin.

'OK, I'm getting up now,' he said, as Justine's worried face appeared at Lucy's elbow. 'I said I'm getting up.'

'Is Daddy sick?' Justine asked.

'Everything is fine.' Lucy pulled Justine out with her. 'Daddy's just feeling a bit dramatic this morning.'

The door closed and he was alone in his old bedroom in his mother's house. He listened to their footsteps descending the stairs, back to normal family life.

In a few minutes he would put on his clothes, shave and wash and then go downstairs. To find his mother humming along with tunes on the kitchen radio; Philip silently gagging on his toast, yearning for the chance to sneak upstairs to play with his trains; Justine sawing at her violin; Lucy planted there like a martyr, stoically waiting for him to come through whatever mid-life crisis he was cultivating at the moment.

Christ. Another fifty years of this stuff ahead of him. It would have been better to have drowned in his sleep.

Then he remembered the two hundred and eighty grand stashed among the trunks of his father's old things in the attic. He saw Mia's green eyes, imagined chilled Bellinis in Harry's bar in Venice.

Two weeks with no mention of Psychodad in the newspapers or on television. As though the gig had never happened.

He picked up his mobile from the bedside table and dialled Pat's number. He heard buzzing tones then an answering click. Instead of Pat's voice in his ear, he received a blast of boisterous party noise, followed immediately by what sounded like someone blowing a trombone. He held the mobile out from his ear until Pat's voice shouted over the din.

'Hey dude, we were just talking about you. Why don't you come round for a few scoops,' he said. 'This vibe is just starting.'

Nine in the morning and they were partying. Pat had been virtually uncontactable since the gig in Howth. Now he sounded like he had forgotten all their plans to lie low for a few weeks.

'Man, we did the laundry and got away clean,' he proudly proclaimed. 'Dez here is talking about buying a Porsche.'

As far as Myles was concerned, this wasn't over till the body washed up. Disappointed, he told Pat he was too busy to come over.

'Hey dude, you need to loosen up,' Pat said. 'Life is sweet, you know?'

'Talk to you later,' Myles said and rang off.

His finger hovered over the first digit of Mia's number but he hesitated. After the events in Howth, she had spent one unsatisfactory drunken night with him, then cut herself off. No 'Thank you for saving me, Myles.' No 'You're a hero, Myles.' Not even 'I love you, Myles.' Instead, she had sung a new song about needing time and space to put the finishing touches to her exhibition. She hoped that he would understand. 'Of course I understand,' Myles had said. 'You mean you're dumping me.'

'No silly,' Mia had laughed. 'I just need to do this right. No distractions. It's important to me.'

'I thought I had already got rid of your distraction,' he said. 'Maybe you missed that bit.'

'Just be patient. It'll be worth it, you'll see.'

She had kissed him, promising to see him on the opening night. Myles blamed Aisling. The ex-Vietnamese princess turned Irish patriot had blabbed to Mia about Lucy and Justine and turned Mia's head around. That was what he got for paying Aisling a compliment.

He missed Mia. It was strange to go through a day without phoning her, meeting her or dropping over to the apartment. Sometimes at night, he imagined the pressure of her lying on him, hair unfurled across his chest like a red forest. Many times during the past fortnight he had come close to dialling her number or driving to Mountjoy Square to park and watch out for her. But he had resisted the impulse, even though there was a hollow in his guts that felt as though it was growing wider by the day. He would see her tonight. He had a surprise for her. At the right moment – in other words, when Aisling wasn't around – he would spring his surprise upon her and she would just melt.

He stood up and went to the wardrobe to find some clothes. He still felt clammy. Then he noticed that he was leaving wet footprints on the wooden floor. His Calvin Kleins were also soaked. For a moment, he panicked. It hadn't been a dream. He had been sleepwalking. All the way to Howth to be dragged into the sea.

The moment passed, leaving him feeling foolish for having allowed his imagination to overwhelm him. He returned to the bed and felt around. The sheets were sodden. Exposed to the air, they now stank like gutted fish. Jesus, he had wet the bed.

He was about to pull them off the bed when the door opened and Justine peeked in shyly.

'Daddy, are you busy?'

'No darling, what is it?'

Justine smiled. 'I wrote something for you.'

He sat down on the bed as she came into the room, carrying her violin and bow.

'That's great, what did you write?'

Justine sniffed the air. 'What's the pooey smell?'

'Oh nothing,' he said. 'I think the cat might have done something. Now what do you want to show me?'

Justine smiled. 'It hasn't got a name yet. I only made it up this morning. Wanna hear it?'

'Of course I do,' he said.

She put the tiny orange violin to her shoulder, carefully placed the bow across the strings and began to saw.

In the lobby of The Oracle Gallery, he stood in line behind a bunch of sad bastards as they signed their names to Mia's invitation book. The same crowd of pseuds, posers and Hooray Shamuses and Sheilas seemed to turn up at every private view, first night and even rock concert. Most of these people would go to the opening of an envelope. One day they'd even start showing up at dogfights in the back room of The Crazy Horse.

Myles pulled his invitation from his pocket. 'Origins', the card proclaimed in big imitation stone letters over a reproduction of a giant stone phallus. Underneath was Mia's name: 'Mia Powell, artist', in smaller imitation stone letters. As Pat would say, this invitation had a 'Flintstones vibe'. The invitation had arrived the other morning, in a sleek white envelope. Myles had managed to put it in his pocket without Lucy noticing.

When it was his turn to sign the book, he wrote 'Mr Tall'. Under occupation he put 'Artist's muse'.

Inside the gallery, the exhibition was mounted on plain white walls, each of the works tastefully framed and hung. Myles passed a New Man wearing a baby strapped to his chest like a live exhibit. As though no opening could be complete without one.

Mia stood in the far corner with Aisling, Stick and Lorcan and some pretentious bald dipstick Myles didn't recognise. She gave him a tiny smile and a wave, which was the most he'd got from her for nearly two weeks. He contemplated approaching her and then decided against it. He didn't want to have to be polite to Aisling or be introduced to the bald dipstick. He would see Mia later. He had waited two weeks, he could hang on for another half-hour.

Myles's penis hung between the giant stone phallus and a tiny pink appendage that looked like a biro stub. He went across to look at it. The painting looked imposing, playful and colourful. Myles felt a gleam of delight as he read the title, 'Mr Tall'. The brochure listed the Mr Tall painting as retailing at £500.

He noticed a group of men a few paintings down from him. 'That's me,' a skinny guy said, indicating a long, skinny blue-veined penis in the shape of a rocket ship that was blasting through the earth's atmosphere. 'Recognise it anywhere.' 'So would I,' his friend said and they all chortled.

Myles looked around him. Each painting appeared to have at least one young man scrutinising it with extraordinary concentration. Myles recognised the fair-haired geek from Roolaboola's, a crestfallen expression on his face as he turned away from an exquisite rendering of a minute limp phallus.

A new painting hung on the wall opposite. He walked across to study it. The painting showed a large, extremely lopsided penis with a tiny pair of sunglasses perched playfully on the helmet. The lopsided penis was titled 'Mr Cool'. According to the brochure, Mr Cool retailed at £700. Why had Mia needed two weeks of time and space to paint a large lopsided langer? Whose langer was it? What had Mr Cool got that was worth £200 more than Mr Tall?

Myles looked around for a potential Mr Cool. The most immediate candidate was the pretentious bald dipstick standing alongside Mia and Aisling. As Myles watched, the dipstick excused himself, heading for the toilets. Without hesitation, Myles followed him. He wasn't sure what he was going to do if he did indeed turn out to be Mr Cool. He sensed that it was imperative to find out, however.

Inside the toilet, the dipstick stood at the urinal alongside a fat playwright in a puffy white suit that made him look like a butter mountain. The playwright urinated holding his penis with one hand, while with his free hand he held up for scrutiny a page of notes for his opening speech.

Myles stood next to the dipstick. Surreptitiously, he glanced down at the dipstick's penis. Straight, skinny and not lopsided at all. Definitely not wearing sunglasses.

While he was at it, Myles checked the fat playwright's equipment as well. He was short and stubby. He would have hated it if the fat playwright had turned out to be Mia's Mr Cool. Myles was about to relieve himself but something made him glance up to meet the gaze of the fat man.

'Can I help you?' the man said.

'No, it's OK, I was just looking for someone.'

Quickly, Myles zipped up and walked away from the urinals.

'Well I hope you find him soon,' the playwright called after him.

Outside, Myles ran into Stick who appeared to have been waiting for him.

'Tall people rule.' Stick gave a power salute.

'You said it,' Myles said.

The fat playwright passed them, ignoring Myles but giving Stick a grin. She took Myles's arm and led him away.

'I don't know where Aisling finds these turds,' she said, indicating the fat man. 'Last time she got some minister with a face like a bag of maggots. The time before it was a defrocked nun who wrote cookbooks, though I suppose that was interesting enough if you go in for that kind of thing.'

'How is Mia?' Myles asked.

'She's gift. Sold half the paintings already which is ace for a first exhibition. She's going to make savage fucking cash.'

'Has anyone said anything about the, eh, you know . . . the subject matter?'

'One or two. Most people think that it's an exhibition of flowers. Though someone did say that *The Sun* are sending a photographer.'

'That should help sales.'

Stick turned to look at Myles. 'So listen,' she said. 'Fancy a Slippery Nipple? We've got a stash of them in the corner.'

'Did Mia send you to look after me?' Myles asked.

Stick thought about it. 'Yes,' she said.

'OK,' Myles said. 'Lead on.'

He followed Stick to the corner where Garvin from Roolaboola's manned a small table containing rows of tall creamy drinks with umbrellas stuck in them. Garvin wore a tasteful brown trouser suit and matching headband. He looked like Lenny Kravitz. For a moment, Myles considered asking him to drop his trousers to check if his penis was lopsided or wore sunglasses.

'Well, here's to Mia,' Stick said and drank.

'Mia,' Myles repeated.

The Slippery Nipple tasted sweet and cold and he drank it down as though it was a cool orange drink. He wondered if he should buy the Mr Tall painting. He decided to wait to see if anyone else showed an interest in it. It would be quite a kick to have his penis portrait hanging in the lobby of the Bank of Ireland or someplace equally prominent and stuffy.

Aisling rang a little bell and everyone hushed. Aisling, Mia and the fat playwright stood in the centre of the floor. After a few words of welcome, Aisling introduced the man who waddled forward.

'It was either me or a politician,' he began, and the Hooray Shamuses and Sheilas tittered politely.

Myles caught Mia's eye and smiled. Nervous but glowing, she smiled back.

He drank two more Slippery Nipples during the playwright's boring, interminable speech about how writing plays and painting occupied the same canvas really when you got right down to it. Stick hesitated when he asked for another Nipple.

'Slow down. There's a big party afterwards.'

When the playwright had finished and the applause had died down, Mia slowly made her way through the crowd. The younger ones shook her hand or gave her kisses or embraced her. Some of the older art-lovers who had just realised the exhibition's true subject matter reacted as though Mia had turned toxic. A middle-age woman in a grey suit actually appeared to revolve across the floor to get out of her way. Mia came over to them. She embraced Stick and Myles, waved to Garvin who blew her a kiss.

'Congratulations,' Myles said. 'It's very impressive.'

'Thanks,' Mia said coyly. 'You say all the right things.'

'Just one more thing,' he said as nonchalantly as he could. 'Who's this Mr Cool?'

Mia met his gaze without blinking. Good sign. Or else she was a brilliant actress.

'How do you know it's not you in disguise?' she asked cheekily.

Everything was alright again. He had been an idiot to worry. Mia was an artist; she had needed some space to create her work. Nothing wrong with that. As he was reaching into his inside pocket to give her her surprise, Aisling appeared. Myles decided that the surprise could wait. Aisling nodded to Myles and he nodded back. A nod was as much as Aisling was getting from him.

'The Central Bank just bought the stone phallus,' Aisling announced. 'They think it's a painting of a tower.'

'Well it is, in a way,' Mia said.

'Too right girl. The Leaning Tower of Penis,' Stick said.

Aisling looked at Myles. 'I don't suppose you've bought anything, have you?'

Myles didn't look at her. 'Well, I was thinking of buying the Mr Tall. Only I don't trust you with my money.'

'Buy it anyway,' Aisling said cheerfully. 'Then you can always keep a spare prick in your house for when you're not around.'

'OK, you two,' Stick said. 'Calm down now, remember this is a celebration.'

If Mia had heard the exchange she didn't let on. 'When I have my next exhibition,' she said, 'I'm only going to invite real people.'

'Savage fucking idea, girl,' Stick said.

Aisling looked offended. 'Who are the real people?' she said sarcastically. 'I suppose you want bikers? Rock stars? Artists? Actors? E-heads and ravers?'

'Don't forget waitresses,' Mia said.

'Interior decorators,' Stick added.

'People who run cappuccino bars?' Myles offered.

'Exactly,' Mia grinned. 'Real people.'

'Well excuse me,' Aisling said grumpily. 'I only hope that these "real people" buy as many of your paintings as the "unreal" people I accidentally invited.'

Mia kissed Aisling on the cheek. 'Only codding. You've done a wonderful job. Thanks.'

Stick handed Mia and Aisling Slippery Nipples. The dipstick arrived to buttonhole Aisling while Stick and Lorcan went over to talk with Garvin. Myles was alone with Mia. Now that he had her full attention, he should make his move.

'What are you doing tomorrow night?' he asked.

'No plans.'

'I was wondering about my chances of taking you to dinner.'

Mia smiled. 'Depends where you're taking me.'

'It's a bit out of the way,' Myles said. 'A surprise. Here, I brought the menu.'

Myles produced a bulky envelope from his inside pocket and handed it to her.

'Ooooh, for me, I love surprises,' she beamed.

She opened the envelope. Two plane tickets for Venice as well as hotel reservations for a double room for three nights at La Serenissima. She studied the reservations and the tickets for a while, and then she put them back in the envelope. She seemed bewildered. He could see that she was simply blown away. She hadn't been expecting this.

'I don't know what to say.'

'I'll take that as a yes?' he said.

She looked at him for a moment. 'You're very sweet,' she said in a preoccupied faraway voice. 'Why shouldn't we go to Venice?' Then she raised her glass to him. 'Cheers.'

'Cheers,' he said.

They clinked their Slippery Nipples.

'You're really sweet,' she repeated.

Soft breezes caressed his face like gentle gusts of air from a carefully aimed hairdryer.

He stood on the deck of the swaying Vaporetto struggling to

hold onto Mia as well as keep his balance. Mia leaned backwards in his grip, head back and eyes closed with her arms thrown out, as though overcome by the scale and majesty of the tall ornate buildings that rose up on either side rather than the six gin and tonics she had downed earlier on the flight. Myles had matched Mia drink for drink and like her had almost fallen down the steps onto the airport tarmac. Now the sight and smells of Venice in the late afternoon had sobered him, only to have the opposite effect on Mia. At least she had stopped singing 'O Solo Mio'.

As the boat turned into the main waterway, Myles noticed that the breeze carried a faint yet sweetly unpleasant odour of rotting fruit.

'You OK?' he asked as Mia stretched in his arms.

She opened her eyes. '*Dante Alighieri*,' she said.

'Pardon?'

'*Antonio Vivaldi*,' she proclaimed, punching the air to emphasise each name. 'James McNeill Whistler, Titian, Percy Bysshe Shelley, Lord Byron . . .'

As Mia continued with her recitation, Myles glanced about him. The passengers nearby gave him knowing grins. Venice intoxicated boatloads of young lovers. Mia's performance was no big thing. The boat passed a long, white rectangular building so flamboyantly brocaded it reminded him of the front of Elvis's Las Vegas outfit. He wished that Mia would calm down so that he could concentrate on enjoying the sights.

'All of those famous people lived or worked here, did you know that?' Mia sighed.

'Of course,' he said. 'You left out a couple of important ones.'

'Who?'

'Mia Powell and Myles Sheridan.'

She looked at him. 'Sorry.' She smiled. 'Now I guess I'll just have to start again.'

'Don't,' he said, but she giggled and began the recitation anew.

When the Vaporetto docked they grabbed their overnight bags and disembarked. He began asking directions to La Serenissima but she took his arm and steered him along the seafront.

'Where are we going?'

'You'll see,' she said.

Harry's Bar was on the ground floor of a rectangular yellow building. From the outside it looked like a travel office. Inside, the clientele was composed of tourists and a few tanned yachty types. Mia led him to the counter where she ordered Bellinis. The barman went to a small white fridge and removed two skinny wide-lipped shot glasses. He added a drop of peach juice to each glass, and then handed them to Mia and Myles.

'To Venice,' Mia said.

'Venice,' he said, and drank.

At first taste, the Bellini made him quiver. It was like pouring liquid frost into his veins. After he had drained the glass, however, he experienced an extraordinary, almost hallucinogenic, light-headedness. Mia gazed at him as though she was savouring his delight.

'Told you, didn't I?' she said and ordered two more.

'Shouldn't we hit the hotel now?' he said.

'Never put off till tomorrow what you can do today. Besides, this is Bellini time.'

After the fourth round of Bellinis, the bar began to fill up. A yachty couple sat down opposite, the man's skin as tanned as copper, the woman's brown and wrinkled like an old shoe. The couple were Dutch, but Mia spoke to them in Italian and soon they were chatting as though they had known each other for years. Myles relaxed, relieved that he was unable to join in the discussion. Last night, when he had announced that he was flying to Venice to write an article, Lucy had shrugged. 'When are you going to take me to Venice,' she had said, leaving the room before he could tell her another bunch of lies. She hadn't even asked what the article was about.

Now he was glad to have made it to Venice, but he felt tired and sticky and in dire need of a shower and some hot food. He wished they could just go to the hotel. Mia had been in a strange humour all day, as though on a mission to get absolutely scuttered. He guessed that she was feeling very emotional about being back in Venice. She probably half-expected to meet the ghost of Barry. Or perhaps she expected Psychodad to climb out of the sea dripping with seaweed to haul her back home again.

After a few rounds, Mia and her new friends got it into their heads that they should teach Myles to speak basic Italian.

'That vay you cood join in ze converzation,' Copperman said.

'A better way would be if you all spoke English,' Myles replied.

'Ah, dat's too easy,' Shoewoman said. 'You wood not learn anyzing.'

'Yes I would,' Myles said. 'I'd learn what the hell you were talking about.'

The couple thought that Myles was hilarious. 'We must teach him to zay dat in Italian,' Shoewoman said. 'He iz such a funny perzon.'

Mia said, 'We'll start off with how to order a Bellini.'

Tired and drunk for the second time that day, and with his stomach performing starvation somersaults every few minutes, Myles was in no mood to learn a new language. Hoping that they would give up quickly if he was really inept, he deliberately failed to grasp anything they attempted to teach him. His efforts only made them laugh harder.

'Just keep drinking those zings and zoon you will be fluent,' Copperman said.

Unable to keep pace with the gaiety, Myles put his head down and closed his eyes.

He found himself being led out of the bar into the glittering night. He stumbled along, holding onto Mia's arm. Mia appeared sober now. She carried her bag on her shoulder and steered Myles through the narrow alleyways, past rows of bright garish shops, every one of which seemed to be hawking white Venetian masks. There was still light left in the pink sky. A shadow of a tall leaning oarsman appeared on the building in front of them.

'Let's take a gondola,' Myles said.

'No,' Mia said firmly. 'I'm surprised at you, Myles. We've already discussed this. Gondolas are too expensive.'

'But it's Venice,' he said. 'Besides, money isn't a problem.'

'You should always be careful with money,' Mia said. 'Anyway, we've already agreed, no gondolas.'

'Since when?' Myles challenged, suddenly belligerent.

'Since always,' Mia said.

Myles stopped. 'I want to go on a gondola.'

'Fine,' she said. 'Go on your own if you want to.'

'But it's romantic.'

'Not to me.'

'OK, I'll go on my own.'

'Fine. Be romantic on your own then.'

They walked in silence for a time, still holding onto each other's arms. After a while Myles felt silly for arguing with Mia in a wonderful place like Venice.

'How about tomorrow?' he said.

'No,' she said. They walked for a few hundred yards before Mia shrugged. 'Then again I could always change my mind.'

They stopped and kissed on a small bridge, only breaking apart when Myles's bag almost toppled into the canal.

La Serenissima was halfway down a narrow alleyway beside a small elegant bridge. At the tiny check-in desk in the lobby, the dapper seen-it-all-before concierge welcomed them to Venice. Ignoring their giggles, Seen-It-All-Before showed them to their room on the second floor.

'Enjoy your stay. There is just one rule you must keep. Please do not feed the birds.' He left the room, closing the door behind him.

Opening a window, Myles looked out upon a narrow cobbled street where the click-clacking of footsteps on cobbles mingled with the bustle and cooing of battalions of grey and brown pigeons who occupied every inch of rooftop, rain gutter and window ledge. In the confined space of the street, the pigeons sounded like clashing armies of football hooligans. When he turned around, Mia lay stretched on the bed, naked.

'When you've finished admiring the birdies,' she said. 'Or maybe you'd prefer to hop on a gondola.'

He threw off his clothes and they began to make love. The sex was awkward, halting and constantly interrupted. At first he couldn't get hard. Then he couldn't get it in. For some reason he hadn't been expecting sex. At least not so soon after arriving. He had presumed that they would shower first, then maybe go out to dinner. Afterwards, drink wine by candlelight. Then would come lovemaking and intimacy. That was the way it had played out in his head for the last few weeks. The reality was a bit too abrupt for him. It required co-ordination bordering on athleticism which was too much for a man who had downed half-a-dozen gins and half-a-dozen Bellinis on an empty stomach. First, he accidentally prodded her with his elbow. Next she kneed him in the stomach. After that, he banged his head into hers.

'Jesus, what are you trying to do, kill me?' she said.

'It's OK,' he assured her. 'I'm just not used to Italian beds.'

Their pathetic failure to get any rhythm going became almost spiritual. They were both too drunk and tired to make love, or else this was the worst sex that either had ever experienced. Eventually, without a word, they spontaneously gave up and rolled over on their sides, backs to each other. Myles dropped off immediately.

He dreamt of babbling water and tall buildings and of a perplexing attempt to paddle up O'Connell Street in a gondola. In the morning he awoke to the squawk and squabble of pigeons throwing a party on the window ledge. From the street below came the sound of somebody singing an aria. For a city without cars or motorbikes or bicycles, the hullabaloo was astonishing.

He felt around for Mia but she was gone. He noticed a scrawled note on the pillow.

'Gone for a walk. Back later. X. Mia.'

He got up and dressed quickly, excitement mounting in him. The first day of his new life as a man of the world. On the flight, he had read about two ninth-century merchants who had stolen the body of St Mark from its resting place in Egypt and brought it to Venice. Venice could attribute much of its later prosperity and success to that act of cunning and theft, the article had argued. Myles reckoned that Venice was an appropriate place for Mia and himself to start a new life of travel, shopping, sun and sex and whatever else they wanted now that he was rich.

He refused to accept that the money he now possessed had

been stolen. The money was dirty in the first place. All he was doing was putting it to good use. In time he would invest some of it in case he and Mia ever decided to have kids. In the same way that the merchants had brought the body of St Mark to Venice to attract money from pilgrims to realise their dream, Myles and Mia would use the dirty money to do something worthwhile with their lives. After all, if you could steal the body of a saint and get away with it . . . By the time he had descended to the lobby his hangover wasn't too bad, just rough enough to kick a hole in a wall.

Seen-It-All-Before nodded to him. That fellow must never stop working, Myles thought. In the small breakfast room, he drank café au lait and ate a chocolate croissant.

Afterwards, feeling ravenous yet alert, he left the hotel and walked through the narrow streets and along the rows of busy shops selling Venetian masks and trinkets. He savoured the aroma of food mingled with the sweet smell from the sea. Soft breezes lapped at his skin. Everywhere the constant clopping of feet on cobbles.

Venetians were quite small, he noticed. Most around five foot five. Here he was Gulliver amongst the Lilliputians. Once, entering an alleyway, he experienced the sensation of a gondola slowly appearing around a corner, majestic and lugubrious, complete with colourful striped-shirted gondolier and the delicious dipping of oars. As though he had stepped through a time portal into a medieval city. He didn't care how much it cost. He was going to take Mia on a gondola ride even if he had to drag her aboard.

St Mark's Square was loud with clattering and awash with fluttering, diving, strutting pigeons. People sat at tables outside lavish cafes that glittered in the harsh sunlight. Outside Florian's a small orchestra played sentimental music on a makeshift podium. A woman stood in the centre of the square, covered in pigeons, as her friends took pictures. On the clock roof of a tall building, mechanical medieval characters clanged a bell.

Walking through the square, a delicious dreamy sensation of serenity overcame him. He felt privileged to have now chimed into a hidden tranquillity that had been the preserve of Venice for centuries. He understood why Mia was so enamoured of the place.

Perhaps they would buy an apartment here. He wondered if Mia was in one of the cafés at this moment, sipping cappuccino. He wondered if she was searching the shops to buy him a present.

In a small square a few hundred yards from St Mark's, he noticed a red-headed mannequin in the window of a clothes shop. The mannequin displayed a bejewelled denim jacket. The jacket was stylish, engraved, and studded with tiny azure and opal gems. On impulse he went inside and bought the jacket as a present for Mia. Once she saw it, she would agree to go on a gondola with him.

Back at La Serenissima, there was no sign of her. Not even a message. He paced about in the narrow street outside, carrying the carefully wrapped jacket. Being in Venice must be hard for her. That was the reason she had got drunk yesterday, and it probably explained why their lovemaking had been so dire. She was thinking about Barry. Myles knew that he must be patient. It was just that he had never expected to have to compete with a ghost.

He went to a nearby café and ordered a cappuccino and three more chocolate croissants. When he had finished he went back to the hotel and dropped Mia's present into their bedroom. Then he went downstairs and checked at the desk for messages. Seen-It-All-Before told him that there were no messages for him and that he had not seen the 'Signorina' since she left this morning at six.

'She left at six?' Myles was astonished. It was lunchtime now. Mia had been on a six-hour walk.

'Yes,' he said. 'She say that she receive a call on her mobile and she must go immediately.'

'Mia doesn't have a mobile,' Myles said, but Seen-It-All-Before shrugged and made a face that implied that as far as he was concerned all women had mobiles.

Myles wandered outside and stood in the street trying to make sense of things. Since when had Mia had a mobile phone? Where could she have disappeared to for six hours? How come she had told Seen-It-All-Before about a phone call, while all she had left for Myles was a note saying that she had gone for a walk? Maybe the pressure had got to her. Maybe her memory had gone. Could she be wandering about somewhere, confused and distraught?

On impulse he walked down to the waterfront and looked around. He paced along the jetty where the Vaporetti docked, and scoured the crowds for her. Retrace their steps from the day before. That was the only plan he could think of.

After a while he made his way to Harry's Bar. With a jittery feeling he walked down the few steps and went inside. Through the tourists, he caught a glimpse of red hair in the far corner. Mia was talking earnestly to someone that he couldn't see because of the crowd. She looked up and saw him and stopped talking. He smiled at her but she didn't smile back. His heart stopped. Confused and afraid of what he was about to find, he moved closer until he had an unimpeded view.

Mia sat beside Pat. They held hands as they looked up at him with a mixture of relief and defiance. Pat's dark eyes were warm but also resolute. There were Bellinis on the table in front of them. Myles knew that he didn't have to look for Mr Cool anymore. He didn't have to ask if Pat's langer was lopsided. He walked up to the table where they sat and pulled up a stool. He sat down facing them. The jitters had gone. Instead he felt numb, as though his emotions had been surgically removed and thrown into the canal.

Mia looked at him with cool green eyes.

'I've got something to tell you,' she said.

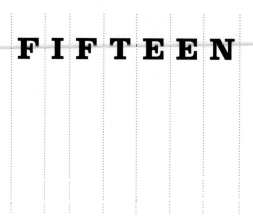

FIFTEEN

Gondoliers

They sat like undertakers waiting for a corpse to be wheeled in. Myles adjusted his chair and was surprised at how calm he felt as Mia prepared the big explanation speech. Alongside her, Pat looked as though he had swallowed a small animal.

'I want us to break up,' Mia said. 'I didn't set out to hurt anyone. The thing with Patrick just happened.'

Myles couldn't see what was so great about Harry's bar anymore. The place looked squeaky-clean and insipid, with all the warmth of an operating theatre. Someone should slap some rudders and sails and mastheads onto the walls, then convert the lounge into a ship's ballroom with fancy chairs and tables. Replace the chandelier with a gondola festooned with lightbulbs. Maybe with a real gondolier in it. That would liven up the place.

Mia continued. 'I should have told you before now that I had found someone else, but I didn't want to hurt your feelings.' She waited for this to sink in.

'Thanks very much,' Myles said.

Pat drew himself up smartly in case Myles tried anything. What could he possibly do in Harry's Bar: stab them with their own Bellini glasses? Beat them to death with a chocolate croissant?

Staring straight ahead as though she might waver in her purpose if she caught Myles's eye, Mia explained that in the beginning she had fought against her feelings for Pat, as Pat had fought against his feelings for her. Beside her, Pat nodded, sighing quietly to show that he had fought the good fight but had had to concede.

'In the end I knew that I had to go with it. It was a once in a lifetime thing,' Mia said.

This Mia was not even a distant cousin of the Mia he knew. She spoke in a flat voice, as though reciting lines from memory. It was obvious that someone had coached and cajoled and brainwashed her until she believed the rubbish she was spouting. Myles wanted to make her laugh. Snap her out of the spell she was under. Suddenly he caught himself. Wait a second here. Mia was breaking it off with him in Venice, city of romance. She had lured him here then betrayed him with Pat. Yet Myles still wanted to comfort *her*. What was wrong with this picture?

Myles looked up to find that Mia had finished speaking and was staring at him, awaiting his response.

'Well I can't say that I'm surprised,' he lied. 'I've known about this for ages.'

Pat and Mia looked at each other.

'You have?' Mia said.

'Of course.' Myles decided to push it a bit further. 'All the little signs gave you away. I saw the looks you gave each other in the nightclub. I knew there was something going on.'

Mia looked stricken. 'You did?'

'Only a complete eejit could have missed it,' Myles said smugly.

Pat turned to Mia, 'I knew we should have been a bit more careful.'

'Why didn't you say something?' Mia asked.

Myles shrugged. 'I've always believed in freedom of choice.' Now that he thought back on it, Myles had indeed noticed certain give-away signs. The night in Roolaboola's when they had staged an argument. The recce to Howth where they had pretended to dislike each other. Mia's drunken behaviour on the trip to Venice. Myles had suspected all along. It was just that he had underestimated Pat's brainwashing abilities. He didn't want Pat to leave here thinking that he had got one up on him. Of course Pat *had* got one up on him – he had stolen Myles's girl – but that was beside the point. At least now Myles could take some solace from having denied Pat and Mia their notions of a totally clandestine affair.

'I hope we can stay friends,' Mia said. 'You don't stop caring about a person just because you happen to fall for somebody else.'

Pat looked uncomfortable.

'Maybe we could talk about this back at the hotel,' Myles said. Mia smiled as though she had been waiting for just this opportunity to put things straight once and for all.

'Myles, you're a nice guy but . . .' she began.

Myles switched off. He didn't hear the rest of Mia's sentence. He didn't need to. No man had ever made a comeback after being called a 'nice guy'. He hoped that nobody in the bar had heard her calling him that.

Now that he thought about it, he could see that Harry's Bar badly needed a soundproof booth in the corner where people could discuss important issues without being disturbed or worried that their words were being overheard. The booth could be fitted with a special panel of buttons that corresponded to pictures of individual drinks. To order a Bellini for instance, you simply pressed the button under the appropriate picture. It would be an exciting new development in barroom technology. He would have to start working on it once he escaped from here. He would probably make millions. That would make a pleasant change – to make big money without having to wear a mask and chase someone off a cliff.

'Anyway, you've got a girlfriend,' Mia announced as a majestic coup de grâce, as though it absolved her of all responsibility.

'It's all over between us.'

'Have you told her?'

'Em, not exactly,' Myles said. 'I don't have to because she knows how things stand.'

'You've got a kid.'

Myles pointed at Pat. 'So what? He's got kids too. Loads of them, all over the place.'

'I know all about Darren,' Mia's face became taut. 'It's not a problem because Patrick's basically single. You're still living with your girlfriend.'

'Well, so are lots of people,' Myles said weakly, not really knowing where he was going with this line of argument. 'Having kids or living with someone never stopped people from behaving like human beings.'

Everyone looked totally confused. Mia opened her mouth to reply but then thought better of it. As she closed it again, her teeth made a little clipping sound like shutting the clasp on a handbag. She took Pat's hand.

'Yeah, well,' she shrugged. 'Whatever.'

Mia was herself again. The middle-class girl with the enchanting smile and the sexy giggle who had grown up with the assumption that she would be rich someday. Except that the vivid green eyes that had once gazed lovingly at Myles were now directed at Pat. Funny how Pat had now become 'Patrick'. As though going with Mia made him respectable. Myles figured that Mia and 'Patrick' must have been seeing each other for at least a month. Maybe longer. The betrayal didn't hurt as much as being played for an idiot. He had been their paper hanky, each had blown their noses on him and now he was being tossed into a bin. Myles wondered how long Aisling had known about this. Or Stick. Or that dweeb of a younger brother, Lorcan. It wouldn't surprise him if the whole town had known. You couldn't trust anyone. He ruminated on when exactly Mia had painted the Mr Cool portrait. Did having a lopsided penis make any difference in bed?

On the table in front of Mia, a pile of empty chocolate wrappers lay carefully folded. Tokens of a morning spent rehearsing. Pat leaned forward frowningly, as though the survival of the human race hung upon what he was about to say.

'I know this is tough. I hope we do not overreact here and lose the run of ourselves. I would absolutely hate it if I lost a friend over this development. All's fair in love and war. Maybe that's not a great way of putting it, but it gets the right vibe across.'

Pat was looking at him expectantly. Myles did not feel bitter or angry. Those feelings could not alter what had happened. The situation was clear to him: Pat had become jealous of Myles and Mia and had set out to take Mia away from him, just to prove that he could. Pat had no great interest in Mia. Taking her away from Myles was the only way that Pat knew to assert his manhood. Pat was a sad bastard really when you got down to it, but Myles could not summon up the energy to feel sorry for him. Mia was the one who deserved sympathy. She was going to get hurt terribly when Pat dumped her.

Myles gave a big shrug, followed by what he hoped was a wry smile. 'What's done is done,' he said, signalling the barman. As Pat and Mia watched him cautiously, Myles ordered a Bellini for himself along with two more for 'my friends'. 'No reason why we can't be civilised about this,' he explained.

'I knew you'd take it well. You're a real gentleman,' Mia said, turning to Pat. 'Didn't I always say that Myles was a real gentleman?'

Relieved that there wasn't going to be an unpleasant scene, Pat spread his arms. 'Sure, you only have to look at the man to know that,' he said.

Myles imagined Pat's plane touching down last night while he and Mia had been having crap sex on the creaky bed in La Serenissima. Pat must have left a message on Mia's secret mobile. First thing this morning she had sneaked away for a lover's tryst with Mr Cool of the lopsided penis while Mr Eejit Myles lay asleep in the small hotel room overlooking the street that was home to the most boisterous pigeons on earth, all cousins to the one he had shot in Dublin. 'Gone for a walk. Back soon. X. Mia.'

'I wouldn't blame you for being angry,' Mia said almost cheerfully. 'I should have been honest with you a long time ago.'

'It's just one of those things,' Myles said.

'Please don't hate me,' Mia said in a small voice. 'Promise you won't.'

He leaned across to her with a concerned expression. 'Well, I'm afraid that this means that there'll be no more lifts home.' Mia looked at him as though he had just plucked off his nose. He spread his arms wide. 'I mean, where am I going to find a horse in this place.'

Mia giggled. In an instant they re-established intimacy. He noticed that her ponytail had loosened, a few curly strands dangling coyly over her right eye. The way she looked sometimes after sex. Even after the crap sex in the hotel. There was still something between them. She hadn't totally surrendered herself to Pat.

Then the barman arrived with the drinks and the contact was broken. He couldn't believe that Mia wasn't with him anymore. He couldn't believe that she preferred Pat. He couldn't believe that Pat would do this to him. He pushed the thoughts away.

'To Venice,' Myles said, raising his glass.

They all clinked glasses and drank. The tension between them eased.

'Here,' Pat said. 'Has anyone noticed the strange Peggy Dell about the place?'

Myles nodded.

'It's the algae,' Mia said.

They both looked at her.

'Algae?' Myles said.

Mia nodded sagely. 'Yes, the algae, you know.'

'Ah yes, that explains everything.' Pat raised his eyes to heaven.

Mia thumped him playfully on the arm. 'I can't believe you haven't heard.'

'We have heard but we've forgotten,' Myles said, throwing Pat a wink, letting on to the sad crinkly-eyed bastard that they were still friends.

Mia said matter-of-factly, 'There's this foul smelling algae all around Venice that is rapidly multiplying out of control. Every week they go out on boats to pour weed killer or algae killer on it but it keeps spreading. Now it looks as though Venice could be overrun in a couple of years.'

'Heavy vibes,' Pat said. 'Venice could end up too smelly for anyone to bother with.'

'I hope not,' Mia said.

'Good news for us, Miss Mint,' Pat said. 'We would just have the place to ourselves.'

Miss Mint?

Something snapped behind Myles's civilised exterior as 'Miss Mint' and 'Patrick' looked into each other's eyes, all lovey-dovey. They seemed to have forgotten about him. As though he had no feelings. As though he didn't matter. Myles decided that the sound-proof booth should be equipped with special trapdoors under the seats. That way, individuals whose conversation proved boring or whose behaviour was unwholesome or who had drunk peppermint tea with someone's girlfriend could be deposited in the canal at the flick of the appropriate switch.

'Oh listen, there's good news from home,' Mia said, as though they were a group of friends on holidays. 'My exhibition has almost sold out. Isn't that brilliant?'

Myles nodded. 'That's brilliant,' he said. He wondered if anyone had bought the Mr Tall painting.

Mia's expression changed to a pout. 'Even though *The Irish Times* reviewer said that "the work of this artist is shallow, vainglorious and preening".'

Pat scratched his beard. 'He the guy who said that the paintings were "well hung"?'

'Well, he would say that, wouldn't he?' Mia sipped her drink. She giggled. 'Some of them were.'

Myles caught a glance that passed quickly between Mia and Pat. They were mocking him. Secretly, they probably called him 'Goalpost'. Suddenly, Myles didn't want to hear any more stuff about 'exhibitions' and he didn't want to spend any more time opposite 'Miss Mint' and 'Patrick'. He felt a strange irrepressible tide of bile rise inside him. He broke into what he hoped was a disarming smile.

'So listen, there's something I have to know,' Myles said, and they turned to him. 'Is sex with Mr Cool here better because his prick is lopsided?'

They looked at him for a long time. Myles noticed a sudden stillness in the bar. The barman had stopped doing whatever he was doing and all of the customers seemed to be looking across at them. Pat stared intently at Myles's face as though picking out a spot to land a punch.

'It's not about sex,' Mia said. 'It's just—'

'I thought we were going to be civilised,' Pat interrupted.

'We are. I was just asking a simple civilised question,' Myles said. 'Is sex better when it's straight or lopsided?'

'You must have a very shallow view of relationships if you think that sex is all that matters,' Mia said.

'Maybe I could go to a gym. I could hang little weights off the side of it to make it lopsided,' Myles said brightly.

'Myles, why are you being like this?' Mia said.

'Like what?' Myles said. 'I bet there are little barbells I could use.'

'There's no need for that kind of talk,' Pat said.

'What's wrong with barbells?' Myles asked. 'Just trying to have a discussion here.'

'Is that going to solve anything?' Mia said.

'Alright, alright, talking about solutions, I've an idea,' Myles said. He waited until he had their complete attention and they were glaring at him. 'I suppose a threesome is out of the question?'

'Now you're asking for a fist sandwich,' Pat said.

'Eh, no thanks.' Myles pushed his chair back as Pat got to his feet.

'OK,' Mia said. 'I'll just leave you two boys to it.' She stood and grabbed her purse.

Suddenly realising that he might be left alone with Pat, Myles rose, blocking Mia's exit. For a moment, the three of them stood and looked at each other.

Myles smiled. 'Stay where you are. I'll go check out the algae. The air outside is bound to be better than in here anyway.' Mia said nothing. Just stood there looking frozen. Pat put his large hand on her shoulder but she shrugged it off. Myles interpreted that as a small victory. 'Miss Mint' and 'Patrick' now had something to remember him by. Now they knew that he wasn't going to be walked on. Myles left them there and walked out of the bar.

Outside, he immediately felt a rush of remorse. He had walked out on Mia. Left her there with Pat. Now he felt sorry for her. Which he knew was thick. The thing with Pat wouldn't last. They didn't have the right chemistry, anyone could see that. Who would be there to catch Mia when she fell? Now there were flies buzzing in Myles's head. He felt confused and his legs felt wobbly. He scoured the jettyside for a place to sit down and think things through.

Just then he heard a voice hailing him. He turned and waited as Pat ran to catch up. Pat didn't seem angry anymore. Instead he appeared friendly. Here comes old pal Pat, anxious not to let a little thing like stealing Myles's girl come between them.

'There you are, I was afraid I was going to miss you,' he said breathlessly.

'How is she?' Myles asked.

'She's fine. You know how they get at big emotional moments.'

'Buy her another Bellini. She likes them.'

'Who are you telling,' Pat paused, suddenly unsure of what he wanted to express. Myles enjoyed the spectacle of seeing the usually confident Pat so wrong-footed.

'We've always been . . .' Pat began and trailed off. 'I just wanted to say that . . .' He stuck out his chin. 'Here look, plant one on me, I mean it. If anyone deserves a fist sandwich, then it's me. Go ahead.'

Myles considered punching Pat's broad, whiskered chin. Break his jaw. Knock out all his front teeth. Change smiling 'Patrick' to toothless Pat. No, he decided. Too lenient. Pat could have his jaw rewired. He could get dentures. He might hit Myles back.

'No, you're alright.' Myles started to walk away but Pat caught up with him.

'Listen, would it be OK if I stroll with you for a while? I don't want it to end like this.'

Myles shrugged. 'Suit yourself.'

They walked along in silence for a few moments. Through the queues of passengers for the Vaporetti. Along the line of handsome hotels and lively cappuccino bars. Past swarms of young couples joyfully exploring Venice. Everywhere ahead of them rows of swaying gondolas next to tall barbershop poles. Their nostrils filled with the sweet smell from the palely rolling sea.

Pat spoke. 'Listen dude. Don't be angry with us.'

'Who says I'm angry?'

'You know it won't last. Maybe we'll get a couple of good years out of it. Maybe only a few months. Love is a temporary condition, but sometimes the vibe hangs around for years, know what I mean?'

'No,' Myles said.

Pat sighed. 'A woman like Mia is never going to stay with anyone, and that's fine. I accept that. My thing is, I go with the flow as long as there's something there. Keep it mellow. I don't expect too much. That way, when the scene gets stale, I'm gone. Like the wind. Do you get me?' He puffed up his cheeks, made a flapping gesture with his hand to show a big wind blowing everything away. 'Anyway, look at the bright side. At least you have the few bob stashed. Hey, we robbed the laundry and got away clean, didn't we? It's not all doom and gloom.'

'How long have you been shagging her?' Myles said.

They stopped and stood awkwardly for a few moments, neither really looking at the other.

'We haven't had sex,' Pat said softly. 'Mia felt that it wouldn't be right until the scene with you was sorted.'

Myles was impressed. Pat must have been chewing his beard in frustration. Probably the first time that anything like that had ever happened to the Casanova of the Inner City. Pat had told him to soften the blow, Myles supposed. That was big of him. Either that or the bastard was lying.

'I wanted to have these few words with you,' Pat said. 'I just thought it was important.'

'Thanks,' Myles said, and thought things over for a moment. 'Look, don't worry about anything. Mia and I were running out of steam anyway.'

Pat nodded sympathetically, anxious to make amends. 'Well, you know,' he began. 'If you were serious about the threesome thing I'm sure we could work something out. I'll have a word with M—'

'No, no, that's OK.' Myles held up his hands. 'Forget all that stuff. I just need some time to myself.'

Pat took a step back, raised his hands. 'No problem. Take all the time you need.'

'Yeah well, I'd better go and get my stuff,' Myles said.

Neither moved. They heard the soft reassuring lapping of water against the quay.

'Good luck,' Myles said.

Pat put out his hand. Myles shook it and before he could react Pat had pulled him close and enveloped him in a big bear hug. Immediately Pat's voice hissed in Myles's ear, firm and menacing. 'Please don't get any strange ideas, sure you won't? I would really hate that. You get me?'

The bear hug tightened.

'I get you,' Myles croaked, and immediately Pat relaxed his grip. He released Myles then slapped him on the shoulder. All smiles again. Pat's eyes crinkled with friendship. He nodded. 'Listen. Maybe in a couple of weeks I'll give you a call. Have a scoop or something.' Pat rumbled a low laugh. 'Hey, who knows, the thing with Mia might be all over by then.' He winked. 'Tell you something though. I am really looking forward to tonight.'

Still smiling, he turned and strolled away. Myles stood and watched him go.

Then he turned and walked back towards the hotel, squinting hard against the breeze to keep the tears from rolling down his face.

Myles took a gondola across the canal to the terminus for the airport. He lay back and told himself that he was enjoying the breeze and the gently swaying motion. The gondolier was a sullen little fellow with huge shoulders. He didn't sing. Perhaps he only did that for couples. Or for huge tips.

At the other side, he paid the gondolier the amount asked for and took a bus to the airport. Making his way through the crowds, he eventually found the right queue for check-in. He heard Pat's words ringing around in his head. 'Really looking forward to tonight.'

The bastard couldn't let things go without having a final dig at Myles. All that talk about 'not wanting it to end like this'. Just to give Myles something to think about for the flight home. He imagined Pat and Mia on a gondola with the sullen gondolier singing to them. He heard Pat call Mia 'Miss Mint'. Heard Mia's answering giggle. 'I am really looking forward to tonight,' Pat leered. Myles had the sullen big-shouldered gondolier bringing his oar down savagely on Pat's head. He saw Pat topple into the canal with a splash.

At the check-in desk the woman attendant changed Myles's ticket reservation without fuss. As though she was well used to the spectacle of jilted lovers returning early and alone from romantic Venice.

'Would you prefer an aisle seat or a window seat?' the woman asked.

'I thought he was my friend,' Myles said quietly. 'He said he didn't sleep with her but I don't believe the bastard.'

The woman looked at him for a moment.

'I'll put you down for a window seat,' she said.

Once in his seat, Myles read the in-flight magazine until the plane took off.

When they were airborne he put the magazine back in the seat rack in front of him. Turning, he found his father sitting next to him. He had a sympathetic expression on his crumpled face.

'You can never rely on the reading material on board these things,' his father said. 'It's always advisable to bring your own.'

'Why didn't you remind me to buy magazines at the airport shop?'

'Because you can't read Italian. Sure amn't I always looking out for your interests?'

'Not that I've noticed.'

Myles fidgeted with his seat belt. He was aware of his father studying his face for tell-tale signs of weakness.

His father adjusted his seat. 'I hope the movie will be good.'

'There's no movie, it's a short flight.'

'Shite. I was looking forward to it. I haven't seen a good film in yonks.' He sighed. 'That's typical of you to go for a cheap European jaunt. Next time you run off with a young one, go to the US or somewhere that's a decent spin away, will you?'

'I'll bear it in mind,' Myles said.

Myles turned away. He didn't want to see his father's lived-in crumpled face. He didn't want to see the army uniform with the shiny buttons on the lapels. In a while, he heard his father giving a long soft sigh, followed immediately by the sound of low rattly breathing. When he sneaked a glance, his father was asleep.

The stewardess brought lunch on a small tray. Myles removed the wrapping. Burnt-looking salmon in a grungy sauce with three mangy string beans and a single slice of yellowing tomato. The side salad carried a faint whiff of rotting fruit. Myles left the food on the tray and picked up the in-flight magazine again. He began to read an article about Singapore but he couldn't concentrate. Spreading the magazine on his lap, he rested his head on the back of the seat and stared out of the window. He daydreamed uneasily and fitfully about the pigeons on the rooftops outside the hotel room, and about Mia's green eyes. He began to feel hot and tired. After a while he fell asleep.

He was a small boy holding his father's hand as he looked up at the strings of coloured beads hung across the trees in O'Connell Street. They stood on a large platform with the lord mayor and some other colourfully dressed people. Tinsel and stars and other Christmas decorations dangled from the poles as well as from the cinema marquees on either side of the wide street. The lord mayor spoke into a microphone to a dark mass of people. Zillions of bright-eyed faces peered back. His father leaned down to whisper in his ear. 'Now watch while I throw a little light on the subject,' he said. His father went over to the front of the platform, pulled a lever and the coloured beads across the trees blazed into dazzling brightness. His father pulled more levers and from every corner and crevice more light poured forth until it was brighter than daylight, all multi-coloured and glittering like a cartoon city. The crowd cheered and the lord mayor led them in 'We wish you a Merry Christmas'. It was as though the people were singing to thank his father for turning on the lights. His father bent down and winked at him. 'I am really looking forward to tonight,' he said.

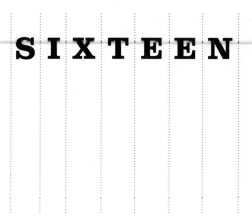

SIXTEEN

Scumbags

Lucy held the bejewelled jacket out in front of her. She turned it and the tiny studded gems caught the light, sparkling like a personal galaxy.

'Oh Myles,' she said, 'it's stunning.'

'Just a little thing I picked up,' he said.

'It must have cost a fortune,' she said, slipping the jacket on. It looked sleek and sexy and trim on Lucy. It could have been specially made for her. As she inspected herself in the mirror, Myles sat down on the bed, relieved. Maybe there was something to be said for falling for a woman who wore the same size jacket as the mother of your child.

'It's really me, isn't it?' She sounded thrilled.

'Yes, it's really you.'

Lucy came over and kissed him. 'Thank you.' She sat on the edge of the bed, a strange inquisitive look in her eye. She smiled. 'So does this mean that it's over?'

Myles played for time. 'Is what over?'

'You and the young one, whatever her name is.'

There was no right answer. If he said no, she wouldn't believe him and he would be admitting to the affair with Mia; if he said yes, he would be leaving himself open. The way Lucy carried on you'd think that they were married.

'Nothing happened,' he said. 'She was just a friend. I don't do that sort of thing anymore.'

There was a silence. Lucy raised a sceptical eyebrow.

Myles held up his hands. 'I swear. You've nothing to worry about.'

'Who says I'm worried.' She fingered one of the tiny green studs on the lapel of the jacket. He could see that she wasn't convinced. He could have told her the truth, but then he would have had a lot of explaining to do. No point in stirring up grief and argument, especially now the thing with Mia really was over. Until Pat broke her heart anyway.

Lucy stood. 'Well anyway. We can talk about it after your mother's birthday party.'

She walked over to the mirror, opening the jacket. 'What do you think? Buttoned or unbuttoned?' She fastened the buttons to show him, then undid them again.

Myles pretended to give the matter deep consideration. 'Unbuttoned.'

'Really?'

'Definitely.'

'Right.'

A final check in the mirror, then Lucy was satisfied. 'Come on, your mother's waiting and Justine wants you to see her bringing in the cake.'

He had got away with it, he thought. Lucy was delighted with the jacket. The worst that could happen now was that she would try to get him to attend another therapy session with that insipid cucumber, Frank Forage. He decided that he would attend just to stop the whingeing. After that, who knows? The thing was to get through the next few weeks. Give himself time to think things through. At least he still had the money. That was something.

They went out of the bedroom, down the stairs and through the side door to the pub. Inside, the place was packed with well

wishers, friends and musicians, as well as the usual shower of
hangers-on who were slobbering for free drinks. Streamers and
balloons everywhere. He ducked as he passed beneath a huge
overhead banner that proclaimed, 'Happy Birthday Stella – Forever
Young'.

Myles said hello to Johnny Bones. Johnny ignored him and
walked past Myles to the piano where he sat down and began to
tinkle the chorus of 'The Night They Drove Old Dixie Down'.
Everyone looked at the side door. Nobody appeared. Johnny went
into the chorus again. Again no Stella. Everyone looked at Philip,
but he just shrugged to show that he couldn't be held responsible
for his mother's actions on her birthday.

Halfway through Johnny Bones' third go at the chorus, Stella
walked into the room wearing a pink southern belle ballgown.
Hair up in a wobbly beehive, pink lips glistening, she looked like
Scarlett O' Hara's mother. The crowd gave her a thunderous
ovation.

Today, mother was fifty years old. She had been fifty years old
on the same day last year. And on the same day the year before last.
Nobody minded. As far as Myles was concerned, if his mother
wanted to stay fifty for the rest of her life she was perfectly entitled
to do so. In a while the musicians would gather and she would
reluctantly allow herself to be pushed onto the stage to sing 'Dixie'
and 'As I Roved Out' and 'Both Sides Now', as well as all her other
favourites. The place would go spare. Then everyone would get
plastered on free drink as six months' profit disappeared into their
gobs. Afterwards, Myles and Philip would clear up the mess. Next
year, God willing, Mother would turn fifty again.

'I'm really glad you're back in time for this,' Lucy said. 'She'd
have murdered me if you had missed it.'

In truth, Myles had forgotten about his mother's birthday. Later
he would have to sneak out and buy a present.

Stella came over, puckering lips that radiated with pink gloss.
'Has my first born got a big smooch for his mother?'

Myles gave her a kiss on the cheek. She received a kiss on the
other cheek from Lucy. Myles noticed that the jewelled eye-
patch that had previously covered his mother's right eye had now

mysteriously switched to her left, the good eye.

Stella did a smiling slow-motion pirouette for them. 'Well, darlings? Do I pass the audition?'

'You look wonderful,' Myles said.

'The ballgown is a stunner. I hope I look as good at fifty,' Lucy said.

'I feel as big as a house. I spent simply ages trying to weld the flimsy fucking thing onto myself. Are you sure that it looks alright?'

'Sure, you'd put all the twentysomethings to shame, isn't that right, Myles?'

'That's right,' he said.

'Ah, you're very kind.' Stella smiled, and then she noticed what Lucy was wearing. 'Lucy, darling, that's a simply glorious jacket. Where did you get it?'

Lucy indicated Myles. Stella gave him a look of astonishment mixed with a begrudging admiration.

'Well, it's about time,' she said. 'Some people don't know how lucky they are.' She nodded to herself then tottered away, beehive leaning precariously. They watched as she was enveloped in a swarm of musician friends.

'Your mother adores you,' Lucy said.

'Not half as much as she adores herself,' Myles said.

'Now Myles that's not nice.'

'It's the truth.'

'That's a bit rich coming from you.'

'OK, then give me back the jacket.'

'No, no, it's alright,' Lucy giggled. 'I don't feel that strongly about it.'

A huge vase of white lilies stood on top of the piano. Myles remembered Mia's bewildered face on the night that they had nearly run her down. The smack of the bouquet of flowers against the car windscreen. Now feelings of regret and guilt suddenly flooded his body as though a tap had been turned inside him. He had let Mia down by abandoning her in Venice. It didn't need a soothsayer to predict that Pat would dump her the same way he had dumped every other girlfriend he'd ever had. Pat's kick had always been to take another fellow's woman. Once that had been accomplished he got bored quickly. Mia had made a big mistake, and when it was over she would be too proud and be in too much pain to admit it. Myles gave Pat and Mia a month.

Justine and Philip appeared, wheeling in a large birthday cake with a tall candle blazing in the middle. They pushed the cake to the middle of the room where everyone gathered to admire it. 'Stella – Fifty Years Young', the cake said in squiggly pink icing.

'Oh, will you look at this for style,' Stella cooed. 'I'm totally spoiled.'

Justine saw Myles and ran to him. 'Daddy, Daddy, Daddy,' she shouted and everyone laughed.

Myles gathered her in his arms. She hugged him, and then he hoisted her up. She leaned over to whisper in his ear.

'Daddy, are you still having your mid-light crisis?'

Stella blew out the candle and everyone cheered – the genuine friends and relatives as well as the freeloaders, losers and hangers-on who were delighted because of the free drink they knew was coming their way.

Myles glanced at his watch. Nearly eight o'clock. In Venice, the restaurants would be throbbing with people. St Mark's Square festive in the dusk, vital with footsteps and laughter, the fluttering of wings and smooth breezes from the sea mingling with the aroma of coffee. A band playing lively music outside the fancy cafés. On the hour, he imagined, little medieval figures would come shuffling out on the ledge atop the bell tower to ding the bell with their tiny hammers.

'OK everyone,' Stella said. 'Come and get it.'

Myles was daydreaming about standing on a gondola pushing Pat under the water with the large end of a paddle when Mixer and Earl emerged from the toilets, carrying swords almost as long as themselves. Yelling and slashing at banners and decorations, the two scumbags rushed at the birthday guests, scattering them like confetti. People made a frantic rush for the side door or huddled together in groups along the walls. Two young mothers ran babies in arms into the toilets. Philip pulled Stella behind the bar as the scumbags hacked her birthday cake to pieces. The scumbags shouted 'hi-ya' and 'ee-yea' in high voices as though they were in a Bruce Lee film. Myles helped Lucy to climb over the counter. Then he handed Justine to her and told them to get down.

'Myles, what's going on?' Lucy asked.

'Keep down,' he said.

'Daddy,' Justine yelled.

'It's alright,' Myles said, and picked up a chair.

When the scumbags had finished with the cake, they went for Myles with their swords raised and he realised that they had come to kill him. He didn't have time to feel shocked. Instead, he shrieked to his brother.

'Philip, give me a hand!' Holding the chair in front of him, Myles backed away towards the main entrance. Mixer advanced, slicing the air in wide arcs with the sword. Bits of pink icing still clung to the blade. Earl broke away to come around on Myles's blind side. Mixer slashed at Myles and half a chair leg went spinning. Myles dodged another series of slashes. Then he tried a swipe at Mixer with the chair. They poked at each other until Earl attacked Myles from the side. He spun the chair round to ward off the blow. The sword blade stuck fast in the hard wood of the chair seat. Myles twisted the chair and pulled the sword out of Earl's grasp, but the effort sent both of them sprawling. He attempted to scramble to his feet but the floor was slippery from spilt beer and he fell again. A woman screamed.

This was the end, Myles knew. He was going to be slashed to pieces by scumbags on the floor of his mother's pub. He tensed, attempting to cover his head with his arms. The best he could hope for now was to lose an arm or a leg. He screamed.

But the blow didn't come.

He sensed someone standing over him.

Through his spread fingers, Myles squinted up to see Mixer grinning down at him.

'Hey Goalpost, watch this.'

Mixer aimed his sword at something on the far wall. With a great effort he threw it from him. Myles heard the hiss of the sword through the air, followed by a thunk as it hit a target.

'Yesssss,' Mixer punched the air.

Philip emerged from behind the bar holding a long window pole in front of him like a lance. Other men fell in alongside. Some carried chairs and one held a smashed bottle. They all looked petrified. Advancing very slowly, as through they had wandered into a minefield, they looked like they would turn and run the moment the scumbags said boo to them.

'Don't go away,' Mixer said to Myles, before he dashed for the door, followed immediately by Earl.

There was silence.

Philip and the other men went to the door to check that the scumbags were really gone. Cautiously, birthday guests unpeeled themselves from the walls. Others slowly emerged from under tables or behind the bar.

As Myles got to his feet, he heard shouting from outside, followed by a clatter of running feet.

'Close it, quickly!' Philip said, and moved faster than Myles had ever seen him move. 'Come on will you.'

Myles ran to help him. Before the door slammed shut, he caught a glimpse of dozens of pairs of shellsuited legs running across the road towards the pub: the Charge of the Scumbag Brigade. In their midst, Mixer waved what looked like a pistol. Philip drew the bolt seconds before bodies, boots and shoulders slammed into the door. It shook on its hinges, quivering and rattling.

'What have you done?' Philip shouted at Myles.

'Nothing,' he said.

As the first bottle came through the window, people crawled back under the tables or dashed for the rear of the room. Bricks followed the bottle, along with iron bars, lumps of wood, bits of piping, bolts, screwdrivers and stones, as well as other hard objects. The television set over the bar exploded. Sparks danced and fizzed on the bar counter. Everywhere thuds and smashes and eruptions. Glass shattering. A silver beer keg sailed through the window and bounced along the floor.

In the midst of the storm a voice shrilled, 'Virgil Kane is my name.' Stella walked through the showering glass with her eyes closed and arms out dramatically as though singing might bring this madness to a halt. She stopped in the middle of the room.

'Now everyone, join in on the chorus,' she called.

Johnny Bones grabbed her and hauled her back behind the bar just as the shooting started.

Slivers of wood from the door spun past Myles's ear. He dropped to the floor where he lay flat. Philip joined him, looking at him with jittery eyes. An evening newspaper was plucked off a table. The paper danced in mid-air as it was ripped to shreds by invisible fingers. Bottles along the shelves buckled and tumbled like felled soldiers. Rivers of liquid ran across the shelves and down the walls. Guinness gushed from a pint on the counter through a small, perfectly formed hole halfway down the side of the glass. The world all around became the intermittent mizzling rain of flying splinters and pieces of glass.

When silence finally arrived once again, it was deafening.

Slowly, people picked themselves up. Someone was crying. The doors to the toilets opened and the young mothers poked their scared faces out. Myles got to his feet, glass showering from him. He looked at the portrait of his father that hung over the bar. The blade of Mixer's sword was buried deep in the portrait's mouth. His father's brows were knotted in disgust.

'Oh my poor cake,' Stella said. 'Look at what they've done to my place. Myles, do you know those young fellows?'

'No,' he said. 'Never seen them before in my life.'

Just then a voice shouted from outside and everyone froze. 'Hey in the pub, are you listening?' the voice shouted.

Everyone ducked, expecting something else to come crashing through the window. Nothing did.

'This one was for Dez,' the voice sing-songed. 'Goalpost is a dead man.'

Later, Myles lay in bed in his old room, unable to sleep. In the darkness, he played with his erect penis as he tried to drive from his mind images of the icing-splattered blade that had slashed at him. For some reason he felt unafraid. Instead, he was curious about why the scumbags had attacked. For a moment, he saw

Mixer's small, grinning face glowing from the middle of the dark ceiling, and then the vision faded. It was possible that the attack was a warning from Pat – a way of keeping him in line. The scumbags had been sent by Dez who had always been jealous of Myles's friendship with Pat. Something nagged at him. Why would Dez bother his arse? Myles wasn't a threat to Dez. Unless Dez had totally lost the plot. One thing about Dez, he had never really seemed to know the plot in the first place. He didn't want to think about what might happen next.

The door opened and Lucy appeared in the light. The last thing he needed now. He stopped playing with his penis and pretended to be asleep. She closed the door and walked across to the bed, where she sat and switched on the bedside lamp. The harsh light was like fingers being thrust into his eyes.

'Must you?' he said.

'Myles, we've got to talk.'

Reluctantly, taking his time, he sat up. 'OK. So talk.'

'Don't snap at me, Myles, I'm just trying to find out what's going on?'

'Maybe you should ask your therapist.'

Lucy looked hurt but she carried on anyway. 'Myles, I've just spent an hour calming Justine, she was terrified.'

He nodded. 'What did you tell her?'

'I told her that it was just bad men who had drunk too much beer.'

'Good,' Myles said. 'Did she believe it?'

'No.'

'Oh.' He had presumed that Lucy would make everything alright, as she always did after a crisis.

'She wanted to know why the bad men were trying to stab her Daddy.'

Myles shrugged. 'I wouldn't mind knowing that myself.'

Neither said anything for a few moments.

Lucy's face softened as she tried another approach. 'You did a great job tidying up. I mean, apart from the broken window and the holes in the front door and the smashed mirror—'

'And the sword stuck in the portrait of Dad,' he interrupted.

'Yes, and the sword, but apart from all that you'd never know there had been a riot.'

'Well, that's something anyway,' Myles said.

By the time Myles and Philip had swept away the broken glass and rubbish and bits of cake, and then boarded up the broken front window with wooden planks, most of the guests had disappeared. Two policemen had arrived, taken details and names then melted into the night as if they had more pressing matters to deal with. Johnny Bones had attempted to restart the party with a strawberry sponge from the all-night Kylemore down the street, but everyone kept looking around, expecting a bottle to come through the window or someone to rush out of the gents waving a sword. Nobody had said a word to Myles. Even though there had been a lot of comment about 'wild young fellas on drugs', there was an unvoiced belief that somehow the whole disaster had been Myles's fault. Stella hadn't even cut him a slice of the strawberry sponge. Eventually, she and Johnny and a few others had taken a bottle of Jamesons into the kitchen, leaving Philip and Myles to close up the battered pub.

'Does Mother still think it was my fault?'

For a moment, Lucy searched for a nice way of answering the question. There wasn't one.

'Yes,' she said.

'Typical. You'd think that I'd get a bit of support from my own mother,' Myles said, realising that he was whingeing.

'Look,' Lucy said. 'If you won't talk to me about it I—'

'There's nothing to talk about,' Myles said. 'It was just a couple of assholes causing trouble.'

'Then why did they say you were a dead man? And who's Dez?'

'Because . . .' he paused. 'Well, because . . .'

'Yes?'

Myles couldn't think of anything. 'I don't know. Maybe they didn't like my face.'

'They called you Goalpost.'

'Yeah, well, lots of people call me that.' Myles's lip curled. 'Especially behind my back.'

Lucy leaned over. 'Look, I've lived with you for six years. I know you're in trouble. Whatever's going on, you've got to stop denying it and deal with it. Do you hear me?'

Myles said nothing. He felt like a little boy being chastised by a schoolmarm. He found the idea quite intriguing – in truth, he found it extremely stimulating. Even though he knew that it was ridiculous and entirely inappropriate, he was excited to feel that his erection had returned.

'You don't have to talk to me,' Lucy said. 'But you need to talk to someone about this. It's up to you. Nobody can help you until you start to help yourself.'

She stood up. He noticed a tiny piece of pink icing that clung to her ankle. Her slim bare ankle.

'I hope that I am getting through to you, Myles. We can't go on like this.'

'I agree,' he said.

Lucy nodded, relieved that at least she was getting somewhere. 'Good,' she said. 'Well that's all I have to say. If you want me, I'll be in with Justine.'

She turned and made for the door.

'Hang on,' Myles said.

Lucy stopped, turned to see what he wanted.

Myles smiled. 'I suppose a ride is out of the question?'

Lucy smiled sympathetically, and then she turned and went out, closing the door behind her.

In the morning, Myles got up at six and left the house without breakfast. He got into the Nissan and drove around the city listening to music and inane disc jockey chatter on the car radio. Scumbags peered slyly at him from every corner. Other scumbags rode bicycles or were disguised as motorcycle couriers.

He parked the Nissan in the multi-storey car park down the street from the *Daily News*. Two scumbags passed him on the street. Neither would meet his gaze.

He remembered that Pat had said Dez was thinking of buying a Porsche. He looked around but didn't see a Porsche or Dez or any more scumbags.

On the steps of the *Daily News*, he paused. A scumbag watched him from the doorway of the sweet shop opposite. The instant that Myles glanced over, the scumbag took off, talking into a mobile. He went up the steps to work. Inside, he ran into Lola Wall on the stairs.

'Did you hear the news,' she said.

Myles's heart stopped. She knew about Psychodad, the attack on the pub, Venice and Mia and Pat and everything. It was all over.

'Bob Casper has been appointed managing editor for features.'

Myles's heart started beating again.

'That's brilliant news. It's about time they appointed someone good.'

'I'm not so sure,' Lola said. 'Wait till you see him. He's going around wearing a yellow tie.'

She told him that Bob Casper had been at meetings for nearly three days and that everyone in features had only caught an occasional glimpse of him.

'They always turn into pigs when they get promoted. It's the way things are,' she said gloomily. 'I should know. Getting fired as features editor was the best thing that ever happened to me.'

'You were features editor?' Myles was amazed. He had always known Lola as a quiet, glum subbie, the kind of person who got nervous ordering a pizza.

'Oh yes, before you came. The job almost destroyed me.' Lola went into deep reflection. 'Afterwards, it took ages before I got the joy back into my life.'

Myles knew that Bob would initially set out to make a good impression on the management types. A man's nature didn't change just because he started wearing a yellow tie. Bob would always be Bob, and that was a good thing for Myles and for the features department.

Lola snapped out of her meditation. 'Anyway, there's drinks tonight in the Nerve to celebrate. Are you coming?'

'I wouldn't miss it. Aren't you?'

'I suppose I'll toddle along. But I bet it'll be crap.'

'Why do you say that?'

'Because it always is,' Lola said solemnly before walking away. Cliff Mangan, Dogbrain and Myles's other colleagues in features were away someplace on a new technology course. Myles had the office to himself. He wondered why he hadn't been invited on the course, but then he pushed it out of his mind as not worth bothering about. For the rest of the day he occupied himself with sub-editing features. Once he caught himself picking up the phone and dialling the first few digits of Mia's number. He dismissed it as an old habit. Occasionally a copyboy brought new features. The copyboys were either scumbags or the brothers of scumbags. Myles didn't talk to any of them anymore. Safest not to even look at them.

Rows of multi-coloured flashing lights and the sound of 'Long Distance Run-around' by Yes greeted Bob Casper, Lola Wall, Dogbrain, Cliff Mangan and Myles. Behind a huge set of speakers and decks in the far corner of the Nerve's upstairs bar hovered a moving beard who was the disc jockey. On the wall behind the moving beard, a large poster proclaimed in large bubble letters: 'Prog Rock Night'.

Bob Casper was delighted. He sang along with 'Long Distance Run-around' as they walked across to a table at the back of the room.

'Now this is what I call real music. I still have this on vinyl,' he said. 'I'm telling you boyos, real music is going to make a comeback.'

They sat at the booth. There were maybe twenty people in the place. Mostly in their late thirties. A couple of hippies stood cosmically rooted in the middle of the dancefloor, making odd windmilling motions with their arms.

'Listen, I meant to say this earlier,' Myles said. 'Congratulations.'

'Thanks,' Bob said. 'Now stop arse licking and buy me a pint.'

The waitress came and they ordered drinks. 'I've been promoted, did you know that?' Bob said to her.

'Congrats,' the waitress said and moved off.

'I don't expect to have to put my hand in my pocket all night,' Bob grinned. 'From now on, you lot can just call me "Sir".'

The moving beard leaned into the microphone. 'Good evening,

prog rockers,' he said in a deep voice over spooky mellotron music. 'Tonight, we have secured all the nefarious ingredients to create a nutritious and indeed most succulent prog rock stew. Start with a pinch of ELP, followed by a slice of King Crimson, then a large helping of Led Zep, a generous dollop of Gentle Giant, a sprinkling of Gleenslade plus a spoonful of Jethro Tull. Maybe some Spock's Beard and a little Porcupine Tree. Listen out for some surprises. For starters, here's something you won't hear on the radio —from the early 70s, it's Gnidrolog from their first album, "In Spite of Harry's Toenail".'

A swirling dreamy intro came through the speakers.

Cliff Mangan choked on his pint. 'I'm not surprised you won't hear it on the radio. I mean what sort of a name is Gnidrolog?'

Myles listened. Lots of moody bass and guitar. A singer wailing in a voice like the cry of a seagull. Something about 'Long Live Man Dead'. Just what he needed.

'Go if you want Cliff, but we're staying. That right, Myles?'

'That's right,' Myles said.

'Fair enough,' Cliff Mangan said, and stood up just as the door opened and two good-looking women in black mini dresses walked in. Cliff Mangan sat down again.

'Then again,' he said. 'This stuff gets better the more you listen to it.'

Bob Casper eyed the women. He leaned over to whisper in Myles's ear. 'How long is it since we had a bit of fun?'

'Too long,' Myles said.

'Tonight's the night boyo,' Bob said.

Myles decided that he would humour Bob for a while, then slip away. The last thing he needed at the moment was another complicated situation with a woman.

'Come on,' Bob said. 'We'll go up together.'

'You go first,' Myles said. 'I don't feel up to it.'

'Lost the old touch, eh?' Bob leered. 'Suit yourself. Your woman in the black mini skirt is giving me the eye bigtime. Maybe I can fix you up with her skinny friend.'

Bob stood up and adjusted his jacket. 'Here we go, here we go, here we go,' he sang under his breath.

'The man's indefatigable,' Dogbrain said.

Lola leaned over. 'Told you this would be crap.'

Myles, Cliff, Lola and Dogbrain watched as Bob strolled over to where the women were seated at the bar. They saw him strike up an animated conversation with the dark-haired woman in the black mini dress. The woman ordered drinks, then handed Bob a foaming pint. They all agreed that Bob was away. Everyone was surprised when he returned immediately to the table carrying the pint that the dark-haired woman had given him, face as hard and unforgiving as granite.

'Well?' Myles said. 'Are you away?'

'Not yet,' Bob Casper said. 'But you are.'

'Huh?' Myles said.

'Here.' Bob handed him the foaming pint. 'This is from her. She say she loves your writing and she's dying to meet you.' Myles took the pint and glanced up at the bar. The girl was dark and beautiful and she liked his writing. Myles's first tabloid groupie. A thrill ran along his backbone.

'Jammy bastard,' Bob said. 'Aren't you going to go over and say thanks?'

'I wouldn't be a gentleman if I didn't, would I?'

Things were coming around again. His spell of bad luck was over. Feeling confident and excited, but eager to maintain a cool exterior, Myles took his fresh pint and walked across to the bar. The women coolly appraised his progress in the mirror. As he arrived, the dark girl turned.

'Hi,' Myles said. 'Thanks for the drink.'

'I thought your article on the cats was great,' she said.

'Thank you.'

'It made me laugh out loud and I love that.'

She was about twenty-five, rows of perfect shining teeth, a strong nose and brown eyes that looked at him with approval.

'I'm Myles,' he said, offering his hand.

'I know who you are.' She shook his hand. 'I'm Fever.'

'Fever is a wonderful name,' Myles said. 'It's like something from a beautiful poem.'

She tossed her hair playfully. 'Yes, everyone says that.' Myles and Fever looked at each other, then they laughed. Fever seemed charmed by the compliment.

'This is Marla. Watch her, she's trouble.'

'Look who's talking.' Marla extended a thin arm.

Marla was skinny, with a thin, pretty face and a vacant gaze, as though she was in a different bar. She held a small mobile phone in her free hand.

'Pleased to meet you,' she said absently, before turning to dial a number on her mobile.

Fever looked at Myles approvingly. 'You're even taller than I thought.'

'Six six and a bit and still growing,' he said. 'I kill chandeliers for a living.'

She gave a full throaty laugh.

'Get away, still growing, that's brilliant. You're a laugh.'

Myles smiled. 'This has never happened to me before. Usually it's the guy who sends a drink to the girl.'

'Well you were taking your time and there wasn't anything else going on so I just thought I'd cut to the chase. Any objections?'

'None at all. Cheers.' He raised his pint.

They drank, then looked at each other for a moment. Myles tried to figure out which way things were going to go. Fever was a stunner. He felt as though his tongue had retracted and his mouth had dried up. Suddenly he was unable to think of anything conversational to say to this beautiful creature. Then the moving beard played 'Used to Know' by Jethro Tull, a slow rock song that Myles knew built gradually to an intense climax and fade out. He could handle the situation now, he decided.

'Would you like to dance?' he croaked.

'Sure.'

Fever came up to his neck. She circled it with her arms. As they danced, she looked up at him and moistened her lips as though he had just given her an orgasm. A charge ran through him, the most erotic sensation he had ever experienced with his clothes on. He held her waist as they danced, taking care not to lean into her in case she discovered that he had an erection. During the wah-wah guitar solo, he accidentally trod on her foot. She gave a little gasp, then pulled him closer so that she could control where he was putting his feet. They moved as though they were stuck together. If she noticed his excitement, she didn't let on.

Other people came onto the floor. Myles and Fever remained slow-dancing while all around them long-hairs performed strange jerky motions with their arms and legs. Someone kicked Myles in the calf. Cliff Mangan appeared alongside, slow-dancing with Marla, her mobile still to her ear. Cliff looked wild-eyed with anticipation. Marla just looked jaded.

When the song faded, they sat at a table across from the moving beard's turntable and drank another couple of rounds. They carried on a half-shouted, half-whispered conversation about nothing much, until mid-way through a long speech by Myles, Fever abruptly leaned across.

'C'mere a moment,' she said and kissed him on the lips.

'Are you cutting to the chase again?' Myles said.

She didn't answer. They kissed for a long time. This time so passionately that he thought she was going to suck the tongue out of his head.

When they finally pulled away, Myles was breathless. He looked across to where Bob and the others had been sitting. The table was deserted. He looked around for Cliff and Marla but they had disappeared as well. A faint chill stroked his cheeks.

'Let's get out of here,' Myles said.

'OK,' Fever said. 'Give a lady a minute will you?'

'Of course,' he said as she stood and walked towards the ladies.

She was gone so long that Myles had to endure the full version of Emerson, Lake and Palmer's 'Fanfare for the Common Man'. Upon her return, she took his arm and led him from the table through the dancefloor, side-stepping windmilling long-hairs.

By the time they got to the landing and began to descend, Myles felt as though he was hovering above, observing himself descending the stairs on the arm of a beautiful woman. He followed himself and the woman outside. Heard their laughter rise in the crisp night air. Watched them entwined by a bus stop for a while. Saw them scour the street in vain for taxis as it began to rain. He watched as the Myles below pulled Fever into a darkened doorway and the couple continued kissing. Myles's hand under her top. Hers deep in his pocket. He felt relieved that he had found someone so soon after his bad experience with Mia. Coming here tonight had been a good thing, he decided. Fever was a confident, sexy and exciting woman.

He saw a gold Jaguar slide into the kerb opposite the kissing couple. From above, he saw Fever pulling Myles towards the car.

'Quick, a taxi,' she said. 'Get in before we're drowned.'

Myles felt kiss-dazed but happy as Fever led him across the street through the rain to the car's open back door. 'Come on,' she laughed, bundling him into the back seat. She jumped in after him, slamming the door. The car squealed away from the kerb and Fever immediately pushed Myles roughly from her.

'I got him,' she said to the taxi driver.

'Good girl,' a familiar American burr said.

It took a few seconds before Myles realised that he was looking at the back of Psychodad's head. Psychodad's tight eyes squinted at him in the rear-view mirror. When he turned to Fever he saw that she was glaring at him granite-faced, a gun pointed at his stomach. The car swished through a rain puddle.

'Good job I happened to be passing,' Psychodad said. 'You might have caught your death in this weather.'

SEVENTEEN

Gnidrolog

'Watch out kiddies,' Psychodad shouted.

The car drove over a bump in the road and the top of Myles's head struck the underside of the low roof. Car roofs, chandeliers, lightbulbs, low doorways – as long as he could remember Myles had been banging his head into things. Why should it be any different sitting in the back seat of Psychodad's Jag?

'Take it easy, Charlie,' Fever said, pointing the gun at the floor of the car. 'I nearly shot your man's goolies off.'

'Sorry, couldn't resist it,' he said. 'He give you any problems?'

'You codding me?' Fever said. 'Except he kisses like a mule. I thought he was going to reef the tongue out of me head.'

Psychodad broke into a dazzling smile. He puckered his lips. 'Poor Button. Did I send you after a guy who kisses like a mule? Forgive me?'

Fever didn't look at him. 'You'll make it up to me.' She paused. 'You'd better.'

Psychodad grinned at Myles again in the rear-view mirror. His smile made his eyes disappear into slits. 'Surprised to see me?' he said in a friendly voice.

'No,' Myles lied.

'Why not?'

'I had a feeling that you'd show up sooner or later.'

'I can see why they call you Goalpost,' Psychodad said. 'You should have been a professional basketball player.'

'The opportunity never arose,' Myles said.

Psychodad gave a quick series of snorts. He could have been laughing, or he might have been trying to blow a scrap of food through his teeth.

Now they would drive him to a quiet place and one of them, probably that treacherous wagon Fever, would blow his head off. That was how it happened in the movies and in the crime reports in the *Evening News*. He imagined a farewell headline: 'Goalpost Finally Loses His Head'.

But it wasn't over yet.

He decided that he would to take the first opportunity to open the side door and throw himself out of the moving car. Either he would roll clear and get away or he could break a leg. He had a vision of himself lying in the middle of the road in agony, unable to budge a muscle, waiting for Psychodad to reverse the Jag over him.

'There's one thing I need to know,' Psychodad said, slitty eyes watching the road. 'Don't try to spoof me or I'll get mad, do you follow?'

'Yes,' Myles said.

'I pride myself on being an open-minded sort, but what in the name of God was that dreadful rubbish they were playing in the bar. Some moron wailing about "Long Live Man Dead"?'

'Lucky you weren't in there,' Fever said. 'I nearly threw up.'

'It was a band from the 70s called Gnidrolog,' Myles said.

Psychodad and Fever laughed together like slates sliding down a corrugated roof.

'Gnidrolog,' Psychodad said. 'That explains nothing, and yet it explains everything.'

'I only went because I was with friends,' Myles said.

'Can you explain to me why people like it?'

Myles shrugged. 'It's just nostalgia. It helps to take people's minds off rap music.'

'What's the matter with people these days? They seem to have lost all sense of artistic value.' Psychodad leaned forward and fiddled with something under the dash. 'I think it's time we had some real music.'

The car filled with Andy Williams singing 'Where the Girls Are'. He pressed a button and the windows rolled down. They drove along the coast road without a word, the song blaring and cold wind rushing into their faces. Like they were off to the seaside on a family outing. Except it was night. And the girl had a gun in Myles's ribs.

Myles promised himself that when he got out of this he would buy the CD of *Andy Williams' Greatest Hits*. Whenever he was thinking of taking an easy score or starting an affair with a ditzy redhead, he could stick on 'Where the Girls Are' and remind himself of the close call he had once had.

'What do you think of Fever? She's something, isn't she?' Psychodad said.

'Stop Charlie,' Fever said dryly. 'You'll only make me blush.' Fever appeared scary and alluring in the flickering light from the street. Ten minutes ago this girl had had her tongue wrapped around Myles's tonsils. Now she was ready to shoot him. Where did women like Fever come from? As though there was an academy for bad girls somewhere churning them out. Mia was a graduate with honours. Fever made her look like a nun. Seemed like bad girls were the only types he seemed to attract anymore.

'Yes, she's something.'

'She's been working for me for years. That right, Button?'

'Working *with* you, Sweetness,' Fever said. 'Not *for* you.'

'Got two parlours of your own now, or is it three?'

'Actually, it's four.'

'I tell you, Fever is going to be a real player soon, aren't you?'

'I'm a real player now. Just doing you a favour tonight, Sweetness.'

These people lived in a fantasy world, Myles decided. They gave each other nicknames so that they wouldn't have to deal with reality. Fever became Button. Psychodad was Sweetness. Mia was

Miss Mint and Pat was Mr Cool. If they killed him, they would be bumping off 'Goalpost' instead of Myles Sheridan. Like rubbing out a cartoon instead of a real person. He should have married Lucy. He would at least have had a future. A long, slow, boring future, but any future was better than a bullet in the skull. Perhaps if he had gone along to more of those therapy sessions, he would have learned how to 'unblock', an activity that he was now prepared to admit was probably a good thing. But who in their right mind would hand over their money to a dandified whingeing scuzzbucket and charlatan like Frank Forage? When he got out of this he vowed to attend proper counselling, as long as it was with proper counsellors.

Psychodad pulled the Jag into a dark car park overlooking the sea. Headlights flared across sandy beaches, flashed across a lifeguard's hut beyond. A few cars were scattered around the car park like forgotten toys. Psychodad stopped the car and pressed a button on the dash. The windows closed automatically. He turned off the engine and they sat for a while in the throbbing darkness, listening to the waves babbling on the rocks in front of them. Like being marooned in a luxury dinghy, tripping out to a tape of New Age sea noises. Psychodad shifted heavily in the front seat until he was facing Myles.

'I'm a reasonable man,' he said. 'The only reason you're still breathing is because you didn't pull the trigger on me in Howth. Got that?'

'I did,' Myles said. 'I missed.'

Psychodad winked at Fever. 'You shot the chandelier. If you had hit me then you wouldn't be in this mess.'

Fever giggled. 'Charlie, you're a riot.'

'I make a living,' he said, delighted with himself.

Lifting his arm up to the pale half-light for Myles to see, Psychodad rolled up his sleeve to reveal a cast with writing and drawings on it.

'I bet you've never tried to climb a cliff with a broken arm, have you, eh?'

'No.'

'Of course not. You wouldn't be up to it. You would have died out there. Your friend Pat, too. It took me twelve long agonising hours but I made it.'

'You're amazing, Charlie,' Fever said. 'There's nobody to touch you.'

'Thanks, Button,' Psychodad said modestly. 'You're a great support to me in my hard times.'

Myles remembered Dez's question in the car after they had arrived with the bags of money. 'Did you see the body?' Pat had lied to Dez. Myles had said nothing. Poor Dez had believed Pat. Dez's tragedy was that he had been the only pro amongst them all along.

Fever poked the barrel of the gun against Myles's ribs. 'You want me to waste this long string of shite?'

Psychodad half-turned to Myles, face ghostly as a priest in a dank confessional. 'That depends on what he has to say for himself.'

They both looked meaningfully at Myles. They probably expected him to plead for his life. Give them a laugh. Make them feel superior to the poor eejit they were going to waste. He tried to think of a lie or a spoof to save himself, but his mind was as barren and as free of ideas as a sand dune.

'Don't kill me,' Myles croaked. 'I made a big mistake.'

'Buddy, you can say that again,' Psychodad said.

'I made a big—' Myles started to say until Psychodad poked him in the chest with his finger. Three hard jabs.

'Where's. The. Money?'

'Pat has it,' Myles lied. 'He took the lot.'

'You expect me to believe that?'

'Pat took Mia too,' Myles said.

'He's lying,' Fever said. 'Want me to blow off a kneecap.'

'No thanks, Button. This one would just blubber like a new-born. Besides, you'd make a mess in my car. But thanks for being so thoughtful.'

'Any time, Sweetness.'

Psychodad appeared to be deep into thought. The process lasted just a few seconds.

'You still in love with my daughter, are you?'

'No,' Myles said.

'That's what they all say, and still she keeps them hooked.'

'She's with Pat now.'

Psychodad ignored him. 'Let me tell you something about my daughter. Why do you think she rides a bike everywhere? Why doesn't she drive a car, eh?'

Myles shrugged. He had never considered the question before. 'Maybe she prefers bikes.'

Psychodad hissed through his teeth.

'Did she tell you that she was driving when her mother was killed? Did she tell you she was driving when her boyfriend Barry was killed? Of course not. My little girl was born crazy. Like her poor mother. She's even picked up her mother's vodka habit. If you're looking for a quick way to see God, just sit in the passenger seat when my daughter is driving.'

'Don't tell him any more,' Fever said. 'You're too generous to him already.'

'Don't I know it.' Psychodad sighed. 'That's the story of my life. I've done my best for that girl. And what thanks do I get? She tries to have me rubbed out. Her own father.'

Fever touched his shoulder. 'Take it easy, Charlie. Don't do this to yourself.'

Psychodad took a moment to reflect. There was a long slow intake of breath, followed by an even longer and slower sigh.

'You have no idea what that bitch has done to him,' Fever said to Myles. 'Are you OK, Sweetness?'

'I'm fine, thanks for asking.' He adjusted himself in the seat.

'Listen, I'm not a hard guy. I don't even hold a grudge about the cliff business. That money you and your pals stole belonged to some heavy friends of mine. Now my heavy friends are putting pressure on me to get their money back. It so happens that I've got a little cashflow problem of my own and because you're such a poxy shot, not to mention a lovesick slob, I'm willing to give you a break. Get my money back for me and you stay alive.'

'How do I do that?'

Psychodad turned back to look out at the dark sea. 'Up to you, Bud. You have twenty-four hours. After that, it's ashes to ashes.'

'You won't get a better deal than that,' Fever said. 'Charlie's on the side of the angels.'

Myles sensed that he was clear. All he had to do was tell a few more lies and they would let him go. It was too easy. There must be a catch. He didn't have time to worry about it now.

'No choice, have I?' he said.

'That's the spirit. Give him the number, Button.'

Fever handed Myles a card.

'Ring the number on the card. Anytime. Day or night,' she said, all business-like. 'I'll tell you where to bring the money. When you get there I want to see you and the money and that's all.'

Myles put the card into his pocket.

Fever nudged the barrel of the gun into Myles's ribs. 'OK, your twenty-four hours starts now. Get out.'

Feeling relieved yet wary of a bullet in the back, Myles opened the door and climbed out. The Jag's engine rumbled. Myles waited for it to move off, but instead the passenger window whirred down. Psychodad's hand appeared, holding a black bowling bag.

'Here, make sure this finds a home.'

'What is it?'

'Something to help you concentrate. Wait till we're gone, then open it.'

Myles accepted the bowling bag and Psychodad withdrew his hand. The window rolled down again. Then the Jag reversed out of the car park, straightened with a squeal of brakes, before speeding down the road. Myles was left standing there with the black bowling bag in his hand. It felt too light to contain a bowling bowl. Myles knew that the sensible thing was to put the bag down and walk away.

Instead, he knelt down, placed the bag on the ground and slowly unzipped the zipper. Pulling aside the flaps, he felt his stomach churn. Inside, beaming up at him with a frozen wide-eyed beatific blood-splattered grin, was Dez's severed head.

Dez winked at Myles. 'Hey Goalpost, what's the weather like up there?'

After zippering the bag shut, he placed it carefully on the ground and walked briskly away, out of the car park and towards the city centre. He felt like throwing up but instead he quickened his step and gradually the feeling passed. He had slowed only when he was panting and his legs were sore.

Just when he was in the clear, they hand him a bag with a severed head in it.

He was finished now. It was clear that the scumbags had attacked the pub because they blamed him for Dez's death. They probably had it in for Pat, too. He recalled the time in The Crazy Horse when Pat had threatened Dez while Mixer and Earl looked on. If the scumbags didn't kill him, Psychodad would. Or maybe Psychodad's 'heavy friends', whoever they were. Even if he returned the money to Psychodad, that still left the scumbags to deal with.

He needed to go somewhere quiet and make an escape plan. He couldn't go back to his mother's. He would walk into town and drink coffee and think out a solution. He wondered if Pat and Mia had returned from Venice.

A thought struck him.

His fingerprints were on the bowling bag.

He stopped. Cars swished past while he stood trying to decide what to do. Keep walking and hope that his prints on the bag were too smudged to be made out, or go back and wipe them?

Then he had a better idea. He should bury the bag in the sand and get rid of the evidence. It would hold things for a while. Give him time to work something out.

He turned around and walked back to the car park. What if someone had found the bowling bag? What if a car had crunched over it and stopped to see what it was?

He panicked and ran.

Even in the darkness he had no trouble finding the bag on the ground where he had left it. Picking it up he stepped over the low wall and descended onto the sandy beach. He stopped beside a large sand dune and searched around for something to dig with. He found a broken slat of wood and began to gouge a hole in the sand. He dismissed the notion of going to the police. What could he tell them? That he had stolen money that didn't officially exist? That he had agreed to bump off a young one's father? That he had chased a man over a cliff to his death, but the man was still alive? That the dead man had given him his life back, then handed him a severed head in a bowling bag?

The police would probably think he was insane. He would end up in therapy with Frank Forage.

He could take off. Head for England or America. But then Psychodad would track him down. The man was indestructible.

And there was Justine. What was he going to do about Justine? He couldn't take the kid with him, and he couldn't just abandon her. The only option was to find Pat and convince him to give back the money.

First, though, he had to get rid of Dez's head.

When the hole was deep enough, Myles wiped the bag with the hem of his coat before tossing it and covering it with sand. When the hole was covered, Myles tramped across it until the sand underfoot felt settled and firm.

A new horror assailed him. What if they found his footprints?

He decided to throw away his shoes first chance he got. Then there would be no traces; nothing to connect him to Dez's head.

He tossed away the piece of wood and crunched his way back to the car park. Walking back to town with sand in his shoes and a sick feeling in his stomach, he wondered what they had done with the rest of Dez.

At nine-thirty in the morning the coffee counter in Bewley's was packed and he had to queue for ages. He bought a steaming mug of white coffee and walked into the bright back room. He needed a hot drink and a warm place to sit after walking all night in the cold. He needed to make some calls. He wanted to put together a plan to save himself.

He sat at a far table and looked around. Nobody he knew in the place. Lots of young Celtic Tigers and Tigresses, some office workers and a few lost-looking student types. He noticed his shaggy-faced father in his captain's uniform skulking behind a potted plant at a table by the wall but he ignored him. He wasn't in the mood to be lectured at.

The coffee warmed him and he felt human again, instead of a walking zombie. Walking around the city usually made him feel alert and creative, but this morning he just felt chilled and vacant.

He pulled out his mobile. He dialled Mia's number in Mountjoy Square and let it ring. No answer and no ansaphone. Next he called Pat's mobile. A deep male voice told him that the user was either powered off or out of range and to try again later.

He phoned Pat's home number but there was no answer. His ma must be off with her dogs. Then he tried Aisling at The Oracle Gallery. It rang for ages. As he listened he went into a kind of trance. He was just drifting off when Aisling's husky voice answered.

'Aisling, it's Myles.'

'What do you want?'

'I've got to find Mia. I'm in Bewley's West and I'm ringing everyone. You've got to help me.'

'Goodbye.'

'Don't hang up, please.'

'Give me one good reason.'

'My life is in danger.'

At first he thought the phone had exploded. Then he realised that it was the sound of Aisling's laughter at the other end.

'You serious that your life is in danger?' she said.

'Yes.'

'Then that's the best news I've heard for years.'

The line went dead.

He had opened himself up, made himself vulnerable to Aisling, yet she had callously dismissed him. She had always been jealous of his relationship with Mia. He suspected now that Aisling was a closet lesbian. That would explain everything. He phoned his mother's house and after a few rings Philip answered.

'It's you,' Philip said.

'Let me speak to Lucy.'

'She's out.'

'Where?'

In the silence he could almost feel the phone shrug.

'Where's Mother?'

'Out.'

'When will they be back?'

'Dunno.'

'OK, thanks,' Myles said, and rang off.

He dialled his office and was glad to head Dogbrain's familiar voice.

'Everyone was looking for you,' Dogbrain said.

'Who was looking for me?'

'Oh, they didn't leave names. Some girl kept ringing though. This bloke as well.'

Myles knew that it was useless trying to get information out of Dogbrain. He never wrote anything down and rarely remembered the names of callers or the messages they left.

'How are you?' Myles asked.

'Me? Oh, grand, I'm grand,' Dogbrain said. 'I have to go and see the Sperm with the Perm this morning. I think I'm going to be promoted.'

Dogbrain sounded so innocent that Myles didn't want to spoil it for him.

'Good luck with that,' he said. 'See you later.'

Myles drank his coffee and bought another, along with an almond bun. He sat down, pulled out a biro and some crumpled paper and made a list of dos and don'ts.

He wrote and thought and crossed things out and wrote down alternatives. Every do was cancelled out by a don't. When the don'ts started winning, he crumpled the paper and dropped it into his coffee cup. He sat there in the early morning clatter of the restaurant without a plan and with no clear idea of what to do next in order to save himself. He was a dead man. It was only a matter of time.

A waitress came over and placed a single red rose in a cup of water in front of him.

'From the girl in the far corner,' she said with a smile, and left.

Myles looked up. Mia was sitting at a table across from him. Her red hair was cut short but she still looked stunning. She gave a little wave and smiled at him and a surge of feeling for her ran through him like a shock.

'Long Live Man Dead' started playing in his head.

EIGHTEEN

Threesome

Mia strolled across the floor to him. She had a lopsided smile on her face, as though she expected him to rise up and run to embrace her. He watched her, trying desperately to remain outwardly unconcerned while inside his guts burned. Reaching his table, she hesitated with her hands on the back of a chair.

'Hello,' she said. 'Are you still speaking to me?'

'I'm thinking about it,' he said.

'Well, can I sit down while you're thinking?'

'I'll think about it,' he said.

She smiled and sat down opposite him. He didn't return her smile. That would be fatal. If he acted too friendly and forgiving she would walk all over him. He was shocked that he felt no anger or resentment. All he could think of was how wonderful she looked, the way her new short hairstyle emphasised the fullness of her lips and made a highlight of her magnificent bumpy nose. He glanced around for Pat but couldn't spot him. He wished that his insides would settle down.

'Do you like the rose?'

'Yes,' he said. 'Thanks.'

'You're welcome.'

They looked at each other.

'Did you miss me?' she said.

'No,' he said.

'Oh.' She shrugged it off. 'Well I missed you.'

'You've a funny way of showing it.'

'Are we going to have a big fight?' she asked cheekily, as though none of this was serious.

'No', he said.

'I'm not saying that we shouldn't. It would be good to clear the air.'

'Some other time maybe,' he said.

'Promise?' She smiled.

He decided to ignore that. 'Where's Mr Cool?'

Mia looked evasive. 'We don't see each other anymore. After you left, it was all a bit of a disaster.'

He nodded. After the thrill had gone, Pat had dumped her, just as Myles had predicted. Pat had only taken Mia away from him to prove that he could.

'Aren't you going to say "I told you so"?'

'No,' he said.

'It's alright, I deserve it.'

'It was your decision.'

'Do you hate me?'

'There's no point in that. I'm just sorry everything went wrong,' he lied, nearly choking on the words. Why was he being so nice to her? What was he trying to prove?

'You're being very understanding,' she said.

He looked at her. 'No, I'm not really,' he said truthfully.

'I see.' She pushed her chair back and stood up. 'Maybe I should go. I can see I'm not wanted here.'

At the prospect of losing her again, he panicked. 'Wait,' he said. 'I'm sorry. It's OK, it's been a hard night. Here, sit down again.'

'You sure?'

'Go on. Sit down.'

'You don't hate me?' she said.

'No.'

'Positive?'

'For Jaysus sake, sit down.'

She smiled. 'Good.'

This woman had lied to him and used him and then callously dumped him to go with his friend, and yet here he was pleading with her to stay. As though it had all been his fault. What was the matter with him? It was this type of ridiculous carry-on that was responsible for all his present problems, and probably contributed to his growth defect. He wouldn't be surprised if he had grown an inch in the past twenty-four hours. So much for his resolution to become ruthless. Trust nobody. Behave as though the world was out to get him. Get his retaliation in first. But he needed Mia to help him convince Pat to hand over the money. That was all. After that he would be done with her. The important thing to remember was that his life now depended on Mia, and how he handled her. He resolved to tell her whatever she wanted to hear, whatever would make her help get him out of this mess. Yet she looked fantastic. Better than he had ever seen her. Those vivid eyes. That bumpy nose. And the short hair made her look more mysterious. Nothing like a trail of broken hearts and a severed head to make a woman bloom.

'How did you manage to find me?' he asked.

'I was in Aisling's when you rang. That's where I've been hanging out since Venice. Lorcan's gone to England with Garvin to open a club so Aisling has been looking after me.'

At the mention of Venice his feelings of anger and rejection surged. It had been a long flight home by himself. He doubted that he would ever be able to feel romantic about any woman again.

'I was a complete bitch, wasn't I? How can you ever forgive me?'

With difficulty, he controlled himself. 'These things happen,' he said.

Now she looked contrite, and suddenly he felt confused again. He was on a weird emotional rollercoaster, fighting to control his expression. He wanted her to stay near him. He was surprised that he still harboured such strong feelings for her. He thought that he had learned his lesson. Going mushy about Mia was what had got him into trouble in the first place. It was just a love hangover, he told himself. It would pass once he got used to having her around again. For now, he should play her at her own little game.

He smiled. 'It's nice to see you again.'

She brightened. 'And you.' Mia fidgeted with her fingernails. 'I wasn't very good for you, was I?'

Myles shrugged. 'Nobody forced me to pretend that I was a gangster.'

'Well, at least you don't have to pretend anymore,' she said.

Despite himself, he smiled. Mia smiled back and something opened up between them. She was trying to get him back. He could feel his stomach climbing into his throat.

'I've been thinking about you a lot,' she said suddenly. 'I sent a present round to your mother's pub last night. Did you get it?'

'I wasn't home last night,' he said. 'I was out with friends.'

She looked hurt, as though he had just told her that he had gone on a date with another woman.

'I was hijacked by your father and his girlfriend. They told me that they wanted the money back. Then your father gave me a bowling bag with Dez's head in it.'

Mia looked stricken. 'His head?'

'I buried it on Sandymount Strand. Then I walked around for a bit, and then I came here.' He gave what he hoped was a sardonic grin. 'Just your typical midweek night, really.'

'I'm sorry you had to go through that,' Mia said. 'I'm glad you weren't hurt.'

He found himself blabbing to her about the attack on the pub and how the scumbags held himself and Pat responsible for Dez's killing. He told her about the deal he had made with Psychodad and Fever. He needed her help to find Pat and convince him to give back the money.

She nodded. 'He thinks it's all over. He's planning to get into films.'

'Films?'

Mia smiled. 'Don't ask.'

He looked at his watch. 'We've got about sixteen hours.'

'I'll ring him, but I think you should talk to him. He might not want to hear from me.'

Mia indicated his mobile and he handed it to her. She took it and began to dial then paused. 'First I have to ask you something,' she said.

'OK,' he said.

She had nothing in her green eyes now except longing, sincerity and a deep sadness that seemed about to overflow. He wasn't going to be taken in by one of her little acts again. Like the black eye in the restaurant. Or her concern for Lorcan in Roolaboola's. Or the way she had pretended to hate Pat when all the time they had had their hands deep inside each other's underwear. He wondered whether she and Pat had made love in Venice. He hoped that they had had a really crap time. He was beginning to feel hatred for them again. This was more like it. Now he felt he could handle the situation.

'What do you want to ask me?' he said.

'I just want to know, when this is over and we are free, what will you do?'

'What do you mean?'

She took a deep breath. 'I mean, do you think that you are ever going to want to see me again?'

'Are you telling me that you made a big mistake?'

She shrugged. 'I suppose so.'

'You either did or you didn't?'

'You've a perfect right to torture me, I deserve it.'

'I'm just asking a question.'

'OK, I made a big mistake.'

'That's better.'

'Satisfied now?'

'It's a start.'

If he wanted to be really cruel, he could string her along with false promises, then break her heart later just as she had done to him. But something in her expression tugged at him. What if they took the money and went away, someplace where Psychodad and his friends would never trace them? What if she really loved him? What if—?

He caught himself. Only minutes in her company and here he was, Eejit Myles again. She was some kind of sorceress. Even if they did work something out, how could he ever feel really certain in his own mind that she would not betray him again? Stop this now. Don't fall into another trap. Humour her for the moment.

'You think we can work something out?' he asked.

'I don't know. What do you think?'

'Maybe it's time I got married and settled down,' he said.

She smiled. 'Maybe it is.'

'Start a new life in Wicklow,' he said.

'A little house or a big house?'

'A little one with potential,' he said. 'And a TV and two and a half armchairs.'

She giggled. 'Don't forget the horse.'

She was so self-obsessed that she couldn't imagine him with anyone else except herself. Well, let her imagine. He would string her along and then dump her the way that she had dumped him. But he couldn't sustain it. The joyous look on her face annoyed him. It was time someone taught her a lesson.

'Lucy has always wanted a quiet wedding in a registry office,' he said softly.

Mia's face plunged. 'Oh, right,' she said.

For a moment he was pleased that he had hurt her. Next moment regret flooded in. He watched her downcast face as she studied the buttons on the mobile. He wanted to reach across, remove the phone from her small pale hands and take back his words. He wanted to tell her that the past was forgiven and that they could work out a way to be together forever, or something equally dangerous and unrealistic and mad.

Abruptly she sat up straight and dialled a number.

'Sorry I didn't mean——' he trailed off.

'It's OK,' she said softly with the phone to her ear. 'I can't stand Wicklow anyway. Too many sheep.'

They sat on a park bench in Mountjoy Square with their arms folded. Myles at one end, Mia in the middle and Pat with his back to them.

From the playground behind them came screams and shouts of children at play, along with the scuffling of feet kicking a ball about on tarmac.

Pat didn't believe that Psychodad was still alive. He didn't believe the stuff about Fever. He didn't want to hear anything that Myles said. He deliberately avoided looking at either of them.

'Are you finished?' Pat said. 'I've got a meeting with some important movie people this afternoon.'

'There's no need to be like that,' Mia said.

'Like what?' he asked.

'How are we going to get anywhere if you have an attitude like that,' she said.

'It must be the company I'm keeping.'

'Hey,' Myles said. 'That's not helpful. I came here to help us save our necks.'

'You're going to save my neck, are you? Well, that's great,' Pat said. 'I feel much safer already.'

'Listen,' Myles said. 'We wouldn't be in this fix if you had checked for a body.'

'Incorrect,' Pat said. 'I would not be in this fix if I had not worked with amateurs.'

They all spoke at once. Myles told Pat that it was alright with him if Pat wanted to commit suicide; Pat told Myles to go and save himself; Mia told them both to keep their voices down and discuss this thing like rational people.

'Rational people is it?' Pat said. 'That's good coming from a woman who paints pricks for a living.'

'Well, yours was the only one that didn't sell,' Mia said.

Pat and Mia got stuck into each other. They argued about something that had happened in Venice. 'Performance anxiety is nobody's fault,' Mia told him. 'It happens to everyone sooner or later.'

'Always pointing the finger,' Pat shouted. 'Forever blaming others for your problems.'

'You have difficulty with intimacy, that's your problem,' she said.

Pat sighed. 'You're not a woman, you're a headwreck.'

Myles felt delight that the relationship between Pat and Mia had turned toxic. It almost made up for some of the pain. But it wasn't going to save their lives. Mia was telling Pat that he had a neanderthal attitude to women when Myles stood up and told them to shut up, that they had important business to discuss. They ignored him. He yelled 'Shut up!' Again they carried on arguing.

'I buried Dez's head this morning,' Myles yelled.

They stopped squabbling. Even the kids in the playground quietened. Mountjoy Square was completely silent.

'What are you on about?' Pat said. 'Dez is in Cairo with his new girlie. I had a goodbye pint with him last week.'

'Maybe the rest of him is in Cairo, but his head is inside a sand dune on Sandymount Strand,' Myles said.

'You're letting the pressure freak you,' Pat said.

'Whose head did I bury then?'

'How do I know, man? Some other bloke's. Maybe some toy head from a joke shop.'

'Are you saying I don't know a real head from a toy head?'

Pat stroked at his beard for a moment. 'Yes,' he said.

'Let's go and dig him up then,' Myles said.

'Don't be soft,' Pat said.

'Yeah,' Mia said. 'We can bring buckets and make sandcastles.'

'That would be just like you,' Pat said.

'Digging up heads is bound to be more fun than this,' she said.

Pat snorted. 'I don't believe any of this vile nonsense.'

Myles shrugged. 'Well, I saw a head and the head was dead. This time I was professional about it.'

'You saying I'm not professional?'

'I'm saying that this time I made sure.'

Pat leaned across Mia to face Myles. 'Listen my friend.'

Myles pointed a finger at Pat's chest. 'I'm not your friend.'

Pat ignored the remark. 'It is a very dangerous thing to aggravate me.'

'Tell that to Psychodad. He already kicked the crap out of you once.'

'I have had enough of you,' Pat said quietly and stood up.

Myles stood to face him and Mia jumped between them.

'Now boys, calm down. This is getting us nowhere.'

'Tell him to shut his jaws,' Pat said.

'Make me,' Myles said.

'Cool it, both of you.'

Pat and Myles looked at each other for a moment. Myles was relieved that Mia had intervened. Pat would have beaten the stuffing out of him and that would have finished everything. Pat also appeared relieved that he wouldn't have to fight Myles. After a ritual hard look at Myles, Pat sat down on the bench. Myles sat down as well. Mia sat between them.

'OK,' Pat said. 'We've had our "rational" discussion, now what?'

'We dig Dez up?' Myles suggested.

'Waste of time,' Pat said.

'So you believe me?'

Pat shrugged.

'Poor Dez,' Mia said.

'I'm kind of sorry that I didn't make more of an effort to get along with him,' Myles said.

'He hated you,' Pat said.

'Well, now that you put it like that, I didn't like him much either.'

'I was kind of going off him myself.' Pat looked at Myles. 'All the time, I'm warning him not to be so flash. But he has to have his Porsche. He has to blow a few grand on slappers and booze. And where does it get him? Inside a sand dune on Sandymount bleedin' Strand.'

'The Sundance Leprechaun Bites the Sand,' Myles said.

Pat thought about this for a moment, and then he laughed.

Myles joined in.

'You're dreadful,' Mia said, but she didn't seem too cut up about Dez anymore either. 'Both of you.'

When the giggles finished, they sat there for a while, like zombies on a day out.

'Listen,' Myles said. 'What's this about the movies?'

Pat shrugged. 'Just a pipedream. I met this girl. She'd worked in films in Amsterdam. She knows this bloke with a camera. We're going to hire a room and lights. You know. Give it the full whack.'

Myles was amazed. 'You're going to make pornos?'

'Typical,' Mia said.

'It would have been a first. Have you ever heard of an Irish porno? Have you?' Pat said. 'It would have been historic.'

They shook their heads.

'I would have been ahead of the posse. It would have been a smash.'

'As long as you weren't thinking of starring in it yourself,' Mia said dryly.

'Hey, you already failed the audition,' Pat said.

They started arguing about Venice again. Myles held up a hand. 'OK, that's enough. We've got work to do.'

They stopped arguing and they all sat in silence for a few minutes.

Pat looked at Myles. 'So what are you saying? We give back the money and then this is over.'

'That's the story,' Myles said.

'How can we be sure they'll keep their word?' Pat asked.

Myles didn't have an answer for that.

'I'll make sure,' Mia said.

'How will you do that?'

'Leave it to me,' she said.

She looked from Pat to Myles and back again with a surprised expression, as though she couldn't believe that they could doubt her.

'After all, he is my father,' she said.

At his mother's house, Philip brushed past Myles.

'What's the matter?' Myles asked.

'You're a shit,' Philip said, and went into the pub.

Outside the kitchen, Myles ran into Johnny Bones.

'How could you? You fecking pervert,' Johnny said.

'What?' Myles said.

'Pervert,' Johnny Bones repeated, and followed Philip into the pub. Myles stood in the hallway perplexed. He had arrived home pleased with himself for having sorted out Pat and Mia. Now he was being attacked for something that he didn't understand. Were they still angry at him for the attack by the scumbags? How did that make him either a 'shit' or a 'pervert'? It didn't make any sense.

Myles found Lucy in the kitchen with Annette. Whenever there was a problem, Annette always showed up to make things worse.

Stella stood at the cooker, smoking. He noticed that Big Paddy's picture had been turned to the wall.

'What's wrong?'

'Say nothing,' Annette said. 'You don't have to talk to him.'

Lucy began to sob and Annette put her arms around her.

'See what you've done,' Annette said.

Stella blew out smoke. 'Thanks be to God that Justine isn't here.'

'Where is Justine?' Myles asked. 'Did something happen to her?'

'I sent her to stay with friends,' Stella said. 'We got the child out of the house the moment that – that – that object arrived.'

'What object?' Myles asked.

Stella indicated the back yard. Myles went to the back door and opened it. Outside in the yard, amongst the bins and cardboard boxes and cases of empties and beer barrels, lay the 'Mr Tall' painting, with sheets of gift wrapping in tatters around it. An envelope addressed to 'Myles' lay on the ground. He picked it up and opened it. 'For Myles with love, in memory of happier times'. It was signed with an 'M'.

He put the card into his pocket and walked across to the painting. He wiped some of the dirt off 'Mr Tall', tucked it under his arm, and then walked back into the kitchen.

'I can't believe you're bringing that filth back into this house,' Stella said.

'I'll get rid of it,' he said as he walked through the kitchen, avoiding Annette's glare.

He went upstairs to the attic. Inside, he placed the painting against the far wall. Then he moved some boxes across to hide it. When this was all over, he would come back for it. He didn't know what he would do with it. He couldn't imagine it hanging in the new house in Wicklow. But then he couldn't imagine the new house in Wicklow anymore.

Fourteen hours left.

He went to where the bags of money were hidden and pulled them out. First, deal with the business in hand. Worry about the other stuff afterwards.

He unzipped the hold-all and took a long, hard look. Inside, instead of the money, were two telephone directories. He grabbed the other bag and opened it. A hardback of *The Satanic Verses* fell out.

He sat on the dusty floor, clutching the bags to him. Now it was official. He was a dead man.

NINETEEN

Cowboys

In the kitchen they were drinking tea. Lucy's face was red-eyed and tear-stained but she seemed to have got over her shock. When Myles asked her if she had found any money in the attic, she looked at him blankly then suddenly started blubbing like a child.

'Now see what you've done,' Annette said. 'You've a lot to answer for.'

'It's only a painting,' he said.

'Sure,' Annette said. 'And the Gestapo were only following orders.'

Myles gave her a look, and then decided not to get into it with her. Stella stood by the window, sipping a cup of tea. As Myles approached, her good eye sought him out accusingly.

'I'm very disappointed in you, Myles.'

'I know,' he said. 'Sorry about that. It's just that I was wondering if you'd seen any money around the place, in the attic, say?'

Stella appeared not to have heard him. 'My heart is scalded with grief, but it's time for you to leave this house.'

If Stella had taken the money, she would have declared it a

gift from Big Paddy in the next world and thrown a huge party.

'Myles,' Lucy said. 'We've got to talk.'

'We will,' Myles said. 'The moment I get back.'

'Creep,' Annette said as he left.

Rattled and confused and aware that time was flitting away, Myles went next door to the pub. He was certain that Philip knew something about the money. His brother had always been a bit shifty, and extremely jealous of Myles's imagination, good looks and height.

'Can I ask you a question?' Myles said.

'No.'

'Did you take my money?'

'Go and bollix.' Philip turned his back on Myles as he went to serve a customer.

Myles walked out of the bar. Once he was out of sight, he rushed upstairs to search Philip's room but found the door locked and bolted. He kicked the heavy door in frustration. Then he wandered about the corridor trying to figure out what to do.

OK, his stolen money was gone. There was no time to look for it. Now what? The house was in an uproar because of the penis painting and his mother wanted him to leave. That shouldn't be a problem. By tonight he would probably be dead anyway – along with Pat and possibly even Mia.

Mia. The cause of all this trouble. Why was it that he could still smell her minty breath? Still taste her lips against his? Feel the way she giggled when he was kissing her?

Big Paddy stood in the corridor watching him with a casual eye. 'Remember, when things get bad, always expect them to get worse.'

'Thanks for the tip,' Myles said.

Big Paddy shrugged before vanishing into the wall.

In a little while, Myles was due to meet with Pat and Mia to arrange the pick-up. He couldn't tell them that his money had been stolen. Pat would take a walk. Mia would leave him to the mercy of Psychodad and Fever.

As he saw it, Myles had very little choice. He could mope about feeling sorry for himself until he ended up like Dez.

Or he could try something.

He rushed upstairs to his old room and fetched a bundle of newspapers, black bin-liners and scissors and went up to the attic. First he cut the newspapers into the sizes of wads of paper money. Next he covered the newspaper with strips of black plastic bin-liner and bound them with rubber bands. Then he stuffed the black bundles into the two bags. As a final touch, he sprinkled fivers and tenners from his own wallet into the bags. He had seen this kind of thing done in a film, though he couldn't remember which exactly. He wasn't sure where the ruse was going to get him but he reckoned that it was better than arriving empty-handed.

At least he was trying.

Before he left the house he removed two spare pairs of socks and a pair of underpants from his chest of drawers and put them into his pockets. Just in case he didn't make it home tonight. He didn't want to end up with rancid feet.

Entering the features department, Myles banged his forehead on the doorframe. Everyone laughed except Lola Wall who made a tragic face.

'Mind your head,' Cliff Mangan said.

'Ooh. Are you OK?' Lola said.

'Grand,' Myles replied, rubbing his forehead. 'Who lowered the door?'

'Where were you this morning?' Lola asked. 'We thought you'd left us for a real job.'

'Dentist,' Myles said. 'Out of my brain with pain. I had to get an emergency filling.'

'You look a bit pale alright,' Dogbrain said. 'Welcome back all the same.'

No sign of Jarlath Boon. At least that was something to be thankful for.

Messages and letters were piled on Myles's desk. He couldn't bring himself to sift through them. Mia's words trailed across his screen saver: 'Whatever is meant to happen will happen. Only a complete spanner fights against the law of the universe.'

A shadow fell across him. Bob Casper stood at his desk with a frown.

'Good of you to show up. What happened to you, boyo?'

'Savage toothache,' Myles said. 'It was an emergency.'

'That's rough,' Bob said, unconcerned. 'Mind you, that was a wild night last night. I don't blame you for having a toothache.' Bob leaned over to whisper, 'Listen, have you a minute? I've got something for you. I don't want to say anything in front of these dweebs.'

'Sure,' Myles said.

He followed Bob Casper out of the department and down the stairs to the second floor. Bob wore a neat pin-stripe suit with a white shirt and mad-looking tie. He looked quite the corporate king.

'What's going on?' Myles asked.

'You'll see boyo.'

Myles was surprised when Bob led him into the Sperm with the Perm's office.

'Where is he?' Myles said.

'Close the door and I'll tell you,' Bob said excitedly.

When Myles had closed the door, Bob spread his hands like a preacher. 'Another victory for the good folks,' he said. 'The Sperm's in intensive care. Brain fucking haemorrhage. Blew a gasket halfway through his sixth pint last night. Fowler wants to keep it quiet for a few days. He doesn't want to panic the place. In the meantime, guess who's the new acting features editor?'

'Em,' Myles began.

'You're looking at him. First the World Cup, next a promotion, and now this. Who would have thought things would have worked out so well, eh?'

'Gosh,' Myles said. 'That's something. Congratulations.'

'Cheers, boyo. Now listen, I've a big job for you. Don't let me down will you?'

Bob handed Myles a piece of paper with a name and address on it.

'This morning in Tallaght an old woman was brutally murdered in her kitchen. Blood everywhere. The Gardai say that they've never seen so much blood in one room in the history of the State. Go out there, Myles old pal, and give me an ace news feature. Start with something like, "Today, fear stalks the heart of Tallaght. An old woman viciously done to death in her own home. Gardai think a sharp instrument was used. Possibly a meat cleaver. Is nobody safe? What animal could have done this? What does it say about the society we live in?" You get the picture. Put your own spin on it but I want it hard, Myles, hard. I want full details of the wounds and what made them.'

Myles nodded.' I know what you're looking for.'

'Good man. Give me six hundred words for the city edition.'

Bob escorted him to the door.

'Listen,' Myles said. 'Can I ask a favour?'

'Ask away.'

'Later, after I do this piece, could we go for coffee or something? I need to ask some advice?'

Bob leaned forward, a hand on Myles's shoulder. 'Is it personal?'

'Yes.'

'Ah,' Bob said. 'In that case my apologies, boyo, but I'll have to decline. You see I'm a grade six now and you're only a grade four. A grade six can't be seen to be socialising with a grade four, it's bad form.'

'Oh,' Myles said.

'I hope you understand. Changing times and all that. Sure, you'll be a grade six one day.'

'You think so?' Myles said.

'Sure you will.' Bob slapped him on the shoulder. 'Of course, by that time I'll have moved up. Anyway, nothing personal.'

'Nothing personal,' Myles said.

Myles and Mia waited by the bandstand in Stephen's Green. There were bags at Myles's feet. Like tourists waiting for directions. An occasional gust of cold wind tossed leaves and sweet wrappers across the grass. Some people sat on benches far away or stood by the duck pond, throwing breadcrumbs at the ducks. Somewhere, amid the late afternoon traffic noise, a ghettoblaster pumped out bass beats.

'Where's God's gift to womankind?' Mia asked.

'He'll be here,' Myles said.

'I don't trust him,' she said. 'What's to stop him running off with the money?'

'Nothing,' Myles said. 'But he won't.'

'How do you know?'

'Because we were in school together,' he said.

'That's no reason. Now you're just messing with me.' Mia appeared too edgy to hold a real conversation. Even though this was a serious situation, Myles couldn't resist winding her up. He watched as she fidgeted with her fingernails and then wandered around the bandstand stretching her arms. In a while, she came back to lean against the railing beside him, moving as close as possible without actually touching him. Myles felt slightly removed from everything. As though Mia wasn't real. As though they were all in some mad dream. He wished Pat would arrive. Things would start to get real then.

'Tell me again what she said?' Mia asked.

'She just said to wait here.'

'You sure there was nothing else?'

'That's all, then the line went dead.'

'I never liked her. She's a bitch,' Mia scowled.

'Maybe she's just misunderstood,' Myles said.

What was it about Mia's edginess that made him so cheerful? There was probably something psychologically wrong with him. When he got out of this he would have to do some work on himself. He was about to apologise to Mia for his teasing when he noticed a figure approaching.

'Here comes Mr Cool,' Myles said.

'Please don't call him that,' Mia said, pained. 'That's all in the past now.'

They watched as Pat walked across the grass to the bandstand. He carried what looked like several large bundles. 'How's it going?' he said.

Smiling a warm smile, he deposited a large hold-all on the ground, along with two rolled up blankets and a bottle of whiskey.

'In case it gets freezing,' he explained. He squatted at the side of the bandstand and glanced about him with an amused expression.

'Good choice for a pick-up. Wide open space. People about. Couldn't have picked a better spot myself. What's the story?'

'We wait,' Myles said.

Pat nodded, 'You know what?'

'What?' Myles asked,

'I've a feeling that everything is going to work out OK.'

Pat looked at Mia, and then at Myles.

'You have feelings?' Mia said. 'Now there's a surprise.'

Pat squinted at her. 'Listen, don't you think it's time we buried the hatchet?' he said. 'After all, we're in this together.'

'If you'd buried the hatchet in the first place, we wouldn't be here,' Mia said.

'A fair point.' Pat smiled. 'But hey, as the fellow says "we've all passed a lot of water under the bridge since then".'

Mia shrugged and stared at something far away. Three lads passed by holding a ghettoblaster. One looked like Earl, Myles thought. But then all scumbags looked alike from a distance. The lads veered off and disappeared down a pathway behind some trees.

'There should be a law against rap music,' Pat said. 'Maybe there ought to be rap-free areas, you know, like No Smoking zones or No Kicking Football on the Grass signs.'

'What has you in such good form?' Myles asked.

Pat sat down on the corner of the bandstand and picked up a small pebble, rolling it between his fingers.

'Oh, I dunno. Life's too short. Or else it's too long, you know. People make mistakes. It's only human. Time to get on with our lives, you know what I'm saying?'

'No,' Myles said.

Mia looked at him. 'You trying to apologise?'

Pat held his hands together. 'If you like. I hate the thought of bad blood between us. We're all here now, but who knows what's going to happen. We may get through this no bother. Or there might be bad stuff. Either way, there's no point holding grudges.'

'I'm listening,' Mia said. 'I haven't heard an apology.'

Pat got to his feet with a slow smile.

'I'm sorry,' he said.

Mia said nothing. She didn't acknowledge Pat, just stared through him as though he were made of air.

'Do I have to get down on my knees?' he asked.

'That would make a pleasant change,' Mia said.

Pat got down on his knees in front of her. 'I'm really, really sorry,' he said. 'I apologise for all the hurt and the pain I have caused.' He got to his feet again. 'Did I pass the audition?'

'We'll let you know,' she said.

'Do I get a hug? I won't believe we're friends again till I get a hug.'

Mia thought about it, then gave Pat a tentative hug. After a few seconds, she broke away.

'OK, that's it,' Mia said. 'Let's not get too excited, given the circumstances.'

Pat walked across to Myles. 'I suppose I'll have to get down on my knees with you as well, do I?'

Myles tried to block any bad feelings for his old friend out of his mind. Somehow, the fact that Pat's betrayal had resulted in disaster seemed to make everything alright again. As though punishment had already been meted out for breaking the laws of friendship. Myles had lost Mia, but Pat had lost her too. Maybe Pat had never wanted her in the first place. Anyway, Mia was the only thing that had come between them, but now it was over for all of them. Pat was right. There was no point in holding a grudge. Hatred got you nowhere.

'It's alright,' Myles said. 'You're forgiven.'

They hugged, and Pat gripped the hair on the back of Myles's head.

'Sorry man,' Pat said. 'For always thinking with my dick.'

'Forget it,' Myles said. 'Let's just get through this.'

Myles's initial discomfort and slight embarrassment at being hugged by a man blew away. It was reassuring to be in the strong embrace of his friend. Now, somehow, they were all going to come through this. Pat and himself may never be really close again but at least they wouldn't be enemies. It felt good to let go of his anger. Well, most of his anger. No point getting totally carried away because of a hug.

'When you boys have quite finished your love-in,' Mia said.

Pat smiled his widest, most engaging smile. They looked at him. 'I'm glad we got this sorted out. You have to admit, forgiveness clears out the old head space.'

Mia, who had been resisting the impulse to smile, finally gave in. 'I've never met anyone like you.'

Pat beamed. 'It's been a mad trip, and it's not over yet.' He indicated two figures approaching from the west side of the green. One of the figures hobbled along with the aid of a crutch. As the figures drew closer, they could see that the figure with the crutch was Psychodad. Alongside him, Fever walked slowly.

Pat turned to Myles. 'Remember that woejus old boot in school. The Irish teacher, what was her name?'

'Miss Ó' Suilleabhain,' Myles said.

'Yeah. Miss O Shule-a-wahn-a-wahn-a-wahn, the lads called her. She was so ugly she used to have to reverse into a room in case she frightened anyone. She looked like the back of a number 14 bus, remember?'

'I remember she was a good shot with the duster.'

Pat turned to Mia to explain. 'Anytime she saw someone nodding off she'd give him a smack of the duster. All these kids going around with chalky heads afterwards, like Albinos.'

Myles and Pat laughed. Mia appeared perplexed.

'What *are* you two going on about?'

Myles saw that Psychodad and Fever were a only a few hundred yards away now. Mia stood straight-backed and tense.

'Miss O' Shule-a-wahn always said that the best preparation for life was to always come prepared,' Pat said.

'She was crazy,' Myles said.

'Maybe. But sometimes the crazy ones have the answers we're looking for.'

With that, Pat produced a joint from his inside pocket and beamed at Myles, seeking approval.

'Ta da,' he sang.

'God, you're not going to light up now?' Myles said.

Pat flicked his lighter. 'Why not?'

He lit the joint and took a deep drag. Mia looked at Myles, fear in her green eyes. What was going on? Pat had lost the plot. It was the pressure.

He passed the joint to Myles, but Myles shook his head. His head was wrecked enough as it was. Pat offered it to Mia. She accepted, examined it briefly, and then took a small pull before passing it back.

'That's savage shit,' she coughed.

'It hits the spot doesn't it?'

They watched as Psychodad and Fever walked to within a few feet of the bandstand and stopped.

Fever came forward alone. Elegant, dressed in black save for a small splash of turquoise on a locket around her neck.

'He won't do business if she's here,' Fever said.

'It's a free country,' Mia said.

'You were supposed to come alone?' Fever said to Myles.

He was about to reply when Pat spoke. 'It's alright. We've brought what you wanted. Take it and we can all be friends again.'

Fever seemed to be weighing things up. Pat smiled to show her that his intentions were good.

'Tell the main man that I want to apologise,' he said. 'I hate to think that there'd be any bad feeling left after this is over.'

Fever sniffed the air. 'Who's smoking dope?' she said.

Pat proffered the joint. 'Care for a blast?'

'No thanks,' she said.

She made her decision. 'Lift your arms.'

Pat raised his arms and Fever walked over to him and gave him a quick body search.

'Hey, that tickles.'

Pat tried to catch her eye and make her smile but she ignored him. When she had finished with Pat she went to Myles and gave him a thorough search. She didn't look at him either. Her hands roamed over his body, poking at him, shaking, probing, patting.

When she was satisfied that Myles was carrying no weapons, she turned to Mia.

'Don't even think about it,' Mia said.

'Come on,' Pat said. 'Be nice. Get this thing over with.'

Mia said nothing. Cautiously, Fever went to her. Mia allowed herself to be searched without raising her arms or giving any indication that a stranger's hands were exploring her body. Fever finished her search, then she nodded to Psychodad. He hobbled over to the bandstand and gave his daughter a hard look.

'See what you've done to me. Are you happy now?'

'No,' Mia said.

'Well that's what you get for working with cowboys,' Psychodad said.

'OK, let's get on with it,' Fever said.

With a friendly smile, Pat lifted the bags and moved them to the centre of the bandstand. Fever looked at Psychodad. He nodded.

As Fever knelt down to examine the bags, Myles tried to remain calm. To his relief she picked up Pat's hold-all first. Maybe she wouldn't bother to examine the other bags. Perhaps once she'd seen that Pat had brought the money, she'd just take them and leave. Myles saw that Mia was staring at Psychodad, her fists clenched by her sides as though about to launch herself at him. Psychodad leered at his daughter.

'Still acting out your little fantasies,' he said.

'This time you were lucky,' she said.

Psychodad laughed and turned to Fever. 'Hear that, Button? This one's still at it. How can a man be lucky with a daughter like her, eh? Can anyone answer me that?'

Fever struggled with the zip on Pat's hold-all. 'Stupid thing,' she said.

'Here, let me give you a hand,' Pat said, and knelt down opposite Fever, joint dangling from his mouth.

'I don't need a hand,' she said.

Pat unzipped the bag. 'We all need help sometime,' he said quietly.

Casually, and with a smooth movement, Pat pulled a small pistol out of a side pocket of the hold-all, pushed the muzzle into Fever's heart and fired. A sharp crack. Fever said 'Oh,' and sat back on the ground with a surprised expression. A beautiful woman made floppy and undignified by a bullet in the chest. Still kneeling, Pat gripped the gun with both hands and quickly shifted his aim to Psychodad.

'Now hold on,' Psychodad managed before Pat shot him. His head snapped back and he jerked twice before flopping. He hit the ground before his crutch did.

Pat stood up and checked Fever's still form. Then he calmly walked across to where Psychodad lay bleeding from a hole in his forehead.

'Hey, you poor fella,' Pat said. 'Let me get you into the shade.' Mia had turned milky-white. She watched with big eyes as Pat grabbed Psychodad under the arms and hauled him up the steps into the middle of the bandstand. Myles looked around. Two people sat on a bench far away. They didn't seem to have noticed anything amiss. Nobody else was around.

'Jesus,' Mia said. 'That was fast.'

'Heavy bastard for such a small bloke,' Pat said to Myles.

'Good job he's only going a short distance.'

Pat dumped Psychodad alongside the still body of Fever.

Humming a tune, he fetched the rolled up blankets, untied the binding and draped them over the two bodies. Then he rolled the bodies in the blankets until Fever and Psychodad looked like two sleeping tramps.

'Now nicely tucked in,' Pat said.

He opened the bottle of whiskey and poured it over the blankets. Then he took a quick slug for himself.

'Like Miss O Shule-a-wahn used to say, "always come prepared",' he said. He offered the bottle to Myles and Mia. They declined.

'Suit yourselves,' he said and poured the remainder of the whiskey around the bandstand until the place reeked of alcohol.

Finally, he took out a handkerchief, wiped his fingerprints off the handle of the gun and then he placed the gun carefully in Fever's lifeless hand. He placed the hand under the blanket.

'She shot him for fooling around with other women. Then she turned the gun on herself. Tragic, isn't it?'

He picked up the hold-all and tossed it into the pond.

'Ha,' he said. 'It's full of newspapers. You didn't think I'd really give these losers my money, did you?'

He picked up Myles's bags. 'Did you bring money?'

Myles shook his head. Mia was astonished.

'I knew it,' Pat said, tossing Myles's bags into the pond.

He turned to Mia. 'Now, has the lady any complaints about this job?'

She shook her head. 'No complaints.' She smiled. 'It's brilliant.'

'Right, let's clear the scene.'

Myles felt as though his legs had turned to wood. He took a step, then another. Mia stayed where she was, staring down at the bodies.

'You coming?' Pat said.

'You go on,' she said. 'I've a few things I want to say to him.'

'Don't wait too long,' Pat said. 'And don't disturb anything.'

'I won't,' she said.

Pat and Myles walked away from the bandstand. Myles turned around to see Mia kneeling by her father's body. She appeared to be speaking animatedly, pointing at the body on the ground.

'Well, that was short and sweet anyhow.' Pat took another long drag on the joint.

'When did you make up your mind?'

'To blow them away? Since day one man. Nobody messes with me, nobody. I have a rep to uphold, you know.'

Pat glanced back at Mia.

'Maybe I should have taken care of her too.'

'Not worth it,' Myles said. 'You did what you had to do.'

Pat beamed. 'I was cool wasn't I? See the way I dropped the pair of them in seconds? The blankets were a neat touch, don't you think?'

'Stroke of genius,' Myles said.

'The only thing that can link me to the gig is your woman, the rich bitch.' Pat stopped. He seemed to be considering whether it was worthwhile to go back and do a job on Mia.

'Come on,' Myles said.

Pat squinted for a moment, then took a last drag on the joint before flicking it away. They walked towards the main entrance to the Green. There were plenty of people milling about, some taking shortcuts, others lounging about on the grass or seated on the benches. A few families were feeding the ducks.

Mixer and a dozen scumbags stood with their arms folded at the entrance. They seemed to be waiting for them. Myles touched Pat's arm and then Pat saw them too.

'Little eejits,' Pat said. 'If they want trouble they can have it.' A sudden rush of footsteps made Myles glance behind him. Earl and the scumbags with the ghettoblaster were running at them. Myles caught a glimpse of something steel and shiny in their hands.

He ran.

TWENTY

Cartoon City

A large hand grabbed Myles's shoulder.

'Hang on a bit. They're only little eejits,' Pat said.

Reluctantly, Myles allowed himself to be stopped and he turned to face his attackers. He was scared. Even Pat's bulky presence didn't reassure him.

'Stay behind me. Hold your ground,' Pat said calmly as he assumed a karate stance.

Pat dodged the first assault and then he smashed a scumbag in the face. Myles swung at a scumbag who slashed at him before peeling away. He looked up as Pat kicked Earl in the face – once, twice, three hard kicks, after which Earl dropped to the ground, face bloodied.

Women screamed at their children to run. There was uproar as people scrambled to get out of the immediate area.

Pat straightened up. Earl and one of the scumbags lay on the ground, groaning. A third stood pasty-faced by the trees, holding a blade. The ghettoblaster lay smashed on the footpath.

'Told you,' Pat said. 'They're just tiny fuckheads.'

Myles watched as Mixer and the others advanced quickly towards them. There were at least a dozen. They were taking blades out of their pockets, staring grim-faced at Myles and Pat.

'Back away into the bushes,' Pat instructed. 'Don't let any of the bleeders get behind you.'

Myles backed away until he felt branches behind him. The scumbags charged in a ferocious rush, yelling like banshees. Then they were on them and Pat was ducking, kicking and punching all around him. A face appeared in front of Myles and he punched at it. The face vanished. He saw a scumbag hurtling through the air like a thrown rag. He kicked at a shape in front of him and felt his foot connect. Something smashed him on the side of the head and he swung around, kicking and punching. A scumbag stood in front of him with a knife. At the sight of the blade, Myles froze. The scumbag thrust forward, the tip of the blade aimed at Myles's chest. Pat grabbed the youth's knifearm and smashed it on his knee. The scumbag screamed and fell away. Pat picked up the knife and spun around in time to slash at a couple of eager young faces.

The attacks kept coming.

'Go through the bushes,' Pat shouted. 'I'll cover you.'

They backed their way through; Myles led, clearing his way until large trees blocked the route. Pat appeared alongside him. Backs against the trees, they prepared for the next assault.

'Come on yis little shites,' Pat yelled.

Shapes and faces appeared then vanished. The scumbags appeared to have stopped for the moment. Myles felt as though his lungs were on fire.

Pat turned around. Not a mark on him. His face was exhilarated. Myles had never seen him enjoy himself so much before.

'Jesus, what a big day,' Pat grinned. 'What do you think Miss O Shule-a-wahn would make of us now?'

They walked away from the trees and headed for the Harcourt Street exit, a couple of hundred yards ahead of them down a narrow leafy path. Behind them, Mixer rallied the scumbags. Pat and Myles walked faster. Myles kept glancing behind him, but Pat stared straight ahead, as though he was expecting the danger to appear in front of them.

'Stay cool,' he said. 'We're almost home.'

Two boys materialised abruptly from an adjoining path and ran out in front of them. Pat moved swiftly and knocked one of the boys down. The other stopped and stared at Pat in amazement. A middle-aged woman appeared, and then she screamed.

'What are you doing to me boy? John, are you alright, John?' The woman ran to the fallen boy who was sitting up stunned.

'Ma, your man clobbered John for no reason,' the other boy said, looking as though he was about to make a run for it.

The woman swiped at Pat with her handbag. 'You louser,' she yelled. 'Crook, criminal, animal.'

'Take it easy missus,' Pat said. 'It was an honest mistake.'

The woman took another swipe at him. 'Terrorist,' she shouted.

While Pat was arguing with the woman, a small scumbag who looked about ten years old sneaked up behind him and planted a knife between Pat's shoulderblades. He stiffened then tried to reach over his shoulder to pull out the knife.

'Get this shagging thing out, will you?' he screamed to Myles.

Myles ran over and tried to pull the blade from Pat's back, but the woman was still raining blows with her handbag and now more scumbags appeared, blades glinting in their hands.

'Serves you right,' the woman said, as she gave up and went back to tend to her fallen boy.

Pat and Myles turned to face the scumbags. This time they didn't have time to get to the shelter of trees. Pat bared his teeth and resumed his karate stance. Even with a blade sticking out of his back and a trickle of blood running down his jacket, he picked up the first two attackers and threw them as though he was tossing bundles of rubbish into a skip. Pat karate-kicked the next one, then smashed his elbow into the face of another.

After that, everything became flailing, slashing, ducking, running and kicking. Every tall guy's worst nightmare – little light guys who buzzed and pinged around and could not be caught. A blade sliced Myles's hand but he felt no pain. Someone thumped him in the chest. He grabbed a scumbag and spun him into another attacker. Alongside Myles, Pat karate-chopped Mixer in the throat. Mixer choked and dropped to his knees, face purpling. Something smashed into Myles's nose and his eyes filled with tears. Then he was struck in the stomach and the wind went out of him. He tried to straighten up, but a blow to the cheek spun him around. He hit the rough ground face first and tried to rise. Around him dirty sneakers kicked out. Dust got into his eyes and he couldn't see. Tasting his own blood, he felt like throwing up. Just as he was about to black out, a hand seized his collar and dragged him roughly along the path towards the trees.

'Come on Goalpost,' Pat said. 'It's no fun without you, man.'

'Look after yourself,' Myles spluttered. 'I'm just getting my breath back.'

Suddenly he was dumped on the ground. He heard slaps and grunts and wallops and the thumps of someone getting a kicking. 'Me eye,' a voice screamed. 'Me eye.' A scumbag ran off holding his face.

Myles sat up and watched as scumbags surrounded Pat and took it in turns to plunge blades into him. No sooner had Pat dealt with one attacker than another lunged to stab him. Pat slowed down, his kicks and punches began to miss and he started to windmill ineffectively. He grabbed a scumbag by the throat but the lad thrust a blade into Pat's stomach before breaking free.

Then the scumbags stood back and watched as Pat swayed before them like a large oak about to topple. They seemed astonished that he was still standing.

'What's the matter?' Pat said quietly. 'You chicken or what?' Slowly, he turned to face Myles. Frothy blood dribbled from his mouth. His eyes seemed glazed. When he saw Myles he gave a crinkly grin.

'Vamoose,' Pat said.

Pat turned to face the scumbags as they closed in again. He became a blur of motion. One scumbag fell holding his stomach. Another toppled into a bush.

Myles scrambled to his feet and wobbled off. He banged into a tree, righted himself and tried to see where he was going. Behind him, Pat disappeared in a crush of youths who piled in like hyenas upon a wounded beast.

In the distance, Myles observed two girls on the path watching the fight. One had red hair. The other wore a beautiful Oriental dress. As he watched, Aisling took Mia's hand and led her away. Mia didn't look back.

Big Paddy appeared beside him.

'Don't look back yourself. Bad for the nerves. Keep going straight and you'll be grand,' he said.

'They'll come after me.'

'Don't worry about them. Never let the other bastards set your agenda. Once you do that, you're history.'

Somehow, Myles stumbled back onto the path and towards the exit a hundred yards away. People he passed either screamed or jumped off the path as though he were contaminated.

The noise of the fight receded. Now all he could hear was the unsteady shuffling of his own footsteps.

'What are you looking at?' he said to a fat woman who held her hands to her mouth like she'd seen a ghost.

'Save your energy,' Big Paddy said. 'Keep walking in a straight line and you're away. Think you can handle that?'

'Course I can,' Myles said.

'That's the lad.'

That was when Myles realised that people were staring not at his face but at his chest.

'Don't look down,' Big Paddy said.

Glancing down automatically, Myles saw the jagged edge of a snapped off blade protruding from the middle of his chest. The blade bobbed up and down as he walked, like it belonged there. There was no blood, which Myles thought was very strange. He felt his left arm going numb.

'What did I tell you?' Big Paddy said. 'What do you suppose would happen if tightrope walkers kept looking down? The hospitals would be overflowing. How do you think I felt when I looked down at me feet in the latrine and saw that grenade? Do you know, I'd say I'd still be going strong today if only I hadn't looked down.'

Myles stumbled and began to cough. A large hand took Myles's right hand and led him forward.

'Jaysus, I don't know what you'd do if you didn't have me to look out for you. By the way, how's your mother these days? Is the wrecked eye any better?'

'She's fine, but the eye's still the same,' Myles said. 'I think she likes the eye-patch too much.'

Big Paddy laughed, a full throaty roar. Myles was glad that he had made his father happy. He tried to think of another funny thing to tell him but he couldn't come up with anything. It was growing dark. He wanted his father to switch on all the lights in the city again, turn the day into Christmas just as he had done that time when Myles was a kid. A cartoon city glowing with neon. That had been magical. All his father had to do was to flick a switch.

'Turn on the lights Dad, will you?'

'In a minute.'

Nearly at the Harcourt Street exit. He could see traffic passing and hear the sound of footsteps on the pavement outside. Big Paddy led Myles through the exit and onto the street. He guided him through a stream of people who were too preoccupied to notice the blade sticking from Myles's chest. At the zebra crossing, Myles tried to halt but was overcome by a sudden weakness. Mia had walked away, he remembered. She had watched Pat and himself fighting for their lives and then she had turned her back on them as though she had grown bored with the entertainment. She had walked off with that bitch, Aisling. A buzzing noise came from his pocket. After a moment's confusion, he realised that it was his mobile. Slowly, with his free hand, he removed the phone from his pocket and brought it up to his ear. He pressed the button.

'Where are you? Where's my shagging six hundred words?' Bob Casper's voice rasped.

'I'm nearly finished,' Myles said, and the phone slid from his grasp.

Then he was falling, his hand slipping out of his father's grip. He felt himself plunging through space. Like the time he fell down the hill on the gig with Pat and Dez. The night he had met Mia. The night when all this had begun.

He hit the road and lay there, exhausted, pain rising in his chest and left arm. A rush of noise in his ears told him that cars were passing within inches of his head. He closed his eyes. Hoofbeats clip-clopped the road in front of him. A small pebble bounced off his cheek. The hoofbeats ceased. A horse neighed above him. Opening his eyes, squinting in the darkness, he saw a gigantic speckled horse standing over him, framed in a glowing circle of light like an old portrait of a famous Grand National winner. He thought he recognised the horse. He must really be dead now.

He heard Johnny Bones' voice telling Sheba to quiet down. Next thing, he felt himself being picked off the road, cradled in someone's strong arms as though he were a baby about to get his nappy changed.

'Dad?' he called.

He was raised high in the air, and held there like a trophy for the entire world to see before being hurled into darkness.

He came to in bed in a room bathed in pure white light. The bed sheets were so dazzling that he couldn't look at them. There was an invisible elephant sitting on his chest.

A palely glowing woman hovered over him.

'There you are,' she said cheerfully. 'Can you sit up, like a good man?'

With a huge effort he tried to sit up. Every part of him felt stiff and immobile, as though his limbs hadn't been used for years. The elephant on his chest turned into a baby elephant, then a bear cub. Finally it became a padded bandage. Eventually, with the assistance of the glowing woman, he sat up fully in the bed.

'Thanks,' he said.

'You had a bad night,' the woman said. 'But you're out of the woods now I'd say.'

'Out of the woods? What woods?' he asked.

The woman laughed and tucked the sheets under his arms.

'Gosh you're a fierce height,' she said. 'How tall are you?'

'I don't know.'

'What do you mean? Everybody knows how tall they are.'

'I've haven't stopped growing yet.'

The woman giggled. 'Oh, you're a character. I was warned about you, so I was.'

The nurse moved off to another bed. A moment later Stella appeared. She was dressed in black, her hair in a beehive. She moved slowly down the beds in the ward, searching for Myles. At the bed next to Myles she halted, her good eye staring with an intensity that convinced the occupant that his time had come.

'Nurse,' the occupant croaked. 'Nurse, help me.'

'Mother,' Myles said.

The jewel in Stella's eye-patch turned, located his position then caught the sunlight to shine at his face like a searchlight.

'There you are. They've moved you again.'

She moved across to his bed in slow motion, milking the drama of having a wounded son in hospital. She seemed disappointed to find that he was awake.

'Oh Myles, darling. I am out of my mind with fretting.'

When she was still a few feet away from him, she closed her eyes and puckered her lips to kiss him. Her aim was off by a couple of yards. She was headed for the wall behind him when he put out his arm to stop her.

'Oh, you've moved again,' she said and corrected her aim. Then she gave him a peck on the top of his head. Her whiskey smell hit him like a slap across the cheek.

'God, I thought you'd gone to join your father. The doctors said they'd never seen a knife so deep in a person's chest before. It's a miracle you're alive.'

Stella stared off over his head as she considered something even more profound. 'They said there was nothing more they could do for my eye. I was hoping I'd have it back working again by the time you woke up.' She sighed. 'But some things are not to be.'

'How's Justine and Lucy?'

Stella opened her purse and took out a packet of cigarettes and a box of matches. She seemed to have lost interest in him now that he was alive and sitting up and able to talk.

'Oh sure they're fine. Why wouldn't they be? Didn't Justine find all that money in the attic in one of Paddy's old bags? It was a miracle. He must have been saving for years. All that time in the Lebanon. Just to surprise us one day, but sure he never got the chance because God called him too soon.'

'Justine found money in the attic?'

'Isn't life marvellous? Full of fantastic twists and turns, just when you least expect it. Now Lucy has the house in Wicklow and I've got my sky-blue kitchen, the one Paddy always wanted me to have, as well as the stage in the pub for concerts and performances. Wait till you see it. Of course, Philip had to go and buy a new train set as well, but sure, that's the way he is.'

Myles was relieved that Justine had found the money. It meant that a pressure had been lifted from him. The money had never been his anyway. It had caused him nothing but trouble. Maybe now some good would come of it.

'Justine will be in later. Johnny said he'd bring her over specially in the horse-drawn carriage. You owe that man your life so be nice to him. Mind you, the doctors did say that you were probably in more danger from the bumpy ride to hospital in his carriage than from the wound.'

There was a rumbling from outside in the corridor, accompanied by raised voices.

'Oh listen darling I hope you don't mind,' Stella said, an unlit cigarette soaking up lipstick from her mouth. 'I've invited a few people.'

Into the ward at a rush came a posse of cameramen and journalists. Myles recognised Cliff Mangan and Lennon the photographer from the *News*. Behind them came radio people with tape recorders followed by a television crew. Soon a crowd was milling around Myles's bed, jockeying for space. Flashbulbs went off like bombs.

'Myles, over here.'

'Hey Myles, smile.'

'Mrs Sheridan, get in close to your son, will you?'

'That's it Myles, look at your ma.'

Stella sat on the bed beside Myles and beamed at the photographers. She alternated between a look of motherly concern for her son and a beam of delight that he was OK. She seemed to have been waiting for this moment all her life.

Cliff Mangan leaned in to him. 'Hey Myles.'

'Hey Cliff.'

'Glad you're better. Listen, how about an interview. An exclusive for the *News*?'

Cliff's precocity irritated Myles. He shook his head.

'Why not?' Cliff appeared outraged. 'It's your own newspaper.'

'I'll talk to Dogbrain,' Myles said. 'Send me Dogbrain.'

'I'll pass on your message.'

Offended, Cliff turned aside, produced his mobile and began to dial. At that moment a doctor and several nurses arrived and herded the journalists, photographers and the camera crew out of the ward.

'He's just woken up,' the nurse told them. 'He needs time and rest.' She ignored all protests as she ushered the posse out into the corridor.

'That was refreshing wasn't it?' Stella said. 'Did I look alright.'

'You looked great, Mother,' Myles said.

The nurse returned. Stella turned to her, indicating her black dress. 'Do you think I look too big in this thing?' she inquired.

'Not at all,' the nurse said. 'I'm afraid that those reporters want to talk to you outside.'

'Oh yes, of course,' Stella said, and adjusted her beehive. 'Sure, why wouldn't they? I've been through a massive ordeal.' She made a big show of blowing Myles a goodbye kiss before leaving.

The doctor, a burly man with glasses, leaned over Myles and checked his temperature.

'Quite the celebrity aren't we?' he said. 'How are you feeling?'

'I feel OK,' Myles said. 'A bit stiff here and there.'

'You've made a miraculous recovery. You should be proud of yourself.'

Myles watched as the doctor examined the bandage on his chest. For the first time, he noticed that he had a bandage on his left hand as well.

'Doctor, did my friend, Pat? Did he—?'

The doctor shook his head. 'By the time he was brought to us there was nothing we could do. I'm very sorry.'

Myles caught a sympathetic look from the nurse. She drew a large screen around his bed as the doctor continued his examination.

'Is it OK if I ask a favour, doctor?'

'Of course,' the doctor said. 'Ask away.'

'Thanks,' Myles said. 'It's just, I was wondering if you could you tell me how tall I am?'

EPILOGUE

Lovers

He stood by the pole on the seafront as the cold breeze ruffled his hair and blew spray across his face.

A year had swept away all traces of flowers or cards. The ragged remains of a Manchester United scarf fluttering in the wind was now the only reminder that the pole had once been Mia's memorial to a dead boyfriend.

This was Myles's first visit in months. At first, as soon as he had been released from hospital and the police had decided that they had nothing more to ask him about the bodies on the Green, he had visited here at least once a week. Expecting to find new bouquets. Expecting to discover a card. Expecting to see a red-head on a bicycle appearing on the seafront road. Instead, all he had found were rotted windswept flowers. Gradually, he had realised that Mia was never going to return, and he had stopped coming.

When the memory and the smell and the images of Mia had finally flown out of his body and out of his mind, he had felt a tremendous sense of uplift and release. A relief that now he could get on with his life. A relief that things were now normal. Aisling had disappeared with Mia. Lorcan was somewhere in London clubland, and Stick had taken a job as a model and was off doing photo-shoots around the world. Last month, he had met Stick outside the Elephant. She had been polite and given him a kiss on the cheek, but she told him that she hadn't heard from Mia for ages. She would be surprised if she ever heard from her again, she'd said.

One day the United scarf would disappear as well, and the pole would revert to being a pole again. Until someone else's lover crashed into it.

He would never see Mia again. He was certain of that. Just as he was certain that he would never again see his father's shagged-out face or hear advice from that husky voice. Just as he was certain that Lucy would never be happy living in the new house in Wicklow with that insipid scuzzbucket, Frank Forage. Just as he knew that his mother's pub was flourishing and that Pat's mother had somehow come into a lot of money and now drove a purple Porsche.

He was content with his new role of editor of small ads and obituaries in the newspaper. It was an easy life, unless he got an obituary wrong, in which case he usually blamed one of the junior subs or even a copyboy. Six months ago, after Fowler suffered a stroke and Bob Casper was appointed editor, Myles had been offered the position of feature writer but had turned it down. There didn't seem to be anything that he was interested in writing about anymore.

With the money from the serialisation of his story in the *Evening News*, he had bought himself a small apartment on Bachelor's Walk. Bedroom, kitchen, small living room with a view of the Liffey and a tiny bathroom with no bath, just a shower that never got hot. A sofa bed in the living room for when Justine came to stay at weekends. It suited him fine. For the moment.

He had given up women. It was the safest thing. The only times he ever got an erection was when he woke suddenly after a deep sleep. It felt as though there was an imitation penis between his legs. He kept the 'Mr Tall' painting on the wall of his bathroom. Just as a reminder. In case he ever got any stupid ideas.

This morning, he had measured himself at six feet seven and a half inches. There had been no further growth since he had got out of hospital. Each morning, he measured himself just in case it started again. Or in case he started shrinking. Sometimes, he felt Pat's large hand clamping his shoulder. Occasionally, when he felt uptight, he heard Pat's voice telling him to 'relax the head'.

A sudden blast of seaspray shook Myles from his reverie. He touched the fluttering scarf. To his shock, it came away in his hand. He tried to stick it back on the pole but the thing was so rotten it began to disintegrate. The remains of the scarf blew away in the wind.

He walked swiftly down the road to where he had parked the Nissan. You can never go back, that was what his father had always said.

Myles opened the door of the car, and then hesitated. He debated whether to turn around for a last look at the pole. Then he decided against it. He told himself that he had no wish to see a figure on a bicycle coming down the road. He told himself that he was over all that shite. He told himself that he would never have to go back to that place again. All he had to do was get into the car, start the engine and drive back into the normal world he had been living in since Mia left. Finally he was free, and it felt good.

Getting into the car, he banged his head.